The House of the Mosque

By the same author

My Father's Notebook

The House of the Mosque

KADER ABDOLAH

Translated from the Dutch
by Susan Massotty

CANONGATE
Edinburgh · London · New York · Melbourne

Published by Canongate Books in 2010

2

Copyright © Kader Abdolah, 2005
English translation copyright © Susan Massotty, 2010

Family tree copyright © Masoud Gharibi, 2005.
Reproduced with permission of De Geus BV.

First published in The Netherlands in 2005 by De Geus BV, Postbus 1878,
4801 BW Breda

First published in Great Britain in 2010 by Canongate Books Ltd, 14 High
Street, Edinburgh EH1 1TE

www.meetatthegate.com

The publishers gratefully acknowledge generous subsidy from the
Foundation for the Production and Translation of Dutch Literature.

British Library Cataloguing-in-Publication Data
A catalogue record for this book is available on request from the British
Library

ISBN 978 1 84767 240 7

Typeset in Sabon by Palimpsest Book Production Ltd, Grangemouth,
Stirlingshire

Printed and bound in Great Britain by
CPI Mackays Chatham ME5 8TD

To Aqa Jaan,
so I can let him go

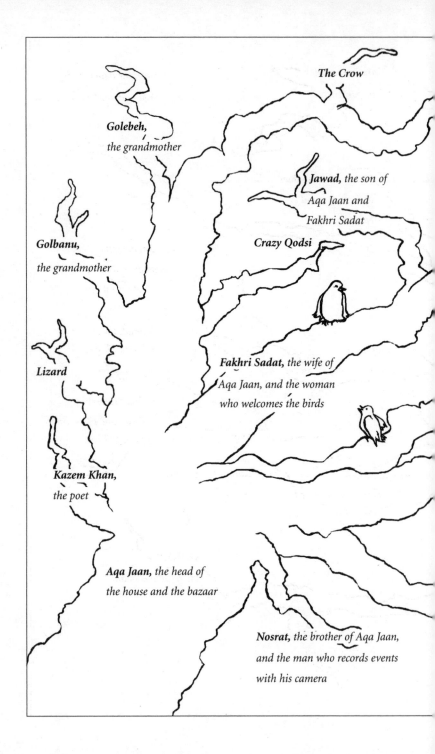

The Crow

Golebeh,
the grandmother

Jawad, the son of
Aqa Jaan and
Fakhri Sadat

Golbanu,
the grandmother

Crazy Qodsi

Lizard

Fakhri Sadat, the wife of
Aqa Jaan, and the woman
who welcomes the birds

Kazem Khan,
the poet

Aqa Jaan, the head of
the house and the bazaar

Nosrat, the brother of Aqa Jaan,
and the man who records events
with his camera

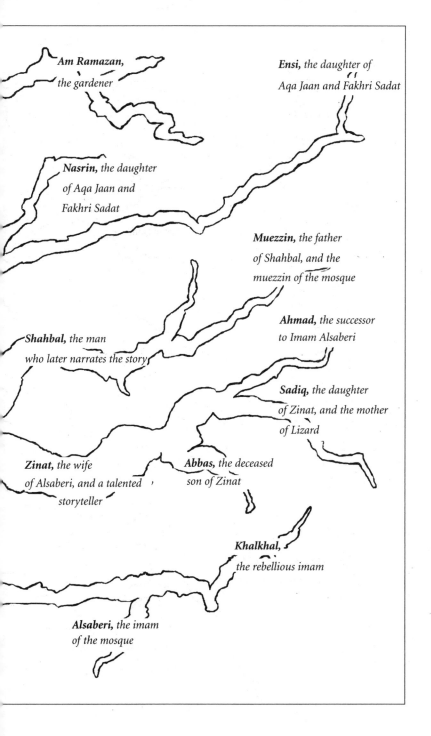

Am Ramazan, the gardener

Ensi, the daughter of Aqa Jaan and Fakhri Sadat

Nasrin, the daughter of Aqa Jaan and Fakhri Sadat

Muezzin, the father of Shahbal, and the muezzin of the mosque

Shahbal, the man who later narrates the story

Ahmad, the successor to Imam Alsaberi

Sadiq, the daughter of Zinat, and the mother of Lizard

Zinat, the wife of Alsaberi, and a talented storyteller

Abbas, the deceased son of Zinat

Khalkhal, the rebellious imam

Alsaberi, the imam of the mosque

Nun, wa alqalame wa ma yastorun.
By the pen and by what you write.

The Pen surah

The Ants

A lef Lam Mim. There was once a house, an old house, which was known as 'the house of the mosque'. It was a large house with thirty-five rooms. For centuries the house had been occupied by successive generations of the family who served the mosque.

Each room had been named according to its function: the Dome Room, for example, or the Opium Room, the Storytelling Room, the Carpet Room, the Sick Room, the Grandmother's Room, the Library and the Crow's Room.

The house lay behind the mosque and had actually been built onto it. In one corner of the courtyard was a set of stone steps leading up to a flat roof, which was connected to the mosque.

In the middle of the courtyard was a *hauz*,* a hexagonal basin of water in which people washed their hands and face before prayers.

The house was now occupied by the families of three cousins: Aqa Jaan, the merchant who presided over the city's bazaar, Alsaberi, the imam of the house and spiritual leader of the mosque, and Aqa Shoja, the mosque's muezzin.

It was a Friday morning in early spring. The sun felt

---

*For an explanation of foreign words see the glossary at the back.

warm, the air was filled with the rich smell of earth, the trees were in leaf, and the plants were beginning to bud. Birds flew from branch to branch, serenading the garden. The two grandmothers were pulling out the plants that had died in the winter, while the children chased each other and hid behind the thick tree trunks.

An army of ants crawled out from under one of the ancient walls and covered the path by the old cedar tree like a moving brown carpet. Thousands of young ants, seeing the sun for the first time and feeling its warmth on their backs, surged down the path.

The house's cats, stretched out by the *hauz*, looked in surprise at the teeming mass. The children stopped playing to stare at the wondrous sight. The birds fell silent and perched in the pomegranate tree, craning their necks to follow the ants' progress.

'Grandmother,' the children cried, 'come and look!'

The grandmothers, who were working on the other side of the garden, went on with their digging.

'Come and look!' one of the girls repeated. 'There are millions of ants!'

The grandmothers came over to investigate. 'I've never seen anything like it!' exclaimed one.

'I've never even heard of such a thing!' exclaimed the other. Their hands flew to their mouths in astonishment.

The mass of ants was growing larger every second, making it impossible to get to the front gate.

The children raced over to Aqa Jaan's study, on the other side of the courtyard.

'Aqa Jaan! Help! We have ants!'

Aqa Jaan parted the curtains and looked outside.

'What's wrong?'

'Please come! Soon we won't be able to reach the door.

There are millions of ants crawling towards the house. Millions!'

'I'm coming.'

He threw his long *aba* around his shoulders, put on his hat and went into the courtyard. Aqa Jaan had witnessed a lot in the house, but never anything like this.

'It reminds me of the Prophet Solomon,' he said to the children. 'Something must have set them off or they wouldn't be swarming in such numbers. If you listen hard enough, you can hear them talking to each other. Unfortunately we don't speak their language. Solomon could talk to ants. I can't. I think they must be performing some kind of ritual, or perhaps spring has triggered a change in their nest.'

'Do something!' said Golebeh, the younger of the two grandmothers. 'Make them go back to their nest before they get into the house!'

Aqa Jaan knelt, put on his glasses and examined the ants up close.

Then Golbanu, the older grandmother, made a suggestion. 'Recite the surah about Solomon talking to the ants – the swarms of ants that covered the valley and brought Solomon's army to a halt. Or read the Al-Naml surah, the part where Solomon talks to the hoopoe bird that brings him a love letter from the queen of Sheba.'

The children waited, curious to see what Aqa Jaan would do.

'Read Al-Naml before it's too late!' Golbanu insisted. 'Tell the ants to go back to their nest!'

The children looked expectantly at Aqa Jaan.

'At least read the love letter,' she pleaded. 'If you don't, the ants will take over the house!'

There was a long pause.

3

'Bring me the Koran,' Aqa Jaan said at last.

Shahbal, one of the boys, ran over to the *hauz*, washed his hands, dried them on a towel that was hanging on the clothes-line and hurried into Aqa Jaan's study. He returned with a very old Koran and handed it to Aqa Jaan.

Aqa Jaan leafed through it in search of the Al-Naml surah and stopped at page 377. Bowing slightly, he began to chant softly, '*Hattaa, edha ataa 'ala wade an-namle, qalat namlaton: "ya ayyoha an-namlo 'od kholaa masaak-enakum, la yahtemannakom solaymano wa jonuudoho, wahum la yash'oruun".*'

They all watched in silence, waiting to see what the ants would do.

Aqa Jaan chanted some more and blew on the ants. The grandmothers fetched two braziers and threw a handful of *esfandi* seeds on the freshly laid fires, so that clouds of scented smoke billowed into the air. They knelt on the ground beside Aqa Jaan and blew the smoke towards the ants, chanting, 'Solomon, Solomon, Solomon, ants, ants, ants, the valley, the hoopoe, the queen of Sheba. Sheba, Sheba, Sheba, Solomon, Solomon, Solomon, the hoopoe, the hoopoe, ants, ants, ants.'

The children waited anxiously to see what would happen.

Suddenly the creatures stopped. They seemed to be listening, as if they wanted to know who was chanting and blowing that fragrant *esfandi* smoke at them.

'Clear the courtyard, children!' said Golbanu. 'The ants are turning back! We don't want to upset them!'

The children trooped upstairs and stared out of the windows to see if the ants had really turned back.

Years later, after Shahbal had left the country and was living in a foreign land, he shared his memory of that day with his friends. After the surah had been read, he told them, he had seen with his own eyes how the ants had crawled like long brown ropes back into the crevices in the ancient wall.

The House of the Mosque

A *lef Lam Ra.* Years went by, but never again had the ants crept out from under the ancient walls in such numbers. The event had become a distant memory. Inside the tradition-bound house life went on as usual.

In the evenings the grandmothers busied themselves in the kitchen until Alsaberi, the imam of the mosque, came home and they had to get him ready for the evening prayer at the mosque.

The old crow flew over the house and cawed. A carriage pulled up outside, and Golbanu rushed over to open the gate for Imam Alsaberi.

The ageing coachman greeted her and drove off. He was the last of his kind, because horses had been banned from the city streets. Any coachman who managed to get his driving licence was given a subsidised taxi, but there was one old coachman who repeatedly failed the test. At Aqa Jaan's request, the man was finally given permission to work as the mosque's coachman. Alsaberi considered taxis unclean, and he also felt that it was unseemly for an imam to have himself driven around in a taxi like an ordinary person.

Alsaberi was wearing a black turban – a sign that he was a direct descendant of the Prophet Muhammad – and a cleric's long brown *aba*. He was just coming home, after performing a wedding ceremony for one of the city's foremost families.

The children knew they weren't supposed to come too close to him. Every evening he led the prayer for hundreds of worshippers, and no one was allowed to touch him beforehand.

'*Salaam!*' the children called out to him.

'*Salaam!*' the imam answered with a smile.

When the children were small, he used to bring them a bag of sweets and hand it to one of the girls. The children would scamper off and leave him to walk to his library undisturbed. Now that they were older, however, they no longer ran up to him, so he gave the bag to the grandmothers, who later divided up the sweets among the children.

As soon as Imam Alsaberi entered the house, the grandmothers washed their hands in the *hauz*, dried them and went to the library to help the imam with his bath. They undressed him in silence. One of the grandmothers carefully removed his turban and laid it on the table. The other helped him out of his prayer robe and hung it up. The imam himself did nothing. He avoided touching his clothes.

The grandmothers had often complained to Aqa Jaan. 'You need to talk to him. It's not normal or healthy, what he does, what he demands of others. We've never had an imam in this house who's been so fanatical about cleanliness. Wanting to be clean is fine, but he goes to extremes. He doesn't even touch his own children. And he only eats with a spoon that he carries around in his pocket. It's wearing him out. He can't go on like this.'

The grandmothers told Aqa Jaan everything that went

on in the house, including the secrets no one else was supposed to know.

The grandmothers weren't actually grandmothers, but servants who'd lived in the house for more than fifty years. Aqa Jaan's father had brought them to the house when they were young, and they had never left. Everyone had long forgotten where they came from. The grandmothers never talked about their past. They had never married, though the whole family knew that both of them carried on in secret with Aqa Jaan's uncle. Whenever he came for a visit, they were his.

The grandmothers belonged to the house, much like the crow, the cedar tree and the cellars. One of the grandmothers had raised Alsaberi and the other had raised Aqa Jaan. Aqa Jaan confided in them, and they saw to it that the traditions of the house were maintained.

Aqa Jaan was a carpet merchant and owner of the oldest establishment in the bazaar in the city of Senejan. He had more than a hundred men working for him, including seven draughtsmen who designed the patterns in the carpets.

The bazaar is a city within a city. You can enter it through several gates. Its maze-like streets, covered with domed roofs, are lined with hundreds of shops.

In the course of several centuries, the bazaars had evolved into the most important financial institutions in the country. Thousands of merchants – dealing mainly in gold, textiles, grain, brassware and carpets – operated out of the bazaars.

The carpet merchants in particular had always played a crucial role in the history of the country. Thanks to his unique position, Aqa Jaan presided over both the bazaar and the mosque.

* * *

The rugs produced by Aqa Jaan's company were known for their extraordinary colours and startling motifs. Any rug that bore his label was worth its weight in gold. Of course his rugs were not intended for ordinary buyers. Special dealers ordered them long in advance for customers in Europe and America.

Nobody knew how the designers came up with such original motifs or such a superb blend of colours. It was the company's greatest asset and the family's most closely guarded secret.

The era of private bathrooms had not yet dawned. There were several large bathhouses in Senejan. The men of the house had always gone to the oldest one, where a special place was reserved for the imam. But Imam Alsaberi had broken with tradition. He refused to set foot in a bathhouse used by dozens of other people. Even the thought of being naked in front of all those men made him sick.

So Aqa Jaan had asked a bricklayer to add on a bathroom. Since the only bathing facilities the bricklayer was familiar with were the bathhouses, the man had dug a hole in the room behind the library and built the imam a mini-bathhouse.

That evening Alsaberi sat down as usual on the stone floor in his long white undergarment. One of the grandmothers poured a jug of warm water over his head. 'It's cold,' he shrieked. 'Cold!'

The grandmothers ignored his cries. Golebeh washed his back with soap, then Golbanu gently poured water over his shoulders, making sure not to splatter.

After rinsing off the soap, they helped him into the bathtub, which was not very deep. He lay down and plunged his head under the water for a fairly long time.

When he resurfaced, his face was ashen. The grandmothers helped him up, then hurriedly draped a towel around his shoulders and another one around his waist and led him over to the stove. Frowning with distaste, he wriggled out of his wet drawers and quickly put on a clean pair. They dried his hair and pulled a shirt over his head, sticking his hands in the sleeves. Then they walked him back to the library, where they sat him down in his chair and inspected his nails under a lamp. One of the grandmothers clipped a ragged edge off the nail on his forefinger.

They helped him into the rest of his clothes, placed his turban on his head, put his glasses on his nose and polished his shoes with a rag. The imam was now ready for the mosque.

Golbanu went outside and rang the bell hanging from the old cedar tree to call the mosque's caretaker. When he heard it ring, he went up to the roof, climbed down the stone steps and walked past the guest room to the library.

He never saw the grandmothers. Just before he came into the library, they would slip modestly behind one of the bookcases. He always greeted them, though, and they always returned his greeting from behind the shelves. Tonight he scooped up the books that had been laid in readiness on the table and escorted the imam to the mosque.

The caretaker walked ahead to fend off any dogs that might unexpectedly come up to the imam. He was the imam's trusted aide – the only person besides the grandmothers who was allowed to touch him, hand him anything or take anything from him. The caretaker was as fanatical about cleanliness as the imam himself. He never went to the municipal bathhouse, but had his wife scrub him at home in a copper tub.

* * *

Outside the mosque a group of men waited to escort the imam to the prayer room. These same men always stood in the first row behind the imam during the prayer. As soon as they caught sight of the imam, they called, '*Salawat bar Mohammad!* Blessings on the Prophet Muhammad!'

Hundreds of worshippers had come to the mosque for the evening prayer. They stood up when he entered and made way for him. He sat down in his usual spot, and the caretaker placed his books on the table beside him.

All eyes then turned to the muezzin, who called out from the top of the centuries-old Islamic pulpit, '*Allahu akbar! Hayye ale as-salat!* God is great! Hasten to the prayer!' The moment he mounted the stairs, the prayer had officially begun.

The muezzin was Aqa Jaan's cousin, Aqa Shoja, who had been born blind. Aqa Shoja had a beautiful voice. Three times a day – just before sunrise, at noon and just before sunset – he climbed to the top of one of the mosque's twin minarets and cried, '*Hayye ale as-salat!*'

No one ever used his name. Instead, he was known by his title: Muezzin. Even his own family called him Muezzin.

'*Allahu akbar!*' he thundered.

The worshippers stood and turned to face Mecca.

Normally it was impossible for a blind man to become a muezzin. He had to be able to see when the imam bent down, when he touched the ground with his forehead and when he got up again. But in Aqa Shoja's case the imam simply raised his voice a bit to let him know he was about to bend down or touch the ground with his forehead.

Muezzin had a married daughter named Shahin and a fourteen-year-old son named Shahbal. His wife had died of a serious illness. Muezzin had no desire to remarry.

Instead, he slipped off every once in a while to the mountains to visit a couple of women. At such times he donned his best suit, put on his hat, grabbed his walking stick and disappeared for days at a time. While he was away, his son Shahbal took over his duties and climbed into the minaret to call the faithful to prayer.

After the evening prayer Imam Alsaberi was escorted back to the house by a group of men. Aqa Jaan always stayed a bit longer to talk to people. He was usually the last to leave the mosque.

Tonight he had a quick word with the caretaker about some repairs that needed to be made to the dome. As he was heading home, he heard his nephew Shahbal call his name.

'Aqa Jaan! May I have a word with you?'

'Of course, my boy!'

'Do you have time to walk down to the river with me?'

'To the river? But they're expecting us at home. It's almost dinnertime.'

'I know, but it's important.'

So they walked down to the gently flowing Sefidgani, which was not far from the house.

'Actually, I don't know how to say this. You don't have to give me an immediate answer.'

'Spit it out, my boy!'

'It's about the moon.'

'The moon?'

'No, not about the moon, but about television. And about the imam.'

'Television? The moon? The imam? What are you trying to say?'

'We . . . er, I mean, the imam needs to know what's going on. He has to keep up with current events. Alsaberi only reads the books in his library, and they're old, written centuries ago. He doesn't read newspapers. He knows nothing about . . . well, about the moon, for example.'

'Make yourself clear, for goodness' sake! What is it that Alsaberi needs to know about the moon?'

'Everybody's talking about the moon these days. At school, in the bazaar, in the street. But we don't discuss things like that at our house. Do you know what's going to happen tonight?'

'No, what?'

'Two men are going to land on the moon tonight, and you don't even know it! Maybe it's not important to you or Alsaberi. But the Americans are going to plant their flag on the moon, and the city's imam isn't even aware of it. He didn't make a single reference to it in his sermon. He should have mentioned it tonight, but he doesn't even know it's happening. And that's not good for our mosque. The mosque is where people should hear about things that affect their lives.'

Aqa Jaan waited.

'I tried to bring it up with Alsaberi,' Shahbal went on, 'but he didn't want to hear it. He doesn't believe in such things.'

'What do you want us to do?'

'The moon landing is being broadcast on television tonight. I'd like you and the imam to witness this historic event.'

'How?'

'On television!'

'You expect us to watch television?' Aqa Jaan was astounded. 'You expect the city's imam to watch television? Do you understand what you're asking, my boy? Ever since television came to this town, the mosque has been warning people of its evils, urging them not to listen to the corrupt shah, not to watch the Americans. And now you're suggesting that we sit and stare at the American flag! You know that we're opposed to the shah and to the Americans who put him on his throne. We don't need to bring the shah's face and the American flag into our home. Why on earth do you want us to watch television? It's a weapon used by the Americans to undermine our culture and religion! All kinds of strange things are being said about television. It's full of disgusting shows that poison people's minds.'

'That's not true! Or at any rate not entirely. They also broadcast serious programmes, like tonight. You ought to watch! The imam ought to watch! If we're opposed to the shah and to the Americans, that's all the more reason to watch it. Tonight the Americans are going to set foot on the moon. You're the most important man in the city, and you should see it. I can rig up an aerial on the roof.'

'You want to put an aerial on our roof? You'll make us the laughing stock of the town. Tomorrow everyone will be saying, "Did you see the aerial on the roof of the house of the mosque?"'

'I'll fix it so that nobody will be able to see it.'

Shahbal's request had taken Aqa Jaan by surprise. The boy knew what their position was on certain issues, but he dared to stand up for what he thought was right. It was a trait that Aqa Jaan had noted earlier in Shahbal. He admired his nephew for it.

Aqa Jaan had two daughters and a son, who was five years younger than Shahbal. And yet when he looked at Shahbal, he saw in him the man who would later take his place at the bazaar.

He tried to involve Shahbal in the important affairs of

the house. He loved him like a son and was raising him to follow in his footsteps.

After school Shahbal always went directly to his uncle's office, where Aqa Jaan told him about the latest developments in the bazaar and discussed the decisions he had taken or was about to take and asked him for advice.

Now, though, Shahbal had broached the subject of the television and the moon. Aqa Jaan suspected that the idea had been planted in his mind by Nosrat, Aqa Jaan's youngest brother, who lived in Tehran.

After Aqa Jaan and Shahbal got back to the house, Aqa Jaan said to the grandmothers, 'I'll have my dinner in the library with the imam. I need to talk to him. Make sure we're not disturbed.'

He went to the library and found the imam on the floor, sitting on his carpet and reading a book. Aqa Jaan sat down beside him and asked him what he was reading.

'A book about Khadijah, the wife of Muhammad. She owned three thousand camels – the equivalent of three thousand delivery vans in today's terms. Undreamt-of wealth. It makes sense to me now: Muhammad was young and poor, Khadijah was old and rich. Muhammad needed her camels – her vans – to launch his mission,' said the imam, smiling.

'That's no way to talk about the Prophet!' Aqa Jaan said.

'Why not? Women were attracted to him, so why did he choose the widow Khadijah? She was nearly twenty years older than he was.'

The grandmothers came in with two round trays, set them down on the floor in front of the men and went out again.

'Shahbal has been talking to me about the moon,' Aqa Jaan said as they ate. 'He thinks you ought to look at it.'

'At the moon?' said the imam.

'He says that the imam of this city ought to be aware of the developments in this country and around the world. He objects to the fact that you don't read a newspaper, that you read nothing but the old books in your library.'

The imam took off his glasses and wiped them casually on the tail of his long white shirt. 'Shahbal has already told me all of this,' he said.

'Listen, his criticism is directed at me as well as you. In recent years we've focused entirely on religion. The mosque should introduce other topics as well, such as the men who will be walking on the moon tonight.'

'That's a lot of rubbish,' the imam said.

'Shahbal thinks you ought to watch. He wants to bring a television in here.'

'Have you taken leave of your senses, Aqa Jaan?'

'He's bright, and I trust him. As you know, he's a good boy. It'll be our little secret. It won't take long. He'll remove the television the moment the programme is over.'

'But if the ayatollahs in Qom find out we had a television in our house, they'll—'

'Nobody's going to find out. It's our house and our city. We can decide how we do things here. The boy's right: almost everyone who comes to our mosque has a television. And although it's taboo in this house, we mustn't lock ourselves inside and close our eyes to what's happening in the world.'

The grandmothers watched from behind the kitchen curtains as Shahbal stole through the darkness and carried a box into the library.

Shahbal greeted the imam and Aqa Jaan. Then, ignoring

16

their curious stares, he took a portable television out of the box and placed it on a table by the wall. Next he took out a long cable, plugged one end of it into the back of the television, carried the other end outside and climbed up a ladder to the roof, where he'd already rigged up a temporary aerial. He attached the cable to the aerial, made sure it couldn't be seen and went back to the library.

First he locked the door behind him, then he placed two chairs in front of the television. 'You might want to sit here,' he said.

After the imam and Aqa Jaan had taken their seats, he turned on the television and switched off the lights. Then he lowered the sound and gave a brief introduction: 'What we're about to see is actually taking place right now in outer space. Apollo 11 is orbiting the moon. The lunar module will be landing soon. It's a historic moment. Look, there it is! Oh, my God!'

Aqa Jaan and the imam leaned forward in their seats and stared at the vehicle as it touched down on the lunar surface. There was a hushed silence.

'Something's going on in the library,' Golbanu said to Golebeh. 'Something important that even we aren't supposed to know about.'

'The boy climbed the ladder to the roof, hid something there and hurried back down,' Golebeh said. 'Then the lights in the library went out. What are they doing there in the dark?'

'Let's go and see.'

They crept through the darkness and stopped by the library.

'Look! There's an electrical cord running down from the roof and into the library.'

'An electrical cord?'

They tiptoed over to the window, but the curtains were closed. They walked softly past the window and stopped at the door. A mysterious silver glow was shining through the crack.

They put their ears to the door.

'Impossible!' they heard the imam exclaim.

'Incredible!' they heard Aqa Jaan exclaim.

They looked through the keyhole, but all they could see was an eerie glow.

Frustrated, they tiptoed away and vanished into the darkness of the courtyard.

Nowruz

Along with spring comes *Nowruz*, the Persian New Year. Originally a royal feast, the lavish celebration of spring dates back to the first Persian kings.

Spring cleaning begins two weeks before *Nowruz*. To welcome the new season, wheat is sown on plates and the *sabzeh* – wheat sprouts – are placed on the table. New clothes and shoes are bought for the children to wear on their visits to relatives, especially grandparents.

The women of the household are in charge of the preparations. Only when everything has been arranged to their satisfaction do they devote some time to their own appearance.

In the house of the mosque a few extra people had been brought in to help the grandmothers clean the house for *Nowruz*. An elderly hairdresser had also come over to beautify the women. Her job was to cut their hair, pluck their eyebrows and remove excess facial hair.

She had been doing this for more than fifty years. The first time she had come – she must have been about ten or twelve – had been in the company of her mother. Later, when her mother died, she took over the business. Before long, she had become a confidante of the women of the house.

Whenever she was there, certain sections of the house were off-limits to the men. The women's laughter could be heard all day long. They walked around the house without their veils and crossed the courtyard with bare legs. The grandmothers pampered them, bringing them lemonade, hookahs and other treats.

The hairdresser told them the latest gossip. Since she made the rounds of the wealthiest families in the city, she had a good idea of what was going on in the women's world. She always arrived with a suitcase full of perfume, hair dye, make-up, nail scissors, hairpins and other products that were for sale. Her wares were not the run-of-the-mill kind you could buy in the bazaar. Her son was a migrant worker in Kuwait, and every time he came home, he filled his suitcase with exclusive products for his mother's clients.

Today she had come to cut the hair of Fakhri Sadat, the wife of Aqa Jaan. Fakhri Sadat was popular in the well-to-do circles to which she belonged. Sometimes she helped the grandmothers in the kitchen or sewed clothes for her children. When they were small, she read out loud to them. In fact, she spent most of her time reading, especially the books and women's magazines that her brother-in-law Nosrat brought her from Tehran.

During the autumn, when there was a spell of good weather, she trapped migrating birds. On those days the grandmothers went down into the cellar and helped her bring up a snare – a large wicker basket attached to a long rope. Then Fakhri Sadat scattered some grain in the courtyard, sat in a chair by the *hauz* and waited for the birds. Eventually a flock of birds flew in from the other side of the mountains and landed in the courtyard. When a bird pecked its way into the basket in search of food, Fakhri Sadat yanked the rope, and the snare snapped shut.

Fakhri Sadat kept the trapped birds for several days in the Bird Room. She fed them, talked to them, examined their feathers and sketched the intricate patterns on a sheet of drawing paper. When she was working, everyone tiptoed around and talked in whispers. Afterwards, when the drawings were done, she set the birds free.

The hairdresser had just finished waxing Fakhri Sadat's legs when the crow flew down and perched on the edge of the roof, cawing loudly to bring its news.

No one knew how old the crow was, but references to it in the mosque's archives went back a century. The crow was part of the house, like the dome, the minarets, the roofs, the cedar tree and the *hauz*, whose water it drank.

Fakhri sat up. '*Salaam*, crow!' she said. 'Do you have good news? Who's on the way? Who's coming to see us?'

As evening fell, the caretaker emerged from the mosque. Behind him was Imam Alsaberi, dressed in festive clothes. They usually entered the house through the courtyard gate, but today they went up the stone steps and walked across the flat roof – perhaps because it was made of a mixture of desert clay and plants that gave off a delightful smell in springtime.

'Do I have time for a quick nap?' Alsaberi asked the grandmothers when he reached the courtyard. 'I don't feel well.'

'Yes,' Golbanu replied, 'you've got about half an hour. We're waiting for Aqa Jaan. When he gets home, we'll go to the banquet room. At midnight we'll all meet in the courtyard for the New Year's prayer. Meanwhile, we're going to lay a few carpets on the ground. I'll wake you up in time.'

A taxi stopped in front of the gate. The children raced outside. 'Uncle Nosrat's here!' they shouted.

Fakhri Sadat opened the window of her second-floor bedroom and looked out. Nosrat wasn't alone; he had brought along a young woman. Fakhri flung on her chador and went downstairs.

Nosrat and the woman came into the courtyard and were met with a stunned silence. The young woman wasn't wearing a chador! She did have on a headscarf, but it was pulled back so far that her hair was visible.

The grandmothers, looking out from the kitchen, couldn't believe their eyes.

'How dare he bring a woman dressed like that into this house!' Golbanu cried.

'Who is she?' asked Golebeh.

'I don't know. Some slut!'

Zinat Khanom, the imam's wife, and her daughter Sadiq joined the group. Shahbal watched the scene from the window. It was brave of his uncle to bring along an emancipated woman, he thought. He admired Nosrat for ignoring tradition and rebelling against the antiquated customs of his family.

This was the first time in the long history of the house that a woman had crossed its threshold without a chador or any other kind of veil.

They stood there, gawking. Should they welcome her or not? What would Aqa Jaan say?

Darkness had just fallen, but in the lamplight the grandmothers could see that the woman was wearing sheer nylon stockings. You could actually see her legs!

Nasrin and Ensi, Aqa Jaan's daughters, cheerfully kissed their Uncle Nosrat.

'I'd like to introduce you to my fiancée,' Nosrat said. 'Her name is Shadi.'

Shadi smiled and greeted the girls.

'That's wonderful news!' exclaimed Nasrin, Aqa Jaan's

eldest daughter. 'When did you get engaged, Uncle Nosrat? And why didn't you tell us?'

'Engaged?' Golbanu said to Golebeh. 'What does he mean, engaged?' She jerked the curtains closed. 'He's lying, the rascal. He's not about to get married. He's brought that slut from Tehran so he can have some fun. Where's Aqa Jaan? He'll soon put a stop to this!'

Fakhri Sadat kissed the woman. 'Shadi,' she said. 'What a lovely name! Welcome to our home.'

'Where's Aqa Jaan?' Nosrat asked. 'Where's Muezzin? Where's the imam? And where's Shahbal?'

'Aqa Jaan hasn't come home yet, but Alsaberi is probably in the library,' the imam's wife told him.

'I'll go and surprise him,' Nosrat said, and he headed towards the library.

Fakhri Sadat led Shadi to the guest room, and all the girls followed them.

The grandmothers waited in the kitchen, where they could keep an eye on the gate. The moment they caught sight of Aqa Jaan, they called out, 'Nosrat's here!'

'Good,' he said happily. 'Just in time for the New Year. So my younger brother hasn't forgotten us. Our celebration will have an added glow tonight.'

'There's something else, though,' Golbanu said anxiously. 'What?'

'He's brought a woman with him.'

'He says they're engaged,' Golebeh added.

'That's good news. At last he's come to his senses.'

'Not quite,' Golbanu said. 'She isn't wearing a chador. Just a skimpy little headscarf.'

'And nylons,' Golebeh added softly.

'Nylons? What are nylons?'

'Long transparent stockings. They make your legs look bare. That's the kind of woman he's brought to this house.

23

Heaven help us! Luckily it was dark when they arrived. Imagine if he'd walked past the mosque with her in the daytime! Tomorrow everyone in the city would be saying, "A woman in nylon stockings is staying at the house of the mosque!"'

'I've heard all I need to,' Aqa Jaan said calmly. 'I'll talk to him. I want you to welcome her as usual and give her an ordinary pair of stockings and a chador, in case she wants to go into town tomorrow. You have so many beautiful chadors. Give her one of them as a gift.'

'I don't think they're engaged. He's just brought one of his girls along,' Golbanu said.

'We don't know that,' Aqa Jaan said. 'Let's hope they *are* engaged. Where is he now?'

'In the library, I think, or else in Muezzin's room.'

Aqa Jaan knew that his younger brother had stopped praying and that he was forever rebelling against religion and tradition. But now that Nosrat had brought home a woman, he hoped he'd make an effort to fit in.

'It will all work out,' he told the grandmothers, and went to see Muezzin.

'Dinner's ready!' called Golbanu.

'Children! Dinner's ready!' called Golebeh.

Everyone gathered in the banquet room.

After the women had seated themselves on the right side of the massive dining table, the men entered in their festive clothes.

Fakhri Sadat introduced Shadi to Aqa Jaan, Alsaberi and Muezzin.

'Welcome, my daughter,' said Aqa Jaan. 'If we'd known that Nosrat was going to bring his fiancée, we would have organised a dinner in your honour. Still, just having you here is a celebration.'

Imam Alsaberi greeted her from a safe distance. Fakhri Sadat described her to Muezzin. 'Tonight we have at our table a woman from Tehran. She's different from the women in Senejan and very different from those women you visit in the mountains,' she said archly. 'Her name is Shadi and she's beautiful, with lovely dark-brown eyes, brown hair, gleaming white teeth and a charming smile. Tonight she's wearing a pretty white chador with green flowers, which was given to her by the grandmothers. What else would you like to know?'

'Ah, so she's beautiful!' Muezzin said, and he laughed. 'Just what I would have expected from Nosrat!'

The grandmothers came in with a burning brazier, into which they threw a handful of *esfandi* seeds that filled the room with a fragrant smell, while the girls carried the food in from the kitchen.

'Aren't we going to wait for Ahmad?' Alsaberi asked.

'Forgive me,' Aqa Jaan said. 'I was so excited at seeing Nosrat that I forgot to give you the message. Ahmad phoned me at the bazaar and told me he wouldn't be coming. They're having their own celebration in Qom.'

Ahmad was Alsaberi's seventeen-year-old son. He was in Qom, studying to be an imam with the great moderate cleric Ayatollah Golpayegani.

The grandmothers had cooked a delicious New Year's dinner, and everyone lingered at the table. After the meal the girls brought in sweets made specially for the occasion.

The women had accepted Shadi and were bombarding her with questions about Tehran and the female half of its population. Shadi had brought them presents: lipstick, nail polish, nylons and fancy bras. The men, finding that they were no longer welcome, retreated to the guest room.

It was nearly midnight when one of the grandmothers announced, 'Ladies! It's time to get ready for the New Year's prayer.'

Nosrat moved closer to Shadi. 'What do we need to do to get ready?' she asked.

'Nothing. I'm not interested in all that mumbo-jumbo,' he whispered in her ear. 'They'll have to pray without me. I'm taking you to the library instead.'

'Why, what are we going to do in there?'

'You'll find out,' he said. He grabbed her hand, led her on tiptoe past the cedar tree and softly opened the library door.

'Why don't you switch on the light?'

'Shh, not so loud! The grandmothers see and hear everything. If they find out we're here, they'll swoop down on us like two ghosts,' he said, and he began to undo the buttons of her blouse.

'No, not in here,' she whispered, and gently pushed him away.

He put his hands around her waist, pressed her against the bookcase, then lifted her skirt.

'No! It's spooky in here.'

'It's not spooky; it's thrilling. The ancient spirit of our house is here. For the past seven hundred years imams have been preparing themselves for prayers in this room. It's a sacred place. A lot of things have happened within these hallowed walls, but not this. I want to make love to you here, to add something beautiful to the history of this room.'

'Oh, Nosrat,' she sighed.

He lit the candle on the imam's desk.

'Nosrat, where are you?' Golbanu shouted from the courtyard. 'Hurry, the imam is ready!'

Two large carpets had been spread out in the court-yard so the family could pray. Everyone was there, except for Nosrat and his fiancée.

'I told you he's a rascal,' Golbanu said. 'He sneers at the mosque every chance he gets, but I won't let him. He simply *must* come to the prayer!'

'Where could they be?' Golebeh asked.

They turned their heads towards the library.

Quietly they crossed the courtyard. The library windows were rattling. Or were they imagining it? No, the curtains were moving too.

The grandmothers tiptoed over to the door, but didn't dare open it. They knelt cautiously by the window, looked through the gap between the curtains and saw to their surprise that the imam's candle, which they never lit, was now burning brightly.

They cupped their hands over their eyes and peered into the room.

The bookcases were jiggling slightly in the candlelight. The two women were so startled by what they saw next that they simultaneously leapt to their feet.

What should they do? Should they tell Aqa Jaan?

No, that wasn't a good idea, not on a special night like this.

But what should they do about the unforgivable sin taking place in the library?

Nothing, they told each other with their eyes.

Like generations of grandmothers before them, their duty was to pretend that nothing had happened. They had been entrusted with so many family secrets they had long ago learned to lock them in their hearts and throw away the key. No, they hadn't seen or heard a thing.

*   *   *

The imam had already begun the prayer. The rest of the family was lined up behind him, facing Mecca. The grand-mothers slipped in unnoticed beside the other women. The house was silent. The only sound was that of the imam's prayer:

Allaho nur-os-samawate wa-alard
mathalo nurehi kameshkaatin feeha . . .

He is light.
His light is like a niche with a lantern.
The glass is like a shining star,
Lit by the oil of a blessed olive tree.
Its oil is almost aglow.
Light upon light!

Khalkhal

The girls in the house had grown up and a few of them had reached a marriageable age. But how could they marry if no man knocked on the door and asked for their hand?

In Senejan strangers never knocked on your door to ask for your daughter's hand. Marriages were arranged by matchmakers – older women who set up meetings between the groom and the family of the bride. These visits usually took place on cold winter evenings.

Some families did without a matchmaker. In that case the women in the family donned their chadors, the men put on their hats and the group set off to pay a surprise visit to a family with an eligible daughter. Families with unmarried daughters didn't want to be caught off-guard by an unexpected knock, so they made sure they were always ready to receive visitors.

Such evenings were filled with long conversations about gold and carpets, the basic ingredients of the bride's dowry and about the house, plot of land or sum of money that the groom would have to give his bride if the marriage foundered.

After the men reached an agreement, it was the women's turn to talk. They discussed the bridal clothes and the jewellery to be presented to the bride during the ceremony. Wristwatches were currently a novelty at the bazaar in Senejan, so every bride was dying to have one.

On cold winter evenings, when the lights shone in the neighbours' windows longer than usual, you knew that they were conducting marriage negotiations. Their living rooms were warm, and their windows steamed up from the hookahs. But those same winter evenings were a torment to the many families with an eligible daughter but no likelihood of a groom.

In the house of the mosque the imam's daughter, Sadiq, was old enough to marry.

The family waited in silence. Perhaps someone would knock, perhaps the phone would ring. But winter was nearly over, and there hadn't been a single suitor.

Finding a suitable husband for the daughters of the house wasn't easy. Not just anyone could ask for their hands in marriage. Ordinary girls had enough young men to choose from: carpenters, bricklayers, bakers, junior civil servants, schoolmasters or railway employees. But such men were not suitable for the daughters of the house of the mosque.

The shah's regime was corrupt, so anyone who worked for the government was automatically excluded. What about secondary school teachers? That was a possibility. But when all was said and done, only the sons of prominent merchants were considered suitable.

With winter almost over, the girls who hadn't received a marriage proposal knew they'd have to wait another year. Luckily, however, life doesn't always follow tradition, but carves out a path of its own. And so one evening there was a knock on the door.

'Who's there?' asked Shahbal, the son of Muezzin.

'Me,' called a self-confident male voice from the other side of the door.

Shahbal opened the door and saw a young imam in a striking black turban standing in the yellow glow of the streetlight. He wore his turban at a jaunty angle and smelled of roses. His long dark imam robe was so new that this was obviously the first time he'd worn it.

'Good evening to you,' said the young imam.

'Good evening,' Shahbal replied.

'My name is Mohammad Khalkhal,' said the imam.

'Pleased to meet you. How can I be of help?'

'I'd like to speak to Imam Alsaberi, if I may.'

'I'm sorry, but it's late. He doesn't receive visitors at this hour. You can see him tomorrow morning in the mosque.'

'But I wish to speak to him now.'

'May I ask what it's about? Perhaps I can be of assistance.'

'I'd like to talk to him about his daughter Sadiq. I've come to ask for her hand in marriage.'

Shahbal's jaw dropped. For a moment he was too stunned to reply. Then he collected himself and said, 'In that case you need to speak to Aqa Jaan. I'll tell him you're here.'

'I'll wait,' the imam said.

Shahbal left the door ajar and went into Aqa Jaan's study, where his uncle was busy writing. 'There's a young imam at the door. He says he's come to ask for the hand of Sadiq.'

'He's at the door?'

'Yes. He says he'd like to speak to Alsaberi.'

'Do I know him?'

'I don't think so. He's obviously not from around here. And he's not your average imam either. He smells of roses.'

'Send him in,' Aqa Jaan said as he put away his papers and stood up.

Shahbal went back to the door. 'You may come in,' he said to the imam, and he led him into Aqa Jaan's study.

'Good evening. My name is Mohammad Khalkhal,' the imam said. 'I hope I'm not disturbing you?'

'No, not at all. Welcome! Do sit down,' Aqa Jaan said as he shook the imam's hand.

Aqa Jaan noticed that Khalkhal was indeed different. He liked the fact that, like the imams in his own family, the young man was wearing a black turban, since that meant that he too was a descendant of the Prophet Muhammad.

Aqa Jaan had in his possession the family's oldest genealogical document: a parchment scroll tracing the male line all the way back to Muhammad. It was stored in a special chest in the treasure room beneath the mosque, along with a ring that had once belonged to the holy Imam Ali.

'Would you like some tea?'

A while later Golbanu came in with a tea tray and a plate of dates and handed them to Shahbal. He poured the tea and placed the dates in front of Khalkhal, then turned to go.

'There's no need for you to leave,' his uncle told him, so Shahbal took a seat in the corner.

Khalkhal popped a date into his mouth and sipped his tea. Then he cleared his throat and came straight to the point: 'I've come to ask for the hand of Imam Alsaberi's daughter.'

Aqa Jaan, who had been about to take a sip, put down his glass of tea and glanced over at Shahbal. He hadn't expected the subject to be broached so abruptly, not to mention that a man didn't usually come on his own to ask for a girl's hand. Tradition demanded that the father of the groom did the talking. But Aqa Jaan was used to dealing with all kinds of people, so he replied in an even voice, 'You're welcome to my home, but may I ask where you live and what you do for a living?'

'I live in Qom and I've just completed my training as an imam.'

'Who was your supervisor?'

'The great Ayatollah Almakki.'

'Almakki?' Aqa Jaan said in surprise. 'I've had the honour of making his acquaintance.'

When he heard the name Almakki, Aqa Jaan knew that the young imam was part of the revolutionary anti-shah movement. The name Almakki was virtually synonymous with the underground religious opposition to the shah. Though many of the young imams who studied under Almakki shunned politics, anyone who had been trained by him was suspect.

Aqa Jaan assumed that the young imam, who wore his turban at a jaunty angle and doused himself with rosewater, was far from neutral. But he refrained from comment.

'What are you doing at the moment? Do you have your own mosque yet?'

'No, I'm a substitute imam in a number of different cities. When the regular imam is ill or away on a trip, I get called in to take his place.'

'Ah, yes,' said Aqa Jaan. 'We also make use of substitutes, except that we always call on the same one: an imam from the village of Jirya. He's very reliable, and comes the moment he's sent for.'

Aqa Jaan wanted to ask the young imam where his parents were from and why he hadn't asked one of his male relatives to accompany him. But he didn't bother, because he knew what the young imam's answer would be: 'I'm a grown man and I can decide for myself who

I want to marry. My name is Mohammad Khalkhal. I studied under Ayatollah Almakki. What else do you need to know?'

'How did you hear about our daughter? Have you ever seen her?' Aqa Jaan said.

'No, but my sister has met her. Besides, she was recommended to me by Ayatollah Almakki. He's given me a letter to give to you.' He took an envelope out of his pocket and handed it to Aqa Jaan.

If he had a letter from the ayatollah, there was nothing more to say. If Almakki approved of him, that was enough. The case was closed.

Aqa Jaan respectfully opened the envelope and read the following note:

In the name of Allah. I take the opportunity of Mohammad Khalkhal's visit to send you my regards. Wa-assalaam.

Almakki

There was something odd about the letter, but Aqa Jaan couldn't quite put his finger on it. The ayatollah had neither approved nor disapproved of the young man; he had merely sent his greetings. Evidently he wasn't all that impressed, or else he would have said so in his note. But Khalkhal did have a letter from Almakki and that meant something.

Aqa Jaan slipped the note into a drawer. 'I'm wondering how to proceed,' he said. 'I suggest we do the following: I'll tell Imam Alsaberi and his daughter that we've met. After that we'll set a date for you to come here with your family . . . with your father. Is that all right with you?'

'Yes,' Khalkhal said.

*　*　*

Shahbal showed Khalkhal to the door and went back to the study.

'What do you think, Shahbal?' Aqa Jaan asked.

'He's different. Very astute. I liked that.'

'You're right. You could tell just by the way he sat in his chair. He's a far cry from a rural imam. But I have my doubts.'

'What kind of doubts?'

'He's ambitious. The ayatollah didn't say anything specific about him in his note. He gave him a letter of recommendation, but then didn't comment on him. I sense hesitation in his note. Khalkhal probably isn't a bad person, but it's risky. Would he be the right man for our mosque? Alsaberi is soft; this young imam is hard.'

'What do you mean by that?'

'Is Alsaberi still up?'

Shahbal looked out through the curtain.

'The light's on in the library,' he said.

'Let's keep this to ourselves for a while. There's no need to tell the women yet,' Aqa Jaan said, and he went outside.

He knocked on the library door and went in. Alsaberi was sitting on his rug, reading a book.

'How was your day?' Aqa Jaan asked.

'The same as usual,' Alsaberi said.

'What are you reading?'

'A book about the political activities of the ayatollahs during the last hundred years. Apparently they haven't been idle: they've always found something to rebel against, always found a way to gain more power. This book is a mirror that I can hold up to myself to judge my own performance. I have nothing against politics, but it's not for me. I wasn't cut out for heroics. And that makes me feel guilty.'

Alsaberi was being unusually frank. Aqa Jaan seemed to have caught him at a good moment.

'I know that Qom isn't happy with me. I'm afraid that if I continue my policy of not speaking out, people will switch to another mosque or stop coming altogether.'

'There's no need to worry about that,' said Aqa Jaan. 'On the contrary, the fact that our mosque doesn't get mixed up in politics will attract *more* people. Most of the men and women who come to our mosque are ordinary, everyday people. The mosque is their home. They've been coming here all their lives, and they aren't about to stop now. They know you too well and have too much respect for you to do that.'

'But the bazaar,' the imam continued. 'The bazaar has always been at the forefront of every political movement. It says so in this book. During the last two hundred years, the bazaars have played a pivotal role. The imams have always used the bazaar as a weapon. When the merchants close the bazaar, everyone knows something important or unusual is about to happen. And I know the bazaar isn't happy with me.'

Aqa Jaan knew perfectly well what the imam was talking about. He himself wasn't all that happy with Alsaberi, but you can't dismiss a man because he's weak. Alsaberi was the imam of the mosque and would be its imam until he died. He knew that there was grumbling at the bazaar, that the merchants expected the mosque to do more, but he couldn't help it if Alsaberi was incompetent. Aqa Jaan had even been summoned recently to Qom, where the ayatollahs had told him in no uncertain terms that the mosque needed to take a harder line. They wanted it to speak out against the shah, and especially against the Americans. Aqa Jaan had promised that the mosque would be more vocal, but he knew that Alsaberi wasn't the man for the job.

Qom was the centre of the Shiite world. The great

ayatollahs all lived in Qom and controlled every mosque from within its sacred walls. The mosque in Senejan was one of the most important in the country, which is why the ayatollahs expected it to take a more active role. Qom asked questions, Qom issued orders, but with Alsaberi as its imam, Aqa Jaan would never be able to change the mosque. Perhaps that's why Almakki had sent the young imam to their house.

'I have a surprise for you,' said Aqa Jaan, changing the subject. 'It fits in with the subject of your book.'

'What is it?'

'Someone has come to ask for the hand of your daughter.'

'Who?'

'A young imam from Qom. A follower of Ayatollah Almakki.'

'Almakki?' the imam said, surprised, and he put down his book.

'He's not afraid of politics, he dresses well, he's confident and he wears his black turban at a jaunty angle,' Aqa Jaan said with a smile.

'How did he find us? I mean my daughter.'

'Everyone in Senejan knows you have a daughter. And everyone is free to ask for her hand. But I suspect that this young man has come not only for your daughter, but also for your mosque and your pulpit.'

'What?'

'There's bound to be a political motive if Almakki is involved.'

'We'll have to consider the matter carefully before we give him our reply. We need to know if he's after my daughter or the mosque.'

'Of course we'll look into it, but I'm not afraid of change. Nor do I avoid things that come my way. I don't believe in coincidence. He knocked on our door for a reason. He'll fit into this house quite nicely. We've had a few fiery imams in our mosque in the past. I'll go to Qom and talk to Almakki. If he approves of Khalkhal as a person and as a husband, I'll agree to the match. And I'll phone your son, Ahmad. He's not at the same seminary, but he probably knows Khalkhal.'

'Do whatever you think best, but be careful. It mustn't be a marriage made for religious and political reasons. I'm not going to give my daughter to the first imam who comes along. We have to make sure he's a good man. I want her to have a good marriage. I don't want to sacrifice her to the ayatollahs.'

'There's no need to worry,' Aqa Jaan said.

'I haven't been feeling well lately. My heart is often filled with sadness. I've become more anxious. I worry about everything, especially the mosque. Sometimes I don't know what to say during the Friday prayer.'

'You're tired. Why don't you go to Jirya for a few days? Take the grandmothers with you and relax for a week. It'll do them good to be back in Jirya too – they haven't been there for a while. You're torturing yourself with those self-imposed rules of yours. Nobody bathes as often as you do. And you're also isolated. At the rate you're going, you won't live very long. Go to Jirya. Who knows, soon you might have a strong son-in-law to lean on,' Aqa Jaan said. Smiling at the thought, he left the library.

The next day Aqa Jaan phoned Ahmad in Qom.

'Do you know a man named Mohammad Khalkhal?'

'Where did you meet *him*?'

'He wants to marry your sister.'

'You're joking!' he exclaimed.

'No, I'm not. What kind of a man is he?'

'I've never met him, but he's made quite a name for himself here. He's very eloquent and has an opinion on everything under the sun. He's not like any of the other imams. As to whatever else he might be up to, I don't know.'

'Do you think he'd be a suitable husband for your sister?'

'It's difficult to say. As far as I can tell, he's tough as nails. The only imam my sister has ever known has been her father. She thinks all clerics are like him.'

'Your sister's happiness is my primary concern,' said Aqa Jaan.

'He's a decent man, very intelligent, but I have no way of knowing whether he'd make her a good husband . . .'

'Thanks, Ahmad, I think I've heard enough.'

Aqa Jaan's next step was to phone the residence of Ayatollah Almakki and make an appointment. Early on Thursday morning his chauffeur picked him up and drove him to the station.

Wearing an overcoat and a hat, Aqa Jaan got out of the car and went into the monumental railway station. As soon as the manager saw him, he put out his cigar and hurried over to him. 'Good morning,' he said politely. 'May your journey be blessed!'

'*Inshallah*,' Aqa Jaan replied.

The long brown train that Aqa Jaan was about to board had arrived half an hour earlier from the south. From its starting point in the Persian Gulf, the train would continue on towards the east, stopping at dozens of stations on the way, until it finally reached the border with Afghanistan. Aqa Jaan had a three-hour train ride ahead of him.

The station was filled with hundreds of passengers and people waiting to pick up the travellers. There were men in hats, women in long coats and a surprising number of women not wearing chadors.

Outwardly, the country had been transformed. Aqa Jaan was struck by the change every time he travelled. The people from the south were freer and more relaxed than the people from Senejan. In the train you saw all kinds of women: women with bare heads (and even a few with bare arms), women who wore hats, women who carried handbags, women who laughed and women who smoked. Aqa Jaan knew that the shah had been responsible for these changes, but the shah was a mere puppet of the Americans. The religion of this country was being undermined by America, and there wasn't a thing anyone could do about it.

The manager invited Aqa Jaan into his office, offered him some freshly brewed tea and, when it was time for his train to leave, escorted him personally to the VIP compartment.

Three hours later the gleaming dome of Fatima's tomb came into view.

The train lumbered into Qom. Arriving at the station was like entering another world. The women were swathed in black chadors, the men had beards and there were imams everywhere you looked.

Aqa Jaan got out. The loudspeakers on the roofs of every mosque were blaring out the Koran recitations of the muezzins. There wasn't a single portrait of the shah in sight. Instead there were banners inscribed with Koranic texts. The shah would never dream of setting foot in Qom, and no American diplomat would even dare to pass through it.

Qom was the Vatican of the Shiites – the holiest city in the country, the place where Fatima, the daughter of

Muhammad, was buried. The golden dome of her tomb glittered like a jewel in the centre of the city.

Aqa Jaan took a taxi to Ayatollah Almakki's mosque. At twelve noon on the dot, the taxi pulled up in front of the mosque, and he got out.

The ayatollah came walking up with his students – young imams escorting him to the prayer room. Aqa Jaan nodded politely. The ayatollah held out his hand. Aqa Jaan shook it, went into the prayer room with him and took a place in the front row.

At the end of the prayer, Aqa Jaan sat on his heels beside the ayatollah.

'Welcome! What brings you to Qom?' the ayatollah enquired.

'First of all, I wanted to see your blessed face. But I also came to talk about Mohammad Khalkhal.'

'He was my best student,' the ayatollah said. 'And he has my blessing.'

'That's all I need to know,' Aqa Jaan replied. He kissed the ayatollah's shoulder and got to his feet.

'But . . .' said the ayatollah.

Aqa Jaan sat down again.

'He's a maverick.'

'What are you trying to tell me?' Aqa Jaan asked.

'Well, simply that he doesn't follow the herd.'

'I understand,' said Aqa Jaan.

'May the marriage be blessed and blessings on your journey home,' said the ayatollah, and he shook Aqa Jaan's hand again.

Aqa Jaan was pleased with what Almakki had said about Khalkhal. The ayatollah had given his approval.

But deep inside, Aqa Jaan still had his doubts.

* * *

When he got home, he called his nephew into his study. 'Shahbal, would you please bring Sadiq in here?'

When she heard that Aqa Jaan wanted to speak to her, Sadiq knew instantly that something was afoot.

'Sit down,' Aqa Jaan said to her. 'How are you?'

'Fine, thanks.'

'Listen, my daughter. Someone has asked for your hand in marriage.'

Sadiq's face went pale. She looked down at her feet.

'He's an imam.'

Sadiq turned to Shahbal, who smiled and said, 'An excellent young imam!'

Sadiq smiled.

'I went to Qom and talked to his ayatollah. He spoke highly of him. Your brother also approved of him. What do you think? Would you like to marry an imam?'

She was silent.

'I need an answer,' Aqa Jaan said. 'You can't greet a marriage proposal with silence.'

'He's handsome,' Shahbal told her. He grinned. 'He wears a stylish imam robe and shiny light-brown shoes. He's the answer to every girl's dream!'

Aqa Jaan pretended not to have heard his remarks, but Sadiq had heard every word. She smiled.

'What do you think? Shall we talk to his family?'

'Yes,' she said softly, after a long silence. 'Let's do that.'

'There's one more thing we need to discuss,' Aqa Jaan said. 'He's not at all like your father. He's a follower of Ayatollah Almakki. Does that name mean anything to you?'

Sadiq looked over at Shahbal.

'He's not a village imam,' Shahbal interpreted.

'Your life is bound to be stormy and difficult at times,' Aqa Jaan said. 'Do you think you could live that kind of life?'

She gave it some thought. 'What do *you* think?' she asked.

'On the one hand, it would be a great honour. On the other hand, it could be a living hell if you didn't support it fully,' Aqa Jaan said.

'May I talk to him first?'

'Of course!' said Aqa Jaan.

A week later Shahbal ushered Imam Khalkhal into the guest room, where a bowl of fruit and a pot of tea awaited him.

Then he fetched Sadiq and introduced her to Khalkhal.

She greeted him, but kept standing awkwardly by the mirror. He offered her a chair. She sat down and loosened her chador, so that more of her face was visible.

Shahbal left them alone and gently closed the door behind him.

The grandmothers stood by the *hauz* and kept an eye on things. Fakhri Sadat, the wife of Aqa Jaan, had caught a glimpse of Khalkhal from her upstairs window. Alsaberi's wife, Zinat Khanom, was in her room, praying that her daughter would have a good marriage. It was all she could do, since no one had asked her opinion. Her thoughts on the subject didn't count. Fakhri Sadat was the woman who made the decisions in this house.

Aqa Jaan's two daughters hid behind the curtains so they could see Khalkhal when he left the guest room.

The meeting between Khalkhal and his prospective bride had gone on for almost an hour when the guest-room door opened and Sadiq came out. She looked happy. She glanced at the grandmothers and went up to her room.

Shahbal gave Khalkhal a tour of the courtyard and introduced him to the grandmothers. Then Fakhri Sadat came downstairs. 'This is Aqa Jaan's wife – the queen of our household,' Shahbal said, laughing.

Khalkhal greeted her without looking directly at her. Then the girls were introduced, one by one. After Khalkhal had met everyone, Shahbal took him to the bazaar, so Aqa Jaan could speak to him.

A few days later Aqa Jaan received Khalkhal and his father in his study. Alsaberi was also present. Their conversation had little in common with traditional marriage negotiations, since not a word was said about money or carpets. The bride would present the groom with a gold-embossed Koran, and she would leave her father's house in a white chador, taking with her a collection of poems by the medieval poet Hafez. After all, everyone knew that the daughters of the wealthy families in Senejan weren't sent to their new homes empty-handed. Of course Sadiq would be provided with everything she needed. And so the rest of the conversation was about the mosque, the library, the books, the centuries-old cellars, the blind muezzin and the cedar tree in the courtyard. Lastly they set a date for the wedding.

'*Mobarak inshallah*,' the men said, and they shook hands.

When they were done, Sadiq came in bearing a silver tray with five silver teacups.

The wedding was scheduled to take place on the birthday of the holy Fatima – one of the best days for a wedding. The weather would be relatively hot, but a breeze from the mountains would cool things down and make you want to take your bride in your arms and crawl under a light blanket. During the summer, most people slept on their roofs. Here and there you saw a gauzy white canopy on the roof, which is where the brides and grooms slept.

There would be a special ceremony, to which the leading

44

families in the city and the bazaar would be invited. After all, this wasn't an ordinary wedding, but the wedding of Imam Alsaberi's daughter. And the groom wasn't an ordinary teacher or a registry clerk or even a merchant. He was an imam in a black turban who came from Qom.

Arusi

The day of the *arusi*, the wedding, had arrived.

Zinat Khanom asked her daughter to come to her room, then closed the door and kissed her. 'Are you glad you're going to marry Khalkhal?' she enquired.

'I don't know . . .'

'You should be. He's handsome and your father says he's very ambitious.'

'That's what scares me.'

'I was scared too when I married your father. Girls are always scared when they have to leave home with a man they barely know, but as soon as the two of you are alone together, your fear will disappear. After all, a girl has to marry and leave her father's house one day.'

Zinat Khanom calmed her daughter with soothing words, but deep in her heart she too had doubts. She didn't know why. Suddenly the ghastly memories of her past came flooding back, though she hid them from Sadiq.

'I still can't believe it,' she said to her daughter.

'Believe what?'

'That you're grown up, that you're going to marry and move away.'

'Why do you sound so sad?'

Zinat's eyes filled with tears.

'I wish you joy,' she said, and kissed her daughter.

*   *   *

Zinat had been afraid of losing Sadiq from the moment she was born. She was terrified of finding her dead one day – in her bed, in the garden, in the *hauz*.

The years of Sadiq's childhood had been filled with anxiety, and those years had taken their toll. Zinat was terrified of going to sleep at night, because she had such horrible nightmares.

Zinat Khanom and Alsaberi were cousins. She had married him when she was only sixteen. First they had a daughter, Orza, born five years before Sadiq. When she was eighteen, Orza married a man from Zinat's family. She now had three children and lived with her husband in Kashan.

Next Zinat had a son, Abbas. The hopes of the family had been pinned on him, for he was to be Alsaberi's successor as the imam of the mosque. But one hot summer's day, when Zinat and Abbas were alone in the house, a dreadful thing happened.

Abbas had just learned to walk and was merrily chasing the cats on his wobbly legs. Zinat had gone up to her room and forgotten about the boy. At some point she noticed that it was quiet outside and looked out of the window. Abbas was nowhere in sight. She raced down the stairs and saw the cats sitting by the *hauz*, and there, floating in the water, was the body of her son. She screamed and rushed to rescue him.

Two men, who had heard her screams, appeared on the roof of the mosque and hurried down to the courtyard to help her. They pumped the boy's stomach, but couldn't revive him. Zinat wailed. They turned him upside down and shook him, but to no avail. Zinat wailed. They lit a fire and held him above it to warm him. But it was too late. Zinat wailed again. The men lay the child on the ground and covered him with Zinat's chador. Abbas, the hope of the house, was dead.

No one blamed Zinat for what had happened. But she retreated to her room, shocked and grief-stricken.

Aqa Jaan went up to talk to her. 'I tell myself it was God's will, Zinat. You should do the same.'

From that moment on, no one in the house ever talked about Abbas. For months Zinat wept in silence, but his name was never mentioned. Zinat thought of the silence as her punishment, and a very harsh one at that.

A year later she became pregnant with Sadiq. She left her room and helped the grandmothers in the kitchen. Only two years later, after the birth of Ahmad, could Zinat hold her head up high again and resume her normal life.

Even so, Zinat never regained her position in the household. She lived in the shadow of Fakhri Sadat and felt herself to be inferior.

If Fakhri Sadat had suffered a similar fate, Aqa Jaan would have stood by her and done everything he could to ease her pain, but Alsaberi was weak. Though he had never blamed Zinat, he hadn't supported her during those difficult years either. At no time had he hugged her or spoken lovingly to her.

If your husband ignores you, everyone else will ignore you too. If you're invisible to your own husband, you become invisible to others.

Zinat was still invisible. Her daughter was about to get married and no one had asked her permission.

'It doesn't matter,' Zinat said to her image in the mirror as she wiped away her tears. 'My time will come.'

*   *   *

48

The house was a beehive of activity. The men had borrowed a curtain from the mosque – the long one that separated the men and women during prayers – and strung it across the courtyard.

Expensive carpets had been laid on the ground, and some men from the mosque had covered the walls of the house with tapestries woven with joyful sacred texts.

The trees were hung with green satin pennants inscribed with the poems of the old Persian masters. The most famous singer of sacred songs had been sent for from Qom. His renditions of rhythmic surahs from the Koran left a lasting impression on all who heard him.

Aqa Jaan had bought a new suit and gone to the barber. He liked being dressed in spotless new clothes. Thanks to Fakhri Sadat, he was one of the few merchants in the bazaar who paid attention to his appearance. His office boy kept his shoes polished, and the grandmothers ironed his shirts. Fakhri Sadat liked to tease him sometimes: 'You're the handsomest man in the city. Nobody who saw you with your clean-shaven face and dashing hat would ever guess that you could reel off the entire Koran by heart!'

The imam was sitting in the library as usual. Soon – after everyone had arrived – he would put in a brief appearance and then go back to his books.

The celebration had begun. The invited guests and the city's most influential men came trickling in. The men stayed on the right side of the courtyard, beneath the cedar tree, sitting on chairs grouped around the *hauz*, while the women went behind the curtain and sat in the beautiful, fragrant garden – the pride of the gardener, Am Ramazan. None of the guests had brought their children, which was unusual. Children were normally welcome at weddings, but this was such a distinguished gathering that they had not been invited.

The guests were served tea and the very best pastries. Both men and women had rosewater sprinkled on their hands.

All of those present – especially the women – were curious to see Khalkhal.

A car drew up to the door. The mayor stepped out and was welcomed to the house by Aqa Jaan. The men stood up when he came into the courtyard and waited until he had seated himself by the *hauz* before sitting down again.

A second car drew up to the door. This one, as they all knew, contained the groom. Aqa Jaan welcomed Khalkhal and led him over to the place of honour by the mayor.

The mayor stood up to offer his congratulations, but the groom looked right past him, as if he hadn't seen him and didn't know who he was. To Khalkhal, the mayor was a lackey of the shah. He refused to sit next to him, much less shake hands with him.

The mayor sat down again and no one commented on the incident. Aqa Jaan had been so busy talking to someone that he hadn't even noticed the snub.

At three o'clock the man from the registry office arrived with two bearded assistants, each of whom was carrying a ledger. They sat at the table where the marriage certificate was to be signed and opened their ledgers. The official part of the ceremony could begin.

Just then shouts arose from the women on the other side of the curtain. '*Salaam bar Fatima!*' they cried. 'Greetings to Fatima!'

This signalled the arrival of the bride. She sat down at the table where the registry clerks were busy writing in their ledgers.

The bride was more beautiful than ever. She was wearing a pale green chador with pink flowers over a milky-white gown. Her eyebrows had been carefully plucked, and she was wearing mascara, so that she looked more like a young woman than a girl.

The registry clerk asked for the bride's birth certificate. Aqa Jaan reached into his inside pocket, took out the document and handed it to him. The clerk meticulously noted the details in his ledger, then asked the groom for his birth certificate.

Khalkhal checked his pockets, one by one, but came up empty-handed every time. He and his father had a whispered exchange, after which he rummaged through his overnight bag. All eyes were glued on the groom, as everyone waited for him to produce the certificate.

'I forgot to bring it,' Khalkhal said.

Horrified gasps were heard from the women on the other side of the curtain. This was an extraordinary situation.

The registry clerk thought for a moment, then said, 'Do you have any other form of identification?'

Khalkhal checked his pockets again, and he and his father had another whispered exchange. No, he didn't have any kind of identification with him.

A scandalised buzz broke out on both sides of the curtain.

Aqa Jaan looked at the mayor and read the mistrust in his eyes. He looked at several of the bazaar's leading merchants. Everywhere he looked he saw disapproval. How could Khalkhal have forgotten to bring the necessary documents to his wedding? Everyone was waiting to see how Aqa Jaan would react. He suspected that Khalkhal had left his identification papers at home on purpose, hoping to force the family into letting their daughter marry him without having the marriage officially registered. That might be customary in the countryside, where the bride and groom simply exchanged vows in the presence of a village imam, and then the man was granted access to the woman's bed. In such a marriage the man was free to take other wives. But marriages of that sort no longer took place in the city and certainly not in the prominent circles to which Aqa Jaan's family belonged.

'Perhaps you left the documents at your father's house,' Aqa Jaan said to Khalkhal.

'No, I don't think so. They're in Qom.'

Aqa Jaan sat down beside the mayor and they conferred briefly.

'You're right,' the mayor concluded. 'You shouldn't go through with it.'

Then Aqa Jaan went over to Alsaberi, who had just emerged from the library and was standing by the cedar tree, next to the caretaker.

'We're going to have to postpone the wedding,' Aqa Jaan said. 'Khalkhal must go to Qom to get his identification papers.'

'In that case he won't be back until after midnight. It might be better for them to say their vows first. Then he can go to Qom and get his papers.'

'No, because once they've exchanged vows, that's that. Sadiq will belong to him and we'll be powerless to help her. He'll take her away, and we'll be left with nothing. You of all people should know that.'

'You're right,' Alsaberi replied. 'Let him go and get his papers.' And he went back into his library.

Aqa Jaan strode over to the registry clerk. 'Without valid identification papers,' he announced, 'there will be no marriage!'

Everyone began talking at once.

Aqa Jaan turned to Khalkhal. 'Don't worry,' he said calmly. 'You can go to Qom to get your papers. I'll wait. We'll all wait.'

Khalkhal was taken aback. 'But that's impossible! There's no train going to Qom at this hour. And I don't trust the buses.'

'I'll arrange for transport,' Aqa Jaan said. He went over to where the mayor was sitting and spoke with him. The mayor nodded several times in agreement.

'It's all set,' Aqa Jaan told Khalkhal. 'A jeep will pick you up shortly. The mayor's chauffeur will drive you to Qom. I'm a patient man, but you'd better not take too much time.'

Khalkhal had been outmanoeuvred. He stood up and stalked angrily to the door to wait for the jeep. For a moment Aqa Jaan thought he saw a flash of pure malice in Khalkhal's eyes, as if he had suddenly dropped his mask and revealed his true self.

A banquet had not been included in the wedding celebration, but Aqa Jaan felt obliged to feed his guests. 'Please accept my apologies,' he announced. 'These things happen. I cordially invite you all to stay for dinner.' Then he sent Shahbal to the restaurant opposite the mosque to arrange for food to be delivered.

Fakhri Sadat asked Aqa Jaan to come to her room so she could speak to him in private. 'Don't you think you were being a bit hard on the boy?'

'Maybe I shouldn't say this, but I don't trust him.'

'But you hardly know him.'

'He's no ordinary imam. He's shrewd. I didn't expect him to show up without identification papers. He has some scheme in mind, though I can't imagine what.'

'You men and your schemes! What on earth could he be up to?'

'Well, what's done is done. He's on his way to Qom now. We'll just have to be patient.'

'That's how it always is. Men make the decisions and women must be patient.'

'That's not true. I'm not about to give away a daughter of this house without a proper guarantee. I thought you'd understand.'

'I do, but what should I say to the women?' she said, avoiding his eyes.

'You know what to say. Welcome them, give them something to eat and keep smiling. Show them you can rise above the occasion . . . and be patient.'

At ten-thirty there was still no sign of Khalkhal. The guests had finished eating hours ago. The servants were going around with tea for the umpteenth time. The hookahs had been passed from hand to hand. The mayor, who had left for a few hours, had come back. The men from the bazaar had gone out after dinner, strolled along the river and assured Aqa Jaan that in his place they would have done the same thing.

Shahbal had been sent up to the roof as a lookout. When he finally saw the jeep, he signalled to Aqa Jaan.

A few minutes later the jeep drew up to the door.

Khalkhal got out, walked straight over to the registry clerk and slapped his birth certificate down on the table.

Someone shouted, '*Salawat bar Mohammad!* Blessings on the Prophet Muhammad!'

'*Salawat bar Mohammad!*' everyone shouted in response.

Aqa Jaan smiled. The men from the bazaar came back from their walk. The singer sang loudly:

By the night when it conceals the light!
By the day when it appears!
By the sun and its morning glow!
By the moon that follows in its wake!
By the day when it shows its glory!
By the sky and He who made it!
By the earth and He who spread it!
By the soul and He who shaped it!

Mahiha

Khalkhal had taken his bride to Qom. No one knew where the couple lived. The family hadn't expected him to keep it a secret, but they decided not to make an issue of it.

'It doesn't matter,' said Aqa Jaan. 'The door of our house is always open to them.'

Although Khalkhal had completed his imam training, he still didn't have a permanent position in a mosque. Once you had your own mosque, you could support yourself. Until then you had to make do with a modest allowance from your ayatollah.

Aqa Jaan had offered to finance him, but Khalkhal had refused. Still, by calling on his vast network, Aqa Jaan always managed to find a mosque where Khalkhal could fill in as a substitute imam.

Sadiq came home from time to time, but Khalkhal had forbidden her to give her address to her family. Occasionally she complained to her mother about her new living arrangements. The house was small, the atmosphere was oppressive and she hadn't managed to make any contact with the neighbours. 'Everything is so different in Qom,' she told her mother. 'People shut themselves up in their own homes with their own families, and the doors and curtains are always closed.'

'It's all part of adjusting to a new life, especially when you've moved to another city, not to mention a religious bastion like Qom. Khalkhal is young. He's just finished his training and doesn't have a permanent position yet.'

'I know, but Khalkhal is different from any of the men I've ever known. He's not like my father, he's not like Aqa Jaan, and he's not like Uncle Nosrat. I don't know how to get close to him. It's hard to have a real conversation. There are long, awkward silences when he's at home, and that scares me. He doesn't talk to me and I don't know what to say to him.'

'You shouldn't compare our life in this house to that in yours. This house is old. It's taken centuries for it to develop a rhythm of its own. But your house is that of a young imam with no history. You have to work at creating a home, at making it warm and hospitable, at seeking contact with your neighbours and showing your husband that you love him and are interested in him.'

'It's easier said than done, Mother. I can give him my love, but the question is whether he wants it.'

'Why wouldn't he?'

'I don't know!'

Sadiq was showered with love when she came home. They bought her shoes and clothes and gave her money and sent her back to Qom with her bags full.

When Khalkhal went off to another city to fill in as imam, he sent Sadiq home to her parents, and when he was finished, he came to collect her. Sometimes they left on the same day, and sometimes they stayed a week, in which case they slept in the Dome Room.

The Dome Room had a balcony, a kind of filigreed wooden porch, where you could sit and marvel at the shadows cast by the dome on the opposite wall – the same wall out of which the ants had once crept.

Eight hundred years ago, when the house had been

built, the architect had designed a room especially for the imam of the mosque. The delightful play of sun and shadows went on all day until twilight. At first all you could see was the shadow of the dome on the wall, but then the silhouette of the minarets came into view. Later the dome disappeared and only the minarets remained. Sometimes the shadow of a pigeon, a crow or a cat was projected onto the wall in the vivid evening light. At dusk the mosque cats liked to sit on the balcony and stare longingly at the bats swooping above the *hauz*.

In nice weather you could put a rug on the floor of the balcony, add a few pillows and sit there reading a book or drinking tea. The guests who occupied the Dome Room were always free to do as they pleased, which is why it was the ideal spot for Khalkhal's visits. He would stay there all day. The grandmothers would bring him food, and everyone else was careful not to disturb him.

Shahbal was the only one in the family with whom Khalkhal had any contact. He was often invited to eat with him. Shahbal had been fascinated by Khalkhal from the start. He'd met lots of imams, but Khalkhal had something the others lacked: he was full of new ideas and talked about exciting things. Shahbal liked to listen to him and to discuss a wide variety of topics.

Khalkhal was well informed. He talked about America as if he knew it like the back of his hand. He explained how the Americans had taken control of Iran and how they ruled it from behind the scenes. He told him how the Americans had first gained a foothold. 'It was like this. America was becoming a superpower and wanted a military base in Iran that could be used against the Soviet Union. But Mossadegh, our democratically elected prime minister, was a progressive politician and a nationalist.

He didn't want to give the land to the Americans, but they were getting impatient. They were afraid the Soviets would invite Mossadegh to Moscow and reinforce his anti-Americanism. So the CIA came up with the idea of staging a coup, and the shah went along with it. The plan was for Mossadegh to be assassinated. The Soviet Union got wind of it, however, and told Mossadegh. He arrested the pro-American military officers who supported the coup and had the shah's palace occupied. The CIA managed to whisk the shah away in a helicopter in the nick of time, and he was flown to the US in a fighter jet.'

'That's fascinating!' Shahbal said. 'I've never heard that before.'

'You won't find it in your schoolbooks,' Khalkhal said. 'The history you're being taught is based on lies.'

'What happened next?'

'To realise its global ambitions, America needed Iran. Our country occupies a strategic position in the Middle East and also shares nearly twelve hundred miles of border with the Soviet Union. So the CIA staged another coup, and this time they had the backing of several Iranian generals. Two days later, when everyone thought it had all blown over, Mossadegh was arrested. The generals seized control of the Parliament, and American tanks were parked at every major intersection in Tehran. Hundreds of criminals and prostitutes were then sent into the streets to wave around portraits of the shah.

'The next day the shah, with the help of a group of CIA agents, was reinstalled in his palace. The shah is a puppet. We have to get rid of him and the Americans.'

Shahbal got goose pimples when he listened to Khalkhal's impassioned descriptions of historical events.

The last time they ate together on the balcony, Khalkhal

told him about the armed struggle of the ayatollahs against the regime. He described the historic day when Ayatollah Khomeini, who had incurred the wrath of both the shah and the Americans, had fought back. Many young imams had been killed that day. Many more had been arrested, and Khomeini had been forced into exile.

Shahbal had often heard the name 'Khomeini', but he knew almost nothing about the man. He must have been about seven or eight years old when the uprising occurred. On his next visit Khalkhal promised to bring him a banned book, which contained an accurate account of the history of the ayatollahs' resistance movement in the last few decades.

That evening Khalkhal said something about prisons that made Shahbal rethink his ideas. 'No one's afraid of going to jail,' Khalkhal said. 'It's become a kind of university, especially for young activists.'

It was a novel concept. Shahbal had always thought of prison as a place for criminals.

'Political prisoners aren't like ordinary prisoners,' Khalkhal said. 'They're people who fight against the regime, people who are embarrassed by the presence of the CIA in this country. They're the most intelligent people, the ones who want to take the fate of the country into their own hands and radically change the political system. That's why the regime arrests them and keeps them in a separate wing, but then they're all thrown together, sometimes ten or twenty to a cell, and they meet people from all walks of life: students, artists, imams, politicians, leaders and teachers, as well as people with new ideas. They start talking and discussing things, so the prison cell becomes a university, where you can learn all kinds of things. Can you imagine what happens when you put so many intelligent people together in one cell? They swap stories and listen to each other's experiences.

Before you know it, you've joined them. Some people go in like a lamb and come out like a lion. I know lots of political prisoners – friends of mine, young imams, members of left-wing or right-wing underground movements. Have you ever heard of these movements?'

'No.'

'What are you doing here?'

'What do you mean?'

'I mean, in this house, in this city.'

'Not much. I go to school and to mosque.'

Khalkhal shook his head. 'I knew it. Nothing's going to happen in this city. It's weak. All over the country people are gradually turning against the shah, but Senejan is blissfully asleep. What else can you expect from a city with such a weak Friday Mosque? What does Alsaberi do all day in his library? Nothing, except let the grandmothers wash his balls! It's a shameful waste of this big, beautiful mosque. It's had a brilliant past. A history. It's time it had a fiery speaker. Do you know what I'm saying?'

Shahbal lapped up Khalkhal's words. He thought of Khalkhal as great and himself as small. He wanted to ask questions, but didn't dare. He was afraid of sounding stupid.

One time he'd hardly said a word all evening. Then, suddenly, just as he was about to leave, he blurted out, 'I'd like to show you something.'

'What?'

'My stories,' he said hesitantly. 'I write.'

'How interesting! Show them to me. Have you got them here? Read one out loud.'

'I don't know if they're any good.'

'I wouldn't know either, but it's good that you write. Go and get your stories!'

Shahbal went to his room and quickly returned with three notebooks, which he modestly handed to Khalkhal.

'You've written quite a lot,' Khalkhal said in surprise as he thumbed through them. 'I knew you were clever from the moment I laid eyes on you! Pick one of your stories and read it to me.'

'I've never shown them to anyone before,' Shahbal said. He flipped through a notebook until he found the page he wanted. 'I hardly dare to read it, but I'll do my best.' And he began to read: 'Early one morning, when I was going to the *hauz* to wash my hands before the prayer, I noticed that the light wasn't on in my father's room. It was the first time this had ever happened. He was always awake before I was and always went to the *hauz* before I did, but that morning everything was different. The *mahiha* – the fish – which usually darted through the water when they saw me, weren't moving, and their tails were all pointing in my direction. Brightly coloured scales floated on the surface, and there was blood on one of the tiles. I realised immediately that something was wrong. I ran to my father's room, pushed open the door, switched on the light and—'

'Very good!' Khalkhal said. 'You can stop now, I'll read the rest on my own. You have talent. Leave your notebooks with me. I'll look at them later.'

He went down to the courtyard and walked over to the *hauz*, where he stared at the sleeping fish in the glow of the lantern. A light was on in the library. The shadow of the imam fell on the curtain. He quietly opened the gate and went outside, towards the river.

Aba

It was five o'clock in the afternoon. The courtyard was covered in snow. Darkness was gradually closing in, and there was an icy wind. As usual the grandmothers were carrying towels and clean clothes into the bathroom so Alsaberi could bathe before the evening prayer.

Even though they'd lit the stove early in the morning, the bathroom was still cold. 'This has got to stop,' Golbanu grumbled. 'It's no longer healthy. He should bathe in the municipal bathhouse. If he goes on like this, he'll make himself ill.'

It was a special night – the anniversary of the night on which Imam Ali had been killed.

Ali was Islam's fourth caliph. On that night he had been in the mosque, leading the prayer with hundreds of believers lined up behind him, when Ibn Muljam came in, took a place behind Ali and started praying along with him. He waited until Ali got to the end of his prayer, then took out his sword and killed him with a single blow to the head. From that moment on, Islam was divided into two factions: Shiites and Sunnis.

The Shiites wanted Hassan, Ali's oldest son, to be his successor; the Sunnis backed a candidate of their own. The Shiites and the Sunnis have been at each other's throats ever since. Ali became the most beloved of the caliphs. Fourteen centuries after his death, the Shiites still mourned him as if he had just been slain.

Tonight the mosque would be filled to capacity. Alsaberi, who had memorised his sermon, was planning to talk at length about Ali. He had come up with a novel approach: after fourteen centuries of enmity between Shiites and Sunnis, he was going to suggest reconciliation.

He'd been practising his sermon all day in front of the mirror. 'There has been enough enmity! We are brothers! Let us be friends. Let us shake hands in the name of friendship and Islamic unity!'

He wanted his sermon to be a surprise, so he hadn't discussed it with Aqa Jaan. Besides, if he'd mentioned it beforehand, Aqa Jaan would have said, 'Why bother? There aren't any Sunnis in Senejan.'

Although there might not be any Sunnis here, and although they might not hear him, tonight he was determined to say something new, something no other imam had ever said before.

The grandmothers had kettles of water heating on the stove and were waiting for Alsaberi.

He was lost in thought. He tested the water with his hand and cautiously stepped into the tub. Holding onto the rim with both hands, he immersed himself in the water. After resurfacing, he exclaimed, 'Sunnis, let us shake hands! We are brothers! It's cold! So cold!'

One of the grandmothers poured hot water over his head while the other began washing him with soap. Meanwhile Alsaberi practised his sermon, all the while shivering with cold. 'Islam is in danger! We must forget our differences and fight side by side against our common enemy! *Cold!*'

He was still wondering whether he should change the last words to 'a common enemy'? It was ambiguous, because what did he mean by 'a common enemy'? The shah? The Americans? If he dared to utter those words, it would be the fieriest sermon he'd ever given, but he was in doubt.

'We're done!' said one of the grandmothers.

Alsaberi stood up. He stepped out of the tub, placing his right foot on the towel that had been spread on the floor, but because he'd let go of the rim, he suddenly slipped and fell, his left leg still in the tub.

'Dead!' he blurted out in shock.

The grandmothers were upset, but they immediately pulled him up and tried to get him back into the tub because, having touched the ground, he was unclean and would have to be washed all over again. Just then one of the cats bolted out from behind the stove. Frightened by Alsaberi's loud cry, it fell into the tub, brushed against his leg, leapt out of the tub and ran outside. The imam's wet, bare leg had been touched by a cat! Just the thought of it made Alsaberi nauseous. Maybe there were mice too. Alsaberi shivered in horror. The bathroom was unclean, the water was unclean, the towels were unclean, the grandmothers were unclean – and all of this on the night of Ali's death! The night on which he hoped to give the greatest sermon of his life. What was he to do? Where could he clean himself before the prayer? There was no time to waste; people were already waiting in the mosque.

'Allah!' he cried, with a lump in his throat. Then he stumbled outside, naked, and raced towards the *hauz*.

'Come back!' Golbanu screamed. 'It's been snowing. Come back!'

Alsaberi plunged into the *hauz* and disappeared under the water.

The fish fled to the far end, the crow screeched loudly and the grandmothers scurried down to the cellar and came back up with clean towels.

'You've been in there long enough!' Golebeh cried.

'Please come out!' Golbanu implored.

Alsaberi came up for air, then ducked back under the water again.

'Come out of there this instant!'

Alsaberi stood up. He momentarily lost his balance, but managed to right himself. Then he stepped out of the *hauz* and went over to the grandmothers, who threw some towels around him. Golbanu raced ahead to turn up the heater in the library, while Golebeh went down to the cellar to get more towels.

The heater was red-hot and the extra towels had been warmed, but where was Alsaberi?

'Maybe he went to his bedroom,' Golebeh said.

'Alsaberi!' Golbanu called.

'May God watch over him! Where on earth did he go? Alsaberi!'

The fish were huddled together in the *hauz*, the crow was screeching non-stop and the cats were peering over the edge of the roof as the grandmothers hurried over to the *hauz*. Alsaberi was stretched out in the snow, with the yellow glow of the lantern lighting up his face. His eyes were closed. On his lips was a frozen smile.

'Alsaberi!' the grandmothers shrieked.

But no one was home, everyone was in the mosque. The grandmothers ran up the stairs to the roof, scattering the cats as they went. Standing by the left minaret, which was Muezzin's usual post, they shouted with all their might, 'Alsaberi is gone!'

Inside the mosque, people heard their cry. Muezzin came charging up to the roof, followed by the caretaker and several men from the bazaar. They hurried down the stairs to the courtyard and went over to the *hauz*. The moment the caretaker saw Alsaberi's lifeless body, he cried, '*Enna lellah!*'

At the familiar words, everyone knew that Alsaberi was dead.

The men carried him into the library. The grandmothers dried their tears, because they knew you were supposed to be restrained in the presence of death. Mindful of their duties, they went to an antique cupboard behind the bookcase, took out a white sheet – the shroud the imam had bought for himself in Mecca – and handed it to the caretaker. He unfolded it and draped it over Alsaberi, all the while chanting a sacred verse.

Aqa Jaan came running in.

'*Enna lellah!*' the men cried in unison.

'*Enna lellah,*' Aqa Jaan replied calmly.

He knelt by the body, gently pulled back the shroud and looked at Alsaberi's face. Then he kissed him on the forehead and covered him up again.

Suddenly Zinat appeared in the doorway. Weeping, her face pale, she threw herself onto her husband's body.

The grandmothers helped her up and led her away.

Voices could be heard from the courtyard. People had hurried out of the mosque to see what was happening.

Aqa Jaan left the library and went to the courtyard. The news had travelled fast. Some men were already there with a coffin, which they carried over to the *hauz*. The imam's body was laid inside and taken to the mosque.

Seven men went up to the roof and cried in unison, '*Hayye ale as-salat!*'

Everyone who heard this call to prayer realised that the imam was dead. Every shopkeeper in the city, except for the bakers and the pharmacists, shut their doors and came to the mosque. A long line of police vehicles drove up, and the mayor's car drew up outside the mosque.

It was a blessed death, everyone said, because Alsaberi died on the same day as the holy Ali.

At nine o'clock that evening the coffin was placed on a catafalque by the mosque's *hauz*. It had been decided to leave the body there until the following day, so that people could pay their respects, and relatives who lived far away would have time to get to the funeral.

Aqa Jaan went back to the house. Before morning, he had to find an imam to lead the prayer for the dead. The most logical choice was Ahmad, Alsaberi's son and intended successor, but Ahmad hadn't completed his training. The other obvious person was the imam's son-in-law, but Aqa Jaan didn't have Khalkhal's address or phone number. Nor could he be sure that Khalkhal would arrive on time.

'We need him early tomorrow morning,' Aqa Jaan told Shahbal.

'We also need to find Sadiq. She should be told of her father's death,' Shahbal replied.

'I'll do what I can. I'll phone Ayatollah Almakki in Qom. This is Khalkhal's chance to show himself in a good light. The whole town will be here, and they're all anxious to meet him. I'll call everyone I know in Qom.'

The next morning Aqa Jaan went to the mosque to finalise the details. Thousands of people would soon be pouring in from the surrounding villages, so it was essential to have an imam of some standing to lead the prayer. To be on the safe side he'd sent a message to the imam in the village of Jirya, who normally substituted for Alsaberi, and warned him to be prepared.

Aqa Jaan was talking to the caretaker when a taxi pulled up in front of the mosque. Straightaway he recognised Khalkhal's black turban and saw Sadiq.

Khalkhal got out, came over to Aqa Jaan, offered his condolences and briefly bowed his head.

Aqa Jaan interpreted his bow as a gesture of reconciliation and an acknowledgement of Aqa Jaan's loyalty to the mosque. Ever since Khalkhal had shown up at the wedding without the necessary documents and Aqa Jaan had made him go to Qom to fetch them, Khalkhal had avoided him. Now he had bowed his head. Aqa Jaan therefore replied, 'I'm proud of you, and I'd like you to be the imam of this mosque until Ahmad is ready to follow in his father's footsteps. Do you accept this offer?'

'Yes, I do,' said Khalkhal.

Aqa Jaan kissed Khalkhal's turban, and Khalkhal kissed Aqa Jaan's shoulder in return.

'Go inside and get some rest. The men from the bazaar will come for you shortly. Shahbal will let you know when it's time.'

It was busy in the house. Many of the guests had already arrived. The grandmothers were bustling about, making sure everything was in order. The moment they saw Khalkhal, they rushed into the kitchen to fetch the traditional symbols – a mirror, red apples and a fire – so he could be properly welcomed to the house as an imam.

At noon carpets were laid on the street in front of the mosque so people could pray. Alsaberi's coffin was carried out and placed on a silk rug. Thousands of people were gathered outside, waiting for Khalkhal to appear. A group of the bazaar's most influential men escorted Khalkhal to the coffin, where he would lead the prayer.

From the roof of the mosque, blind Muezzin shouted, '*Allahu akbar!*'

At this signal, everyone lined up in rows behind Khalkhal.

Imam Khalkhal loosened his black turban so that the end dangled against his chest – a sign of mourning – then turned towards Mecca and chanted:

> *Oh, you shrouded in your garments!*
> *Stay awake, but not all night,*
> *Half of it or a bit less,*
> *Or a bit more.*
> *By the night when it retreats!*
> *We have sent you a messenger,*
> *As we once sent a messenger to Pharaoh.*
>
> *Oh, you cloaked in your mantle!*
> *Stand up and deliver your warning!*
> *By the moon,*
> *And by the morning when it dawns.*

Family

According to tradition, Alsaberi's death was to be followed by forty days of mourning. During this period, relatives who lived far away and had been unable to attend the funeral would come and stay for a week. These family gatherings were special. Everyone ate together and stayed up until the small hours, talking in groups and moving about from room to room.

One of the guests was Kazem Khan, Aqa Jaan's ageing uncle and the oldest male member of the family. He was treated by everyone with love and respect.

Kazem Khan never came by himself, but was always accompanied by a group of villagers. Nor did he ever take a bus or taxi. In the old days he and his contingent of villagers arrived on horseback. Later, when he was too old to ride, he was driven to Senejan in a jeep.

He always got out of the jeep in front of the mosque, went into the courtyard, brushed the dust from his clothes and washed his hands and face in the *hauz*. Then he climbed the stairs to the roof, paused to get his breath, took off his hat, said *salaam* to the crow and to the storks nesting on the minarets, put his hat back on his head and went down the stairs to the courtyard.

When the mourners saw Kazem Khan on the roof, they raced over to the stairs to greet him. Then, surrounded by the group of men as if he were an ancient king, he made his way to the Opium Room, where an opium kit and a brazier had been made ready for him.

Women and children adored Kazem Khan. His pockets were always full of poems for the women and banknotes for the children. He was a famous village poet, an eccentric who lived in the mountains. He'd been married once, but his wife had died young. Since then he'd lived alone, though plenty of women welcomed him to their beds.

He ate sparingly, looked healthy and enjoyed life. He had seen everything, done everything and lost a great deal, but there were three things in his life that never changed: his love of poetry, his love of opium and his love of women.

The moment he arrived, the grandmothers dropped whatever they were doing and catered to his every whim. They had an uncanny ability to sense when he was coming, and the first thing they did was to air out the Opium Room.

Next they got out a special teapot and placed it on a tray so they could serve him a glass of freshly brewed tea. As soon as he crossed the threshold, they heated his opium pipe, sliced the opium, arranged the slices on a porcelain plate and set the plate beside the brazier, in which a pile of cherry twigs burned with a soft, blue flame.

When Kazem Khan came for a visit, the grandmothers put on their best clothes and daubed themselves with scent. Everyone knew they did it specially for him. Then they waited to be summoned. When they heard him call out 'Khanom!' – the Persian word for 'lady' – the grandmothers went to his room. Not at the same time, but one by one. Golebeh stood guard outside the door when Golbanu was inside and vice versa.

It had been that way from the beginning. They had known Kazem Khan since they were girls, and had been brought down from the mountains to work in the house as maids. Kazem Khan had promptly claimed them both. In those days how could any girl have resisted his charms? The first time they'd met – when he entered the house in the company of his horsemen – he had laid his hands on the two maids and received them, in turn, at night in his bed.

The hours they spent with Kazem Khan were the happiest the grandmothers had ever known in that house. In their younger years, they sparkled when he was there, skipping across the courtyard and singing as they worked in the kitchen.

Now that they were old, they could no longer be heard giggling in the kitchen, but if you looked carefully, you could see the smiles on their faces and smell their delightful rose perfume.

After Kazem Khan had rested for a while, eaten a bit and smoked enough opium to relax him, he got up and went into the courtyard to greet his relatives. First, however, he went up to the old cedar tree, poked the trunk with his walking stick, inspected the branches and touched the leaves. Then he went over to the *hauz* and recited his latest poem:

> *Del-araaie del-araaie del-araa,*
> *Samman-qaddi, boland-baalaa, del-araa . . .*

> *Darling, darling, my darling,*
> *My tall, jasmine-scented darling,*

73

The clouds are crying lover's tears,
The garden is a sweetheart's laugh.
The thunder grumbles as loudly
As I do at this early hour.

The children raced over when they saw him standing by the *hauz*. He patted them on the head and read them a new poem, which he'd written specially for them:

A deaf man thought:
I can sleep a bit longer,
Until the caravan passes by.

The caravan passed by,
In a billowing cloud of dust,
But the deaf man didn't hear it.

Kazem Khan provided the children with a brief explanation: 'The caravan is a symbol of fleeting time, and the deaf man represents people who fritter away their precious time.'

At the end of the poetry session he handed each child a banknote, pausing longer by the girls, who were encouraged to give him a kiss, for which they received an additional red banknote.

Then he turned to the women. Fakhri Sadat, the wife of Aqa Jaan, was obviously accorded the most attention. He always had a poem for her – the beauty of the house. He handed it to her and she smiled and tucked it in her sleeve.

Eyes that strike your soul like the lash of a whip.
And so green that they look like apples.
Your eyelashes have stolen my heart.

Your lips speak of justice, but your eyelashes steal.
Now you demand a reward for the stolen goods.
How odd: I, who was robbed, must fence them for
    you?

The cats were addicted to Kazem Khan's opium. A row
of them always sat up on the roof, where they could keep
an eye on him. The moment he headed towards the Opium
Room, they jumped down and waited expectantly by the
door. Every time he took a puff, he blew the smoke in
their direction. The cats were overjoyed by the clouds of
smoke.

Today, after his afternoon nap, Kazem Khan went down
to the cellar to pay his customary visit to Muezzin. He
liked to go down to Muezzin's studio to have a chat and
drink some tea.

'My greetings to Muezzin!' he boomed in a poet's voice
as he entered the studio. Muezzin stood up, but because
he was up to his elbows in clay, he didn't come out from
behind his pottery wheel.

'How are you?'

'Fine.'

'And how's your son Shahbal?'

'Also fine.'

'And your daughter?'

'She leads her own life, now that she has her own
family.'

With his acute hearing and keen sense of smell, Muezzin
didn't miss much. Some people claimed that he wasn't
blind at all, that from behind his dark glasses he saw
everything that went on. But Muezzin had been born blind.
He never went anywhere without his sunglasses, which
Nosrat had brought him from Tehran, or without his hat
and walking stick.

'How's your clock?' Kazem Khan asked him. 'Is it still ticking?'

'Yes, thank goodness.' Muezzin smiled.

The odd thing about Muezzin was that he always knew what time it was. It was a gift. He had an internal clock that was extremely accurate. Everyone in Senejan knew about it. 'What time is it, Muezzin?' people asked when they ran into him. And he always told them the right time. Children especially enjoyed asking him for the time when they saw him out walking. 'Do you know what time it is, Mr Muezzin?' the boys and girls would ask, and then burst into giggles when he told them the exact time.

He considered it his duty to share this divine gift with others.

Muezzin was the official muezzin of the mosque, but he spent most of his time in the cellar making pottery. It wasn't his job; it wasn't his hobby – it was his life. If it weren't for his clay, he didn't know what he'd do with himself.

From time to time Shahbal would deliver his father's wares to a shopkeeper in the bazaar who sold them on consignment. Muezzin was the only traditional potter for miles around, which may be why his vases, pots and dishes sold so well.

He had made the huge flowerpots in the mosque's court-yard as well as a giant vase in the square outside the bazaar, which was filled with red geraniums in the spring.

Pottery-making kept him from being bored. And yet there was something else that made his life even more meaningful: a transistor radio.

He kept it hidden in his pocket, since radios were forbidden in this house. They were thought to be unclean.

A true believer would never touch a radio, which was looked upon as a propaganda tool of the shah. A radio didn't belong in the house of the mosque, but Muezzin had kept it tucked in his pocket for so long that it felt like a part of him.

Nosrat had given it to him.

Nosrat was an unusual man. Nobody knew what he did in Tehran. Some said that he worked in a cinema, to his family's great shame, while others claimed that he earned his living as a photographer. Nosrat was well liked. He always had some news to report and was forever coming home with novelties. He surprised them all with his strange lifestyle, showing the residents of the house a side of life they had never seen.

Once, during one of his spring visits, he saw Muezzin going down to the river before the sun was up and wondered what he was doing. He followed him, staying well back so Muezzin couldn't hear his footsteps.

Muezzin crossed the bridge and hurried through the wheatfields and vineyards on the other side. It was still dark, though dawn was not far off. He kept walking until he reached the almond grove, where the boughs were sagging under the weight of the blossoms.

After a while Nosrat lost sight of him. He stole through the almond grove as quietly as he could, but didn't see Muezzin anywhere. He stopped by one of the trees. All was still. Then a glimmer of light pierced the darkness and thousands of birds began to sing. A moment of great beauty.

Suddenly he saw Muezzin, standing motionless amid hundreds of almond trees, his head cocked to one side as he listened to the birds.

The air was filled with the scent of the blossoms and

the birds were welcoming the morning with their song. Muezzin, still clutching his walking stick, stood transfixed, like a man of stone, in the middle of the almond grove.

When the first golden rays of light struck the almond trees, the birds stopped twittering and flew off in a rush of wings towards the mountains.

After the birds had gone, Muezzin returned home.

That evening Nosrat went to his room. 'Have you got a moment, Muezzin?'

'Come in. I've always got a moment for you.'

'I'd like to show you something. Or rather let you listen to something.'

He took a radio out of a bag and plugged it in. A small green light went on. Nosrat turned the knob, searching for a station. Suddenly the room was filled with music. Nosrat closed the door and said, 'Listen to this.'

Muezzin listened. You could see him straining his ears, trying to discover where the sound was coming from. When it came to an end, he took a deep breath and asked, 'What was that?'

'A symphony! What you heard this morning by the almond trees was a symphony, too – a symphony of birds. What you heard just now was a symphony made by people. I saw you standing by the trees this morning, listening to the birds. I think you need a bit of music in your life.'

The next time Nosrat came home, he brought Muezzin a transistor radio. Late that night he slipped it into his brother's hands. 'Now you can listen to music whenever you want to. And to the news and to other people.'

'A radio in this house? What would Aqa Jaan say?'

'You're a grown man,' he said. 'Put it in your pocket

and don't tell him about it. You don't owe anyone an explanation! I have something else for you, too, something no one in Senejan has ever seen.' And he handed him a tiny gadget with a set of wires.

'These are earphones. When you want to listen to the radio, you put them in your ears. Stand up and I'll show you how they work.'

Muezzin hesitated. Nosrat put the radio in Muezzin's pocket, threaded the wires under his sweater, stuck the earphones in his ears and switched on the radio.

'Can you hear it?'

'Yes!'

'Excellent! And remember, if anyone asks you what it is, don't answer!'

Ever since then Muezzin had gone everywhere with his earphones in, and when anyone asked him what those things in his ears were, he didn't answer. After a while everyone got used to them and assumed they were some kind of extension to his dark glasses.

At the end of the forty days of mourning, the men of the family gathered together in the Opium Room. They sat round the brazier and smoked with Kazem Khan.

The grandmothers had taken seven opium pipes out of a trunk in the cellar and had warmed them in the embers.

The men smoked opium, sipped tea, sucked sugar crystals and reminisced about Alsaberi while the smoke spiralled up out of their mouths and drifted through a half-open window.

The women were in the dining room, smoking a hookah. Zinat was the only one who wasn't there. Ever since Alsaberi's death, she had spent hours in the mosque's library, reading. Aqa Jaan was aware of it, but had decided to let her cope with her grief in her own way.

Before it got dark the men took a walk by the river, then went to the mosque to hear Khalkhal speak.

During the last few weeks, Khalkhal had spoken in the mosque every Friday. As these sermons were intended to let the worshippers get acquainted with him, he had deliberately chosen neutral topics. He was waiting patiently for the right moment to show the men of the bazaar what kind of a man he was and how the pulpit could be used as a weapon when the need arose. But the time was not yet ripe. Until the shadow of Alsaberi's death had passed and he'd won everyone's trust, he had to keep a low profile. Tonight he was planning to talk about Alsaberi and focus on the long history of the mosque. Aqa Jaan had provided him with the necessary documents a while ago and he had examined them in detail.

After their walk, the men performed their ablutions in the *hauz* and hurried over to the mosque. It was customary for the men of the family to stand at the door and welcome the guests.

The grandmothers had repeatedly warned the women that it was time to go, but they were still in the dining room, eating fruit, drinking tea and smoking the hookah. After Aqa Jaan had issued his final warning, the grandmothers bustled into the dining room. 'The prayer, ladies!' they chided. 'Hundreds of women are waiting for you in the mosque and you're sitting around smoking a hookah! Hurry, or Aqa Jaan himself will come and fetch you!'

Fakhri Sadat flung on her black chador, and the rest of the women followed her to the mosque. Zinat emerged from the library and trailed along behind the others.

The only person who had so far failed to arrive was Nosrat. Still, he usually turned up unexpectedly: he never phoned, he never knocked, suddenly you'd see him standing in the middle of the courtyard or strolling past the rooms, snapping pictures of everyone when they least expected it.

He hadn't come to Alsaberi's funeral. They hadn't been able to reach him by phone and the telegram had arrived too late. But he'd let Aqa Jaan know that he would be home tonight for sure.

Now that everyone had gone to the mosque and the house was quiet, the grandmothers washed their hands and face in the *hauz* and sat down on the bench, beneath the lantern.

'I don't feel like going to the prayer,' Golbanu said.

'Let's rest here for a while before they all come back,' Golebeh replied.

Since Alsaberi's death, they'd had no reason to be in the library, and because they weren't close to Khalkhal, they didn't dare to go in when he was there. As long as Alsaberi had been alive, the library had been their private domain. Khalkhal had robbed them of that. They disliked him because of it and longed for the day when Alsaberi's son would finish his training and be installed as the mosque's imam.

'Alsaberi was like a pearl that slipped through our fingers,' Golebeh said. 'Khalkhal is arrogant. He struts around like a sultan, keeps his distance from everyone, and doesn't even sit with the other men. He's the most conceited imam this house has ever had. He holes himself up in the library and expects Kazem Khan to come to *him*. Aqa Jaan knew it from the start. It was sensible of him to send Khalkhal back to Qom to get his identification papers.'

The grandmothers were greatly offended, and now with Alsaberi gone, they realised that they weren't going to live for ever either. They had been so busy with the funeral that the last few weeks hadn't been too awful. But what would they do when all of the guests had gone?

Since Khalkhal had taken over the library, they'd been forced to spend their days and evenings in the kitchen, but they couldn't stand being cooped up there much longer. If they couldn't escape to the library occasionally, the house would finish them off for good.

More than once they'd decided to pour their hearts out to Aqa Jaan. But why bother? They realised that the imam's death was the end of an era.

Sometimes they went into his empty bathroom and wept silently.

Kazem Khan was their only hope. Yet he too was getting old. When he died, the light would go out of their lives for ever.

The grandmothers sat on the bench by the *hauz* for a long while without talking. The sky was clear; one by one the stars came out. They could hear the bats squeaking. A stranger looking down at the two figures from the roof of the mosque would no doubt assume they were statues.

They would have fallen asleep if the silence hadn't suddenly been broken by a rustling in the darkness by the trees. 'Did you hear that?' Golebeh whispered to Golbanu.

Kazem Khan, they thought, might have stayed in his room instead of going over to the mosque.

They padded over to the Opium Room, but the door was locked. From the courtyard came a muffled giggle.

'What was that?'

They hid behind the cedar tree and listened to the sounds of the night. Again there was a girlish giggle.

This was followed by the opening of the door to one of the guest rooms. 'It's probably Nosrat!' Golebeh whispered.

'Mercy!'

They caught sight of a silhouette in the light coming from the room and recognised Nosrat's shadow.

'When did he get home? Why didn't we see him? And who's that woman?' Golebeh exclaimed.

A woman in a black chador was briefly visible in the green glow of the minarets before being engulfed again by the darkness.

'Maybe it's that woman from Tehran.'

'No, that rascal never stays with anyone for long. Besides, the woman from Tehran was short; this one is tall and has on a chador. It's a different one.'

'What are they doing?'

'I haven't the faintest idea.'

Nosrat led the girl over to the courtyard steps.

'Come on, sweetie,' he said to her.

'I'm not going up on the roof! I wouldn't dare!' the girl said, laughing.

'Don't be scared,' Nosrat said. 'Nobody's going to see us. They're all busy reciting their prayers. The house is empty.'

'I'm not going up there: it's too high!' she said.

'Why's he taking her up to the roof?' Golbanu whispered.

'The devil himself doesn't know what Nosrat is thinking,' Golebeh replied.

There was a silence, then a few moments later they saw Nosrat and the girl on the roof. The grandmothers tiptoed over to the stairs, climbed up to the roof, crawled over to the dome on their hands and knees and crouched behind it.

Nosrat opened the trapdoor in one of the minarets, to reveal a set of increasingly narrow and rickety stairs.

'I don't dare climb up those stairs!' the woman exclaimed.

'Don't be such a scaredy-cat,' Nosrat said gently. 'It'll be fun! Besides, you promised. Come on, I want to take you to the top of the minaret, I want to kiss you and make love to you in that holy green glow right at the top.'

'I won't do it! Somebody will see us.'

'There's no need to be afraid. Once we're up there, no one can see us.'

He helped her through the trapdoor, while she laughingly repeated, 'I won't go, I don't dare, I don't want to!' Once she was safely on the first stair, he crawled into the minaret and closed the trapdoor behind him.

The grandmothers, from their hiding place behind the dome, looked at each other in astonishment.

'Lord have mercy!' they muttered.

In the green light high up in the minaret, they saw Nosrat and the girl. Their shadows fell on the wall on the other side of the mosque.

The wind caught the girl's chador, and it fluttered out of the minaret like a black flag. 'Stop that!' the girl moaned. And because she was so high up, her words echoed over the mosque.

Nosrat's giant shadow began making rhythmical movements on the wall. The grandmothers clapped their hands to their mouths and trembled at the sight. At a certain point he pushed the girl against the edge of the minaret, so that she exclaimed with a nervous laugh, 'Stop it! I'll fall!'

Her laughter rang out over the mosque, but was quickly drowned out by Khalkhal's sermon, which was being broadcast over a loudspeaker. The girl moaned again. Then there was an unexpected silence and the shadows disappeared from view.

The grandmothers slipped out of their hiding place and crept down the stairs. They unfurled their prayer rugs on the floor of their room, put on their chadors and hurriedly turned to face Mecca.

The Sermon

During the first few months, Khalkhal had managed to keep things on an even keel in the mosque. He knew that agents of the secret police were attending his sermons in order to find out what he was up to.

In everyday life he had few social skills and came across as a stiff and stern imam, but the moment he climbed into the pulpit he was transformed into a witty man with a ready smile who spiced up his sermons with humour, so that it was a pleasure to listen to him.

In his first sermons he deliberately focused on neutral topics, often taking a surah from the Koran and explaining the historical and narrative aspects of the text. Sometimes he took the analysis a step further and talked about the power of the language and the poetry of the surahs. He gave examples and read melodious passages in his beautiful voice.

His listeners enjoyed his interpretations. The majority of the mosque-goers couldn't read the Koran, much less understand it. The Koran had been written in Arabic, which bore little resemblance to Persian. Besides, the language in which it had been written was fourteen hundred years old, which meant that many of the historical references in the surahs couldn't be understood without some measure of expertise.

Khalkhal was not only knowledgeable, but he could also explain the Koran in a simple way that ordinary people could understand.

The agents of the secret police enjoyed his humour and were satisfied with his sermons. They sent positive reports to the main office.

The bazaar was also satisfied with Khalkhal. The merchants praised his knowledge of history and his skill in translating the ancient texts, though, as some of them occasionally hinted to Aqa Jaan, they had expected more fireworks. 'He's a substitute imam,' Aqa Jaan always told them. 'We can't be too demanding. In a year or two, when Alsaberi's son has finished his training, we'll have a permanent imam, and then we'll know where we stand.'

The bazaar might grumble, but Khalkhal had stolen the hearts of the worshippers by gradually bringing up new and startling topics. Sometimes he discussed things the merchants had never heard of before.

Recently he'd talked about migratory birds – a topic not usually discussed in the mosque. He described how the birds could always find their way back home. Even fledglings, he explained, could fly an unfamiliar route and still find their way back to their parents' nest.

People listened to him in wonder as he described the hierarchy in the ant kingdom and the precision with which the ants worked together. He showed them traces of God's greatness.

Aqa Jaan admired Khalkhal for his fresh approach and was pleased that his modern subjects were attracting a younger crowd: more and more youngsters were coming to the sermons on Fridays.

Khalkhal had learned a bit of English. He could barely speak it, but he was able to read English texts. He bought a scientific journal published in the UK and spent hours in the library, looking up words in the dictionary and trying to understand the articles. Then he formed his own opinion and turned it into an exciting sermon.

In one of his sermons he talked about aeroplanes and the history of aviation. He praised Orville and Wilbur Wright for trying to fly like birds, but hastened to point out that the ancient Persians had attempted flight long before the Americans. He gave the story a humorous twist. 'The Americans,' he began, 'always want to be the first in everything. They began to fly fifty or sixty years ago, but the roots of aviation lie deep in our own soil.

'Long ago Nimrod, one of our earliest Persian kings, decided that he would fly. He was so powerful he thought he could do whatever he wanted. He even thought he could compete with God. One day he decided he would go into the sky to do battle with God. He ordered the scientists of his day to make a vehicle that could fly. They came up with a spectacular invention: a rudimentary aeroplane based on a chariot. The four corners of a specially designed wicker chair were attached to four powerful eagles by means of long, strong ropes. Nimrod seated himself in his royal chair, and four pieces of meat were dangled high above the heads of the eagles. The birds spread their wings and tried to grab the meat, in the process pulling the chariot into the sky. And that's how the world's first aeroplane came into being.'

Another time Khalkhal talked about Einstein and his theory of relativity. None of his listeners had ever heard of Einstein. They had no idea that light could travel, let alone that it travelled at a speed of almost 300,000 kilometres per second.

Khalkhal, aware of their ignorance and hoping to impress them, started off by reading a quotation in English. He might, in fact, have been the first imam in the country to use an English quotation in a sermon: 'Einstein said,

"One thing I have learned in a long life: that all our science, measured against reality, is primitive and child-like – and yet it is the most precious thing we have."'

He didn't explain the quotation, but told them about the theory of relativity, or at least as much of it as he himself understood. 'Let's suppose we have a plane that can fly 300,000 kilometres a second and that it's parked up on the roof of the mosque, waiting for passengers. Let's also suppose that we divide the passengers into two groups: one with boys and one with girls between the ages of twelve and fifteen. The girls are asked to stay here in the mosque and the boys are sent up to the roof as passengers.

'The pilot revs the engines, the plane takes off and the boys are hurled into space. Don't forget that the plane is flying at the speed of light. Listen carefully now. The boys fly for three hours, then come back and land on the roof of the mosque. According to their watches they've been in the air for three hours. The boys get out of the plane, walk down the stairs and go into the prayer room. They pull back the curtain between the men's and women's section and can't believe their eyes. The girls have turned into old women, into toothless hags!'

His listeners stared at each other in puzzlement and disbelief. How could the girls have aged so much in the three hours the boys were gone?

'Relativity,' Khalkhal explained. 'The relative speed of light. A different logic applies when you travel at the speed of light. That's why I chose that quotation. Traces of God are everywhere. Power upon power, light upon light.'

Meanwhile, Khalkhal's fame had spread throughout the city. He was especially popular with the young people, and the women doted on him.

Even though he was married, he was surrounded by veiled women who slipped him love letters as he strode through the mosque's dark corridors. He tucked the letters into his robe without so much as a backward glance.

'You're a handsome imam,' said one woman, when she chanced upon him alone in the corridor.

'I want to fly into space in Einstein's aeroplane with you,' said another in passing.

'You smell so good. Where do you buy your cologne?' asked a young woman from out of the darkness, making sure to keep her face concealed.

'You look so handsome when you wear your turban at an angle,' whispered another.

The curtain separating the men's and women's sections ran down the entire length of the prayer room. The pulpit was on a platform between the two. The young women usually sat in the first few rows so they could get a better look at Khalkhal. He revelled in their attention.

Khalkhal waited patiently for the birthday of the Prophet Muhammad, when he would be able to make his true feelings known. According to custom, that's when issues of vital importance were discussed. It was no coincidence that much of the protest in the holy city of Qom had taken place on the Prophet's birthday. Everyone was curious to know what Khalkhal was going to say on that day.

Khalkhal entered the prayer room on the Prophet's birthday escorted by Aqa Jaan and Shahbal. He sat down in his chair and, after a brief silence, began to recite the melodious Earthquake surah:

Edha zolzelati alarzo zelzaalaha . . .

When the earth is shaken to its foundations,
And people are like scattered moths,
And the mountains are like carded wool,
You will ask: what is wrong with it?
On that day it will declare its tidings.

The tone of Khalkhal's voice had changed. His words sounded more powerful than ever.

The mosque was filled to overflowing and everyone was listening intently to his words. 'Imam Alsaberi has left us,' Khalkhal said, 'but the mosque has remained. One day all of us will pass away, but the mosque will remain.

'Is that true? Will the mosque be here for ever? No, not even the mosque will be here for ever. Imams come and go, mosques come and go, but the voice remains.'

The men exchanged puzzled glances. Aqa Jaan and Shahbal looked at each other: 'The voice remains? What does that mean?'

But Khalkhal was right, Aqa Jaan thought. Alsaberi had been forgotten and none of his words had remained, because he'd had nothing to say. Alsaberi's father had been different. He'd been a remarkable imam who'd given fiery speeches, a man who wanted to make things happen, to change things. A man who dared to call a spade a spade. During his time as imam, he'd had the city in the palm of his hand. With one small gesture he'd been able to stir the bazaar to action. Alsaberi's father had been dead for decades, but his voice remained. His voice lived on in the city's memory.

He'd once preached a fiery sermon on the Prophet's birthday against Reza Khan, the father of the present shah. Reza Khan had outlawed chadors and had ordered his soldiers to stop any veiled woman they saw on the streets and take her down to the police station. Alsaberi's father had been arrested and banished to the city of Kashan. After that the secret police had boarded up the doors of the mosque.

Aqa Jaan remembered the arrest as though it had been yesterday. Several military vehicles had pulled up to the mosque, and armed soldiers had leapt out. Then an officer arrived in a jeep. Tucking his baton under his arm, he got out and strode into the prayer room with his shoes on, intending to arrest the elderly imam and haul him off to jail.

Aqa Jaan, then a young man who had only just been put in charge of the mosque, calmly went up to the officer and said, 'If you leave the mosque now, the imam will come out by himself and go with you quietly. If you don't, I'm afraid you'll have a riot on your hands. Consider yourself warned.'

He said it so clearly and firmly that there was no room for doubt. The officer looked at the worshippers, who had formed a circle around the imam. He got the message. 'Bring me the imam,' he said, poking his baton in Aqa Jaan's chest. 'I'll wait outside.' He stalked out of the prayer room and waited by the gate.

Aqa Jaan, his head held high, escorted the imam to the jeep, followed by dozens of worshippers. The officer waited for the imam to get in, then he himself slid behind the wheel.

Meanwhile, the soldiers ordered everyone to leave the mosque and proceeded to board up the doors.

Not until three years later, when the British forced Reza Khan to leave the country and go into exile in Egypt, did the mosque open its doors again.

*　　*　　*

Aqa Jaan smiled and waited anxiously to hear what Khalkhal would say next. But Khalkhal sat there in silence, staring at his audience. Suddenly he uttered a single word, totally unconnected to what he had been talking about before: 'America!'

It was as if he'd hurled a rock into the hushed audience. There were gasps on both sides of the curtain, because it was forbidden to talk about America in the mosque. The word itself was fraught with political overtones. The ayatollahs didn't see America as the rest of the world did. America was evil. America was the enemy of Islam.

The young shah had been about to flee the country – thereby ending 2,500 years of monarchy – when a CIA-backed coup had restored him to his throne. Since then the ayatollahs had referred to America as 'Satan', and the mosques had become a hotbed of anti-American feeling.

An imam who uttered the word 'America' was in effect firing a bullet and shouting, 'Down with Satan! Down with America!'

'Times have changed,' Khalkhal thundered. 'Reza Khan is gone, and now America is everywhere. In Tehran. In Qom!'

He'd made a statement, and yet at the same time he hadn't made one. Basically all he was doing was announcing an innocent truth: 'Times have changed. America is everywhere.'

The city's wise men weighed his words and noted that he was a clever orator. He knew that you had to use words in a certain sequence in order to heighten the suspense.

Khalkhal stared at his listeners. They were hanging on his every word, curious to hear what he would say next. He broke the silence by uttering two short words: 'Allah, Allah!'

Those two words could mean almost anything. When you saw something you admired, you said, 'Allah, Allah.' When you were up to your ears in trouble, you said, 'Allah, Allah!'

But Khalkhal had used those words in an altogether different context. By mentioning Qom and America in the same breath, he had added a new dimension to his statement. Qom! America! Allah, Allah! It was as though he'd fired *three* shots into the mosque.

Then Khalkhal changed tack and switched over to the Victory surah:

You will see them bow and prostrate themselves.
The marks of prostration are on their foreheads.
In the Torah and the Gospel they are likened
To a seed that sends forth shoots
And is made strong.
It then becomes thicker
And rests firmly on its stalk,
Which fills the sowers with delight.

Aqa Jaan and Shahbal exchanged glances.

Khalkhal didn't linger by the Victory, but moved smoothly on to the Rome surah:

The Romans have been defeated
In a land that is close by.
But after this defeat they shall be victorious,
Soon as well as later.
And on that day you shall rejoice.
He is Almighty.

And that was the end of his sermon.

His sermon had been highly suspect, open to various interpretations, and yet it had been worded in such a way that the secret police wouldn't be able to lay a finger on him. He'd started out with the Prophet Muhammad, then slipped in the word 'America' and finally mentioned the decline of the Roman Empire. Clearly, he had no intention of explaining what he meant or where he was headed.

Aqa Jaan realised that the mosque was in for another exciting time – something he had long been waiting for.

Khalkhal got to his feet and stepped down from the pulpit. Hundreds of worshippers stood up for him. Aqa Jaan walked over to him, took him in his arms, kissed him on the left shoulder and proudly escorted him to the door.

The Cinema

Khodaa ya tu busideh-ye hich gah
labb-e sorkh-e faam-e zani mast-ra?
Be pestane kaalash zadi dast-ra?

God, have you ever kissed
the blushing lips
of a drunken woman?

Have you ever touched
her unripe breasts?

One day when Aqa Jaan was walking by Khalkhal's desk, he happened to see a poem lying there. He picked it up and read it. He couldn't believe his eyes: *Khodaa ya tu busideh-ye hich gah . . .*

It was a shocking poem. God, kisses, a drunken woman, unripe breasts – and all of that on Khalkhal's desk!

The poet's name was printed at the bottom: Nosrat Rahmani. Aqa Jaan had never heard of him.

Who was he?

How dare he write such blasphemous words?

'Things are out of hand,' Aqa Jaan mumbled to himself. The shah encourages this kind of rubbish, but what's Khalkhal doing with it? And why does he bring such things back to the library?

There were other poems on the desk. Aqa Jaan began to read one. It was a remarkable poem, because it had been written by a woman:

> *My thirsty lips*
> *Search yours.*
> *Take off my clothes,*
> *Embrace me.*
> *Here are my lips,*
> *My neck and burning breasts.*
> *Here is my soft body!*

He heard Khalkhal's footsteps in the courtyard. There wasn't time to finish reading the poem, so he swiftly put it back on the desk and hurried over to a bookcase, where he pretended to be searching the shelves.

Khalkhal came in. Aqa Jaan removed a book at random and quickly left the library. Still mulling over the poems, he went into his study. He couldn't get the last one out of his mind. It bothered him so much he couldn't concentrate on his work:

> *Here are my lips,*
> *My neck and burning breasts.*
> *Here is my soft body!*

Who was this female poet?

Had the country changed so much that women could talk openly about themselves and express their innermost feelings? Had it changed so much that they could now talk intimately about their bodies? Why hadn't he noticed the change? Who were these women? Why hadn't he ever met them? What did they look like? And where did they live? In Tehran?

The shah! It was all the fault of the shah and the Americans! American culture came pouring into their homes via radio, television and film.

The regime did whatever it could to lure young people away from the mosque and transform them into supporters of the shah and his ideals.

The shah had launched his 'White Revolution'. He had published a thin volume in which he'd outlined his hopes for the country. In an effort to combat illiteracy, he'd sent young women to the villages to work as teachers. They'd taken off their veils, donned hats, and gone into the mountains, much as the shah's soldiers had done, to set up schools in remote villages.

Yes, everything had changed. Aqa Jaan hadn't noticed . . . or hadn't wanted to. The country was being industrialised at a rapid pace, which is why so many foreign investors had been granted permission to build factories in Tehran and other major cities.

Senejan was no exception. Dozens of Japanese and European companies had seized the opportunity to take part in this new development. A tractor factory was being built on the outskirts of the city. Soon it would be employing hundreds of young people from Senejan and the nearby villages.

The management of the factory would be in the hands of the world-famous Japanese manufacturer Mitsubishi. The idea was to produce a small tractor that could be used in the mountains. Thanks to a government subsidy, every farmer would soon have one of those tractors. And so the farmer and the shah would be bound together by Mitsubishi.

No, Aqa Jaan wasn't up on the latest trends; on the contrary, he was far behind. He never listened to the radio and had never owned a television. If he'd seen the shah's wife, Farah Diba, on television, he'd have a better idea of what was going on in his country. She was working hard to improve women's lives. Aqa Jaan didn't realise how popular she was with women, even those who went to mosque every day.

Farah Diba was the shah's third wife – the one who finally bore him a son. His first two wives had failed to give him the crown prince he longed for. He'd met her at a party in Paris, where she was a student, and now she was the queen of Iran. She was hoping to improve the position of women, to free them from their bonds.

Until now things had gone well, and it seemed as if the shah was managing to keep the ayatollahs in line. Secure in this knowledge, Farah Diba flew to Paris once a month to shop at the famous boutiques where Hollywood celebrities bought their clothes.

While the *New York Times* described the country under the shah's rule as an oasis of peace, Farah Diba made an appointment with a clinic in France to have her Persian nose shaped into a French nose. She came back home with a new hairdo as well.

No newspaper dared to mention the nose job, but every hairdresser in Iran had immediately set about imitating the hairstyle. Farah's hair was the talk of the town. Even Fakhri Sadat, the wife of Aqa Jaan, had succumbed to the *Farahi* – the Farah cut – though Aqa Jaan hadn't even noticed.

In Senejan people were busy setting up a women's clinic. According to the latest statistics, the numbers of women suffering from female disorders were higher in the more religious cities and villages, and yet devout women refused to be treated by male doctors. As a result the authorities in religious cities decided to open a clinic staffed exclusively by female physicians. The clinic in Senejan was to be the first and largest women's clinic in the country.

Farah Diba's royal cultural institute supported the plan, and Farah herself was scheduled to come to Senejan to open the clinic.

Khalkhal, who kept abreast of developments across the country, had gradually started including the everyday life of the city in his sermons. Recently he'd criticised the mayor because there wasn't a decent public library in Senejan and the kiosks were selling Farsi translations of trashy American novels.

Another time he attacked the city's theatre for putting on a play in which an imam was ridiculed. The play was aimed at schoolchildren. Every day a new group was brought in to see the performance. Khalkhal was incensed. 'It's a disgrace to the honourable city of Senejan. How dare they turn an imam into a figure of fun to entertain our youth? I warn the bazaar: a cunning attack has been launched in this city against Islam. Have you looked in your children's schoolbags lately to see what kind of blasphemous ideas are being taught at their school? Are you aware of the poisonous poetry being assigned to your daughters in the name of literature? My hands shook when I read some of those poems. Out of respect for the women sitting on the other side of the curtain I won't tell you what those poems were about. War has been declared on our faith. Don't play with fire. I warn you! Don't play with fire!'

The mayor heard the harsh words being hurled from the pulpit. To keep the situation from escalating, he ordered the theatre to stop performing the play.

The incident had barely died down when rumours of

a plan to build a cinema in Senejan spread throughout the city.

Senejan's oldest bathhouse had fallen into disuse, and the owner of a number of large cinemas in Tehran had purchased it with the idea of converting it into a cinema. It was a landmark, a unique place for cultural activities, the perfect spot for a cinema.

Khalkhal immediately let the mayor know that a cinema in a religious stronghold like Senejan was unacceptable, and the mayor let *him* know that the city had not been consulted: the decision had already been taken in Tehran. The royal cultural institute was touting it as one of its pet projects, and Farah Diba had personally approved the plan.

When the cinema owner heard that Farah Diba was going to come to Senejan for the opening of the women's clinic, he vowed to finish the renovation on time so that she could open the cinema as well.

He contacted the authorities in Tehran and arranged for Farah to open the cinema after presiding over the opening of the clinic. Given the fact that Senejan was such a religious stronghold, it was decided to wait until the last minute to announce the news.

On a sunny Thursday afternoon a helicopter flew over the city and circled above the bazaar three times. Schoolchildren lined the streets of the route that Farah Diba's open limousine would take to the clinic.

The children cheered, clapped their hands and shouted, '*Jawid shah!* Long live the shah!' Three jets also thundered overhead, trailing smoke in the three colours of the Iranian flag. Dozens of plainclothes policemen mingled with the crowd, and army vehicles filled with soldiers were stationed at every corner, ready to quell any signs of unrest.

Farah Diba waved and smiled at the crowd, while a fresh breeze toyed with her hair. She radiated power. As the limousine passed by, the teachers and the clinic staff removed their veils to reveal their Farah cuts. They squealed in excitement and waved their veils.

A camera crew was on hand to capture the scene, which would be broadcast on the evening news, so everyone could see how the women in the pious city of Senejan had rallied round Farah Diba and embraced her as their role model. Since this was Farah Diba's first visit to a religious stronghold, it was a litmus test for the regime. If Senejan could be won over, the other devout anti-shah cities could be won over as well.

Everything had gone smoothly. So smoothly in fact that the television station decided not to wait until the eight o'clock news, but to use her trip as the lead story on the six o'clock news. The visit was considered a resounding victory over the ayatollahs. But the broadcasters had over-looked one thing – a minor detail that at first glance hadn't seemed at all important.

A number of young women from Senejan had been hired to work as nurses in the new clinic. They were standing by the door in their crisp white short-sleeved uniforms. As Farah Diba stepped out of her royal limou-sine, the photographers rushed over and aimed their cameras at the nurses, who bowed and presented the queen with a beautiful bouquet of flowers. But their uniforms were made of such sheer nylon that you could see the nurse's pale-blue underpants. The bazaar was stunned, and when Khalkhal heard the news, he was so angry he couldn't eat.

Khalkhal saw it as a slap in the face of the ayatollahs and a deliberate insult to the bazaar. The incident had taken place in *his* city, the city in which he was the imam of the influential Friday Mosque. He felt compelled to comment on it in tonight's sermon.

As evening fell, Aqa Jaan's phone rang. A man from Qom asked to speak to Khalkhal. It was a short, one-sided conversation. Khalkhal listened for a long time, then just before hanging up said, 'No, I didn't know. Yes, I understand. Right, I have all the information I need. So do you.'

Aqa Jaan had no idea what they'd been talking about, nor did he ask Khalkhal whom he'd been talking to. Later, when he glanced through the library window, he saw Khalkhal pacing back and forth.

The news broadcast seemed to suggest that Farah Diba had left the city after the opening of the clinic and had gone back to Tehran. In fact she was still in Senejan. A helicopter had flown her to a historical site on the outskirts of the city, at the edge of the desert, so she could view a citadel that had been converted into an inn. Once upon a time it had been a caravanserai on the Silk Road, where merchants and wayfarers could spend the night.

Farah, who had studied architecture in Paris, was now in charge of the restoration of several of the country's historic buildings. Much of her time had been spent on the improvements to the citadel.

She was scheduled to go back to Senejan later that evening for the opening of the cinema. For this special occasion the cinema owner had sent to Tehran for a Hollywood love film that had never been shown before in Iran. He had told no one of the royal visit, saying only that a few VIPs from Tehran would be on hand for the opening.

As Farah Diba sat down to dinner in the ancient citadel, Khalkhal slipped into Aqa Jaan's study to make a phone call. He had a short, whispered conversation with someone in Qom.

At seven o'clock he was ready to go to the mosque. When Shahbal came to the library to escort him, he noticed that Khalkhal was restless.

'Is anything wrong?' he enquired.

'No, why do you ask?' Khalkhal replied, as they headed out the door.

'What are you going to talk about tonight?'

'I haven't decided. I've been too preoccupied with the visit of that slut.'

Shahbal wanted to ask, 'What slut?', but didn't, for the simple reason that he couldn't bring himself to utter the word 'slut'.

'Where's Aqa Jaan?' Khalkhal asked.

'In the mosque.'

They went into the mosque. The prayer room was full. In fact, there were more people than usual. Everyone was curious to see how their imam would react to Farah Diba's visit.

Khalkhal calmly climbed into the pulpit, took his seat and began to talk in a quiet voice about the mosque and the role of the imam. He saw the mosque as the heart of the city and the imam as the wakeful conscience of the faithful.

He made no reference to the opening of the clinic. Nor did he mention the television broadcast of Farah Diba's visit. Instead, he aimed all of his arrows at the cinema.

'Beware!' he suddenly exclaimed and raised a warning finger. 'You must know what's going on!'

He paused dramatically. 'In the name of the mosque, in the name of the city, in the name of the bazaar,' he resumed, 'I ask you, I beg you, I warn you not to continue. Put a stop to these diabolical plans! Senejan is no place for promiscuous American culture. No place for sin. Put a stop to it, or we will do it for you!'

'*Allahu akbar!*' someone shouted.

'*Allahu akbar!*' the worshippers replied in unison.

No one knew exactly what Khalkhal was talking about, but everyone understood that he was voicing his anger at the cinema.

The men of the bazaar nodded in satisfaction at Aqa Jaan. They approved of Khalkhal's reaction.

Aqa Jaan was proud of him too. He realised, though, that at some point Khalkhal was bound to move on. He was too ambitious to remain the imam of a mosque for long. He needed more breathing space. One day the walls of the mosque would prove too confining, and he would decide to spread his wings. But their mosque was a good place for him to start.

The cinema owner had expected Khalkhal to rant and rave about his cinema, but he wasn't afraid. He knew that both the secret police and the local police would be on hand to protect him. On this particular Thursday evening he was glad the faithful were sitting in the mosque and listening to Khalkhal, for it meant that he could welcome Farah Diba to the opening without having to worry about her safety.

And yet he had underestimated his enemy, for Khalkhal was well informed. He knew that the queen would be at the opening.

*   *   *

Khalkhal looked at his watch. The queen would be arriving at the cinema shortly. So he relaxed, stroked his beard and smiled. Aqa Jaan assumed that Khalkhal had finished talking about the cinema and would now start in on another topic, that he would be satisfied with merely issuing a warning. But Khalkhal surprised him by quoting the fiery Abu Lahab surah, the one about the woman to whom God had spoken in anger. Khalkhal began chanting calmly and quietly:

> Break the hands of Abu Lahab!
> Destroy Abu Lahab!
> Destroy his fortune!
> Destroy the wife of Abu Lahab!
> Abu Lahab shall burn in a blazing fire!
> And his wife shall carry the faggots!
> Around her neck is a cord of palm fibre!
> Destroy Abu Lahab!

Aqa Jaan caught his breath. Suddenly he realised that Khalkhal was going to do more than issue a warning.

Abu Lahab had been Muhammad's uncle – his father's brother – and also the sworn enemy of Muhammad and the Koran. Once, during Islam's early years, Muhammad had been trying to convince Mecca's rulers of his mission when Abu Lahab had cursed him and left the gathering. Abu Lahab's wife had done likewise: she had cursed Muhammad and said offensive things about the Koran. Not content to stop there, the two of them had taken their hostility to the bazaar, cursing the Koran and especially Allah. Muhammad had suffered greatly under their attacks but had been unable to stop them. Then one night the Abu Lahab surah had been revealed to him:

Tabbat yada abee lahabin!

Around her neck is a cord of palm fibre!
Destroy Abu Lahab!

When someone quoted Abu Lahab, you knew that things were serious. Khalkhal continued his tirade:

Break the hands of the man who bought the bathhouse.
Break the hands of the man who turned it into a cinema.
Break the door of the bathhouse.
Break the legs of the men now assembled in the bathhouse.
Place a cord of palm fibre around the necks of the wives
Of the men now assembled in the bathhouse.

Aqa Jaan was unable to lift his head. Instead of looking at Khalkhal, he found himself staring at the patterns in his prayer rug. He had the feeling that Khalkhal was holding him from behind and pressing his head to the ground.

Khalkhal had surprised him. Aqa Jaan supposed he ought to be pleased, but he felt torn. Why hadn't Khalkhal told him he was going to talk about the cinema? Why had he suddenly adopted that harsh tone? Would it be good for the mosque? What effect would it have on the city?

But there was no time to ponder all of this now. He took a deep breath, raised his head and looked around.

There was a hushed silence. All eyes were focused on Khalkhal. 'I warned the authorities long ago,' he said.

'I also warned the new owner of the bathhouse. But they wouldn't listen. Now they've even gone so far as to show a sinful American film in the bathhouse tonight. Tonight of all nights! Do you know what day it is today? It is the anniversary of Fatima's death!

'I, Khalkhal, the imam of the mosque, forbid it. I, Khalkhal, the imam of the Friday Mosque, forbid you to enter that cinema! I, Khalkhal, will hold the Koran up high and board up the door of that sinful place!' he thundered. And he took his Koran out of his pocket.

'*Allahu akbar! Allahu akbar! Allahu akbar!*' the crowd roared.

'To the bathhouse!' Khalkhal cried, and he jumped down from the pulpit.

The crowd stood up for him.

Aqa Jaan, who hadn't been expecting this sudden turn of events, was rooted to the spot. Khalkhal had deceived him: he had taken control of the mosque. But it wasn't too late. After all, Aqa Jaan was more experienced than he was. Somehow he had to take command again, in order to uphold the prestige of the mosque. Khalkhal's reputation didn't count, only that of the mosque.

He turned and raced after Khalkhal. 'Run!' he shouted to Shahbal. 'Stay with him. Don't let him out of your sight!'

The tension had mounted to fever pitch and the crowd was now out of control. 'I've got to do something,' Aqa Jaan mumbled to himself. 'I'm the only one who can put a stop to this madness.'

Khalkhal was striding towards the cinema, holding his Koran high above his head. The faithful were following behind, chanting '*Allahu akbar*'.

The agents of the secret police, caught off-guard by the demonstration, ran in panic down the dark streets. 'A riot's broken out!' they shrieked into their walkie-talkies. 'Guard the cinema!'

After a while, two patrol cars came roaring up, but the patrolmen had no idea what was going on or where the crowd was headed.

A couple of army lorries were blocking the street leading to the cinema. Armed soldiers leapt out and formed a line to hold back the demonstrators.

A helicopter landed in the square by the bathhouse, ready to fly Farah Diba to safety.

The mayor's car screeched to a halt by the kerb. The mayor jumped out and ran over to the demonstrators with his hands above his head. He scanned the sea of faces until he saw Aqa Jaan. 'What the hell do you think you're doing?' he roared. 'You've walked into a trap! Call off the demonstration, or there will be a bloodbath!'

'What do you mean? The authorities don't listen to a thing the mosque says these days! They insult us by building a cinema and now you're threatening us with a bloodbath?'

'No, you don't understand. I'm not threatening a bloodbath, I'm asking you to help me prevent one! There's something you need to know, but I can't say it out loud.' He whispered it in Aqa Jaan's ear: 'Farah Diba is inside the cinema. Believe me, if these people come any closer, the army is going to open fire. Do something! Stop them!'

The armed soldiers held back the demonstrators, while the commanding officer shouted into a megaphone, 'Turn around! Go back!'

Khalkhal ignored him. Holding his Koran high above his head, he strode past the officer and tried to push through the line, but the officer stopped him. 'Turn back!' he warned, 'or they'll shoot.'

'Then let them shoot!' Khalkhal cried, and tried to break through the line again.

The officer grabbed him by the collar, pulled him away from the line of soldiers and shouted into his face, 'If you don't turn back, I'll ram your turban down your throat and haul you off to jail!'

Khalkhal flew into a rage, shoving the officer so hard the man stumbled and nearly fell. The officer whipped out his gun.

Aqa Jaan quickly grabbed hold of Khalkhal and dragged him away. 'Get him out of here!' he yelled to Shahbal.

But Khalkhal didn't want to go. He twisted free of Aqa Jaan's grasp and headed back towards the officer, but before he could reach him, Aqa Jaan grabbed him again. 'That's enough! Stop it!'

Khalkhal shook him off and lunged at the officer, but once again Aqa Jaan caught up with him, seized him and said, 'Don't forget, *I* make the decisions round here!'

Taking the megaphone from the officer, he shouted, 'Quiet, everyone! I have good news for you!'

The crowd quieted down.

'I've just talked to the mayor. The authorities have backed down. There won't be a cinema in this city! So go back to the mosque!'

'*Allahu akbar!*' the crowd shouted.

The event had made quite an impression. Much to Aqa Jaan's satisfaction, people had milled around outside the mosque for a long time afterwards.

The mosque had taken its battle to the streets, and he had been able to prevent a bloodbath. It had been a direct attack from an unexpected corner on the plans of the shah, and a slap in the face of his prime minister. The shah was hoping to wrest power from the religious cities and foist decadent Western culture on them. Tomorrow the incident would be reported in every major newspaper: MUTINY IN SENEJAN!

The Friday Mosque in Senejan had once more let its voice be heard. The ayatollahs in Qom would sit up and take notice, and every imam in the country would be talking about the disturbance.

It was midnight. Everyone had gone home. The mosque was empty and the caretaker had locked the doors. Aqa Jaan was sitting in his study, writing in his journal. 'After a long silence, our mosque has again let its voice be heard,' he wrote. 'Perhaps we have found the way back to our true path.'

He was still writing when two cars pulled up in front of the mosque. One of them parked under the trees, while the other switched off its lights and drove quietly down the alley to the house.

Three men, who looked like plainclothes policemen, got out. The driver stayed inside the car. The man in charge went up to the gate and rang the bell while the other two men stayed by the car.

Aqa Jaan heard the bell and was immediately on the alert. He'd expected the police to come by the bazaar tomorrow, but not to appear on his doorstep in the middle of the night.

The grandmothers also heard the bell. They knew that something unusual was happening and that it would be better for them to stay in their room and let Aqa Jaan take care of it.

Shahbal, who had also heard the bell, immediately went to Aqa Jaan's study.

'It's probably the police,' Aqa Jaan said softly. 'Go and

warn Khalkhal. Tell him he has to leave and then help him sneak out over the roof.'

Khalkhal had been expecting the police, so he was still in the library when the doorbell rang. He swiftly turned off the light, tiptoed out of the library and started up the stairs.

Aqa Jaan put on his hat and coat, and went into the courtyard. He saw Khalkhal's silhouette by the stairs, so he waited until it had been enveloped by the darkness.

The doorbell rang again.

'I'm coming!' he called as he headed towards the gate.

The women were watching from behind the curtains in their rooms.

'Who's there?' Aqa Jaan called before unlocking the gate.

'Open up!'

He swung open the gate. The man in charge and the two men by the car were clearly illuminated in the glow of the streetlight.

He knew instantly that they were agents of the secret police. No local policeman would have dared to knock on his door in the middle of the night. They must be new, or else from another district. It was obvious from their attitude that they didn't know who he was. They didn't even bother to greet him civilly.

'What brings you gentlemen to my door in the middle of the night?' he asked.

'We're looking for the imam,' the man in charge said. He flashed his badge. 'We've been ordered to bring him in.'

So the situation was serious. To gain time, Aqa Jaan stepped outside and quietly shut the gate behind him. 'The imam isn't home,' he said. 'If it's urgent, you can speak to him tomorrow morning at the mosque.'

The agent, caught off-guard by Aqa Jaan closing the gate, belatedly bellowed, 'Leave it open!'

'Keep your voice down. Everyone's asleep,' Aqa Jaan said.

'Open this gate!' the agent ordered, and he banged on it with his fist.

'Calm down! I told you – the imam isn't home. He's gone. And gone means gone! He'll be at the mosque tomorrow morning.' He raised his voice so Khalkhal would be sure to hear him. 'Have you got that?'

'Open the gate this instant, or I'll shoot the lock off!' the agent said. And he unsnapped the black holster of his gun.

Suddenly one of his underlings came running into the alley. 'He's on the roof of the mosque!' he shouted. 'Let's go!'

The other two agents climbed up the gate and onto the courtyard wall. Within seconds they were on the roof, running towards the minarets.

Aqa Jaan opened the gate and was about to race up the stairs to the roof when one of the agents barked, 'Stay where you are!' So he went over to the guest room and stood beneath the trees, where he had a good view of the roof.

'I saw a shadow behind the dome!' one of the agents called up from the street.

'Come out with your hands up!' the man in charge shouted from the roof.

Aqa Jaan was sure they'd spotted Khalkhal. He ran over to the cedar tree to get a better look at the roof. In the green glow of the minarets he saw the man in charge walking towards the dome with his gun drawn, but he couldn't see Khalkhal.

'There's no one here!' the man in charge shouted to the agent in the street.

'I saw his shadow just a minute ago,' the agent shouted back. 'He can't be far away.'

Aqa Jaan was relieved. He moved into the circle of light by the *hauz*. 'Agent!' he called up to the roof. 'The shadow you saw was that of the mosque's caretaker. He'd just been to see me when you came. You're making this much more complicated than it needs to be. Since you're from another district, you aren't familiar with the layout of the mosque. I can assure you that anyone trying to escape from the roof would be spotted by the men posted in the street. Here, let me show you.' And he went up the stairs.

'As I already told you,' he said to the man in charge when he reached the top, 'the imam isn't here. He took the night train to Qom. Call the station and check, if you like. He's well known there. Don't make this any harder than it has to be. There's nothing on this roof except the dome and the minarets. Take a look round, then get out! Have I made myself clear?'

The man shone his torch around the roof, but made no reply.

'And now get yourself and your filthy shoes off the roof of this mosque!' Aqa Jaan snapped. He pointed to the stairs. 'And get out of my house!'

The agents muttered all the way down the stairs and into the courtyard.

'No one has ever dared to enter this house uninvited,' Aqa Jaan said, 'and now four of you bastards have come bursting in. I've had it. Get out, all of you!'

But the man in charge, unfazed by Aqa Jaan's hostility, issued an order to his men: 'Search every room. Now!' The agents rushed boldly into the house.

'Shahbal!' Aqa Jaan called.

There was no reply.

'Phone the mayor!' he called again, knowing full well that Shahbal had left with Khalkhal.

He hurried into his study, rifled through his papers until he found the mayor's phone number and dialled. 'Get these bastards out of my house,' he said, 'or I'll get my rifle and shoot them!'

The agents dragged blind Muezzin out of his room and looked in every nook and cranny.

'Bastards!' Muezzin yelled. 'All of you! Get out of my room! Get out of this house!'

The door to the library was locked.

'Give me the key!' the man in charge demanded.

'I haven't got one,' Aqa Jaan called from where he was standing on the other side of the courtyard.

'Give me the key or I'll break the door down!'

The grandmothers emerged from the darkness, opened the door and switched on the light.

One of the agents was about to enter the library when Golbanu screeched, 'Take off your shoes!'

He ignored her.

'Take off your shoes, you bastard!' she shrieked.

The agent didn't go in, but hovered on the threshold, clearly impressed by the antiquity of the library. He stared at the centuries-old bookcases and the imam's antique desk, then turned and went into the courtyard.

The other agents stormed into the Carpet Room, where a half-finished carpet was hanging on the wall. They peered behind the carpet, opened the antique cupboards and threw spools of wool on the floor. Then they left the Carpet Room and started in on the Opium Room.

A walkie-talkie crackled. The man in charge went over to the *hauz* and mumbled something into his walkie-talkie. After a moment he came back. 'That's enough,' he called to his men. 'Let's go!'

They met in the courtyard, slammed the gate shut on their way out and drove off.

Aqa Jaan locked the gate and switched off the lights.

'Is there anything to eat?' he asked the grandmothers. 'I'm starving. And dying of thirst.'

He had just sat down when Shahbal came in.

'Where is he?' Aqa Jaan asked.

'In the mosque.'

'Where exactly?'

'In the oldest crypt. The caretaker let him in,' Shahbal said.

'He's safe for now, but those agents are bound to come back. This isn't going to blow over. They'll be keeping an eye on the mosque. We've *got* to send him to Qom. Tomorrow, when the doors open for the morning prayer, they'll come in when everyone else does, and we won't be able to stop them. We've got to come up with an escape plan.'

The grandmothers came in, bearing a silver tray. They unfolded a clean cotton napkin and laid it on Aqa Jaan's desk. On top of that they carefully arranged two glasses, an antique gold-rimmed teapot filled with fragrant tea and a delicate porcelain plate heaped with warm bread and cheese. Then they left. Aqa Jaan looked over at Shahbal and smiled.

'Apparently they approve of your actions,' Shahbal commented as Aqa Jaan poured him some tea.

'Grab a chair and have a bite. We've got work to do. We won't be getting any sleep tonight!'

After they'd eaten, Aqa Jaan rummaged through the cupboard in his study and came back with a hat, a suit and a pair of scissors. He placed them on the table in front of Shahbal. 'I have a plan,' he said. 'In a little while I'll go and stand outside the mosque. I'll pretend to be waiting for someone. I know the secret police are keeping watch from their cars, so I'll do my best to attract their attention. Meanwhile, you'll go up to the roof and slip over to the mosque, taking the clothes and the scissors with you. Then you'll help Khalkhal trim his beard and tell him to put on the hat and the suit. The sun will be coming up soon, and people will start arriving for the morning prayer. Because of last night's events, I'm expecting more people than usual. At the end of the prayer, when everyone is leaving, I want you and Khalkhal to walk out behind me. I'll take care of the rest. Is that clear?'

'Absolutely.'

It wasn't cold, but at that hour of the morning a brisk wind was blowing from the mountains. Aqa Jaan took up his position outside the mosque and noticed that the streetlight, which had been broken for months, was now shining brightly. The caretaker had complained repeatedly to the electricity company, but the light had never been fixed. Aqa Jaan himself had phoned several times to complain to the manager, but had never been put through.

The street was empty, except for two men standing on the corner smoking a cigarette. When they realised that Aqa Jaan had spotted them, they slipped into the darkness.

A car with four men inside drove past the mosque, turned and drove past again without stopping.

The two men who'd slipped into the darkness came back into the glow of the streetlight. They strolled towards Aqa Jaan, still smoking their cigarettes, and passed him without a greeting. Obviously they were not from around here; otherwise they would have recognised him, even in the darkness, and said hello.

As he waited, Aqa Jaan realised more than ever how much the city had changed in recent years. Strangers were now in charge. Until a few years ago he had known everyone in a position of authority in Senejan: men from good families, sons of the merchants in the bazaar. And when he went into a government office, the director himself always jumped up to welcome him. He didn't know any of the new directors, who avoided all contact with the mosque. They wore tight suits and ties and smoked fat cigars. The city appeared to be divided in two: on the one side, the traditionalists, the historical buildings and the bazaar; on the other side, the new directors, the new policemen, the modern buildings, the theatres and the cinemas. In the old days he could get anything done with the wave of a hand. Nowadays he couldn't even get a streetlight fixed.

Only now did he understand the mayor's warning: 'Remember, Aqa Jaan, I can't help you the way I used to.'

He – who didn't frighten easily – was now afraid. Until a few short hours ago he thought he'd eventually be able to work things out, even if Khalkhal did get arrested. All it would take, he had assumed, was one phone call to the chief constable and Khalkhal would be released. Now he knew he'd been wrong.

Apparently the brisk mountain air blowing across Senejan had cleared his head and helped him to think straight. Even Khalkhal was a stranger, he realised, and an untrustworthy one at that. Who was he really? An unknown imam who had come from Qom to ask for the hand of Alsaberi's daughter. What else did he know about him? Nothing.

The mountain air had done its work – the mist had

lifted from his eyes and he now saw everything in a clear light. Khalkhal had been playing a dangerous game. He had known that Farah Diba would be in the cinema, but had deliberately neglected to tell him. His aim had been to create chaos in the city. He'd lured the unsuspecting mosque-goers to the cinema so that Farah Diba would walk into his trap, the country would be turned upside down and the event would be world news. And Aqa Jaan hadn't suspected a thing. Thank goodness he'd been able to defuse Khalkhal's plan in time. Khalkhal had deceived him and was now hiding in the crypt. His fate was in Aqa Jaan's hands.

Despite the cold, he could feel the sweat on his forehead. To allay his fear, he began to chant:

> By the morning light,
> And by the night when it is still!
> He has not abandoned you.
> Did He not find you an orphan and guide you?
> And find you in need and make you rich?
> Did He not lift the burden from your shoulders?
> He spread your fame, for with hardship
>   comes ease.

He turned to the window and noticed that it had grown light. Hordes of people were heading towards the mosque. Feeling his heart grow lighter, he squared his shoulders and went inside.

Never before had so many people attended the morning prayer, and they were still pouring in. Aqa Jaan hadn't listened to the radio, but others had heard that a riot had broken out in Senejan and that the city had been turned upside down by a fanatical imam.

All of the morning papers carried reports of Farah Diba's royal visit to the clinic and mentioned her presence at the cinema. Here and there it had been hinted that the mosque-goers had been mobilised by the imam for the most dubious of reasons.

And that's why they had all come to the mosque: to experience what was left of the excitement.

The caretaker came out and greeted Aqa Jaan, then the two of them took a short stroll so they could go over their plan. On the way back, Aqa Jaan stole quietly into the cellar and headed towards the crypt. Suddenly Shahbal loomed up out of the darkness.

'Where's Khalkhal?' Aqa Jaan asked.

'In the storeroom.'

'Go upstairs and ask your father to start the *azan*.'

He cautiously opened the storeroom door. 'It's me,' he said.

In the dim light of the candle Khalkhal was totally unrecognisable. He was wearing the suit and the hat, and his beard had been clipped short.

'The secret police are looking everywhere for you. I'm sure I don't have to tell you why. I'll do what I can to help you escape, but first there's something I need to get off my chest: I'm not pleased with that demonstration of yours. You deceived me. You should have told me what you were doing, but you deliberately kept me in the dark. We'll discuss this some other time. Now we need to concentrate on your escape. Shahbal will come for you after the prayer, and the two of you will leave the mosque along with everyone else. The caretaker's cousin will be waiting for you outside the bazaar. You'll get on the back of his motorcycle, and he'll drive you to the village of Varcheh. The imam of Varcheh will somehow get you to Kashan, and the imam of Kashan will make arrangements for your trip to Qom. Here's some money,' Aqa Jaan said. 'I'm going now.' He turned and walked off without waiting for a reply.

He had wanted to lash out at Khalkhal, to say, 'You deliberately put the city, the mosque, the house and the family at risk. My faith in you has been destroyed. I knew from the start that you couldn't be trusted, but luckily the damage isn't irreparable. Now get out. I don't want to have to see you for a long, long while.' But he hadn't said it. He was glad he'd managed to keep his temper under control and had softened his language.

As soon as Aqa Jaan entered the prayer room, everyone stood up for him. They'd heard that the house had been raided last night and that Khalkhal had escaped.

A group of prominent merchants escorted Aqa Jaan to the place where the imam usually led the prayer. 'I'm going to need your help,' Aqa Jaan whispered to them. 'This is a critical moment for the mosque. Khalkhal is in danger. I'll lead the prayer. I know it's unusual, but this is an emergency. I'd like all of you to stay here afterwards, so we can walk to the bazaar together.'

Aqa Jaan went over to the pulpit, mounted the first step and said, 'Listen, everyone. Imam Khalkhal had to go to Qom suddenly, so we're without an imam. I know it's unusual, but I'll take his place today. The morning prayer is short. Follow me!'

There was a buzz of consternation, but at Muezzin's cry of 'Hayye ale as-salat', everyone fell silent and turned towards Mecca.

The morning prayer is the shortest of the day. It consists of standing up two times, bowing two times and touching your forehead to the ground two times.

At the end of the prayer, the merchants solemnly walked over to Aqa Jaan and escorted him to the courtyard, where they were joined by Shahbal and Khalkhal, who had emerged from the cellar and were mingling with the crowd.

Aqa Jaan had invited only a few of the men to walk with him to the bazaar, but others had apparently sensed the air of urgency and were now walking silently behind Aqa Jaan.

Everywhere you looked there were policemen who had no idea why such a large group of people were strolling so casually down the street towards the bazaar.

The caretaker's cousin was waiting with his motorcycle by the streetlight at one corner of the square. Khalkhal slipped away from the crowd and seated himself on the back of the motorcycle. The cousin revved the engine and off they drove, without so much as a backward glance. Shahbal watched until the motorcycle was safely out of sight. Then he rejoined the crowd, sidled up to Aqa Jaan and whispered, 'He's gone.'

The Birds

Ha Mim. Autumn was drawing to a close, and Sadiq had gone to Qom to be with her husband before winter set in. The first snow of the season had already covered the mountaintops. Everywhere you looked, you could see white peaks jutting up from the villages.

In the house of the mosque Khalkhal's name was rarely mentioned any more. They all had other things on their minds. Soon the migratory birds would be arriving, and maybe this time one of them would be special.

Aqa Jaan woke up one day and said to his wife, 'Fakhri, I had another one of my wonderful dreams. You know I'm always in touch with the dead, and, believe it or not, last night I saw my father. I don't remember the exact date of his death, but he still comes to me in my dreams. They're hard to explain. In last night's dream my father had died and we'd buried him in the cemetery, but when I got home I found him lying in his bed with a white sheet over his body. I knew it was my father, even though we'd just put him in the ground. I knelt by the bed. Somehow I knew that he wasn't dead, that he was about to get up. After a while he moved, stuck his head out from under the sheet and tried to sit up. I went over and helped him stand, then handed him his hat and stick. He left the room and walked over to the *hauz*, where he sat on the bench and stared at the fish.'

'You were thinking about him,' said Fakhri Sadat.

'You're always thinking about the dead. That's why you dream about them so often.'

'I don't think about them all the time. I do think about my father sometimes, but I dream about dead people I've never even met, like my father's father, or my father's grandfather. It's strange. During the day, I'm in the world of the living and at night I'm in the world of the dead.'

'Maybe it's because of those mosque reports you're always writing in your journal.'

He got out of bed and went over to the window. 'Fakhri!' he exclaimed.

'What?'

'The *Tamuz* sun has just come up!'

Fakhri Sadat looked at the sun – a red circle peeping out above the top of Mount Zardkuh, Yellow Mountain.

'I've been looking at Mount Zardkuh every day,' said Fakhri Sadat, 'hoping to see the *Tamuz* sun. I was afraid we weren't going to have one this year.'

'I've been so wrapped up in that business with Khalkhal that the *Tamuz* sun completely slipped my mind.'

Winter had arrived. Sometimes on the last day of autumn or the first day of winter a bright red sun appeared above Mount Zardkuh. It was called a *Tamuz* sun because it was like the suns you see in *Tamuz*, July.

This unexpectedly mild day was always awaited with great anticipation in Senejan. The migrating birds, who knew it was coming before the people did, made use of it to fly over the snow-capped mountains. They began their migration in the cold regions of Asiatic Russia. For as long as anyone could remember, the birds had followed the old Silk Road, where the air was the warmest, and crossed the huge stretch of desert in one go. By the time they arrived in Senejan, they'd finished the most difficult part of their journey. They continued on towards warmer climes until they finally reached their nests in the palm trees of the Persian Gulf.

The day of the *Tamuz* sun was an important day for the family. It was also of importance to the bazaar and the carpet trade as a whole, for on that day Fakhri Sadat and the grandmothers stayed at home to trap birds.

The house drew its inspiration for the patterns and colours of their carpets from the feathers of migrating birds. Years of experience had taught the residents of the house that there were always a few birds in the flocks with unusual markings or striking colours on their feathers.

No one knew how Aqa Jaan dreamed up such inimitable patterns for his carpets or such an exquisite blend of colours. And through the ages it had been the women of the house who had made it possible.

Today, as in previous years, the grandmothers got to work quickly. They fetched the wicker snares from the cellar and set them out in the courtyard, on the same side of the garden as the library and the Opium Room.

The migrating birds who left the desert and headed towards Senejan usually set their sights on the minarets of the Friday Mosque. There were always four storks on the mosque, two on each minaret. No one knew exactly when the old storks died and the new ones took their place, but there were always four storks. They were a defining feature of Senejan. When the migrating birds saw them from afar, they knew they were nearing the city.

Once the birds reached Senejan, they circled noisily for a while, then landed on the roof of the mosque. The old crow perched on top of the dome and watched their every move.

The caretaker had already scattered some grain on the roof and set out bowls of water for the birds. All of Senejan knew about the grain and the water, but no one knew that Fakhri Sadat set traps for them.

Fakhri Sadat sat in a chair by the *hauz*, holding the ropes attached to the snares. The grandmothers hid in the library and peered through the gap in the curtains.

A flock of birds landed by the snares and started to eat the scattered grain, and as they ate, they were lured into the baskets by the raisins that had been placed there to tempt them further. The moment they stepped into the baskets, Fakhri Sadat yanked the ropes, and the snares snapped shut, trapping the birds inside.

The grandmothers hurried into the courtyard and knelt by the first basket. Golebeh lifted the lid, took out a bird and handed it to Fakhri Sadat, who studied its feathers.

This time the catch consisted of seven new types of birds. They put them in seven cages and carried them into the house.

Aqa Jaan came home after dark and went directly to his study, where Fakhri Sadat was waiting for him. 'How did it go?' he asked. 'Did you catch anything special?'

'The birds are beautiful! We saw lots of them up close,' Fakhri Sadat replied.

'I can't wait to see them,' he said. 'Where are the grand-mothers?'

'They're bringing in the cages,' said Fakhri Sadat.

The four of them worked until the early hours of the morning.

Golbanu took one of the birds out of its cage and put

a black hood over its head, so it would sit quietly on the table and not be frightened by the bright light.

Aqa Jaan examined its wings and feathers. 'This one has beautiful markings, though they're not all that unusual,' he said, and he lifted one of the feathers with the tip of his pencil so Fakhri Sadat could see it too. Then he turned to the grandmothers. 'Would you like to take a look?'

They put on their glasses, came closer and inspected the feathers. 'The colours are a bit different, but we've seen markings like this before,' said Golbanu. They took the bird out of Aqa Jaan's hands and put it back in its cage, then they took out another bird and handed it to him.

'Oh, these feathers are magnificent! See the pattern on the tip of this one? It's a crisscross of red and green lines. I'm sure our designers can do something with this.'

Fakhri Sadat studied the feathers under a magnifying glass. 'They're definitely special. The shine on them makes them even more beautiful. Why do the birds in this species have such totally different feathers? Each one has a unique pattern.'

Aqa Jaan looked through Fakhri Sadat's magnifying glass and nodded. 'Put this one aside.'

They examined two more birds, but the feathers were quite ordinary. When the grandmothers took out the next bird, they knew right away that it was a special case. The bird refused to sit still and struggled to get free. 'This one's strong!' said Golebeh. 'Look, its feathers are also thicker than usual.'

'This bird is indeed different,' Golbanu agreed. 'It has little blue dots that glitter like jewels.'

'I looked at it briefly in the daylight,' Fakhri Sadat said, 'but now that I see it here on the table under a strong lamp, it looks even more beautiful.'

'A masterpiece!' Aqa Jaan exclaimed. 'Where does so much beauty come from?'

Fakhri Sadat picked up a pencil and began to draw one of the feather patterns, peering at it from time to time through the magnifying glass. When she finished the sketch, the grandmothers got out an old palette and some paintbrushes.

The women didn't realise that they were artists. In their eyes they were simply carrying on a family tradition, one that involved the carpet trade. They wanted to create the most beautiful carpets in the country, the most beautiful in all of the Middle East. They considered it their duty, and didn't give it a second thought.

Fakhri Sadat sketched the patterns and tried to capture the magical colours of the feathers on paper. She painted with thin brushes, with her fingers and with the helpful advice of the grandmothers ringing in her ears. 'Try this colour, Fakhri, that dark blue by this pale green. Don't mix them, but draw a thin green line over the blue,' Golebeh said.

Fakhri did as the grandmothers suggested.

'But I want to capture that purple sheen. How can we turn it into strands of wool that can be woven into a carpet?' she asked.

'It won't be easy,' Aqa Jaan said. 'You can't achieve the same effect with wool that you can with paint.'

'Bring me some wool,' Fakhri Sadat said to the grandmothers.

They trotted off to the Carpet Room, came back with several spools of wool and laid them on the table.

'Would you hand me a strand of blue?'

'I don't think a single strand is going to do the trick,' Aqa Jaan observed. 'You need to use a handful of blue and combine it with a few thin strands of red.'

He laid a handful of blue wool on the table and wove a few strands of red through it. 'See what I mean?'

'No,' Fakhri Sadat said.

'Wait,' Golbanu said, and she wove a few more strands of red through the blue wool.

'And now?'

'That's more like it,' Fakhri said.

'We'll never be able to get the effect we want here on the table. Only when it's made into a carpet will we know if we've succeeded. Once thousands of red strands have been woven into the blue, a purple sheen will emerge from the carpet. That's how it always works,' Aqa Jaan remarked. 'Take another look at the feather through the magnifying glass. When you examine it closely, you see a splash of blue, dozens of tiny red lines and a few green ones. That automatically creates the effect we're trying to achieve.'

They stared at each other in silence.

'It's too early to celebrate,' he said, 'but I think we may have a winner.'

Fakhri Sadat finished her sketches, Aqa Jaan assembled his notes and the grandmothers returned the spools to the Carpet Room and tidied up the study.

Early the next morning, as the first rays of dawn struck the house, the grandmothers swept the courtyard and brought the birds outside. They fed them, let them drink out of the *hauz*, gave them each a kiss and set them free.

The birds circled halfway round the mosque and flew off towards the south, hurrying to catch up with the flock. If they flew without stopping, before nightfall they would reach the Persian Gulf, where it was warm and huge sharks sliced through the water like submarines.

Janeshin

My thirsty lips
Search yours.
Take off my clothes,
Embrace me.
Here are my lips,
My neck and burning breasts.
Here is my soft body!

After carrying the poem around in his pocket for weeks, Aqa Jaan had hidden it in the drawer of his desk at the bazaar. More than once he'd been tempted to toss it into the wastepaper basket, but something had held him back. It was a sinful poem, and yet he felt the urge to read it over and over again. The poem had lodged itself in his memory without his wanting it to. He could even recite it by heart.

He could rattle off dozens of classical poems, but this one was different. This poem wouldn't let go of him; the words were always on his lips. How dare a woman commit such thoughts to paper? Who was she?

Her name was Forugh Farrokhzad, and she was well known in Tehran as a contemporary poet. She was a beautiful young woman whose first volume of poetry had caused quite a stir. One of her poems had shaken the traditional world of men's poetry to its foundations:

> *I looked into his eyes,*
> *Which concealed a secret.*
> *My heart pounded*
> *At his questioning look.*
>
> *Allah, oh Allah!*
> *His lips sparked desire*
> *On my lips.*
>
> *And I said:*
> *I want you.*
> *Oh, my God, I'm sinning.*
>
> *My naked body,*
> *In that soft bed*
> *Arched above his chest,*
> *Colliding flesh.*

Some saw her as a shiny new star in the firmament of Persian poetry. Others considered her a whore, who sold her body both in bed and on paper.

An ayatollah in Qom berated her publisher for printing such blasphemy. In one of his sermons he offered it as proof that the henchmen of the regime were out to undermine Islam. 'They're insulting our women,' he roared. 'Our daughters are no longer safe in this sinful country!'

Tehran was immune to such barbs. Tehran had its own agenda. The papers were full of blasphemous writings, and the cinema screens were filled with scantily clad women with enormous breasts.

Every day Farah Diba opened a new cultural centre, where bare-legged girls danced for her and young women recited poems about their bodies.

Aqa Jaan, having just hidden Forugh's poem under a sheaf of papers in his drawer, fished it out again. This poem should be part of my mosque reports, he thought. I'll add it to my journal.

There was a knock on the door and in came his office boy. 'The imam is here. Shall I show him in?' he asked.

Aqa Jaan remembered that he had an appointment with Janeshin, the substitute imam. 'Send him in,' he said, and he hastily slipped the poem back into the drawer. This was the first time Aqa Jaan had ever asked the imam to his office.

Janeshin was in his early fifties, with greying temples and streaks of grey in his beard. You could tell from his awkward demeanour that he was a rural imam.

'Do sit down,' Aqa Jaan said, pointing to the chair in front of his desk.

The imam seated himself with great modesty and tucked his arms in his robe. The office boy brought them tea on a silver tray and offered the imam chocolate from an elegant, brightly coloured box.

The imam selected a chocolate, stuck it in his mouth and began to chew.

He was visibly impressed by the regal-looking office, with its antique furniture, leather chairs, crystal chandelier and mammoth desk, behind which sat Aqa Jaan, the head of dozens of carpet workshops in Senejan and the outlying villages.

Janeshin was the regular imam of the mosque in the mountain village of Jirya.

Aqa Jaan trusted him.

In the past, whenever Imam Alsaberi was ill or away on a trip, Janeshin had filled in for him. It was always for short periods, but now that Khalkhal had fled, he would probably stay on longer. After Khalkhal's escape, Aqa Jaan had immediately sent his jeep to collect Janeshin, who had arrived in time to lead the evening prayer.

Normally Janeshin slept in the mosque's guest room, but now that he would be staying on for a longer period, he would need more space, which is why Aqa Jaan had invited him to come in for a chat.

'How are you?' Aqa Jaan asked.

'Fine, praise God.'

'And how's your family – your wife and children? Aren't they upset that you're going to be away longer?'

'Women always complain, but I'll go home for a day now and then.'

'Are you satisfied with the mosque?'

'I am, as long as you are.'

'I'm satisfied—'

There was a knock at the door.

'Come in!'

Seven bespectacled old men in work clothes entered the room. Their hands and clothes were smeared with paint. The oldest unrolled a sheet of paper and laid it on the desk: an intricate carpet design. 'Here are the initial results,' he said. 'There's a purple sheen over the sketch, like a fine mist, and we think it will look even better in the carpet.'

Aqa Jaan studied the drawing, and the seven men leaned over the desk to examine it with him.

'Incredible!' Aqa Jaan exclaimed. 'I didn't expect it to be this good. It's exactly how I pictured it! I don't want to wait any longer. If you can get it ready, I'd like to have it registered this afternoon. Do you think you can finish it today?'

'We'll do our best,' the men promised, and they left.

'Excuse the interruption,' Aqa Jaan said to Janeshin. 'I've been looking forward to this design for weeks. Those seven men are my draughtsmen, my carpet designers. They're magicians, really. Their names are known throughout the Middle East. Carpets designed by them are worth a fortune. But that's enough of that. I gather that you're willing to stay with us for an extended period of time?'

'Yes.'

'You realise that it might be a year or two? After all, Alsaberi's son still has to finish his imam training.'

'I know, but I think of it as a great opportunity. I've always wanted to be an imam in an urban mosque, but unfortunately I never got the chance. That's why I'm glad you offered me this position. I won't be able to manage without your help, though.'

'Don't worry, I'll give you all the help you need.'

'I'll be grateful for that. I mean, preaching a sermon in a village is not the same as giving a speech in the city. In the village you talk about small things, about everyday matters like cows or fodder. In the city you have to talk about big things, like politics. I think it's interesting to talk about such subjects and to speak with more power when influential men are present. I'd like to elevate the tone of my sermons. I'd like my listeners to look up to me in admiration.'

Aqa Jaan smiled. He knew what the man meant, but, to be honest, Janeshin wasn't made of the right stuff. He didn't have the proper attitude or the gift of words or the necessary charisma. He was a village imam, with big hands and a heavy brow. You had to be a Khalkhal to get both old men and young women to support you.

'I'm sure they will,' Aqa Jaan said, 'but after the confusion of Alsaberi's death and Khalkhal's escape, I wouldn't mind having a bit of peace and quiet in the mosque again. Go ahead and talk about trees and plants and your experiences in the country. City folk will be fascinated by such topics. Just be yourself and everything will be fine.'

The imam smiled and hung his head.

'I mean it,' Aqa Jaan said. 'I'm curious to hear what you're going to say on Thursday evening. Talk about Jirya, for example. About the mountains, the almond trees, the rare breed of mountain goats, the saffron. If you have any questions, you can ask the caretaker to get in touch with me. By the way, I've asked him to make arrangements for your stay here. Is there anything else you'd like to know?'

'Not that I can think of.'

The office boy came in and ushered the imam to the door.

That evening, when Aqa Jaan was lying in bed beside Fakhri Sadat, he suddenly chuckled.

'What's so funny?' Fakhri Sadat asked.

'Nothing. I was thinking about the substitute imam. He's a simple man, with lots of ambition, but he has no idea how to realise his dreams.'

'So you're laughing at the poor man?'

'No, not at all. I appreciate the fact that he wants to make something of himself. It's just that he has the build of a peasant.'

'You can hardly blame him for that,' Fakhri Sadat said, smiling.

'You're right. But I know from experience that you won't get very far without talent. It's not enough to have the lamp – there has to be a genie inside. I won't bore you with the details, but, you know, he set his turban at an angle and said, "I'd like to elevate the tone of my sermons."' Aqa Jaan roared with laughter.

'You *are* laughing at him,' Fakhri Sadat said.

'No, I'm not really, I'm just feeling happy. Everything is going the way it should. The mosque is doing well, the imam is right for the job, the business is rolling along as usual, and the new design is finished and it's beautiful. Orders are pouring in and people can hardly wait to see our new carpets. Everyone wants them. It's going to be a good year. Besides, we're all in good health. What more could anyone want?'

He turned and laid his hand on Fakhri Sadat's breasts. 'Plus I have you,' he said, 'and I'm in the mood for love. What more could a man want?'

Fakhri Sadat batted his hand away, turned over on her side and lay with her back to him. He slipped his hand underneath her nightgown and caressed her bottom. 'Take off your nightgown,' he said softly. 'I want you naked.'

Fakhri Sadat pulled the blanket over her head. 'Are you crazy?' she said. 'What's got into you that's made you want me naked?'

He pressed his hand between her warm thighs and whispered:

> *My thirsty lips*
> *Search yours.*
> *Take off my clothes*
> *Embrace me.*
> *Here are my lips,*
> *My neck and burning breasts.*
> *Here is my soft body!*

'What did you say?' Fakhri Sadat said in surprise. She pushed back the blanket and sat bolt upright in bed.

'It's a modern poem,' he said, and kissed her neck. Then he carefully pulled her nightgown over her head and lay her down on her back. 'If I recite the poem,' he whispered, 'will you repeat it to me?'

'No, I won't. You're scaring me. What do you want?'

'I want *you*.'

Fakhri Sadat closed her eyes.

Zinat

One Wednesday evening, when the family was gathered together, Zinat told them a magical tale:

And Allah fell in love with his creation. He fell in love with the stars, with his Milky Way, with his sun, with his moon and especially with his beautiful Earth. He was so proud of the Earth that He wanted to go and live there himself. But how could He do that?

One night Allah had a brilliant idea. He asked his messenger Gabriel to go down to Earth and bring him back some clay. Gabriel did as he was told, and Allah fashioned a man out of the clay, exactly as He wanted him to be. Then He asked the spirit to enter the body, but the spirit refused. The spirit thought he deserved something better than a body made out of clay. So Allah appointed Gabriel as his go-between.

'Step into that body!' Gabriel ordered the spirit.

The spirit refused.

'I order you in the name of Allah to step into that body!' Gabriel said.

'Now that you've invoked Allah's name, I will,' said the spirit. And with a shiver of distaste, the spirit stepped into the body. As the spirit was passing through the chest, the man unexpectedly stood up, then lost his balance and fell over.

Allah smiled. 'He hasn't learned how to be patient,'
Allah said to Gabriel.

The man was given a name: Adam.

Adam sat in the same spot for seven days and
waited. Allah sent him a golden throne studded with
jewels, a silk carpet and a crown. Adam got dressed,
put the crown on his head and seated himself on the
throne. Then the angels lifted Adam and his throne
onto their shoulders and carried him down to Earth.
At that time Creation was 1,240 years old.

Wednesday evening was storytelling time. Every Wednesday
the family ate together, then listened to Zinat. The grandmothers lit the candles, switched off the lights and passed
round a bowl of nuts.

Zinat Khanom was a born storyteller. She had a warmth
in her voice that made you want to listen to her. Her
stories were drawn from old books, particularly those with
extensive interpretations of the Koran. The Koran is a
stark, but highly evocative, book. The stories are never
told in great detail. As a result many books have been
written to explain and flesh out the bare bones of the
stories, and it was from these books that Zinat drew her
inspiration.

For the most part Zinat was quiet and withdrawn. Nobody
knew about her storytelling talent until the day she told
a couple of children a short story she knew by heart.

After her son Abbas had drowned, Zinat had taken
refuge in her room. Only when she became pregnant again
with Sadiq had she emerged from her self-imposed isol-
ation, venturing into the courtyard more often and going
to help the grandmothers in the kitchen.

After Sadiq's birth, Zinat was plagued by so many fears

that she couldn't sleep. During this time, the grandmothers never left her side. They were her main source of comfort and strength. Night after night they sat by her bed until she fell asleep.

When Ahmad was born, her fears were rekindled. One day she handed the baby to Golbanu. 'Watch him for me!' she said. 'I'm afraid of losing this child too. I'm going to the mosque. I need to pray.'

Since then Zinat had gone faithfully to the mosque every day.

When Alsaberi was still alive, he used to retreat into his own world in the library and not get involved in the life of his wife and children.

Zinat's children thought of Aqa Jaan as the head of the household, which is why they called him 'Father'.

After Alsaberi's death, Zinat spent hours and hours in the library of the mosque. Everyone thought she was going to the mosque to mourn the loss of her husband, but she was actually preparing for a new phase in her life.

At first she kept to herself, but later she met a couple of women in the mosque who took her along to their devotional meetings.

An odd thing happened to Zinat Khanom when she became a widow. All of a sudden she seemed to have been liberated, though no one could have said from what. Before then, she had felt like a balloon whose string had become snagged on a tree, but now she felt herself soaring into the sky. It was a wonderful – and terrifying – feeling.

The moment the summer holidays began, she gathered up her children and went to her parents' house in the mountains, where she hoped to find some peace.

* * *

Zinat had never thought of Alsaberi as a real man, as a husband. He had been more of an imam than a family man.

When she compared her marriage to Fakhri Sadat's, Zinat realised that she didn't have a family life. Instead, she was merely a woman who had given birth to a son, a successor.

Fakhri Sadat had Aqa Jaan, and she had a real life. Zinat's bedroom was on the same floor as hers. Late in the evening, when she walked past Fakhri's door, she invariably saw Aqa Jaan lying beside his wife in the reddish glow of the nightlight. And sometimes she heard Fakhri giggling in the middle of the night.

But Alsaberi had never lain beside Zinat. He had slept with her only when he needed her, and he hadn't needed her all that often. After the birth of Ahmad, he had never again gone to Zinat's bed.

Zinat had accepted the fact that Fakhri was the lady of the house. Wherever Fakhri went, the wives of the other businessmen treated her like a queen, but no one showed the slightest interest in Zinat.

Fakhri was the one who snared the birds, the one who was entrusted with the secrets of the carpet designs. Zinat's job was to cook for the family.

That's simply the way things were. Zinat had never been asked what she thought of the situation. She had accepted her role and found some measure of peace in prayer. Still, she knew her life wouldn't go on like this for ever. One day she would come into her own, and everyone would say, 'Look, there goes Zinat!'

When she started attending the devotional meetings, Zinat had been a mere pupil. Gradually, however, a circle of like-minded women gathered round her, and she began to devote more attention to them and to explain the devotional texts.

She had become their confidante. They listened to her and followed her advice.

Zinat was pleased with her new status, but she still hadn't found the peace she'd been looking for. Something was lacking.

One afternoon, on her way back from the bathhouse, she stopped at the mosque. It was late. There was rarely anyone there at that hour. She slipped into the empty prayer room, then came back out, washed her hands in the *hauz* and splashed her face with water.

What was she doing in the mosque that afternoon, long before the prayer? Why had she washed her hands in the *hauz*? She had never done that before, not once in all the years that her husband had been the imam of the mosque. Besides, since she'd just come from the bathhouse, it wasn't even necessary.

The substitute imam, who was staying in the mosque, came out into the courtyard. Zinat was startled by the sound of footsteps behind her.

'*Salaam aleikum*, Zinat Khanom!' he said.

Zinat returned his greeting, without looking at him. Then she dried her face on her chador and fled into the busy street, away from her sinful thoughts.

Last night as she lay in bed, she couldn't help thinking about the substitute imam. She'd thought about him before, but this time the image was so graphic she couldn't block it out. It was the first time she'd ever thought about another man. Alsaberi, whom she'd married when she was sixteen, had been the only man she'd ever known intimately. She'd given her life to him and had never even noticed other men.

To banish all thoughts of the substitute imam, she pulled the covers over her head and murmured:

> *Qol, a'uudhu be-rabb-en-nas,*
> *Malek-en-nas,*
> *Elah-en-nas.*
>
> *Refuge,*
> *Refuge,*
> *Refuge from the evil*
> *Of the sly whisperer*
> *Who whispers in my heart.*
> *He is a jinn.*
> *He is a jinn.*
> *He is a jinn.*
> *The King of mankind,*
> *Refuge, refuge.*

When she got to the end, however, the image of the substitute imam appeared again. This time he was standing beside her bed, looking down at her, his eyes moving from her face to her breasts.

Alsaberi had never looked at her like that.

Zinat threw her arms over her breasts and muttered a few words to herself, words that could conceivably be the start of a good poem, words that came straight from her heart. She knew nothing about the female poets whose work had recently caused such a stir in Tehran, poems in which they described their emotions and their bodies. If she had, she would have grabbed a pen and committed her words to paper:

Someone will come,
Someone who will look at me
And ask:
Will you take off
Your chador for me?
Will you show me
Your hair?

Zinat couldn't remember exactly when she'd first started fantasising about the substitute imam. She had a certain amount of contact with Janeshin, since she frequently discussed devotional texts with him and asked his advice when she couldn't answer the questions posed by the other women. On these occasions he received her in the prayer room after the prayer, advised her and took the time to answer her questions.

She also ran into him sometimes in the courtyard of the mosque, when he was strolling around, smoking a cigarette.

It wasn't as if she went looking for him, and yet she kept bumping into him. He seemed to know when she was coming to the mosque, for whenever she entered its dark corridors, she inevitably saw him standing there.

Sometimes when she passed his office, she noticed that the door had been left ajar and that Janeshin was sitting in his chair without his turban, reading the Koran. She didn't really want to look into his room, but she couldn't resist the temptation. Every time she peeked in, their eyes met. Zinat couldn't help feeling that he deliberately left the door ajar for that very reason.

Of course it was all right for her to talk to him. After all, he was now the imam of the mosque, filling in for her late husband and her son Ahmad, while he was studying to be an imam in Qom.

She was not the only woman who came to his office. Many others popped in to talk to him. One of the imam's tasks was to welcome the women, listen to what they had to say and offer his advice.

The second time Zinat met with the imam she noticed that he was wearing a special scent – the one known as the Mecca scent. Her late husband had also brought back a bottle from Mecca, so she recognised it instantly. She also knew that it was worn only on special occasions.

The imam had sat in his chair, and Zinat had sat across from him. The door had been left ajar, as usual, since he never shut it when he had a female visitor.

Most women discussed their personal problems with the imam, telling him things they wouldn't dream of telling their husbands or doctors. But Zinat went to him so he could explain religious texts that she didn't understand.

One day she went to his office again after the evening prayer to ask him about a couple of verses in the Al-Adiyât surah. She understood what it meant, but she thought – or rather sensed – that there must be some profound, mysterious subtext that she had failed to grasp.

With the imam sitting across from her as usual, Zinat laid her Koran on the desk, leafed through it until she found the right surah, then slid the book over to him.

Janeshin put on his glasses and ran his finger down the page.

'Would you read it out loud?' he said. 'I'd like to hear you reading it.' And he gently slid the book back over to her.

Zinat hesitantly began to read:

By the charging and snorting stallions
Whose hooves make the sparks fly,
And by the raiders in the morning,
Sending up clouds of dust and
Breaking through the battle array.

'You're right,' he said. 'There *is* a hidden meaning. When you read it aloud, I could see what you were getting at. Your voice forced me to listen to it carefully and think about it. You're a special woman. I rarely meet women like you. As I listened to you read, I ran alongside those snorting stallions whose hooves make sparks fly. I've read that surah many times, but this is the first time it's ever touched me so deeply. I owe that to you.'

Zinat soaked up his words like a desert soaks up a sudden rain. And his last sentence did its work. That night, as she lay in bed, she thought of his 'I owe that to you.'

She felt a kind of warmth, a kind of sensitivity, in his words: 'You sent me running alongside those snorting stallions whose hooves make the sparks fly.'

She flipped on the light, got out of bed, went over to the mirror and looked at her hair. It was no longer black, but it wasn't entirely grey either. She looked at her eyebrows. They were still black. Her brown eyes were tired, but that night they were shining with an unaccustomed glow. She ran her fingers over her face and across her lips. She might have aged, but she wanted to start all over again.

It was only right that she should try and get back some of the years she had lost in that house.

Even so, Zinat curtailed her visits to the imam and tried to avoid running into him. Then one evening he spoke to her out of the darkness: 'Zinat Khanom! Why have you stopped coming to see me? Your questions are always on my mind.'

Three days later Zinat found herself sitting across from him again, talking about her interpretation of a certain passage. He stared at her in silence, listening to her words, then suddenly interrupted her. 'Zinat Khanom,' he said calmly, 'your eyes glow like two candles in the night when you're talking to me . . . I mean, talking about the text.'

Zinat pretended not to have heard him. She went on talking, though she could barely concentrate. He didn't pursue the matter, but behaved like any other imam who was counselling a troubled woman.

Janeshin realised that he'd have to wait until she was ready to hear the rest of what he wanted to say. Luckily he didn't have to wait long, because two evenings later he found Zinat waiting by his door.

'Come in,' he said. 'I don't have any plans for tonight, and I'm bored. Did you bring another text to discuss?'

Zinat sat down and began to read the text she'd brought with her.

The imam listened. 'You read so well,' he said. 'You bring the dead words to life. I hear them, I feel them, I see them on your lips.' And he pointed to her lips, almost brushing his hand against her lower lip as he did so.

Zinat packed her suitcase and went for a week to her father's house in Jirya, where she hoped to banish Janeshin from her mind.

She did a lot of soul-searching while she was there and concluded that she didn't want to get involved with him. After all, he was married, with children. He was also the imam of the mosque that her son was going to take over one day.

But when she returned, things didn't go as she had planned.

She was shopping in the bazaar, staring at a jewellery display case, when Janeshin's reflection suddenly loomed up beside hers in the glass. 'Zinat Khanom,' he whispered in her ear. 'I miss you. The chair you usually sit on in my office is empty.'

Zinat didn't say a word. She didn't even turn to look at him. She simply stood with her back to him and listened.

His voice was hard to resist. And yet for the next two days she stayed away from the mosque, skipping both the morning and the evening prayers. Then she couldn't hold out any longer. After the caretaker had locked up and gone home, she put on her black chador, went up the stairs to the roof and walked over to the mosque.

On her way to the prayer room, she passed the imam's office.

'Is that you, Zinat?' he called calmly from within.

'Yes, I'm on my way to the prayer room to get a book.'

'You're welcome to come in, if you like. I've made a fresh pot of tea.'

Zinat continued on to the prayer room, found the book she was looking for, snatched it up and started back down the corridor.

'I always hear your footsteps in the night,' Janeshin said from inside his office.

Zinat went in, sat down on the chair and laid the book on his desk.

Janeshin stood up. He closed the door softly and turned the key. Then he lit a candle, set it on the desk and switched off the light.

Zinat sat quietly in her chair and waited.

He took out his prayer book and looked for the words

that you recite when you want to sleep with a woman who isn't your lawfully wedded wife. According to the teachings of Islam, once he had uttered the *ankahtu* marriage vow and Zinat had said '*Qabilto*' (I consent), he would be allowed to take her to bed.

He softly began to recite the words.

Zinat closed her eyes.

'*Ankahtu wa zawagto*,' the imam chanted, bowing over his book.

Zinat was silent.

'*Ankahtu wa zawagto*,' he chanted a second time.

Zinat was silent.

'*Ankahtu wa zawagto*,' he chanted a third time.

'*Qabilto*,' Zinat said slowly, and she dropped her chador to her shoulders.

The imam put down his Koran. Then he touched her lips and caressed her warm neck.

The Kaaba

The grandmothers, having awakened early, grabbed their brooms and watering cans and tiptoed outside. First they sprinkled water on the ground, then they began to sweep. They couldn't remember how old they were when they first started to sweep the path to the gate, but they did it in the greatest of secrecy because they wanted to go to Mecca.

Millions of Muslims dreamed of making the pilgrimage to Mecca, but not all of them got there, because you had to be well-off to afford the trip.

The grandmothers had no money at all. They'd never thought about money and didn't need any, because the family saw to their needs. And yet they'd known since childhood that the only way a poor person could go to Mecca was by sweeping. There were three conditions: first, the path had to be swept every day before sunrise for twenty years; second, no one must see you doing it; third, it had to remain a secret.

On the last day, the Prophet Khezr would appear and present you with your reward. The legendary Khezr, one of the first prophets, had lived long before Muhammad, Jesus, Moses, Abraham, Jacob and David.

But just how Khezr would arrange the trip to Mecca was a secret between the prophet and the sweepers.

The grandmothers had swept the path every day for twenty years, but the prophet hadn't come. Perhaps they'd done something wrong, they reasoned. Perhaps they hadn't counted properly or had overslept once or been seen by someone who guessed their secret.

So they began all over again for another twenty years.

Their labour might be in vain, but what else could they do? The one thing that kept them going was their goal of seeing Mecca. It gave meaning to their lives. There was always the hope that they would awaken to a new dawn and have one more day in which to await the coming of the prophet.

According to their calculations, they had now reached the end of their second twenty years, and yet there was no sign of the prophet.

At the end of their first twenty years, they had still had the energy to go to Mecca. When they began the second round, however, they knew that at the end they'd be so old that they probably wouldn't have enough energy to make the pilgrimage. But they went on sweeping anyway.

A few days later the grandmothers were sitting gloomily in the dark on the floor of the Carpet Room.

'If someone took away our brooms, we'd drop dead,' Golbanu said. 'We can't stop sweeping now. We have to go on, even if all we can do is crawl to the gate with a broom in our hands.'

'We must have made a mistake,' Golebeh said. 'Maybe we counted wrong again.'

'We couldn't have. Every year we write an X on the wall. Here, count them. We're long past the twenty-year mark.'

'Maybe we broke one of the rules.'

'What rules? There are no rules. Get up early, sweep, keep it a secret.'

'I think I know what the problem is.'

'You can think all you like, but what do you know for sure?'

'We've made a big mistake,' Golebeh said. 'Both of us.'

'What did we do wrong?'

'We weren't supposed to tell anyone our secret,' she said.

'But we didn't.'

'Yes, we did. We shared our secret with each other. You know my secret and I know yours. That's against the rules! You aren't supposed to know mine, and I'm not supposed to know yours. We should have done our sweeping separately.'

'Oh, do be quiet!'

They had jointly decided to sweep the path so they could meet the Prophet Khezr together and go to Mecca together, but so far their plan had failed.

Dejected, the grandmothers sat in the Carpet Room, talking. The two figures eventually blended in with the darkness. No one, it seemed, would ever come to their rescue. Their brooms slipped out of their hands.

No longer visible, they were merely two shadows in the dark Carpet Room. The crow screeched, breaking the silence.

Crazy Qodsi suddenly appeared out of nowhere and peered into the Carpet Room. 'I heard the grandmothers talking,' she muttered to herself. 'But where are they? I thought I heard their voices. I'm sure I did.'

Startled, the grandmothers scrambled to their feet. If Crazy Qodsi had overheard their conversation, she was bound to tell everyone, because blabbing secrets was her speciality.

'How are you, Qodsi?' they began cautiously.

'Fine.'

'How's your mother?'

'Fine.'

'And your sister?'

'My sister? She's crazy. And she's getting worse.'

'Would you like something to eat, Qodsi?' Golbanu asked, and they took her to the kitchen, hoping to find out if she'd overheard their conversation. But before they could say a word, Qodsi slipped away.

'Qodsi?' the grandmothers called, but she had already left.

How old was Qodsi? Thirty? Forty? Older, younger? Nobody knew.

In any case she looked young. Young and simple-minded.

She came from a traditional family. Her father, a distant relative of Aqa Jaan, was a rich nobleman who owned a couple of villages in the mountains. But something was amiss in his family: they were all crazy.

After the birth of her first child, his wife had had a nervous breakdown and never recovered. His son was retarded, his oldest daughter was a basket case and Qodsi roamed the city like a tramp. After his death, there was no one to look after them. Aqa Jaan kept an eye on the family, dealt with their finances and stopped by periodically to see how they were doing.

They were still living in their father's house. Every so often the mother went to the bazaar to buy necessities, venturing forth as if she were a princess. You could tell by her bearing that she'd been born into a wealthy family, but if you took a closer look, you could see that something wasn't quite right. She was accompanied on these shopping expeditions by Qodsi and her elder daughter. Whenever she wanted to cross the street, the two girls ran ahead and stopped the traffic, so that no wagon, car, bus or bicycle could drive on until their mother had safely reached the pavement on the other side.

Qodsi's brother, who was older than she, was named Hashem. He went around in an army uniform, with a field-marshall's baton clamped under his arm. He kept his uniform spotless, and the bronze lion – the symbol of Persia – on his officer's cap always gleamed.

From early morning to late at night, he stood guard at the entrance to the bazaar. He saluted every policeman who went by, and otherwise stood as still as a statue. People accepted him; children didn't even tease him. Everyone looked upon him as a kind of city monument.

The moment he saw Aqa Jaan entering the bazaar, Hashem always saluted and snapped out a military-like 'Hel-lo!' And when Aqa Jaan left, he repeated the performance. After the salute, Aqa Jaan would go over to him, shake hands and say a few words.

'How are you doing, Hashem?'

'Fine.'

'And your mother?'

'Fine.'

'And your sister?'

'Fine.'

'Give my regards to your mother. If you need me for anything, just send Qodsi.'

'I will.'

'Excellent!' said Aqa Jaan.

Qodsi knew almost everything that was going on.

'Got any news, Qodsi?' people asked when they ran into her.

You had to ask her very politely about her mother and her sister, or else she ignored your question.

She didn't pass on her information for free either. First you had to give her a few copper coins, which she promptly stuck in her mouth. Only then did she tell you the latest news. 'Old Qasem is dead, Miryam had a daughter and Sultan's hen had seven chicks.'

Early in the morning Qodsi began with an empty mouth. Then she went from house to house, relating her news and kept going until her mouth was so full of coins she couldn't talk any more.

No one knew what she did with her money. Some people said that she put it in a jar and hid it in the cellar, because if her mother ever found out that she was begging, the poor woman would drop dead on the spot.

'Qodsi,' Aqa Jaan said to her repeatedly, 'you come from a good family. You're a lady. You can't just waltz into other people's houses.'

But she ignored him and kept on going through every open door she saw.

She never sat down, but instead walked in and out of rooms and listened to people's conversations before moving on to the next house – which is how she gathered her news.

Sometimes she crossed the bridge and went to the vine-yards on the other side of the river.

'You mustn't go there!' Aqa Jaan warned her. 'A young woman has no business being in the vineyards.'

'I promise I won't go there any more,' she said, but she went anyway.

She used to cross the bridge and head straight for the vineyards, which was the favourite haunt of suspicious-looking men, men who would slip a handful of shiny copper coins into her mouth.

Whenever one of these men saw her, he led her behind

the trees, filled her mouth with coins and kissed her. Qodsi didn't say a word. He fondled her breasts, but Qodsi didn't respond. He slipped his hand under her clothes and touched her body. Qodsi didn't move a muscle, but the moment he tried to pull down her underwear, she tore herself away and ran back to the bridge.

Qodsi popped in often to see Aqa Jaan at the bazaar. When no one else was there, the office boy didn't stop her from going in. Today she sat down as usual on the chair beside his desk.

'Tea for Qodsi Khanom!' Aqa Jaan called out, as he always did.

The office boy brought her a glass of tea and some chocolate on a silver tray.

'Have you got any news for me?' Aqa Jaan asked.

Qodsi leaned in close and, in a hushed voice, imparted her news. 'I crossed the bridge and went to the vineyards.'

'Again?'

'Two men grabbed me, but I screamed and screamed until they ran off into the mountains.'

'Didn't I tell you not to go to there? If you go to the vineyards again, I'll have to tell your mother. This has got to stop. Do you hear me?'

'Yes. I promise not to go there again.'

'Good! Is there anything else you'd like to tell me?'

'Yes,' she said, and she rattled off the rest of her news without stopping to take a breath: 'Constable Ruhani beats his wife every night and smokes those nasty things and the shoemaker locked his mother in the chicken coop and she was crying because she wanted out and Azam Azam always takes a knife with her when she goes to bed with her husband and Am Ramazan's donkey is sick and the grandmothers thought they'd get to go to Mecca this year, but he didn't come, that's the second time he hasn't come, and that made the grandmothers cry.'

'What was that about the grandmothers? Who didn't come?' Aqa Jaan asked.

'The Prophet Khezr. This is the second time he hasn't come.'

Aqa Jaan was shocked.

'What are you talking about? What do you mean?'

'I've got to go,' she said.

She stood up, crammed a chocolate into her mouth, took a gulp of tea and raced off.

'Wait a minute!' Aqa Jaan shouted.

That night in bed Aqa Jaan told his wife that Qodsi had stopped by again.

'What did she have to say?'

'The usual gobbledegook. She mixes things up and says the first thing that comes into her head.'

'I know, she makes half of it up. In that way she's a bit like our Zinat.'

'You shouldn't compare Qodsi to Zinat. Qodsi has a screw loose.'

'Don't get me wrong, I'm not comparing them. I just meant that Zinat can't sit still either, and her head is also full of fantasies.'

'True, but Qodsi's stories are total gibberish.'

'They may be gibberish, but she tells them well. Still, you never get the whole story. She gives you bits and pieces and rattles them off, one right after another, which adds to the suspense. What did she tell you today?'

Aqa Jaan thought for a moment. He'd been thinking all day about what she'd said about the grandmothers, but he didn't feel like mentioning it to Fakhri yet.

'She makes me so angry,' he said. 'She went to the other

side of the river again. She says that two men grabbed her and that she screamed and screamed until they ran off into the mountains.'

'My God, not those men again! I'm afraid they'll do something to her, and if they do, you'll be the one who has to deal with it. Maybe I should talk to her and scare her a bit, so she'll stay away from them.'

'She also said that Am Ramazan's donkey is sick and that Azam Azam takes a knife with her when she goes to bed with her husband.'

Fakhri Sadat laughed. 'What did she mean by that?'

'I don't know. She makes things up. She goes into a house, sees something and turns it into a story. For all I know she did see a knife or something like it in Azam Azam's bed. She also said that Constable Ruhani beats his wife every night.'

'That might be true. You ought to do something for that poor woman. Her husband's not only corrupt, he's an addict. Tell Zinat. She'll know who to contact in the mosque. She's good at arranging those kinds of things. She could drop by Azam Azam's house and find out what's going on. You should tell Zinat. Anything else?'

'The shoemaker locked his mother in the chicken coop.'

'That can't be true! What kind of person would lock his elderly mother in a chicken coop?'

'People are so cruel sometimes. They're capable of *any*thing.'

'Ask Zinat to go and visit her. Maybe she can find out if it really happened.'

'Qodsi only remembers things that make an impression on her, then she tells them in her own way. But it occurred to me just now that she might have a different motive. Maybe she comes to see me when she has something important to say, something she can't share with anyone else. The difference between her and Zinat is that Zinat tells ancient stories. Qodsi takes a strand of truth and weaves it into a story. There's *some* truth in what she says. That's all I meant to say.'

Fakhri Sadat laid her head on his chest and closed her eyes. 'I don't want to hear another word about Qodsi,' she said. 'Tell me something else, something beautiful, something sweet . . . I don't mean to complain, but you haven't been spending much time with me lately. We used to go away on trips more often. You took me to Mashad for a week, and we stayed in that guesthouse by Imam Reza's tomb. And we went to Isfahan together, but it's been years since we've taken a trip. You go off by yourself and I stay here. Sometimes I think I've grown old, and that you—'

'She mentioned something else.'

'You haven't been listening to a word I've said, have you? Are you still talking about Qodsi?'

'She said something about the grandmothers. About how the Prophet Khezr had let them down.'

'Who let them down?' Fakhri said, and sat up in bed.

'The Prophet Khezr! I'm quoting Qodsi, and she must have been quoting someone. My guess is that she overheard a conversation between the grandmothers. I think they have a secret.'

'What makes you think that?'

'It's just a feeling I have. Qodsi said, "Khezr didn't come. It's the second time he hasn't come, and that made the grandmothers cry."'

Only now did he realise that for years he'd often seen the grandmothers early in the morning, sweeping, but he'd never stopped to think that they might have been doing it secretly.

*   *   *

Just before dawn, Aqa Jaan slipped out of bed, went over to the window and watched the door to the grandmothers' bedroom.

Before long it opened and out came two shadowy figures with brooms.

He'd spent all night thinking about the grandmothers and coming up with a plan. He now knew how to make their dream come true. He smiled to himself and climbed back into bed.

Fakhri Sadat's bare leg caught his eye. He could also see her pomegranate-red pants in the glow of the night-light. She was right – he had been spending less time with her, and it had been quite a while since they'd taken a trip together. He no longer came back with presents for her either. It had been ages since he'd come home from Damascus with that box of underwear in seven different colours. He crawled under the covers, gave her a hug and began to pull down her pants.

'Not now!' Fakhri Sadat said sleepily.

He ignored her as usual and tugged her pants even lower.

'Not now,' she said again, softly.

And then she fell silent.

Eqra!

A few weeks later, the grandmothers were out sweeping when they heard a strange sound coming from the alley. They peered into the darkness, but didn't see anything, so they went back to their sweeping. All of a sudden a horse whinnied. Again they peered into the darkness, but their ageing eyes couldn't make out a thing.

'Did you hear a horse whinny?' Golbanu said.

'Yes, and I heard hooves too,' Golebeh said.

The sounds came closer. The grandmothers clutched each other's hand, stared into the alley and stood rooted to the spot. A black horse suddenly appeared in the glow of the streetlight. High up in the saddle was an Arab in a white robe. The grandmothers bowed in respectful silence.

The horseman cried in Arabic, '*Yaaa ayoohaaaal nabe-ii, waaa salaaaaamooo namazooooo Khezr wa al-Mekka!*'

The grandmothers didn't know a word of Arabic, but the horseman's message was clear enough. The words 'Mecca' and 'Khezr' were all they needed to hear.

Again they bowed to the Arab on the horse.

'*Waaa enne-ii waa jaleha,*' the horseman continued. '*Waaa enne-ii yaa,* Golbanu. *Waaa enne-ii yaa,* Golebeh!'

The grandmothers trembled with excitement. The horseman had said their names. Had they heard him correctly?

'*Yaaa eyyo haaannabe-ii. Eqraaa esme-ii,* Golbanu!' said the horseman.

No, they hadn't been mistaken. He'd clearly said 'Golbanu!'

What were they supposed to do?

Golbanu stepped forward and bowed her head. The horseman took a letter out of his pocket and held it out to her.

Golbanu approached him hesitantly and accepted the envelope.

'Golebeh!' the horseman called.

The other grandmother went up to him and received a white envelope as well.

'*Waaa enna lellaah. Waaa Allaaho samaad,*' the horseman cried. Then he tugged the reins, wheeled around and vanished into the darkness.

Daylight came. The astonished grandmothers were still standing on the path, clutching their envelopes.

They didn't dare move. They were afraid they'd been dreaming. But they couldn't have been, because the crow flew down to the streetlight and cawed as loud as it could.

Back in their room, the grandmothers locked the door, turned on the light and opened the envelopes. The letters were identical, but they couldn't read them: the Prophet had evidently written them in a secret language. They would have to show the letters to someone, but who? Aqa Jaan? Fakhri Sadat? Zinat Khanom? No.

'Let's ask Shahbal,' Golebeh said.

They went to his room.

'Wake up! Are you still in bed? Haven't you said your prayer? Shame on you. I'll tell Aqa Jaan you slept in like a sinner. Here, *eqra*! Read this. Read us the letters!' Golbanu said.

Shahbal sleepily examined the letters. 'I can read the words, but I don't know what they mean. It's in Arabic.'

Perhaps they'd have to show the letters to Aqa Jaan after all, but he'd gone to Jirya, and it would be ages before he returned. So they put on their chadors and went to the mosque to show their letters to the substitute imam.

Janeshin had just finished his morning prayer and gone back to his room to sleep for another hour. When he heard a knock, he thought it was Zinat Khanom, so he called sleepily, 'Come in!'

Instead, the grandmothers came traipsing into his room. 'What's the matter, ladies?' he said in surprise. 'What can I do for you?'

'We've received a highly confidential letter. Or rather two letters. Would you please read them to us?'

'Gladly. Have a seat.'

They handed him the letters.

He took his turban from the nightstand, put it on and sat down on his chair in his long cotton shirt. 'Do sit down, ladies,' he said. 'Hold on, I need my glasses.'

He put on his glasses and perused one of the letters. 'A letter in Arabic?'

'Can't you read it?'

'I should be able to, but it's not as if I read a letter in Arabic every day. Of course I can read the Koran, but the language in the Koran is different, it's the language of God. I can read the Koran well enough to understand it, but if you handed me an Arabic newspaper, I probably wouldn't be able to tell you what it said. Or to put it another way, if I flew to Mecca today, I doubt if I could talk to the people there. Wait, there's an address at the bottom of the letter. Are you supposed to go somewhere? Where did you get these letters? They seem to be formal documents of some kind. I can also make out a name: Hajji Aqa Mustafa Mohajir.'

'We know Hajji Aqa Mustafa Mohajir,' said Golbanu. 'He has an office at the bazaar.'

'Well, that settles it. Apparently you're supposed to go and see this hajji. *Wa-assalaam!*'

The grandmothers were unable to control their excitement. They snatched back their letters and hurried outside.

They wanted to set off for the bazaar immediately, but Golbanu said, 'I think it's too early. Let's wait until the sun's a bit higher. Besides, we ought to put on our good clothes, if we're going to the bazaar with such important letters.'

All of a sudden the house looked different. It was bathed in bright sunlight, as if every object were smiling and everyone was in on their secret. The old cedar tree had no doubt heard the hoof beats, and the *hauz* had thrilled to Khezr's voice.

The flowers in the garden looked reverently at the grandmothers, the sun sparkled on the library windows and the crow circled above their heads, cawing cheerfully. 'Thank you, crow, thank you,' the grandmothers cried. The red fish leapt out of the water. 'Thank you, fish, thank you,' said the grandmothers.

'I hear happy footsteps,' Muezzin called up from the cellar. 'What's put you two in such a good mood?'

Golbanu and Golebeh went down to his studio to say hello. He was standing at his workbench, kneading a lump of clay.

Should they tell him? Were they allowed to reveal their secret? No, first they had to go and see Hajji Mustafa, Golbanu thought. Only then would they know if their lifetime dream was about to come true.

'Good morning!' said the grandmothers merrily.

'And a good morning to you too, ladies. I know you're dying to tell me something,' Muezzin said.

'It's true, we have the most wonderful news!' Golebeh began, but Golbanu quickly changed the subject before Golebeh could spill the beans. 'These vases look new, Muezzin,' she improvised. 'They're absolutely gorgeous.'

'There's no need to overdo it. I've been making vases my entire life. It's just that you're seeing them through different eyes today.'

The grandmothers exchanged smiles.

'We've heard some very good news. We'll tell you soon, and then you can shout it from the rooftops.'

'Such secrecy!' Muezzin said.

The grandmothers all but skipped up the stairs and went back into the courtyard.

They were so happy that they didn't know what to do, where to go or who to visit. They saw Fakhri Sadat walking towards the kitchen and waved – a bit awkwardly, since it wasn't something they ordinarily did. One of the cats walked by and they chased after it. Alarmed by their odd behaviour, the cat fled to the roof.

The grandmothers put on their good clothes, powdered their cheeks and donned their most beautiful chadors. Then off they went, in the direction of the bazaar.

Hajji Mustafa was an old friend of Aqa Jaan. He was also a powerful man in the city, since he had the exclusive right to arrange trips to holy shrines in other cities and to organise the pilgrimages to Karbala, Najaf, Medina, Damascus and Mecca.

His travel agency was in the middle of the bazaar. Hundreds of prospective pilgrims stopped by every day to plan their trips. The grandmothers went in, but didn't have to queue like the others. After all, they had a personal letter for Hajji Mustafa.

They peeked through the window of his office. Although

they'd seen him in the mosque only once, they recognised him immediately. He was sitting at his desk, talking on the phone. He motioned for them to come in, and they cautiously opened the door.

'What can I do for you?' Hajji Mustafa said, as soon as his call was over. The grandmothers handed him their letters. 'We have a message for you,' Golbanu said.

He put on his glasses, opened one of the envelopes and carefully perused the letter, peering occasionally at the grandmothers over the rim of his glasses. After reading the second letter, he took off his glasses and sat without moving for one long minute.

The grandmothers exchanged questioning glances.

He put the letters back in their envelopes, touched them reverently to his forehead and slipped them into a drawer.

'Please sit down,' he said solemnly.

The grandmothers seated themselves in the two old-fashioned leather chairs beside his desk.

Hajji Mustafa rummaged through some papers, jotted down a few words and made a mysterious phone call. Then he went out, leaving the grandmothers alone in his office without saying a word to either of them. Fifteen minutes later he came back in and took a thick ledger out of a mahogany filing cabinet. He opened the ledger and said solemnly, 'Golbanu.'

'That's me,' said one of the grandmothers, and she stood up.

He put an old-fashioned ink pad in front of her. 'Place the tip of your index finger on this ink pad,' he said, 'then press it here in this ledger.'

With trembling hands, Golbanu did as she had been instructed.

'You may be seated.'

He filled in a few lines, then said, 'Golebeh.'

'That's me,' the other grandmother said in a quavering voice, and she stood up.

'Press here and here.'

She pressed her finger on the ink pad and then again on the line in the ledger to which Hajji was pointing with his pen.

'What's your address?' he asked.

'The house of the mosque,' Golbanu said.

'Do both of you live there?'

'Yes,' they said.

When he was finished writing, he stamped the two entries with a rubber stamp, then stood up. 'Follow me,' he said.

The grandmothers followed him down a hallway, through a narrow room, into a larger office and down a dim corridor, until at last Hajji stopped in front of a closed door. He took out a key, opened the door and turned to the grandmothers. 'Please take off your shoes before entering.'

Golbanu and Golebeh found themselves standing on the threshold of an extraordinary room. Banners inscribed with sacred texts lined the walls. Rows of wooden racks were filled with battered leather suitcases. The familiar smell of books and leather gave the place an aura of holiness. An antique rug stretched from one end of the room to the other. Off to one side was a small alcove with a big stack of ledgers. The ones on the top were covered with a thick layer of dust.

The hands of the grandmothers shook beneath their chadors. They removed their shoes and went inside.

'Sit down,' said Hajji, pointing to some chairs grouped around an antique table. Suspended above it was an exquisite silver chandelier with seven candles. The grandmothers' hearts soared.

'Everything that has happened so far, everything we've

said to each other and everything you've seen up till now are to be kept secret,' Hajji said. 'If you breathe a word of this to anyone, your trip will be cancelled.'

'We won't tell a soul,' Golbanu said.

He disappeared behind a curtain and came back with two brand-new suitcases, on which a picture of the Kaaba had been embossed. He set the tan suitcases beside the grandmothers with such an official flourish that they nearly fainted from excitement.

Hajji sat down across from them. 'Everyone at home is probably going to ask you a lot of questions,' he said calmly. 'But don't answer them. I repeat, don't answer them.'

'We understand,' Golbanu said.

'On the anniversary of Fatima's birth, the two of you are to wait with your suitcases at the entrance to the bazaar,' Hajji said.

'We will,' Golbanu promised.

'If you have any questions, now is the time to ask,' he said, 'because you won't get another chance.'

The grandmothers looked at each other uncertainly. Did they have any questions? No, they didn't.

'Oh, wait,' Golbanu said hesitantly. 'I do have one. What time are we supposed to be at the bazaar?'

'Early in the morning, just before dawn,' Hajji replied.

Golebeh had a question as well, but she didn't dare ask it, so she whispered it in Golbanu's ear.

'Excuse me,' Golbanu said, 'but you haven't given us any proof. It might be good to have some kind of document with our names on it.'

'The suitcases are your proof!' Hajji said. 'They already have your names on them.'

They looked at the suitcases and, to their surprise, saw their names written in big letters on a piece of paper encased in a transparent plastic holder.

'So they are!' Golbanu said, and she scowled at Golebeh for asking such a silly question.

'You will receive your travel documents on the day of the trip,' said Hajji. 'Any other questions?'

The grandmothers exchanged glances. No, they had no more questions.

Beaming with joy and hiding their smiles behind their chadors, the grandmothers picked up their suitcases, left the travel agency and made their way through the busy bazaar.

At home they hid the suitcases in one of the trunks in the cellar and pretended nothing had happened. But the secret weighed heavily on their hearts. They couldn't sleep; they tossed and turned for hours. The days seemed longer and the nights went on for ever. Was it really going to happen? Would they be able to pack their bags one day and set off on their journey? Were they strong enough to undertake such a long trip?

They were afraid they weren't going to live to see the day, that they would have an accident or break a leg or die. But they had been patient for forty years, so a few more months would hardly matter.

The Treasure Room

Oh, you cloaked in your mantle!
Stand up and deliver your warning!
Magnify your Lord.
Purify your garments.
Shun abomination.
Be patient!

A group of seven men emerged from the alley. Four of the men bore a large basket, suspended from two poles, on their shoulders, while the other three walked on ahead. They were villagers from Jirya, transporting Kazem Khan to the house of the mosque.

One of them knocked. It took a while for Golebeh to open the door. 'Yes, gentlemen?' she said, surprised to see a makeshift litter.

'We have Kazem Khan with us,' one of them said, pointing to the basket.

'Golbanu!' Golebeh shouted, upset. 'It's Kazem Khan!' As soon as she saw the litter, Golbanu knew what needed to be done. She showed the men to the Opium Room, and they carefully transferred Kazem Khan from the litter to the bed. His eyes were closed, his face was pale and he was emaciated. The men went into the courtyard and gathered round the *hauz* to smoke their pipes. Golebeh wept softly, while Golbanu did what was necessary.

She covered Kazem Khan with a blanket, placed a Koran and a hand mirror on the shelf above his head and went into the kitchen to make breakfast. After setting the table with bread, cheese, jam, a bowl of fruit and a teapot, she called to the villagers. 'Gentlemen, time to eat!'

Meanwhile, Aqa Jaan had come home and gone straight to the Opium Room. He took one look at Kazem Khan and knew there was no point in taking him to hospital. Instead he went into the kitchen to greet the villagers.

They stood up to show their respect, and one of them told the story: 'We hadn't seen Kazem Khan in the teahouse for several days, but we thought he was away on a trip. Then last night we heard his horse neighing and assumed he was back, but the horse didn't stop neighing. So we went to his house and found him lying in bed, almost dead. This morning we put him in the litter and brought him here by bus.'

'Thank you. I'm grateful for all you've done for my uncle,' Aqa Jaan replied.

That evening he placed a chair by Kazem Khan's bed and sat next to him for hours, quietly reading the Al-Fatiha surah to him.

Kazem Khan was the heart and soul of the house, despite the fact that he had never formed an attachment to either the house or the mosque. He was the kind of person Aqa Jaan would never be. Aqa Jaan was the head of the household, the mosque and the bazaar, and had numerous other obligations; Kazem Khan, on the other hand, was as free as a bird, and now he was dying like a bird, for old birds suddenly plummet out of the sky, close their eyes and never wake up again. Kazem Khan was a poet who had always thrown convention to the winds. He had done all kinds of things, things Aqa Jaan didn't dare think about.

Aqa Jaan reached into Kazem Khan's pocket and took out his poetry book. He leafed through it until he came to the last poem, which he softly read aloud:

> If those sweet lips, that goblet of wine,
> Yes, everything, ends in non-existence,
> Then remember, for as long as you exist,
> That you are only what you will be one day:
> Nothing. It's impossible to be less than that.

For the past seventy years someone had always prepared the opium kit for Kazem Khan the moment he stepped through the door. Now that long-standing custom had come to an end.

The grandmothers sat in the kitchen, talking and weeping silent tears. The man they loved was about to die. When had they first met him? One afternoon more than a half-century ago, when they were young girls and the poet Kazem Khan had come riding into the courtyard on his horse. Before that time they had never even heard a poem. A few days later Kazem Khan had written two poems, one for Golbanu and one for Golebeh. Poems about their eyes, their long plaits, their smiles and their hands, which were pleasantly warm when they lit the fire in the opium kit. The next time he came to the house, the two women were his for all eternity.

Am Ramazan appeared in the doorway. He was the man who looked after the garden. Every day at dusk he stopped by to see Muezzin in his studio. He kept track of the clay and ordered a new supply when Muezzin was running low. Am Ramazan lived alone; his wife was dead and he had no children. All he had was a donkey. He earned his living by mining sand from the river and transporting it to his customers on his donkey.

Am Ramazan whispered a greeting to Aqa Jaan, who returned his greeting and motioned for him to come in. 'Listen,' he said. 'Kazem Khan hasn't had any opium for a while. His body is crying out for it. The grandmothers are going to prepare the opium kit. If you could smoke the pipe and blow the smoke into his face, it might give him some relief.'

Am Ramazan smoked opium from time to time, but couldn't afford to buy it for himself. He was delighted to accept Aqa Jaan's offer, because he knew that Kazem Khan smoked the best opium in the mountains. Am Ramazan and his friends smoked a dark-brown opium that stank to high heaven, but Kazem Khan smoked a yellowish-brown opium that smelled of wildflowers.

Aqa Jaan handed half a roll of opium to Am Ramazan, who slipped it in his pocket and went outside to help with the fire.

Before long Golebeh came in with a pot of tea and a brazier filled with glowing embers. She looked at Kazem Khan with tears in her eyes and set the brazier on the floor. Am Ramazan stuck the pipe in the hot ashes and cut the opium into thin slices.

When the pipe was hot, he put one of the slices on the tip, secured it with a pin, picked up a glowing ember with a pair of tongs, and held it up to the opium. He started out with a few gentle puffs, then inhaled more and more deeply. For a moment he forgot he was smoking the opium for Kazem Khan. Then his eye caught Aqa Jaan's and he stood up, holding the pipe in his left hand and the tongs with the glowing ember in his right hand.

Leaning over Kazem Khan, he heated the opium in the

pipe with the glowing ember, then inhaled deeply and blew the smoke in Kazem Khan's face.

He smoked patiently for half an hour, until the room was filled with a dark-blue cloud of smoke.

The door opened and Crazy Qodsi came in. The grandmothers tried to stop her, but Aqa Jaan gestured for them to leave her alone. She walked over to the bed, leaned down, peered into Kazem Khan's face, mumbled something and tiptoed out, without saying a word to Aqa Jaan.

'That's enough,' Golbanu said to Am Ramazan. 'If you would care to leave, we'll read to Kazem Khan from the Koran.' Aqa Jaan, having grown a bit drowsy from the smoke, roused himself and left the room along with Am Ramazan.

Golebeh took the Koran from the shelf and sat down on the floor beside Golbanu. Reading ordinary books wasn't a problem, but the Koran was much more difficult. Fortunately they both knew a number of surahs by heart. Golbanu opened the book and stared at the page, then began to recite a surah by heart, while Golebeh repeated the words after her:

> By the pen and by what you write.
> We put the owners of the gardens to the test.
> In the morning they called out to one another:
> 'Go early to your field,
> If you wish to gather the fruits.'
> And they set off early,
> But when they saw it they said:
> 'We must have lost our way.
> No, we have been dispossessed!'

Golebeh brought her mouth to his ear and whispered, 'Kazem Khan, you have begun your journey. Sooner or later we will follow. We have a secret. We aren't supposed to tell anyone, but we'll tell you. A few weeks from now we'll be going to Mecca. We owe it all to the Prophet Khezr. We were planning to go to Jirya to say farewell. I kiss you, Kazem Khan. We both do. You made us happy.'

Golbanu and Golebeh kissed Kazem Khan on the forehead and left the room.

On the third night Aqa Jaan noticed that Kazem Khan's end was nearing. He went into the room alone, shut the door and kissed his uncle on the forehead. 'You can let go now,' he whispered. 'We will remember you always. I will put your shoes and your poems in the treasure room. I'm here beside you, holding your hand.'

Shahbal tiptoed in and remained standing by the door.

'Would you bring me a glass of black tea and a spoon?' Aqa Jaan asked him.

When Shahbal returned with the requested items, Aqa Jaan put a slice of opium in the glass and stirred it until it dissolved. 'Here,' he said to Shahbal, 'put a spoonful of this in his mouth, his body craves it. This way his soul can depart his body more peacefully.'

Shahbal carefully spooned the yellowish-brown liquid into Kazem Khan's mouth.

Aqa Jaan put his hand on his uncle's bare shoulder. 'He's going,' he said, and he leaned down and kissed Kazem Khan again on the forehead. Slowly, the life ebbed out of the old man. 'He's gone,' Aqa Jaan said, his voice filled with sorrow. 'Will you let the others know?'

The grandmothers were the first to enter the room. They offered their condolences to Aqa Jaan and stood quietly by the bed. The next to arrive were Fakhri, Zinat and Muezzin, all crying. Aqa Jaan gathered up Kazem

Khan's shoes and his poems and carried them through the darkness to the mosque.

The mosque had a treasure room, a secret chamber in the crypt, where items of value to the house had been stored for centuries, such as deeds, parchment rolls, letters, the robes and shoes of the mosque's imams from the past to the present and hundreds of journals filled with mosque reports written for centuries by men like Aqa Jaan. Every object had been arranged in chronological order and placed in chests.

The treasure room was a gold mine of information. You could trace the country's religious history in its archives. Many personal items that had belonged to the residents of the house were also stored there.

The archives and personal items should probably have been given to a museum for safekeeping, but they constituted a unique – and more importantly – personal history of the house and the mosque.

The head of the household was obliged to carry the key to the treasure room at all times.

The only other person aside from Aqa Jaan who knew about the treasure room and its contents was Shahbal. Aqa Jaan had told him about the journals. 'When I die – and God is the only one who knows when that will be – you will become the keeper of the key,' Aqa Jaan had said to Shahbal. 'You will write in the journals, and you will decide what happens.'

He himself had been a mere twenty-seven years old when he entered the treasure room for the first time.

After the death of his father, he'd taken a lantern and gone down to the crypt in the dark of night. With trembling hands he'd inserted the key in the ancient lock, opened the door and gone inside.

He had felt as if he were in a dream world, for that vaulted room was like nothing he had ever seen before. An old pomegranate-red carpet had been laid over the stone floor. One corner contained a chair and a table, on top of which stood an inkpot, a quill pen and a journal, opened to a blank page. The wall was lined with dozens of pairs of dusty shoes, each labelled with the name of the deceased imam to whom they had belonged. Across from the shoes were rows of coat-racks, and on every hook was an imam's prayer robe and black turban. Next to some of the coat-racks were walking sticks and small chests, in which the personal belongings and important documents from that particular imam's era had been stored.

Aqa Jaan didn't know exactly how old the mosque and the house were, though he could have found out easily enough. All he had to do was to take his lantern and walk past the coat-racks to the darkest recesses of the crypt, where he would no doubt find the oldest chest and the very first journal. The blueprints of the house and the mosque might well be in that chest.

There was a dark passage at the far end of the room, which made Aqa Jaan suspect that there were even more nooks and crannies, with even more ancient chests. He decided to explore. The first thing he saw when he held up his lantern were parchment documents hanging on the wall, though the light was too dim to make out the words.

Just as he was about to step into the passage, he saw a thick layer of dust on the red carpet, thicker than that on the chests, prayer robes and other items. For the last hundred years or so, no one had ventured any further than where he was now. Aqa Jaan didn't feel that he could go any further either. The dust represented a kind of seal that wasn't meant to be broken.

He would have liked to stroll past the robes and read the names of the former imams and occupants of the house. Who were those people? What kind of clothes had they worn? What sort of rings had they worn on their fingers?

He wanted to open one of the chests and examine its contents, to smell the clothes, try on the rings, read the entries in the journals. What had people written about back then? What had gone on in the house, the mosque, the bazaar? What colour were the *hauz's* first fish? What type of tree had grown in the middle of the courtyard before the cedar tree? Which crow had been the predecessor of the one they had now?

He wanted to spend weeks or even months in the cellar, journeying back to the past, finding the answers to his questions. But that was impossible. The treasure room was a secret that lay in the dark, a secret that was bound up for ever with the mosque, a secret that was more suited to the Koran and the long-lost past. The past was a room to which you had no access. Once Aqa Jaan had reached this conclusion, he was able to curb his curiosity.

Tonight he tiptoed into the treasure room and laid Kazem Khan's poetry book in a chest. Then he placed his uncle's shoes at the end of the row and blew out the lantern.

Kazem Khan had stated in his will that he didn't want to be interred in the crypt, so the villagers looked around for an appropriate burial site. They chose a spot at the bottom of his garden, where an old almond tree shed myriad blossoms in the spring.

The next day dozens of villagers came to the city to collect the body of their poet and take it home to Jirya.

Aqa Jaan, Fakhri Sadat, Zinat Khanom, Muezzin and the grandmothers went with them.

Exactly forty days after the death of Kazem Khan, the grandmothers were scheduled to begin their trip to Mecca. After the morning prayer they donned their chadors, picked up their suitcases and went out to stand by the *hauz*.

'We're leaving!' Golbanu shouted.

'On the trip of our lives!' Golebeh added.

The grandmothers had been terrified that the trip would be cancelled if anyone discovered their secret. Today, however, they couldn't stand the strain any longer.

Muezzin was the first to hear their cries. He rushed upstairs. 'What trip?' he asked.

'To Mecca!' they said in chorus.

'Really?' he said. 'Mecca?'

'We aren't allowed to talk about it, Muezzin. You'll just have to take our word for it.'

He ran his hand over their suitcases. They were indeed embossed with the holy Kaaba. 'The grandmothers are going to Mecca!' he hollered.

It seems that everyone was already awake, because when Aqa Jaan switched on the lights in the courtyard, they all came trooping out in their best clothes. Laughing and crying, they hugged and kissed the grandmothers.

Fakhri Sadat came over to the grandmothers with a brazier full of fragrant *esfandi* seeds. Her daughters, Nasrin and Ensi, carried a mirror and some red apples, while Zinat Khanom bore the traditional bowl of water that was used to wish the travellers a safe journey.

Shahbal went to the library to fetch the antique Koran and handed it to Aqa Jaan. Golbanu and Golebeh picked up their suitcases. Aqa Jaan kissed them, held the Koran above their heads and escorted them to the gate.

Zinat threw water on the ground behind them, and everyone wept, as if the grandmothers were leaving the house for good.

Sayeh

Aqa Jaan had seen Zinat slip out of her room at night sometimes like a *sayeh* – a shadow – but he had no idea where she went. Zinat's bedroom was on the second floor, and to reach the stairs, she had to go past Fakhri and Aqa Jaan's bedroom.

Late one evening, Aqa Jaan was reading in his study when he heard the door at the top of the stairs open. He thought it was Fakhri, but when he didn't hear any footsteps, he looked out through the chink in the curtains and saw someone stealing through the darkness.

He opened the door and stepped into the courtyard, just in time to catch a glimpse of a black chador by the stairs. It might be Zinat, but what was she doing up so late at night?

He went back inside. Suddenly the crow screeched.

The crow's warning reminded Aqa Jaan of the woman from Sarandib:

Once upon a time there was a merchant from Sarandib, whose wife was named Jamiz. She was so beautiful that people could hardly believe she was real. Her face glowed like the day of victory, and her hair was as long and as dark as the night in which you wait for a lover who never comes.

Jamiz was secretly having an affair with a famous artist who could do magical things with his brush.

She slipped out occasionally to visit him, and together they experienced the most beautiful of Persian nights.

Then one night she said to him, 'It's becoming harder and harder for me to steal away from my house, and even harder for me to have to wait so long. Think of something, so I can visit you more often. After all, you're an artist!'

'I have an idea,' said the artist. 'I will make you a veil. On one side, it will be as clear as the reflection of the morning star in a pool of water. On the other side, it will be as dark as the night. At night you can wear the dark side of the veil, so that when you come to me, you will blend in with the night. In the morning you can turn it round to the clear side, so that when you go back home, you will merge with the morning.'

With the grandmothers away, the house entered a new phase. The rhythm they brought to the house had been broken. A sure sign of this was that the antique clock stopped ticking. When the grandmothers were at home, the kitchen was abuzz with activity, the crow cawed to announce the arrival of visitors and the library was always neat and tidy. But those days were over.

It was the grandmothers who woke the children and helped Fakhri Sadat clean her room. It was the grandmothers who told Aqa Jaan what was going on in the house. And it was the grandmothers who kept an eye on Muezzin's studio. While they were away, their tasks were left undone.

No one could fill their empty shoes. If the grandmothers had been here, they would already have followed Zinat to the roof.

* * *

Aqa Jaan was satisfied with the substitute imam. Janeshin carried out his work with enthusiasm and seemed to be happy. During their initial talk, Aqa Jaan had noticed that he was ambitious, but had doubted that he would accomplish much.

The man still couldn't talk about anything but rural matters, though he did that well enough. Not long ago he'd criticised the Minister of Agriculture for doing too little to help the poverty-stricken villages.

Janeshin had never been to Tehran, but in one of his sermons he made a remark that was quoted on the front page of the local paper: 'I've been told that everyone in Tehran has a telephone in their home, and yet hundreds of mountain villages are without a single phone. If you cut your finger in a kitchen in Tehran, you can call an ambulance, but what am I supposed to do if I find my father on his deathbed? I'm warning you, Tehran! Take heed! We are all equal in the eyes of God.'

The secret police smiled at his innocent barbs. They valued such criticism; in fact, they even encouraged it.

Janeshin's remarks were becoming increasingly popular and were often quoted in the local paper. Aqa Jaan was so satisfied with him that he gave him a bit more leeway. One time, after the paper had printed a photograph of Janeshin and an excerpt from one of his sermons, a colleague of Aqa Jaan's had observed, 'The man's naïve, but sometimes he hits the nail on the head.'

Never before had the paper printed a picture of an imam. A photographer had been sent to the mosque, and Janeshin had been photographed on the roof, standing between the two minarets.

The next day, when the imam saw his picture in the paper, he was so excited he couldn't sit still. His dream had come true. Ever since he was a little boy, he'd dreamed of speaking in a big mosque. Now that his sermon and his picture had appeared in the paper, he was suddenly a local celebrity.

According to the laws of the sharia, Zinat and Janeshin were doing nothing wrong and didn't need to be so secretive. If a Muslim is away from his lawfully wedded wife for any length of time, he may take a temporary wife, a *sigeh*. But Janeshin knew that it was risky and that Aqa Jaan would send him packing if he found out.

Zinat was uncomfortable with her status as a *sigeh*. She was ashamed of herself for going to bed with Janeshin in the same mosque in which her husband and dozens of his predecessors lay buried. She refused to come to him every night, as he begged her to, for fear that Aqa Jaan would find out.

When she saw Janeshin in the daylight, she found it hard to believe that she had let him undress her and make love to her. It was different in the dark. She couldn't see him then, she simply felt his hands, his shoulders, his back, his thrusting hips. He was as strong as an ox.

The moment it was over, Zinat would snatch up her chador and scurry home, wanting nothing more to do with him. She couldn't bear to hear him utter another word. But the next night, after she'd turned off the light and crawled into bed, she missed his body.

Alsaberi, her late husband, had never kissed her breasts or bitten into her buttocks in an animal frenzy. Janeshin, by contrast, brought her to such blissful heights that she forgot everyone and everything.

Recently he'd taken her down to the crypt, where he had undressed her and made love to her on the cold hard tombstones. She had protested, spluttering that she didn't want to do it on the tombstones, but he had insisted, and she'd thrown her arms around him, clung to him and surrendered herself.

'I'm never going to do it again, I'm never going back to that man,' Zinat always told herself as she tiptoed back to her room. 'It's over. I'm lucky no one has found out. I have to stop, and I will. I'll go away for a while, I'll go and visit my daughter in Qom and stay with her for a few weeks. I'll go to Fatima's tomb to show my remorse and beg for forgiveness. Yes, that's what I'll do, I'll leave tomorrow, I'll pack my bags and go.'

But she hadn't gone and was now on her way to his room again.

Janeshin heard her walking softly towards the steps. For a moment she was swallowed up in the darkness of the stairwell, then she emerged to wash her hands in the mosque's *hauz* and splash some water on her face.

Janeshin wanted to take her down to the crypt again, but she refused. Then he put his big hands around her waist and lay his head between her breasts, and she melted. He scooped her into his arms, opened the door to the cellar and carried her downstairs.

Deep in the darkness a candle was burning on top of a tall headstone. He took off her clothes, her shoes and her socks and led her barefoot into the candlelight, where he took off his imam robe and laid it on the headstone. Out of nowhere he suddenly produced a bunch of purple grapes, which he placed on her breasts and ate one by one. The juice ran down her breasts and over her belly, and when he lapped it up, Zinat thought she'd die of ecstasy.

They were so engrossed in what they were doing that they didn't notice the person striding past the cellar window with a lantern.

Janeshin was drunk, from both Zinat and the grape juice. As he lay on top of her he recited the Al-Falaq surah:

> *I seek refuge with Him,*
> *The Lord of the early dawn,*
> *From the evil He created,*
> *And from the evil of the night,*
> *As darkness falls.*

He spoke and Zinat listened with her eyes closed, unaware that a man with a lantern was coming down the cellar stairs.

Suddenly she saw a flash of light and heard footsteps. She pushed Janeshin off her, grabbed her black chador and hid in the darkness.

Janeshin wheeled around and saw a silhouette holding a lantern high above its head.

'Imam! Pack your bags!'

The Hajji

Aqa Jaan sent for another substitute imam, an elderly man from Saruq who took things easy, devoting many of his sermons to the lives of the Muslim saints. Aqa Jaan was satisfied. The last thing the mosque needed right now was another firebrand.

Three months had passed by. It was now time for the pilgrims who had gone to Mecca to come home.

Aqa Jaan was planning to celebrate the grandmothers' return with a party, to which the whole family would be invited.

Welcome-home parties for pilgrims were always special occasions. The house of the pilgrim was decorated with coloured lights, rugs were spread out in courtyards, sheep were sacrificed. For an entire week friends, relatives and neighbours dropped in to congratulate the pilgrims, and everyone was invited to eat. During such a *mehmani*, the honorary title of 'hajji' was bestowed on the pilgrims – a title they would proudly bear for the rest of their lives.

Aqa Jaan wrote to Nosrat:

Dear brother,
You've been gone a lot lately. Please come home more often. I've invited everyone to the grandmothers' welcome-home party, and I'm hoping you'll come too. Try to be on time.

The grandmothers have put their entire lives into this house, so the least you can do is be there for the most important celebration in their lives.
The children all miss their Uncle Nosrat.
See you soon!

A few days later Nosrat phoned. 'I'm sorry, but I can't come. I've got an important appointment. I promise to visit another time to make up for it.'

The evening the grandmothers were expected home, Nosrat was scheduled to go to Tehran's largest theatre, the one on Lalehzar Street, where the legendary singer Mahwash was to be performing. The theatre had hired Nosrat to take a series of artistic photographs of her, and Nosrat was determined not to miss the appointment. If his portraits turned out well, his reputation as an artist would be made.

Mahwash was a star who had changed Tehran's nightlife for ever. It wasn't so much her voice as the way she moved her arms, her breasts, her hips. She was the dream of every Persian male, the symbol of an era in which women had cast off their chadors and gone outside without their veils.

Men burned with desire as they watched her perform. She bewitched them with the movements of her bare arms and undulating breasts. Her high heels, slinky low-cut dress and red-lipsticked mouth drove them wild. She revealed the secrets that no decent Persian woman had ever before revealed to the masses of men who crowded to the theatre to see her. Tehran's theatre owners treated her like a goddess, and photographers bumped and jostled each other to get a good shot.

Mahwash was the first woman in the history of the country to show her breasts and wiggle her hips on stage in a conspicuously tight dress. She would raise her plump, bare arms and shake her ample behind. At a certain point she would stick out her backside and sing in her sensuous voice:

> To ke az Hend aamadi
> baa machin-e Benz aamadi.
> Aan qadr budi, aan qadr shodi.
> Jun-e man, begu,
> in kun kajeh?

> Here you are just back from India,
> Driving your fancy Mercedes-Benz.
> A nobody when you left, a big shot now.
> Darling, be honest for once and tell me,
> Do you think my backside's too big?

'No, no, who told you that?' the men shouted happily.

'*Madar shuhar*, my mother-in-law!' she shouted back.

'*Baa tu lajjeh*, she's just jealous!' the men bellowed in return.

Even though Mahwash's picture appeared in the newspapers almost daily, no photographer had ever made a portrait of her. Nosrat had persuaded the owner of the Mulan Ruzh (Moulin Rouge) Theatre, who was a friend of his, to let him take some photographs that would truly immortalise her.

She had agreed to receive him in her own home, because the theatre owner had assured her that Nosrat wasn't like other photographers, that he wasn't doing it for the money, but for her.

Just as Nosrat was entering Mahwash's house, Aqa Jaan and Fakhri Sadat were driving to the railway station to

189

welcome the grandmothers. Behind them was a procession of cars filled with friends and relatives.

The train they were meeting was full of returning pilgrims. They had been travelling for three weeks. First they'd been driven in buses from Mecca to Medina, where the Prophet Muhammad is buried. Then they'd gone from Saudi Arabia to Iraq to see the holy cities of Najaf and Karbala. The tomb of Hussein was in Karbala, and that of Ali in Najaf. Finally they'd taken a boat across the Arvand River, which marked the border between Iran and Iraq, and boarded the train that was to bring them home.

Everyone was thinking of the grandmothers, especially the children, who were looking forward to the presents the pilgrims usually brought back from Mecca, such as watches that glowed in the dark like lanterns and alarm clocks that played sacred songs. There would be rings and bracelets for the girls, and belts decorated with proverbs for the boys. The unforgettable presents were treasured by one and all, for they weren't ordinary gifts, purchased in any old shop, but gifts from Mecca, the city where the Kaaba, the House of God, was located. The city where Muhammad had been born and where his wife Khadijah, the richest woman in Mecca, had once owned three thousand camels.

The train they had come to meet was a special one that stopped at every major city in the country. It had been designed with the pilgrims in mind. Green was the colour of Islam, so green flags adorned the railway carriages, green banners fluttered from the windows and every hajji had on a green scarf.

The train blew its whistle long before it reached a city and pulled into the station, its headlights gleaming.

The moment it stopped, an army band would strike up a welcoming song.

Aqa Jaan parked his car in the square outside the station. The manager, dressed in a special uniform, welcomed him at the top of the stairs and waited for the rest of the family to arrive before ushering them into the VIP lounge, where servants offered them tea and biscuits on silver trays designed especially for the railway. Mosque singers sang melodious verses from sacred texts into hand-held microphones, while old crones tossed *esfandi* seeds into braziers, filling the room with a fragrant smoke. The waiting relatives treated everyone to sweets and fruit drinks, and railway employees poured rosewater out of silver jugs over the hands of the visitors.

At last the train pulled into the station, and hundreds of pilgrims waved their green scarves at the crowd on the platform. The three railway carriages occupied by the group from Senejan stopped exactly in front of the door to the main hall. One by one the hajjis emerged with their bulging suitcases, while the manager welcomed them back over the loudspeaker.

'Where are the grandmothers?' Fakhri Sadat asked.

'Still in the train, I suppose,' Zinat Khanom replied. 'You know them, they're probably tidying up the compartment so they can leave it spick and span.'

'Shahbal, why don't you go and see what's holding them up?' Aqa Jaan said. 'I'm afraid the train's going to leave with them still on it.'

Shahbal searched through the three railway carriages, but didn't see the grandmothers. 'They're not here!' he called through one of the windows.

'Look in the other carriages. Maybe they got lost in the crowd.'

It was a long train, so Shahbal ran from one carriage to the next.

Aqa Jaan approached the manager. 'My passengers haven't alighted. They're probably sitting in the wrong compartment and don't realise they're supposed to get out here.'

The manager wrote down their names, went into his office and switched on the loudspeaker. 'I have an important announcement for hajjis Golbanu and Golebeh. You should get out here. I repeat: hajjis Golbanu and Golebeh, get out here!'

After ten minutes there was still no sign of the grandmothers.

Shahbal came running up. 'I've looked through every compartment and haven't seen them anywhere. Maybe they got out earlier, in another city.'

The pilgrims were leaving. When the platform was nearly empty, the engine driver climbed back into the train and shut the doors.

The manager's voice rang out over the platform one last time: 'I have an urgent announcement for Miss Golbanu and Miss Golebeh. Please report immediately to the manager.'

The conductor waited a moment, then looked at his watch and blew his whistle. The train chugged slowly out of the station, leaving Aqa Jaan and his whole family behind on the platform.

For one solid week Aqa Jaan phoned every railway station between the Arvand River and Senejan, but no one had seen the grandmothers.

He visited all of the recently returned hajjis, but they had no news for him either. The last time anyone had seen the two women had been in Mecca. Everyone had assumed they'd gone off with another group.

The only thing to do was to wait for the travel guides to submit an official report, but they weren't due back for several weeks.

It didn't usually rain during the summer, but a few dark clouds had gathered over Senejan and were moving towards the desert. Just as the first drops began to fall, there was a knock at the door.

Shahbal switched on the light and looked out. Hajji Mustafa, the man who'd organised the pilgrimage, was standing by the gate with a suitcase in each hand.

'Good evening. Is Aqa Jaan at home?' the hajji asked.

'Please wait. I'll let him know you're here.'

Shahbal went away and came back a few minutes later to usher Hajji Mustafa into Aqa Jaan's study.

Hajji Mustafa put down the suitcases, embraced Aqa Jaan and launched into his tale: 'Nothing like this has ever happened before. It's a strange story. I can't decide if it's a blessing or a tragedy. It's a blessing if they lost their way in the House of God, but a tragedy if they're somewhere else.'

'What happened?'

'Here are their suitcases. The grandmothers disappeared in the desert of Mecca like two drops of water. I searched everywhere, went to every police station, hospital and mosque in Mecca, but I could find no trace of them. They simply disappeared. Up until the last day they were part of the group and were doing fine. They were healthy and happy. Then a strange thing happened. An hour before we were to leave for Medina, they came to my office, left their suitcases by my desk, adjusted their chadors and left, without saying a word. I thought they'd gone to the bazaar one last time to buy some souvenirs, but they never came back. Here are the suitcases. I'm sorry, maybe I should have taken better care of them. Please accept my apologies. I'll do whatever I can to find them. I promise to keep you informed.'

After Hajji Mustafa's departure, Aqa Jaan was left alone in the study with Shahbal. 'I don't believe for a second that they're lost or are wandering round Mecca,' Aqa Jaan said.

'What do you think happened?'

'I think they probably hid behind the sacred curtain in the Kaaba. My guess is that they had no intention of coming back.'

'But why hide?' Shahbal asked, surprised.

'They want to die in Mecca. It's the most wonderful death any Muslim can imagine. I think the grandmothers talked it over and decided they'd lived their lives. They had a choice. They could either go home and wait to die an ordinary death, or they could die in the House of God. Anyone who dies in the Kaaba goes straight to Paradise. So what would you do if you were the grandmothers?'

'I *still* can't believe they decided to stay in Mecca. Why do you think they did?'

'It's hard to explain. They've lived in this house for over fifty years. For fifty long years they've been listening to ancient stories. Now they want to write a story of their own.'

Shahbal smiled.

'Let's open the suitcases,' Aqa Jaan said. 'Maybe they left us a letter.'

Shahbal opened the suitcases to find them full of gifts: watches, rings, gold bracelets, brightly coloured garments that glittered in the light of the overhead lamp – lovely gifts from Mecca for every person in the house.

'This proves it,' Aqa Jaan said. 'There are no personal belongings in the suitcases. They didn't even pack their

Mecca shrouds. Everyone dreams of buying a shroud in Mecca. It's the first thing every hajji buys. The grandmothers must have their shrouds with them. Perhaps they're even wearing them under their clothes.'

'But what should we tell the others?' Shahbal asked.

'The truth. Please put the suitcases behind the desk and ask everyone to come in here.'

Shahbal dealt with the suitcases and went off to find the rest of the family.

'Hajji Mustafa was just here,' Aqa Jaan informed the assembled family. 'Unfortunately he had nothing new to report. He's been in touch with the police in Mecca. The moment he hears anything, he'll let us know.'

They listened to Aqa Jaan in stricken silence.

'Does this mean we'll never see them again?' asked Nasrin, Aqa Jaan's elder daughter.

'It's not as though they could go anywhere,' said Jawad, Aqa Jaan's son. 'The police ought to be able to find them.'

'I know. Hajji Mustafa is doing all he can. Who knows, they might have taken a train to some other city. There are millions of pilgrims in Mecca, so maybe they got lost in the multitude. Still, the grandmothers have done a very generous thing: they left your gifts with Hajji Mustafa. To me, that's proof that no harm has come to them,' Aqa Jaan concluded. 'Shahbal, open the suitcases!'

Shahbal placed the suitcases on the desk and opened the lids. Everyone marvelled at the splendour and magnificence: watches, alarm clocks, gold necklaces, slippers, headbands, perfumes, colourful chadors, distinctive blouses and handbags. Every gift was labelled with the name of the recipient. For Nasrin and Ensi there were bright blouses; for Jawad a watch and a cap; for Fakhri Sadat a make-up bag; and for Muezzin a collapsible walking stick – something none of them had ever seen before. Zinat Khanom was given a volume of poetry written by poets from Mecca, Aqa Jaan a fountain pen with a picture of the holy Ali on the cap and Shahbal a watch and several yards of a navy-blue pinstripe that could be made into a suit.

They were delighted. They were remarking on the grandmothers' good taste and noisily discussing each other's presents when they heard shouts coming from outside. One woman yelled something, and another one began to scold her like a fishwife. Women's quarrels were never conducted outside, so this was unusual. The two women were apparently standing on the roof of the neighbour's house, hurling insults at each other. 'It's the wives of Hajji Shishegar,' Zinat Khanom said.

Hajji Shishegar was a man in his early sixties. He had gone to Mecca at the same time as the grandmothers and had therefore returned only recently. He was a glass merchant who owned a large shop in the bazaar.

Hajji Shishegar had two wives: an older one named Akram, and a younger one named Tala. Akram had borne him seven daughters, but he wanted a son and had spent a long time looking for another wife. At last he had found a young woman and married her, but so far she hadn't produced any children.

'Don't!' Tala begged. 'Don't hit me! I'm sorry! I didn't know, I really didn't.'

Akram wasn't about to stop. She screamed and pulled Tala's hair and struck her again.

'Don't! I haven't done anything wrong! Your children are my children too. I beg you, stop!'

Zinat Khanom had gone up to the roof to see what she could do. 'What's going on here?' she said. 'What are you two fighting about?'

'Nothing,' said Tala, the hajji's younger wife.

'Then why is Akram hitting you? And why in God's name are you quarrelling out here on the roof?'

'Because Hajji is at home and has company,' Tala said. 'And I . . . I'm . . .'

'You're what?'

'Pregnant,' she said softly.

Akram, Hajji's older wife, burst into tears and ran off into the darkness.

'Tala is pregnant!' Zinat cried.

'*Mobarak!* Congratulations!' Nasrin and Ensi shouted from the dark courtyard.

When Hajji Shishegar was at the Kaaba, he had asked God to grant him a son, and God had answered his prayer by giving him two sons – twin boys.

In the house of the mosque the weeks and months slipped by. And there was still no sign of the grandmothers.

The Return

One morning, as Shahbal was going to the kitchen to eat breakfast, he saw a woman with a suitcase sitting on the bench by the *hauz*. Only when she lowered her chador to her shoulders did he recognise her.

'Sadiq, is that you?'

When Khalkhal had fled Senejan in the aftermath of the cinema riot, Sadiq had gone to Qom to be with her husband. She had not been home since.

Zinat hugged and kissed her daughter, and asked her what had been going on and why she had come home looking so sad. Sadiq lay her head on Zinat's shoulder and wept, but offered no explanation for her return.

Zinat knew that her daughter was unhappy with Khalkhal. He had never given her a normal family life or let her have visitors in her own home. She lived in fear of him.

He was away often, leaving her at home all by herself. He never told her what he was doing, and he forbade her to discuss anything with her family.

The smile that had always graced Sadiq's lips was now gone. A veil of sorrow had fallen over her face.

'What's happened?'

Sadiq was reluctant to speak.

'Have you left him?'

Silence.

'Did you two have a row?'

She shook her head.

'Then tell me what's happened.'

But Sadiq's lips were sealed.

She walked around the courtyard, pondering her life.

Khalkhal had been gone for several months. He had left her on her own, without saying where he was going or when he would return. One day she got a letter from him. 'I won't be coming home for a while,' he wrote. 'In fact I'll probably be gone for a very long time. Go back to your family and don't breathe a word of this to anyone!'

Sadiq didn't, but they all knew she'd come home to think about her troubled marriage. She was struggling with a difficult question: if he did come home, did she want to go back to him? Back to that horrible house in Qom? Did she want to live with him again? To share her bed with him? But she knew that, as a woman, she had no choice. If he asked her to come home, she *had* to go back.

No, I won't go, she thought. And if he makes me, I'll scream until everyone in the mosque runs up to the roof to see what's going on.

She went into the kitchen. It felt so empty without the grandmothers. When they had lived here, the kitchen had always been neat and tidy. Now it was a mess. Nothing was where it should be. The rubbish bin was full, the spice jars were all over the place instead of in the cupboard where they belonged and the kitchen was no longer filled with the delightful smell of fresh fruit, which had always stood in the bowl on the counter. Sadiq began to clean up. She carried out the rubbish, wiped off the spice jars and arranged them on the shelf. She put away the dishes, swept the floor, washed the windows and watered the plants.

Then she got out a frying pan and began to cook.

* * *

That evening, when everyone came home, they saw a light on in the kitchen, and the house was filled with the tantalising smell of food.

Sadiq set the dining-room table. For the first time in a long while the family ate together.

They were careful not to ask her any questions or to mention Khalkhal's name. They knew that Aqa Jaan would talk to her when the time was right.

It had been an enjoyable evening, and they all mentioned how much they had missed eating good food. After dinner Sadiq went back to the kitchen and stayed there until bedtime. After doing the washing-up, she sat by the window for a long time and stared into the darkness. Her suitcase was still by the *hauz*. Zinat had offered her a bed in her room, but she didn't want to share with her mother.

Sadiq peered at herself in the kitchen mirror, the same one the grandmothers had always used. The mottled old mirror told her that a new phase of her life was about to begin. She'd been dithering all day long, but now she'd finally made up her mind. Sadiq stood up, switched off the kitchen light and went down to the cellar.

'Who's there?' Muezzin called.

She jumped.

'Is that you, Sadiq?'

'Yes, it's me.'

'I wasn't sure at first. Your footsteps have changed so much I almost didn't recognise them. What are you doing down here in the middle of the night?'

'Looking for a key. It must be in one of those old trunks.'

'The key to what?'

'The room next to the stairs. The one between the stairs and Aqa Jaan's study.'

'Do you need it right now?'

She searched through the trunks, but didn't find the key.

'Look behind that archway,' Muezzin said. 'There's another trunk in there. Take the lantern, or you won't be able to see a thing.'

There was a lantern in a niche, with a box of matches beside it. Sadiq lit the candle in the lantern and used it to light her way to the trunk, which she rummaged through without finding the key.

'There's a box in here, in the cupboard,' Muezzin told her. 'The key might be in that.'

She switched on the light in the studio and saw Muezzin taking some vases out of his kiln.

'Don't touch them,' he said. 'They're still hot.'

She edged her way past the newly fired vases and opened the cupboard. Inside were a couple of old-fashioned men's jackets and two walking sticks.

'Did you find it?'

'No, all I can see are clothes.'

'It has to be in there somewhere. I heard keys jingling once when the grandmothers were clearing out the cupboard.'

She pushed aside the jackets. Suddenly she heard a dull jangle.

'You found them!' Muezzin exclaimed.

Sadiq went back to the courtyard. She walked past Aqa Jaan's study and stopped in front of the third door. She tried the keys in the lock, one by one. Only one key in the bunch fitted, but she couldn't get it to turn.

She went back to the cellar to get Muezzin. He oiled the lock and tried the key again, but it still wouldn't budge. 'This room hasn't been used for ages,' he said. 'The key and the lock are rusty.'

He was dying to ask, Why does the door have to be unlocked *now*, in the middle of the night? If you want to sleep, use the guest room. But instead, he poured a little more oil in the lock and tried it again.

'I think it's loosening up, yes, here it comes, it's turning. No, wait, it's still stuck. I need to tap it with a hammer, but I'm afraid I'll wake everybody up.'

And yet he had no choice, so he went back to his room and got a hammer. He gave the key a couple of taps, then turned it. There was a sudden click. 'At last!' he exclaimed. 'It's unlocked now, though heaven only knows why you're so anxious to get in here at this time of night!' Then, without waiting for an explanation, he went back to his room and shut the door behind him.

Sadiq gently pushed open the door.

The room was dark. She felt around for the light switch, but it wasn't working. So she went back to the cellar, got the lantern and returned to her room.

White sheets had been draped over everything, even the carpet. They were covered with a thin layer of dust. Sadiq carefully removed the sheets and piled them up outside.

There was a bed, and next to that an old mirror. A chador was hanging on a coat-rack, and beneath it lay a worn pair of slippers. On the bedside table was a comb, a compact and a small make-up bag. The two shelves on the wall above the bed held a number of books. There was also a wood-burning stove – on top of which stood a tea glass and a bowl – and a cupboard with several dresses hanging inside.

Sadiq took two clean sheets out of the laundry room, fetched her suitcase, went back to the bedroom, set the suitcase down beside the cupboard, made up the bed, crawled under the covers, closed her eyes and went to sleep.

Early the next morning everyone saw her giving the

room a thorough cleaning. She beat the carpet and washed the windows, and also had Shahbal fix the wiring.

That evening a light could be seen in the window of the room by the stairs. The coloured panes of glass cast a red, green and yellow glow on the ground beneath the window.

One night, after Aqa Jaan had seen Sadiq standing in the doorway with the red, green and yellow lights shining on her abdomen, he wrote in his journal, 'Sadiq is pregnant.'

Guerrillas

At the entrance to the bazaar policemen were busy putting up WANTED posters. Underneath the black-and-white pictures of four men with glasses and moustaches was written: 'Escaped prisoners! Armed Communists! A reward of 10,000 *toman* offered for any tips as to their whereabouts.'

The same pictures had been printed on the front page of the local newspaper. 'Four dangerous terrorists at loose in our city!' read the caption.

People had crowded round the entrance to the bazaar and were standing in little groups, talking. They didn't know the first thing about Communism, but they did know that Communists were dangerous people who didn't believe in God.

The paper also printed an interview with a goatherd, who claimed to have seen the fugitives.

'Were they armed?' the interviewer asked.

'Yes, they had rifles slung over their shoulders.'

'Where did you run into them?'

'I didn't run into them. I was gathering my flock, chasing after a goat, when suddenly I saw four men on horseback. I could tell right away that they were strangers, because they were sitting in the saddle like sultans. You don't see people like that in the mountains very often.'

'Did you talk to them?'

'Not at first. Only later. I didn't get a look at their faces. They were going up the mountain, so I only saw them from behind. They were heading for the pass. I guess they were hoping to cross the border into Afghanistan. Suddenly one of them turned, rode down to where I was standing and asked me if I could give him some bread and milk.'

'And did you?'

'Yes, but I didn't know they were Communists. I wouldn't have given it to them if I'd known.'

'Didn't you ask him who he was?'

'No, that's not something you usually ask a stranger. I just got out a pail and went looking for a goat to milk.'

'What did he do when you gave him the milk and the bread?'

'He shook my hand and said, "Please forgive me, but I can't pay you."'

'Did he say anything else?'

'Yes, he said that he'd remember my face.'

'What did he mean by that?'

'I don't know, but the next day I saw the WANTED posters at the police post in our village. Four terrorists! And I gave them my bread!'

Ordinary people didn't know what was going on, but those who listened in secret to Radio Moscow's Persian-language broadcast knew the reason for the manhunt.

The fugitives who were attempting to flee the country were the four most important members of a leftist underground movement. They had been arrested a few years ago during an uprising in the forests of the northern region of Shomal, where they'd been in charge of an anti-American guerrilla movement. Their aim had been to spark a rebellion in the north that would eventually topple the shah. One of those men was Hamid Ashraf.

Most of the mountain people lived in poverty. Their villages lacked even the most basic facilities: there were no schools, no telephones and no doctors. The authorities did nothing at all for the village of Farahan, because that's where Ashraf had been born. The village was paying the price for his political activities.

Ashraf had studied physics at the Technical University of Tehran – a hotbed of leftist discontent in the country. He was a young leader who had abandoned the traditional Communist Tudeh Party and set up an underground movement known as Fadai, whose followers were engaged in an armed struggle against the shah.

Because of its long opposition to the regime, Farahan was known as the Red Village. The villagers were proud of Ashraf and of the town's nickname.

There were no radios in the other mountain villages, and yet the people of the Red Village listened to Radio Moscow. The moment they heard that Ashraf had escaped from prison, they spread the news through the entire mountain region.

The people of the Red Village claimed that the newspaper interview was a pack of lies, that the goatherd didn't exist. They were convinced that the whole story had been fabricated by the secret police. But others swore that the goatherd had been sent by the Red Village to throw the police off the track.

Leftist sympathisers throughout the country talked about the Red Village so much that it had taken on mythical proportions. They claimed that the villagers were all

Communists, that on holidays the red flag fluttered over every door and that the shah's gendarmes didn't dare set foot there.

Although most of the people in the mountains were illiterate, it was said that everyone in the Red Village could read, that leftist sympathisers had secretly gone to the village and taught people how to read and write.

In Radio Moscow's report of the escape, it was hinted that Hamid Ashraf and his comrades might be hiding in the Red Village.

The next day fourteen armoured vehicles roared into the village, and two helicopters circled above. Since the mountain people had never seen a helicopter at such close range, they dropped what they were doing and raced up the hills to get a better look. The helicopters were flying so low they could see the armed men inside.

The people of the Red Village climbed up on their roofs to protest, leaving their doors wide open so the police wouldn't break them down.

The policemen searched every house and questioned everyone they found on the roofs. They kicked in a lot of doors anyway and turned the village upside down, but didn't find a trace of the fugitives.

They did, however, arrest a number of young men who couldn't prove that they lived in the village or had been visiting relatives. Only when darkness fell did they call a halt to the search.

Shahbal didn't come home that night. Muezzin, who had listened to the news on his radio, was worried about his son. He went to Aqa Jaan to let him know that the boy hadn't come home.

Aqa Jaan had seen the posters in the bazaar and heard the news of Hamid Ashraf's escape. He owned several small carpet workshops in the Red Village, where people wove rugs for him. He knew the village well, and the villagers knew and respected Aqa Jaan. Still, it had never occurred to him that Shahbal might be mixed up in its Communist activities. He stayed up till midnight, waiting, but there was no sign of Shahbal.

'Do you have any idea where he might have gone?' he asked Muezzin.

'He came downstairs this morning to say that he was going out and that he'd be home late, but I didn't expect him to be this late.'

'Perhaps it's stupid of me to ask, but do you think he's involved somehow with this business in Farahan?'

'In the Red Village?'

'Apparently the police arrested a lot of people. At least that's what I heard at the bazaar.'

'What's that got to do with Shahbal?' Muezzin asked in surprise.

'Everything's tied up with everything else these days. There was a lot of unrest in the city this afternoon. Everyone was talking about the Red Village. Anyway, it's midnight now. All we can do is wait. We should stay calm and try to get some sleep, and see what the morning brings.'

Muezzin nodded and started to walk away, but Aqa Jaan was suddenly struck by an idea. 'Wait a minute,' he said. 'If Shahbal *was* in Farahan this afternoon and did get arrested, we should search his room before the police do. They're bound to come here sooner or later.'

Aqa Jaan went into Shahbal's room and started looking through his things. To his surprise he found a stack of books beneath the bed and in the cupboard – books they didn't have in their own library, such as novels, short stories and contemporary poems. There were also clandestine books, in which the shah was criticised for being an instrument of American imperialism.

He leafed through the books, but didn't have time to examine them, so he crammed them all into a bag and hurried through the darkness to the river.

Shahbal didn't come home that night, and no policeman knocked on their door.

The next morning Aqa Jaan went to work as usual, as if nothing out of the ordinary had happened. At about ten o'clock the phone rang. It was the chief constable, asking Aqa Jaan to come in for a talk. Aqa Jaan put on his hat and had his chauffeur drive him to the station.

He sat down in the chair proffered by the chief constable. 'We've arrested your nephew,' the chief constable informed him, 'along with a group of foreigners.'

'Arrested?' Aqa Jaan said in as calm a voice as possible. 'What for?'

'We picked him up in the Red Village. When we searched him, we found a transistor radio and a book on him.'

'What of it? Everyone has a transistor radio these days.'

'It was tuned to Radio Moscow.'

'There must be some misunderstanding. He lives in the house of the mosque. There's no need for anyone in our house to listen to Radio Moscow.'

'I agree. That's why I've asked you to come here.'

'Thank you. I'm very grateful to you,' Aqa Jaan said.

'But I'm still wondering what he was doing in Farahan.'

'We have a few carpet workshops there. We employ dozens of the villagers. I often send my men there to inspect the work. Shahbal went to Farahan at my request.'

'But he had an illegal book in his possession,' the chief constable said.

'What was it about?'

'The Russian Revolution.'

'What's so illegal about that?'

'It was written by Maxim Gorky.'

'Who's Maxim Gorky?'

'A Russian writer. Any student who's found with a subversive book like that in his possession gets sentenced to six months in jail. But luckily for your nephew, you and I know each other. We need each other in this town, so I'm letting him go. As a favour to you.'

'Thank you, I understand. I'll speak to him when he gets home and warn him not to do it again,' Aqa Jaan said, and he stood up.

When Shahbal came home a while later, Aqa Jaan called him into his study. 'You own a transistor radio and you listen to Radio Moscow. What's the meaning of this? Why didn't I know about it?'

'The police overreacted. Everyone has a television these days, and radios are everywhere. People listen to broadcasts from all over the world. I listen to everything I can. Not just the Iranian channels, but also Radio Moscow, the Voice of America and the BBC.'

'They found a Communist book on you.'

'It was a novel, a made-up story. Books are books, what does it matter? Besides, the chief constable can't tell me what I can and cannot read!'

'Oh, yes he can. He had you arrested!'

'He can arrest me, but he can't force me to do what he wants.'

'What were you doing in the Red Village so late at night?'

'That's another story. I should have mentioned it, but I couldn't decide whether or not to tell you. Something's been bothering me, but perhaps this isn't the best time to go into it. I don't want to hurt your feelings. Then again, not telling you is just as bad.'

'You can tell me, Shahbal.'

'I've been struggling with this for a long time. I'm filled with so many doubts that it's all I can think about.'

'Doubts about what?'

'About everything! I hesitate to tell you, because I still can't make up my mind. But the thing is, I . . . well, I've stopped going to mosque.'

'No, you haven't. I see you there every day.'

'I don't mean physically, I mean mentally. I'm there all right, but when I turn to face Mecca, I'm thinking about completely different things.'

'What kind of things?'

'I don't dare put them into words. That's why I think that it might be better for me to take a break from the mosque and the prayers.'

'Everyone has doubts. That's no reason to get so upset.'

'I'm past the doubting stage,' Shahbal said. 'I don't feel at home in the mosque any more. I've lost my faith.'

Shahbal watched as Aqa Jaan slumped in his chair and slipped his hand in his jacket to touch his pocket Koran.

'I've hurt you,' Shahbal said softly. 'I'm sorry.'

'Your news does indeed hurt me,' Aqa Jaan replied, 'but I went through a similar phase once. It will pass. Young people are especially prone to doubts. In my day there were no radios or televisions or tempting books, all of which have a great influence on people. But I'm not worried, because I haven't filled your head with strange ideas that would cause you to turn your back on God. All I can do is wait. But you should remember this: I'm not mistaken, I trust you, I believe in you. It's only human to have doubts. But you're tired. Go and get some sleep. We'll discuss it another time.'

Shahbal turned to leave. He had tears in his eyes. Yet Aqa Jaan surprised him with one last question: 'Do you know anything about those four escaped men?'

'No!' Shahbal said. But Aqa Jaan could tell from the tone of his voice that he was hiding something.

Early the next morning Aqa Jaan was on his way to the bazaar when he ran into Crazy Qodsi.

'How are you, Qodsi?'

'Fine.'

'How's your mother?'

'Fine,' she said.

'Do you have any news for me?'

'The Moshiri girl sometimes goes down the street with her bare bottom hanging out.'

He didn't understand what she was saying. Moshiri was one of the richest carpet merchants in the bazaar. His twenty-four-year-old daughter was mentally ill, which is why he never let her leave the house.

'The Moshiri girl sometimes does what? Would you repeat that?' Aqa Jaan asked.

Qodsi brought her face close to his and whispered, 'You have ghosts in your mosque.'

'Ghosts? Bare bottoms? Come now, Qodsi. You can do better than that!'

But she had already disappeared through the nearest open door.

The police had received a tip about some suspicious goings-on in the cellar of the mosque. They were convinced that the guerrillas were hiding in the crypt. So one evening two policemen slipped into the mosque disguised as young imams and lined up for the prayer along with the other worshippers.

Afterwards the policemen lingered and struck up a conversation with the substitute imam. They told him that they were from Isfahan, and that they were spending the night at an inn in Senejan before going on to the holy city of Qom.

The elderly imam invited them to his rooms for tea. He explained that he was only filling in for Alsaberi's son, who, if all went well, would graduate from the seminary at the end of the year and take his father's place. The policemen sipped their tea and kept their eyes on the courtyard.

'Does anyone else live here, or do you live alone?'

'I'm the only one living in the mosque, but the caretaker is around a lot. The mosque is his life. I'm grateful he's so dedicated; he does the work of ten men. He gets here early in the morning and goes home late at night.'

'I think I hear a noise in the cellar,' said one of the policemen, inventing an excuse to go outside and look around.

'This mosque is old, very old. It has many secrets. Don't ask me who goes in and out of the cellar. Ancient mosques are always full of mystery. Sometimes I hear strange sounds, like footsteps in the night, or faint voices. The mosque has a life of its own. You have to ignore such sounds when you sleep here. You have to bury your head in your pillow and close your eyes.'

At the end of the evening, the policemen heard footsteps in the courtyard. They stood up, said goodbye and stole through the darkness to the cellar, where they crouched down and peeked through a small window.

The shadow of a man with a candle in his hand glided into the cellar. He seemed to be looking for something, or perhaps he was carrying out a ritual. In any case he was holding an object in his left hand, though they couldn't tell what it was or see exactly what he was doing. He was either talking to himself or to someone else as he headed towards the darker regions of the cellar. They heard a door open, and the shadow disappeared.

They tiptoed into the cellar, crept cautiously down the stairs and stood stock-still, listening to the silence. They didn't dare switch on their torches. They inched their way towards the place where they had last seen the shadow, taking care not to trip over the tombstones. As they approached the door, they heard a faint voice and saw a yellow strip of light beneath it.

They stopped. The voice – or voices – wasn't very clear. It sounded like someone reading something aloud or telling a story. They pressed their ears to the door and heard snatches of something that made no sense to them at all:

> *Suckle him.*
> *If you fear for him,*
> *Cast him into the river.*
> *Fear not,*
> *And do not grieve,*
> *For We shall restore him to you.*

Suddenly they heard a woman scream. They stared at each other in sheer terror, not knowing whether the shriek had come from the mosque or from the cellar. They raced up the stairs, making as little noise as possible, and hurriedly left the mosque.

It was Sadiq who had screamed. She'd been standing next to the *hauz* when she suddenly went into labour. A stabbing pain had gone from her belly to her back and left her feeling dizzy. She'd screamed and crumpled up in agony.

Aqa Jaan, Fakhri, Zinat and Muezzin had gone on a pilgrimage to a nearby village that evening and wouldn't be back until tomorrow. Luckily Shahbal had heard Sadiq's scream. He ran to the *hauz*, helped her up and brought her to her room. There, in the bright light, he saw drops of blood on the floor.

'Phone the doctor!' he yelled to Nasrin, Aqa Jaan's elder daughter. 'I'll go and get the midwife!' He jumped on his bicycle and pedalled as fast as he could in the direction of the river.

When the midwife finally arrived, she took one look at Sadiq and said, 'This is serious. I can't deal with it on my own. You'll have to send for a doctor.'

'He's already on his way,' Nasrin informed her. 'I'll go and wait for him.'

Sadiq was in agony. She screamed so loudly that the midwife decided she'd have to do what she could or Sadiq would lose the baby.

'The baby's trying to come out, but something's holding it back. I can't see anything in this light. Nasrin, get me a lamp and some clean towels.'

Nasrin hurried out and came back with a lamp and a stack of towels.

'Shine the light over here. Don't be so clumsy. Concentrate!'

Nasrin stepped closer to the bed, but avoided looking at Sadiq as she held the lamp over the midwife's head. 'I think I hear the doctor,' she said.

'Shut up and hold that lamp still!'

A car stopped outside the gate. Nasrin's hands were shaking. To calm her nerves, she began to hum.

The midwife told Sadiq to keep breathing and to push harder. 'The baby's turned the wrong way,' she explained. 'It can't come out. We're going to have to try something else.' Sadiq let out a loud cry and fainted.

Just then the doctor came into the room.

'The doctors are always the last to arrive!' the midwife muttered. 'They're always tucked up nicely in their comfy beds.'

It was a difficult birth, but a few hours later, with the help of the midwife and Nasrin's humming, the doctor delivered the baby. 'It's a boy!' he said.

The midwife held the baby upside down. 'He's not breathing.' She shook him a few times until at last he began to cry. 'Thank God!'

The doctor went over to Sadiq, took out his stethoscope and listened to her heart. 'She's exhausted, but doing all right,' he said to the midwife, who was washing the baby in a basin that Nasrin had filled with water.

'There's something wrong with its back,' the midwife said, and she carefully laid the baby on its stomach.

The doctor put on his glasses and ran his finger along the baby's spine, examining the bones. 'A severe deformity,' he muttered.

'Just as I thought,' the midwife sighed.

The doctor left.

'Both mother and baby are asleep,' the midwife said to Nasrin. 'I'm sorry I snapped at you. These situations are always difficult. I'm going home to get a few hours' sleep, but I'll be back first thing in the morning. There's a problem with the baby. The doctor will phone Aqa Jaan tomorrow.'

The house had settled down again. There was still a light on in Sadiq's room, and the windowpanes were casting their multi-coloured glow onto the stones in the courtyard.

Shahbal was awed by the baby's birth.

In the past, when a child had been born in the house of the mosque, Aqa Jaan had always recited a melodious surah into the baby's ear, because, according to one of the Prophet's sayings, 'The first words that a child hears remain in his memory for ever, like a sentence carved in stone.'

Shahbal went into the library, took the oldest Koran out of the cupboard and tiptoed back to Sadiq's room. She was fast asleep. The baby lay in its cradle by the wall. Shahbal opened the Koran and leafed through it in search of a melodious surah. Then he changed his mind and put it aside. Leaning over, he whispered a poem in the newborn's ear, a verse by the famous contemporary Persian poet Ahmad Shamlou, which Shahbal knew by heart:

> *Bar zamin-e sorbi-sobh*
> *savaar*
> *khamush estaadeh ast*
> *Wa yaal-e boland-e asbash dar baad.*

> *A man on horseback*
> *sits motionless*
> *in the lead-grey morning*
> *while the wind ripples his horse's long mane.*

> *Oh God, horsemen shouldn't sit still*
> *when danger is headed their way.*

The baby opened its eyes.

Lizard

Lizard was now a year old. He crawled over to the *hauz* and played with the water. It was the first time he'd ever ventured so far from his room.

In the beginning everyone used to watch him like a hawk, but after a while no one paid any attention to him. He stared into the water at the red fish, who stared back at him with their blank eyes. Lizard opened and shut his mouth in imitation of the fish, then giggled. He was happy. He crawled closer and suddenly fell into the water.

Everyone was stunned. Sadiq ran over and tried to pull him out, but Lizard didn't want to go. Instead, he paddled through the water, chasing the fish. So Shahbal stepped into the *hauz*, scooped him up and handed him to Sadiq, who carried the crying child to her room.

Owing to a congenital spinal defect, Lizard was unable to sit up, but he grew quickly and started exploring his surroundings at an early age. He often crawled under the bed and under the blankets like a giant lizard. It didn't take him long to find his way to the courtyard, where he liked to crawl between the plants in the garden. Later they discovered that Lizard was unable to talk.

Aqa Jaan's children didn't want him coming into their rooms and crawling under the blankets, so they began to lock their doors. They found him repulsive and were ashamed of their feelings, but it was hard to shake them off. It took time to adjust to his deformity, to get used to holding a child who looked more like a reptile than a human being.

Still, Lizard had his own favourites: the moment he saw Am Ramazan, he would crawl over to him as fast as he could. Then Am Ramazan would pick him up, put him on his shoulders and walk around the courtyard, pointing out the flowers, the trees, the crow, the cats.

Lizard also felt at ease with Muezzin. He liked to crawl across his room and lie under his bed.

'Is that you, my boy, or is it the cat?' Muezzin always said with a laugh.

Lizard would hand Muezzin his walking stick. It was his way of saying he wanted to go for a walk, so Muezzin would stroll around the courtyard, with Lizard crawling along behind.

Nobody knew how he got his nickname. Aqa Jaan had forbidden his children to call him 'Lizard', but it suited him so well that it had stuck.

Officially his name was Sayyid Mohammad, but he didn't respond when he was called that. He only crawled over to those who called him 'Lizard'.

He was a creature who was closer to the world of cats, chickens and fish than to the world of people. Everyone had accepted this fact. Even his mother had stopped fighting it and resigned herself to her fate.

Khalkhal had disappeared from their lives but come back in the form of Lizard, who had his father's face. Lizard crawled into Sadiq's bed and tugged at her to get her attention. She didn't want him, but she had no choice. He was her child.

The day that Lizard fell into the *hauz* turned out to be an important day in the history of the house.

Ahmad, the son of the late Alsaberi, had finally completed his imam training in Qom and had come home to assume his father's position.

In a few days he would be installed as the imam of the mosque. The entire family had gathered for this once-in-a-lifetime event. It would be the beginning of a new era in Senejan, as the relationship between the mosque and the bazaar was bound to change. Everyone was curious to see how the mosque would fare under Ahmad's leadership.

Last week Aqa Jaan had gone to Qom to attend Ahmad's 'robe presentation' and had spent the night, so that he and Ahmad could have a quiet talk about his installation ceremony and his future duties.

Ahmad's inexperience was obvious to Aqa Jaan. But he was a handsome young imam who dressed neatly, carried himself erectly, doused himself with cologne and wore a modish turban.

He also had a powerful voice, a good delivery and a natural gift for reciting the melodious Koran passages by heart. Time would tell how competent he was in other matters.

Ahmad arrived with his suitcase the night before the festivities. Aqa Jaan immediately took him into the library to discuss his speech, but Ahmad had other priorities. He laid his suitcase on the table, unlocked it, took out his beautiful new imam robe and looked around for a place to hang it up. 'Why isn't there a coat-hook?' he asked, annoyed.

'You can hang it in your bedroom,' Aqa Jaan replied.

Ahmad jammed a pencil between two bookcases and hung his robe on that. Then he began to unpack his suitcase.

'Where can I put my clothes?' he said. 'I'll need a chest of drawers in the library.'

'You can keep your personal belongings in your bedroom,' Aqa Jaan patiently reiterated.

'I want my things in here,' Ahmad said.

Aqa Jaan realised that this wasn't a good time to go over Ahmad's speech.

'I think you need to rest. I'll talk to you tomorrow in my study,' he said and left.

Late that night he wrote in his journal: 'The new imam begins tomorrow. Ahmad has arrived, and I can see from the way he behaves that times have changed. He's very different from his father and the other imams I've known. I mustn't doubt his abilities. After all, he's young and has a lot to learn. One thing I can say with absolute certainty, however, is that we now have a charming imam in our house. I like him and I am curious to see where he'll lead us.'

On Friday the bazaar closed at ten o'clock, and thousands of people flocked to the mosque for the special prayer service. The installation of a new imam was a simple, yet festive, occasion. The prayer was to be held outdoors, so dozens of rugs had already been spread on the ground.

Policemen were patrolling the area, and vans filled with armed soldiers were parked in the side streets. This level of security was unusual for Senejan, but during the last two or three years the situation in Iran had changed drastically. Students at the University of Tehran were demonstrating against the shah and chanting 'Down with America!' The regime was afraid that riots could break out at any moment.

Aqa Jaan went through the details with Ahmad for the last time, put on his hat and left for the mosque.

'May your day be blessed!' exclaimed his neighbour, Hajji Shishegar, who was also going to the mosque with his twins.

'God willing!' Aqa Jaan cheerily replied.

'If there's anything I can do for you today, I'm at your service,' said the hajji.

'Thanks, but everything's been taken care of. How are the twins?'

'Children grow up so fast these days!' he said. 'Your son too.'

'That's true. Jawad is now a young man.'

Aqa Jaan caught sight of Crazy Qodsi. 'It's good to see you again, Qodsi,' he said. 'Is your mother coming today?'

'She bought a new black chador especially for the occasion.'

'I'm looking forward to seeing her,' Aqa Jaan said.

'But she's not coming.'

'Why not?'

'She can't find her new chador,' Qodsi said.

'Has she lost it already? Or did you hide it from her?' he asked, smiling.

'No, I didn't hide it.'

'Then where is it?'

'I don't know. She was up all night looking for it, but she couldn't find it anywhere.'

'I'm sure it will turn up and she'll be able to come,' Aqa Jaan said, and he started to walk off.

'That crazy Moshiri girl likes to go down the street with her bare bottom hanging out,' Qodsi whispered. 'She did it again last night.'

'I tell you what. Why don't you go into the house?' Aqa Jaan said to her. 'Ahmad has just put on his new robe. He'll give you a few copper coins. Go on, go!'

Qodsi walked off towards the house and Aqa Jaan went

into the street, where a large crowd was waiting for the ceremony to begin.

A man shouldering a film camera broke away from the crowd and aimed his lens at Aqa Jaan. 'You're looking elegant in your hat and navy-blue pinstripe suit,' the cameraman remarked.

'Nosrat, is that you?' Aqa Jaan exclaimed delightedly. 'I'm so happy! I didn't think you'd make it. When did you get here?'

'I just got in. I took the night train.'

The deputy mayor shook Aqa Jaan's hand and offered his congratulations.

'What are those military vehicles doing here?' Aqa Jaan demanded.

'They lend importance to the ceremony,' the deputy mayor replied. Together he and Aqa Jaan walked over to the door of the mosque, to greet the chief constable, the head of the gendarmerie, the provincial officials, the director of the hospital and the headmasters of the local schools.

Nosrat trailed behind Aqa Jaan, filming everything. Aqa Jaan was pleased to see that the city officials had turned out in full force, though he was a bit surprised. In the old days they would have shown up as a matter of course, but in recent years they rarely bothered to attend functions at the mosque. Oddly enough, he didn't recognise a single one of them; all of the faces were new.

Nosrat filmed Aqa Jaan talking to the chief constable. Suddenly Crazy Qodsi tugged at his sleeve. 'My mother can't come,' she whispered in Aqa Jaan's ear. 'Someone stole her black chador, and the Moshiri girl likes to go down the street with her bare bottom hanging out.'

Aqa Jaan motioned to his nephew. 'Shahbal, will you see to it that Qodsi joins the other women?'

In the distance he spotted a procession of black Mercedes-Benzes. He signalled to Muezzin, letting him know that the elderly Ayatollah Golpaygani would be arriving shortly.

'*Allahu akbar!*' Muezzin sang out. And the crowd responded: '*Salla ala Mohammad wa ale Mohammad!* Blessed be Muhammad and the House of Muhammad!'

Nosrat went up to the roof so he could film the welcoming ceremony from above.

Ayatollah Golpaygani was one of the most influential ayatollahs in the nation. He had come specially from Qom to solemnise Ahmad's installation as the imam of the mosque.

Aqa Jaan, the municipal representatives and a group of schoolchildren stepped forward and officially welcomed the ayatollah. Aqa Jaan helped him out of the car, handed him his walking stick, kissed him and offered him his arm, to escort him to the special chair reserved for him.

Suddenly Qodsi was standing beside him.

'Shahbal!' Aqa Jaan called, annoyed. Qodsi, protesting loudly, was once more led away by Shahbal.

Now that the ayatollah had arrived, the ceremony could begin. Ahmad, accompanied by six young imams, came out and stood on the doorstep.

'*Allahu akbar!*' Muezzin shouted.

'*Allahu akbar!*' the crowd repeated after him.

Ahmad and his escorts went up to the ayatollah, knelt before him and solemnly kissed his hand. The ayatollah placed his hand on Ahmad's black turban and chanted:

Qol, a'uuthu be-rabb-elfalaq,
Men sharre ma khalaqa . . .

I seek refuge with the maker of the dawn,
From the evil of the night,
As darkness falls,
And from the evil of the women
Who blow on knots.

Aqa Jaan handed him the ceremonial robe, which he had brought up from the treasure room. It was covered with precious gems. For centuries it had been worn at the installation of every imam in the family.

After donning the robe, Ahmad strode over to an ancient prayer rug. Aqa Jaan and Ayatollah Golpaygani went over and stood behind him, and the crowd moved along with them.

'*Allahu akbar!*' Muezzin repeated.

Ahmad turned towards Mecca and began his first official prayer.

At that exact moment a young woman wearing a brand-new black chador and a pair of red high heels emerged from the alley. She made a beeline for Ahmad and stopped a few feet in front of him.

Aqa Jaan saw her and wished he could shoo her away, but it wouldn't be right for him to interrupt his prayer.

The woman lifted up her chador and stuck out her right leg. It was bare.

Ahmad closed his eyes and tried to concentrate on his prayer.

'*Allahu akbar!*' Aqa Jaan said loudly, hoping it would scare her into leaving. It didn't. Instead, she suddenly twirled around, so that her black chador flew up and revealed not only her bare legs, but also her bare bottom!

'*Allahu akbar!*' Aqa Jaan exclaimed.

Ayatollah Golpaygani had his eyes closed and was so wrapped up in his prayer that he didn't see it. Only when

Aqa Jaan cried '*Allahu akbar!*' for the third time did he open his eyes. But since he wasn't wearing his glasses, he saw little more than a black blur.

The woman lowered her chador to her bare breasts and twirled again, looking incredibly proud. Aqa Jaan, now forced to break off his prayer, went over to her and was about to pull her chador back over her head when she suddenly flung it to the ground and ran naked into the crowd. Aqa Jaan bounded after her and grabbed her round the waist. Shahbal picked up her chador and threw it to him. He caught it in mid-air and wrapped it around her in one smooth motion. Then he called his wife: 'Fakhri!'

Fakhri Sadat, already hurrying to his side, led the woman over to the women's section.

Thanks to Ahmad, who had maintained his composure throughout, the prayer continued, and the crowd followed him.

But now that Aqa Jaan had touched a naked woman, he wasn't allowed to finish his prayer. He went into the courtyard and over to the *hauz*. He, who had never even looked at another woman, had held that naked woman round the waist. He could still feel the warmth of her soft breasts on his hand. He took off his coat, rolled up his sleeves, knelt by the *hauz* and plunged his hands up to his elbows in the cool water.

It wasn't enough. He leaned forward, stuck his head under the water and held it there for a long time. Then he came back up, took a deep breath, got to his feet, dried his face on a handkerchief, put on his coat and calmly rejoined the crowd.

Nosrat had filmed the entire incident.

Opium

Once again light shone in the library windows.
From time to time there were the usual confrontations with the imam, especially when it came to meeting his demands.

Now that the house had a permanent imam again, everyone realised how much the grandmothers had always done. The house had functioned like clockwork, and now even five women couldn't get it ticking the way it used to.

Several times Zinat Khanom had suggested hiring Azam Azam, the woman who had threatened her husband with a knife, but Fakhri Sadat wouldn't hear of it. And yet Sadiq, who now had Lizard to take care of, couldn't do as much work as she used to. Fakhri Sadat finally sent to Jirya for a maid.

The maid's name was Zarah. She was very capable and immediately took charge of the household, though the kitchen was still Sadiq's domain. Sadiq felt comfortable there; she found it peaceful, and spent most of her time cooking for the family.

Now that they had Zarah, the house was again running like clockwork. She was a hard worker, but she was reserved and shy. So shy that she never looked you directly in the eye when you talked to her.

'It's just as well,' Zinat observed, 'or we might have a problem on our hands, what with all the young men in this house.'

Zarah was a beautiful girl – or rather young woman, since she was nearly twenty-one. She had married an older man when she was sixteen, but after four years, when she had failed to produce a child, her husband had sent her back to her parents. They were glad their daughter had found a job as a maid in the house of the mosque and hoped she'd be able to work there for a long time.

In the past the grandmothers had spent much of their time looking after Imam Alsaberi, but Ahmad didn't need that kind of help.

Zarah quietly went about her business. No one noticed her, she never disturbed anyone. She entered the rooms unobtrusively, tidied them up, collected the dirty dishes, helped Sadiq with Lizard, washed the windows, fed the fish, swept up the dead leaves and went down to the cellar to see if Muezzin needed anything.

She dusted Ahmad's desk, changed the sheets on his bed and ironed his shirts.

After the morning prayer, Ahmad usually crawled back into bed and slept until noon, or sometimes even until two o'clock, something no other imam in the house had ever done. Actually, he stayed in bed until Zarah knocked on the door and said, 'Your lunch is ready, Imam.'

Every morning before he got up to lead the prayer, she would bring him bread, butter and honey. She would knock on the door and whisper, 'Are you awake?'

'Come in,' Ahmad would call sleepily, and she would shyly set the tray on the bedside table and leave.

It wasn't her job to serve Ahmad, but it had quickly turned into a routine. And Ahmad was pleased with her.

One morning Zarah woke him up in time for the prayer, but he rolled over and went back to sleep. The second time she woke him, he threw on his clothes and raced outside, only to stop suddenly by the *hauz* and pee into the drain. Zarah stared at him in horror. It was strictly forbidden; nobody ever did such a thing. She knew she mustn't tell anyone what he'd done.

One time when Zarah brought Ahmad his breakfast, she set the tray on the bedside table as usual, but Ahmad grabbed her hand and drew her gently towards the bed. She resisted for a moment, then surrendered.

Ahmad put his arms around her and pulled her into bed with him. She instantly clamped her thighs together.

'*Ankahtu wa zawagto*,' Ahmad whispered in her ear.

There was no reply.

'*Ankahtu wa zawagto*,' Ahmad whispered again.

Still no reply.

'*Ankahtu wa zawagto*,' Ahmad whispered for the third time.

'*Qabilto*,' Zarah said, and she welcomed him into her arms.

A while later she got up and put on her chador. 'It's late,' she murmured. 'You have to go to the mosque.'

Many young women came to the Friday prayer especially to see Ahmad.

His sermons were not at all like those of his father or Khalkhal. He had an interesting way of sneaking politics into his sermons, and he preferred to stimulate the minds of his listeners rather than threaten them with the wrath of God.

As far as the secret police could tell, he wasn't in touch with any dangerous religious movement in Qom. He was more of a pleasure-seeker than a rebel, but it was still not clear what kind of person he would become or how his character would be shaped by his position as the city's imam.

In one of his sermons he talked about an Islamic state in which the Koran would be the cornerstone of society. But he didn't elaborate on the idea or explain exactly what he meant by it. It seemed more as though he'd thrown a stone in the water to fathom its depths.

On another occasion he made a masterful move: he unexpectedly dropped the name of Ayatollah Khomeini into his sermon. It had been done so innocently that no one knew whether he'd said it accidentally or on purpose. Even so, Aqa Jaan could tell that he was sympathetic to Khomeini.

Ayatollah Khomeini was a fierce opponent of the shah. In his last public sermon he'd said that the shah had humiliated everyone in the country. 'We're ashamed of him,' he said. 'He's not a shah, but a lackey of the Americans.'

A riot had broken out in Qom afterwards. People had gone into the streets, shouting anti-shah slogans. The army had been called in, and soldiers surrounded the mosque where Khomeini had delivered his speech.

Hundreds of young imams had snatched up the rifles stockpiled beneath the mosque and climbed onto the roof. Street fighting had broken out. Dozens of imams had been killed and countless others arrested. After the rebellion had been put down, one of the generals went in person to the ayatollah's house to arrest him.

The group of imams guarding the ayatollah stopped the general at the door and ordered him to remove his boots before entering the ayatollah's study. The general, who knew that even the US army couldn't have helped him in this situation, took off his boots.

'And your cap!' one of the guards snapped.

The general tucked his cap under his arm and went into the room. He bowed his head and said, 'I've been ordered to arrest you!'

Khomeini was exiled that same day. He moved to Iraq

and bided his time, waiting for the right moment to spark off a revolution against America and overturn the kingdom of the shah.

After the uprising, no one dared to mention his name. For years it was as if he didn't exist. Now his name had started to crop up here and there. Pamphlets written by him were making the rounds, and in Qom pictures of him were once more hung surreptitiously on the walls of the mosques.

Khomeini had been exiled, but the young imams had kept the flame alive, honouring his name at every opportunity and by any means possible.

Ahmad's fame gradually spread, even to other cities. He was invited more and more often to speak in other places. Recently he'd given a speech in Khomein, the birthplace of Khomeini.

He used his trips to spice up his sermons, innocently telling his listeners about his jaunts. 'I was in Isfahan recently,' he said. 'What a magnificent city! I send my greetings to the Isfanhani. My next destination was Kashan, a city much loved by its inhabitants. I send my greetings to the Kashani. Last week I was in Khomein. This was my first visit to that most fortunate of villages. Khomein is a unique place, with wonderful people. I send my greetings to Khomeini.'

And by 'Khomeini' he meant the inhabitants of Khomein, but the allusion was not lost on his listeners, who immediately shouted, 'Salaam bar Khomeini!'

Aqa Jaan beamed with joy.

He knew that Ahmad's remark had not been accidental, but the result of careful planning. Ahmad was no doubt following orders from Qom.

*　　*　　*

Aqa Jaan had received a secret message from Qom, informing him that Khalkhal had crossed illegally into Iraq and joined Khomeini.

Khalkhal was clever. He'd gone to Iraq for a reason, no doubt sensing that Khomeini would one day seize power and realise his long-cherished dream of establishing an Islamic Republic.

Aqa Jaan now understood why Khalkhal had abandoned his wife and child.

On the streets, however, there was no sign of a transfer of power or an approaching revolution. The shah was experiencing the best years of his reign. In a recent interview in *The Times*, he'd said that he didn't feel threatened at all and that his country was an oasis of peace.

Fearing Soviet expansion, America was content to let the shah rule Iran. He was always the first to buy the latest American fighter planes and weapons, and he deposited a large part of the nation's oil revenues in American banks.

The shah was convinced that he was the best head of state the Americans could wish for, which is why he thought he could count on their unconditional support. He felt sure that they would never let him down and saw no reason to worry about someone like Khomeini, sitting out his exile in Iraq.

And so he quietly and confidently prepared his son for that far-off day when he would accede to the throne.

While Ahmad was throwing himself wholeheartedly into the activities of the mosque, Shahbal was preparing to go to the University of Tehran. He wanted to study Persian literature, but Aqa Jaan had advised him against it. 'You can study Persian literature at home; you don't need a university to do that. You have talent. Study mathematics or engineering or business administration. We already have more than enough classics in our family library. What this house needs is the spirit of modernity.'

When it was time for Shahbal to leave for Tehran, Aqa Jaan drove him to the station. 'I've noticed a couple of things, but I'm not sure if I should tell you about them,' he said to Aqa Jaan in the car.

'What sort of things?' Aqa Jaan asked.

'Well, I've bumped into Ahmad up on the roof a few times, standing behind the dome and smoking. He's old enough to know whether or not he should smoke, but those cigarettes of his have a funny smell . . . like something an imam shouldn't be smoking. He also sneaks off occasionally to strangers' houses to smoke opium. I thought you ought to know.'

'I'm glad you told me,' Aqa Jaan said after a long silence. 'I'll see what I can do. Is there anything else I should know?'

'Not really. Women are his weakness. I've noticed him once or twice in the mosque taking more liberties with women than an imam ought to.'

'I've noticed that too. He needs to be careful. We have a lot of enemies in this town.'

At the station he escorted Shahbal to the train in silence.

Shahbal had not talked about his religious doubts again since the night he'd first mentioned them. Aqa Jaan had tried to broach the subject, but Shahbal wasn't ready to discuss it further, so he left him in peace.

Now that they were standing on the platform, Aqa Jaan wanted to tell him to be careful at the university, but Shahbal didn't give him the chance. He hugged Aqa Jaan, kissed him and boarded the train.

Aqa Jaan waited on the platform until the train had moved off and disappeared from view.

*   *   *

Aqa Jaan kept a close watch on Ahmad.

One evening he saw Zarah taking a tray of tea and dates to the library at an unusual hour. He knew that Ahmad was in there reading, so he followed her. Through the chink in the curtains he watched her lean over Ahmad and set the tray on his desk. Ahmad slid his hand up her blouse. She stood still and let him touch her. Then Ahmad stood up, lifted her skirt and pressed her against a bookcase.

The next morning Aqa Jaan called Zarah into his study. 'Sit down,' he said, pointing amicably towards a chair.

She took a seat, shyly.

'I'll get straight to the point. I'm very happy with your work here. We couldn't wish for a better maid. But I'm giving you a choice: you can either stay away from Ahmad, or you can pack your bags and go! Is that clear?'

Zarah was too stunned to reply.

'Is that clear?' he repeated.

She nodded mutely.

'So which is it going to be? Do you want to stay here, or shall I send you back to your parents?'

'I want to stay here,' she said, her voice trembling.

'Fine. And now get back to work. Muezzin needs some assistance, so if you're not too busy, you can help him. That's all. You may go.'

That evening after the prayer Aqa Jaan asked Ahmad to walk down to the river with him. As they strolled along the banks in the waning light, he gave Ahmad a severe talking-to, making it clear that he wouldn't tolerate his vulgar behaviour to women and that his use of opium was an affront to the mosque. If Ahmad was not prepared to heed his advice, he would have to curtail his freedom.

Ahmad listened to Aqa Jaan in silence.

'Don't you have anything to say in your defence?'

Even that failed to get a response out of Ahmad.

A few days later Aqa Jaan approached the father of the oldest carpet merchant in the city to discuss the possibility of a marriage between his daughter and Ahmad.

One month later the family of the bride held a wedding banquet. At midnight the bride was brought to the house in a decorated coach. Though one of the bedrooms on the upper floor was to be hers, the guest room had been readied for the seven nights of the honeymoon.

Ahmad was given a week off, and the family went to Jirya, so that he and his bride could spend some time alone. Lounging round the house in baggy cotton clothing that didn't restrict his movement, Ahmad acted like a prince who had brought his young bride to a castle.

His wife was named Samira. At eighteen, she was a classic beauty. On the first night Ahmad charmed her and made love to her until dawn, only falling asleep when it got light.

At one o'clock that afternoon, Am Ramazan welcomed him to the Opium Room, where the pipe had already been laid out for him. Ahmad had asked Am Ramazan to arrange for a seven-day supply, since opium was said to be an aphrodisiac.

After Ahmad had smoked a quarter of a roll of yellow opium, he went back upstairs and crawled into bed with his bride, who was fast asleep.

Samira bore him a daughter, Masud. Everyone was delighted with the little girl, but the house was waiting for a son and successor to Ahmad.

People still flocked to the mosque. Ahmad's sermons were exciting to listen to, for he was a born storyteller. He had wonderful things to say about the tales in the Koran. He transported you with the magic of his words to the past, to the time of the prophet Muhammad, who used to make love to his young wife, Aisha, on the roof of his house. One time Ahmad told the following story:

Muhammad had declared street musicians taboo. No Muslim was supposed to listen to their music. Then one day, as he lay with his young wife Aisha on the roof, he heard music drifting up from the street. Aisha begged him to let her take a look: 'Let me see, let me see, let me see!' Love won out. Muhammad bent down, and Aisha stepped onto his back and peeped over the balustrade at the musicians down below.

This was the first time an imam had ever told such a tale in the mosque, but Ahmad was forever coming up with unusual stories that left his audience spellbound. Instead of an imam, he probably should have become a storyteller, an actor who charmed the crowds at the bazaar with his tales.

Ahmad scheduled even more trips to important religious bastions such as Kashan, Arak, Hamadan and Isfahan. Sometimes he was gone for a whole week. And yet he always came back with two bags: one filled with money and gold, and the other with love letters and presents that veiled women had surreptitiously slipped into his pockets, such as socks, vests, underwear, colognes, soaps and rings.

Although Ahmad had promised Aqa Jaan that he would stop, he continued to frequent clandestine opium dens throughout the city.

To escape Aqa Jaan's watchful eye, he accepted as many speaking engagements as possible in distant cities. There he met men who spirited him off to their favourite haunts, where they caroused with women and smoked opium until dawn.

In Senejan Aqa Jaan kept him on a tight leash, which is how he came into contact with the underworld. What he didn't realise, however, was that the secret police were laying a trap for him.

Opium had been outlawed a year ago. Addicts were allowed to collect half a roll of opium from a chemist's twice a month, provided they were registered with the authorities. Since he couldn't go through the legal channels, Ahmad got his supply illegally.

One night, he and two other men were smoking opium and enjoying the company of women in the cellar of a house in Senejan, when all of a sudden the secret police burst in. They took several pictures of Ahmad, seated beside two unveiled woman and an opium kit. After planting a few more illegal rolls of opium, they photographed the scene from every angle, clapped handcuffs on Ahmad and drove him to an unknown location, where an agent was waiting to speak to him.

Ahmad had nothing to say. He knew that he'd been framed and that it wouldn't be easy to get out of this predicament.

'You can sleep in your own bed tonight and lead the prayer in the mosque tomorrow morning as usual,' the agent told him, 'on one condition.'

'What's the condition?' Ahmad asked, his voice trembling.

'That from now on you and I will keep in touch, if you know what I mean.'

'No, I don't know what you mean.'

'In that case things are going to get complicated, because I'll have to send you straight to jail, where the morning edition of the paper will be brought to you at breakfast with your picture plastered across the front page. Maybe then you'll figure out what I mean.'

It was a long night. Ahmad wept soundlessly. He hadn't expected his life to take such a terrifying turn.

When dawn finally arrived, the agent came to his cell. In the meantime the photographs had been developed, and he showed one of them to Ahmad. 'What's it going to be?' he asked. 'Shall we have some copies made, or shall you and I have a little chat?'

Ahmad had no choice. If the picture of him with the two unveiled women and the opium was published in the newspaper, his career would be over, and he would bring shame upon his family. So he went with the agent to his office, where he was given a chair and asked to fill in a form. 'Provided we can reach an understanding, this will take only five minutes,' the agent said. 'After that I will personally escort you home. What we want you to do is simple. We want you to keep in close touch with Qom and to pass on whatever information we ask for. That's all.'

Half an hour later a car delivered Ahmad to the gate of the mosque. He stepped out. 'You'll be hearing from us,' the agent said, and he drove off.

Several months went by and nothing happened. Ahmad hoped and prayed that the secret police had merely wanted to scare him into submission. They had not forgotten Khalkhal's campaign against the cinema and the riot he'd triggered during Farah Diba's visit. No doubt they were trying to take revenge by holding Ahmad hostage.

He hoped they'd dropped the idea of using him as an informer, because he wasn't cut out for the job. It would be highly inappropriate for him, as an imam and as a person. But what kind of information could he pass on if he had to?

He knew that the secret police were blackmailing him so he wouldn't stir up trouble. Their little game had worked. He no longer dared to say anything about the shah or the rumblings in Qom.

He cautiously allowed himself to feel happy again, and his fears gradually faded. But one evening, just after the prayer had ended, he suddenly saw the agent kneeling beside him in the prayer room.

'How are you?' the man whispered, with an intimidating smile.

Horrified, Ahmad turned to see whether Aqa Jaan was sitting in the row behind him. He wasn't.

'What do you want?' he asked in a low voice.

'As you know, Qom is in an uproar again. We want you to go there, make the rounds of the ayatollahs and find out what's going on. I assume you still have my phone number?'

'Yes,' Ahmad said, his face ashen with fear. He leaned over and touched his forehead to the ground, as if he were continuing his prayer.

When he sat up again, the agent was gone.

With trembling hands, he slipped on his *aba* and hurried home, his shoulders hunched as if he were in the grip of a fever.

The first thing he did when he reached the house was to go into Aqa Jaan's study and fall to his knees. 'Save me, Aqa Jaan!' he wailed. 'I've been framed!'

Aqa Jaan, astonished at the sudden outburst, stared at his nephew.

'The secret police have taken pictures of me! Dirty pictures, with women, opium! They want me to go to Qom and be an informer. If I don't, they'll publish the pictures in the paper!'

Aqa Jaan sat speechless in his chair. This was the last

thing he'd expected. 'Where did it happen?' he finally asked.

'In a cellar here in town.'

'The opium isn't a problem, but who were the women?'

'*Siegeh* women.'

'The secret police are trying to even an old score. Have you cooperated with them in any way or worked for them before?'

'No! Never!' Ahmad said.

'Have you ever passed on any information to them?'

'No, none!'

'I repeat,' Aqa Jaan said, with emphasis, 'have you ever told them anything?'

'No, I haven't said anything. I haven't done anything,' Ahmad replied.

'Consider yourself lucky, because if you had, I would have kicked you out of the house this instant. However, if we act quickly, I think we can keep the damage to a minimum. Don't breathe a word of this to anyone. In the next few months I'll make sure you're never left alone. I'll go down to their headquarters tomorrow and see what I can do. They need us to keep the peace in Senejan, so they're not about to print those pictures in the paper. They're just using them to blackmail us. Don't say a word. And no matter what happens, stick close to me.'

'I have another confession to make,' Ahmad said. 'I can't preach a sermon without smoking opium first. I'm sorry, I know how much this must hurt you.'

'It does. It pains me even more than your other news,' Aqa Jaan said sorrowfully. 'Anyone can make a mistake, but your addiction is an insult, a humiliation to us all. I can't bear to think that the imam of our mosque can't preach unless he's smoked opium first. You've hurt me to the quick. I'm not going to compromise on this, you're going to have to kick the habit, even if I have to lock you in a cage. From now on you're not to step foot outside this house unless I say so!'

The next day Aqa Jaan cancelled all of Ahmad's appointments and called the family doctor to ask if he could come in for a confidential chat.

Going directly from the doctor's office to the headquarters of the secret police, he demanded to see the director immediately, even though he hadn't made an appointment. He was ushered into the office and seated in a big leather armchair. The director showed him the photographs of Ahmad. Aqa Jaan had no choice: he had to make a deal. He promised to keep the mosque free of the trouble that was now plaguing Qom and, in return, the director agreed to keep the photographs in his drawer.

That evening Aqa Jaan opened his journal. 'The imam of our mosque is addicted to opium,' he wrote. 'We are in for hard times.'

Quiet Years

A long time passed in relative tranquillity.
Aqa Jaan got Ahmad back in line by making him follow a strict set of rules and not letting him travel to other cities by himself until he was sure that he had conquered his addiction.

Though the matter of the photographs had been taken care of, Aqa Jaan thought of it as a turning point in the history of the mosque.

At first Shahbal came home from university at least once a month, and then his visits tapered off. Sometimes he phoned Aqa Jaan at the bazaar, but all they did was talk about business: 'How are you? How's the work going?'

'What can I say? The world has changed, my boy. We need a man with new ideas. I'm getting old.'

'You? Old? You're not old!'

'Well, maybe not old, but old-fashioned. You can't compete these days at an international level with the traditional methods we use here. Study hard; I need you. We'll talk about it the next time you come home.'

But when Shahbal did come home, it was late at night, and the next evening he'd take the night train back to Tehran, so there was never any time to discuss the carpet trade and the bazaar.

Shahbal had not yet told Aqa Jaan, but he was no longer interested in business and certainly not in carpets.

At the university he had joined an underground student movement – a different group from the one he'd been involved with in the Red Village.

He soon found himself appointed to the editorial board of the clandestine student newspaper, where he felt at home. Since he wrote well and was more mature than his fellow students, he was quickly regarded as a man with leadership potential.

Shahbal had changed, but so had the world around him. The bazaar, which used to play such an important role in Senejan, had been relegated to the sidelines. Persian rugs were no longer the determining factor in either the economy or in politics; their place had been usurped by gas and oil.

Aqa Jaan had once wielded a great deal of power in the bazaar, and the authorities had always held him in high regard. Now they had grown so bold that they dared to send secret policemen to the mosque and to suggest that the imam be used as an informer. The mayor used to call him at least once a week to maintain contact between the bazaar and the local government, but the new mayor hadn't even invited Aqa Jaan to his inaugural banquet, much less phoned him. Some of the other merchants had been invited, however, which meant that the regime was attempting to destroy the unity of the bazaar. Meanwhile the bazaar was losing its dominant position as the producer of carpets. Several new carpet factories had sprung up in the city. In the old days no one would have dreamed of buying a cheap factory carpet that reeked of plastic, but nowadays everyone seemed to have one.

Until only a few short years ago, having a television aerial on your roof was taboo in Senejan, but times had changed. Once, when an enterprising businessman had decided to convert the old bathhouse into a cinema, all it took was Khalkhal to rally the faithful and rout out even Farah Diba. Recently someone had bought the oldest garage in the city and transformed it into a modern cinema. Every night hundreds of young people queued up to buy tickets.

So many attractive businesses had opened in the city that the younger generation had lost touch with the bazaar. A few years ago, young people used to go to the bazaar just to take a stroll. Now the city had built a broad boulevard, to which they flocked during the evening prayer, eating ices and strolling beneath the trees in the garish neon light.

The shah had finally conquered the city. Posters of him were plastered on every government building, and his voice could be heard on every radio station in the country. In the past, shopkeepers used to keep their radios under the counter, for fear of offending their customers and losing trade. Now they displayed their radios prominently on a shelf, so that everyone could hear the broadcasts.

Some of the traditional carpet merchants in the bazaar even had portraits of the shah hanging in their shops. Only a few years ago, that would have been unthinkable, but things had changed so rapidly that sometimes you didn't recognise your own city.

The focal point of Senejan was no longer the bazaar, but the new boulevard, where a large equestrian statue of the shah had been erected.

The shah's voice now reached almost every home in Senejan; even the thick old walls of the house of the mosque could no longer shut it out. Every time the shah gave a new speech in some part of the country, the authorities parked a jeep next to the mosque and broadcast the speech through a loudspeaker. All day long the shah's voice would echo through the courtyard. Fakhri Sadat couldn't understand why Aqa Jaan didn't speak up and why Ahmad didn't protest.

Recently the shah had visited the grave of Cyrus, the first king of the ancient Persian Empire, and said with great hubris, 'Cyrus! King of kings! Sleep quietly, for I am awake!' The jeep outside the mosque had broadcast the speech non-stop for an entire week.

'Such gruelling days! Such gruelling nights!' Aqa Jaan wrote in his journal. 'It's a great humiliation to us all, but there's nothing I can do about it! I'm so ashamed that I hardly dare to show my face at the mosque.'

No one could keep the shah out of the house any longer. Even the pictures of him, which a helicopter had scattered over the city, had been blown into the courtyard by the wind. Lizard had picked up a couple of them and put them on Aqa Jaan's desk.

One day Aqa Jaan was standing in the courtyard when he heard loud music coming from the house of Hajji Shishegar. Music in the house of the pious Shishegar? It must be a special occasion.

Aqa Jaan looked over and thought he saw a television aerial on Shishegar's roof. A television aerial on the roof of one of the most respected glass merchants in the bazaar? Surely his eyes must be deceiving him?

There was another burst of noise.

Aqa Jaan went up the courtyard steps and carefully picked his way through the darkness until he was directly opposite his neighbour's roof. No, his eyes hadn't been deceiving him. A long aluminium aerial was poking up from the roof!

Hajji Shishegar had decided that he and his sons needed

to keep abreast of the latest developments. He had been invited to the mayor's inaugural banquet, where each of the guests had been given a portrait of the shah to take home. And that portrait, now in a gold frame, had been placed on the mantelpiece, directly above the television.

But why was such loud music coming from the hajji's house?

Aqa Jaan crept over to the edge of the roof and peeked into his neighbour's courtyard.

The hajji was giving a party, to which he'd invited his many friends and relatives. It was a hot evening – too hot to sit inside. Shishegar's twin sons, dressed in long cotton tunics, were lying next to each other on a wooden bed, which had been carried out into the courtyard and set down by the *hauz*. A group of street musicians was playing an American pop song with a strong beat, and a few of the men were dancing hand in hand.

Apparently they were celebrating the circumcision of the hajji's sons. The mother of the twins was talking gaily to her guests with her chador down around her shoulders and only a wispy scarf on her head. There was no sign of the hajji's first wife and her seven daughters.

Bowls of biscuits and sweets had been placed here and there, and the children were chasing each other round the large courtyard. The hajji chatted with his guests and offered them biscuits. Every once in a while he snatched the camera out of the photographer's hands, took a few shots of his sons, then flopped down on the bed beside them for the umpteenth time and shouted, 'Take a picture of the three of us!'

At a certain point he rounded up a couple of other men, went into the living room and came back out with a huge cabinet television. They set it down by the *hauz*, under the tree that was sheltering his sons. The hajji switched it on and a group of female dancers from Tehran filled the screen. Everyone crowded round and stared at the dancers in awestruck silence.

Aqa Jaan retraced his steps until he was standing by the big blue dome. He touched its cold glazed tiles, then walked over to the edge of the roof, where he could look down into the courtyard of the mosque and see the *hauz* and the trees. He looked up at the minarets, but noticed to his surprise that there didn't seem to be any storks, or even any nests. Maybe it was too dark to see them from where he was standing, Aqa Jaan thought, so he walked over to the other side of the roof to view the minarets from that angle. No, he hadn't been mistaken: there was no trace whatsoever of the storks.

He opened the trapdoor in one of the minarets, climbed up the narrow stairs and stood at the top. There was a snap of twigs beneath his feet – all that remained of the stork nests. Something inside him snapped as well. He had grown old. This unexpected realisation took him by surprise. He looked out over the city. Coloured lights twinkled everywhere, and the giant portrait of the shah near the entrance to the bazaar was lit by floodlights. The cinema's red and yellow neon lights were flashing on and off in the new centre of town. Although it was late, he could hear music and women's voices drifting over from the boulevard.

When had the sounds of surahs disappeared from the city? He knew that the mosque, the bazaar and the Koran were up against a powerful enemy, but he hadn't expected the regime to conquer Senejan quite so easily.

Where were the ayatollahs who had fought against the shah?

What had happened to the guerrillas who had been organised enough to arrange an escape from prison?

What changes had been brought about by the clandestine books read by Shahbal?

Where were the radios that had once railed against the regime?

Where was Khalkhal, who had fought the shah with such ferocity?

Where were the students who had wanted to change the world?

And where was Nosrat, who could have filmed all these changes?

These were quiet years. How could Aqa Jaan have known that a new era was going to dawn with dizzying swiftness? Or that a storm of destruction was heading his way? A raging storm that would lash him so hard that he would bend in trembling fear.

He climbed down the stairs, shut the trapdoor behind him and went into the courtyard, a broken man. He wanted to crawl in bed beside his wife and forget his troubles, but decided to go down to the river instead.

It was dark and quiet. Even the river wasn't making a sound. He looked at the vineyards and at the mountains on the opposite bank. All was still. As he walked, he thought about his life.

He had been born in that house. He had devoted his life to the mosque and worked long hours at the bazaar, putting all of his energy and talent into the carpets. His daughters were grown, and Jawad, his only son, was no longer a boy, but a young man, studying for his exams so he could go to university. Aqa Jaan reminded himself that he had not yet been to Mecca, although it was his duty, as a man of means, to make the pilgrimage at least once in his life.

Everything had changed, and on top of that, Ahmad had damaged the reputation of the mosque.

There was an unexpected caw from the vineyard, and the crow flew back across the river. Aqa Jaan heard men's voices and saw the silhouette of a veiled woman detach itself from the trees and walk towards the bridge.

Crazy Qodsi, he suddenly realised.

The silhouette stopped in the middle of the bridge.

'Qodsi!' Aqa Jaan called.

She hurried off. 'Qodsi! Wait!' he called. 'What are you doing here so late at night?' And he ran after her, stumbling through the darkness.

'They will all die,' Qodsi suddenly prophesied in a crow-like voice. 'All of them except you.'

The Television

As Lizard grew up, he became even more of an enigma. People were never sure if he was a disabled child or an animal. His head, hands and feet were human, but his movements were like those of a reptile.

The older he got, the more reptilian he became.

Sadiq tried to teach him how to talk, but he never learned. He wasn't interested.

Lizard did things his own way and paid little attention to other people's behaviour and habits. He refused to eat with everyone else, go to bed at a normal hour or use a knife and fork. He ate his meals like a cat.

'I can't stand it another minute! I'm exhausted. I don't want this strange child any more!'

'You mustn't say that!' Aqa Jaan protested.

Sadiq burst into tears. 'I've had one misfortune after another!' she lamented. 'Why has everything in my life gone wrong?'

'You're still young, my daughter; you have a long life ahead of you. No one expects life to be a bed of roses. Remember: there's a reason things happen the way they do. If anyone has a right to complain, it's Muezzin. He was born blind, but you don't hear him moaning about it. He's accepted the fact that his eyes are sightless, and so have we. He can't see, but he has two keen ears, two sensitive hands and two strong legs that remember the way. If you ask me, he sees everything, even things you and I will never see. Don't cry, my daughter! Your son is a natural part of life. I'm glad we have him. I think of him as a gift to our house. I mean that. We must need him for some reason; otherwise he wouldn't have been sent to us. Hundreds of people have lived in this house, and he isn't the first unusual creature to be born here. Trust in life. We must need your son, or else he wouldn't have been sent to us!'

'I wish I were as trusting as you are,' Sadiq said between sobs.

The next day Aqa Jaan summoned Lizard to his study and made it clear to him that he was to come there every day after the morning prayer. He had decided that he would spend the next few years teaching him how to read. All that was needed was patience and old-fashioned discipline. Lizard's response was unexpectedly positive: he took to crawling over to Aqa Jaan with a book between his teeth, dropping it in his lap and making him read every word of it.

Once Lizard had learned to read, he spent much of his time lying in the garden in the shade of the cedar tree. When that got too hot, he crawled up to the roof with his book, seeking the shadow of the dome. During the winter, he went down to the cellar so he could sit by Muezzin's stove and read.

Ahmad let him come into the library, where he spent hours among the books. No one ever knew if he understood a word of what he was reading or whether he simply made up stories of his own.

His world was the world of the house. He rarely left it, going outside only when Am Ramazan took him for a ride on his donkey. As they passed the grocery shop, the old men lounging around outside always stopped the donkey so they could get a better look at Lizard. Everyone had heard of the boy. They doffed their hats and joked with him. Lizard enjoyed it and responded enthusiastically to their attention.

Later Am Ramazam started taking him along to the river when he was mining sand. He would dig a hollow in the warm sand, and Lizard would curl up inside it and read his book. Lizard felt comfortable with Am Ramazam.

At first Sadiq had stopped Am Ramazam and asked him not to take Lizard with him.

'Why not?' Am Ramazam had asked. 'There's no need to hide him.'

Zinat was often away from home these days. She spent a lot of time in the countryside, giving Koran lessons to rural women. The moment she got home, however, she went looking for Lizard. She liked to tell him ancient tales, and he never tired of listening to them.

Zinat looked after Lizard more than the others did. She thought of him as a punishment for her sins. Lizard never learned to talk, but he had an acute sense of hearing and could move with extraordinary speed. He compelled everyone to interact with him in some way.

Nosrat avoided him during his visits. He stroked Lizard's hair and gave him a few sweets, but that was all, and he slept with his door closed so Lizard wouldn't come in.

One night Lizard crawled in anyway. He lay down in the corner of the room and took out his book. Nosrat didn't know what to do. For a while he simply sat in his bed and stared at him. He wanted to help the boy in some way, but didn't know how. Suddenly he had a flash of inspiration. 'Come with me,' he said.

Nosrat went into the courtyard and down into the cellar,

with Lizard scuttling along behind him. 'Listen, Lizard. Shahbal brought a television into this house a number of years ago so that Aqa Jaan and Alsaberi could see the moon. Alsaberi was an unsophisticated imam who fell into the *hauz* and died, but that television ought to be here somewhere. It's yours, if I can find it. You were born in the wrong house, you know. The world is changing, but everything in this house is forbidden. Do you understand what I'm saying?'

Of course he didn't. Lizard stared at him blankly.

'Still, you're lucky. If you'd been born to any other family, you would have been sold to a circus long ago. This family gives you love, and people need love. But in many ways they're backward. They're God-fearing people who are afraid of everything – radios, TVs, music, the cinema, the theatre, happiness, other women, other men. There's only one thing they like: cemeteries. They feel at home among the dead. I'm serious! Have you ever gone to a cemetery with them? Suddenly they get all happy and excited, absolutely in their element. That's why I left when I was young. Anyway, let's see if we can find that television; it must be in here among all this junk. Let's hope the grandmothers didn't throw it out. Ah, the grandmothers. It's a pity you never knew them. They were very dignified. They didn't approve of me, but that's beside the point. They went to Mecca and never came back, the crafty old biddies. Oh, I think I've found it! Look, Lizard, here's a portable TV for you! As soon as I've rigged up the aerial, your life will change for ever. Hmm, let me think. Where can we put it so you can watch without being disturbed? I know: in the shed behind the dome. It used to be my secret hideout, the place where I went to read dirty books. Later Shahbal added a bed. Now that he's gone, *you* can have the shed.'

Lizard crawled up to the roof behind Nosrat. Nosrat set the television on the table next to Shahbal's bed.

'From now on this bed belongs to you. Go ahead and lie on it. I'll show you how to use the TV.'

Lizard climbed onto the bed. Nosrat strung the cable through the window and carefully screwed the tiny aerial onto the end of a beam, where no one could see it.

'Now watch closely,' he said, and switched on the television.

A young woman wearing heavy make-up and a sleeveless red dress appeared on the screen.

'Don't be scared, my boy! The world outside of this house looks very different. Do you like women? Oh, oh, don't ask *me* that question! One of these days I'll take you to Tehran. Actually, this TV is too small. The next time I come I'll bring you a bigger one. Meanwhile, you'll have to make do with this one. It's yours, and no one can take it from you. If anyone tries to take it away, bite him. Sink your teeth into his ankle and bite down hard. Is that clear?'

For an entire year Lizard managed to keep his hideout a secret, but one night Aqa Jaan tiptoed up the stairs and flung open the door. Lizard was so surprised that he bounded from the bed to the television in one leap and draped himself over it like a cat, with his feet dangling over one side and his head over the other.

Aqa Jaan stood for a moment in the doorway. Then he shut the door, walked over to the stairs and went down to the mosque.

The Locusts

It was an extraordinary day. More things happened than anyone could have expected.

Lizard, having heard the doorbell, opened the gate and looked up to see two big brown horses staring down at him in the late afternoon sun. To get a better look, he grabbed hold of the gate and pulled himself up until he was standing. A large horse-drawn wagon containing two coffins had stopped outside.

'A delivery for Aqa Jaan!' bellowed the coachman in a long black coat and black hat.

Lizard crawled quickly over to Aqa Jaan's study, where he pointed at the gate and neighed like a horse. When Aqa Jaan saw the coachman, he put on his hat and went to the gate.

'*Enna lellah!*' the coachman said.

'*Enna lellah,*' Aqa Jaan replied. 'How can I help you?'

'I have two dead people for you.'

'Dead people? For me?'

'I beg your pardon, I don't mean actual people, just the remains.'

'Of whom?'

'Two women from Mecca.'

'The grandmothers!' exclaimed a horrified Aqa Jaan.

'Sign here,' the coachman said, and handed him the documents.

'I need my spectacles,' said Aqa Jaan.

Lizard scurried back inside and fetched Aqa Jaan's reading glasses.

One of the documents was an official letter in Arabic. It consisted of a few Koran verses, followed by a short statement explaining that the bodies of the grandmothers had been found in a cave in Hira Mountain near Mecca.

Hira Mountain is the most sacred mountain in the Islamic world – the mountain that Muhammad used to climb every night to speak to Allah. It's also the mountain where the archangel Gabriel first came down from Heaven to reveal Muhammad as the prophet.

There was a small cave in Hira Mountain. Muhammad had hid in this cave when he'd been forced to flee from Mecca to Medina in the middle of the night, because his enemies had sworn to kill him in his bed.

Ever since then the cave and that night have played a crucial role in the history of Islam. The Islamic calendar dates back to that night, or that day, on which Muhammad had fled to Medina.

Later the cave became known as the 'spider cave', because every time Muhammad went in, a spider spun a web across the entrance so no one could see that he was inside.

The grandmothers had hidden in that cave. It didn't seem possible, but they had. The police had found their wills beside their bodies.

It was an incredible story. Every year millions of pilgrims went to see the cave. Visitors weren't allowed to enter, but only to view it from a distance. If the story was true, the grandmothers must have had an amazing adventure.

Aqa Jaan felt sad. Yet at the same time, his mind was taken up with an entirely different matter: his son Jawad was due home that night after an absence of six months. Now a student at the University of Isfahan, he had never been away from home for so long. He was studying applied physics, so he could become a petroleum engineer.

A huge deposit of natural gas had been discovered near Senejan, and an American oil company had acquired the drilling rights. The university was therefore offering a new course of study. Hundreds of students had applied and taken the rigorous entrance exam, but only twelve had been admitted. Jawad had been one of the lucky ones. They were going to be taught special courses by American oil engineers. Although they were registered as students at the University of Isfahan, they were soon going to be transferred to the Shahzand oil refinery, twenty-five miles outside of Senejan, where they would continue their course work under the supervision of the oil company. They would be housed in a dormitory and speak only English.

Jawad was guaranteed a job after graduation, and would now be closer to home as well. Things couldn't be better. When they heard that Jawad had been accepted, Fakhri Sadat had been so happy she couldn't sleep that night, and Aqa Jaan had glowed with pride.

Aqa Jaan and Fakhri had been getting ready to go to the station to collect Jawad when the coachman knocked.

'Why did you bring the coffins here?' he asked the coachman. 'You should have taken them to the mosque. And you should have phoned me beforehand and let me know you were coming. You can't just show up on someone's doorstep with two coffins. What am I supposed to do with them?'

'I beg your pardon,' said the driver. 'I'm not bringing you two corpses, but two sacks.'

'Two sacks? What's that supposed to mean?' Aqa Jaan answered testily.

The coachman hopped onto his wagon, opened the lid of one of the coffins and took out a small sack. Then he opened the second coffin and took out another one. Holding them up, he said, 'You see? The Saudis sent only these two small sacks! Do you want them, or should I send them back?'

'Why are you transporting two small sacks in two full-size coffins? Why have you brought them in a horse-drawn wagon? And why have you come so late in the afternoon?'

'I understand how you feel, but I'm only the coachman.'

Aqa Jaan quickly stuffed a few banknotes in the man's pocket, took the sacks from him, went into the courtyard and shut the gate.

'What's going on?' Fakhri Sadat called from upstairs.

Aqa Jaan hid the sacks in the garden under a few large pumpkin vines. 'Nothing!' he told her. 'Nothing important. Are you ready? We've got to leave now or we'll be late.'

The red sun was sinking below the desert horizon when Aqa Jaan got behind the wheel of his Ford and drove to the station with his wife.

Fakhri Sadat wept with joy when she saw her son emerge from the train. He had always been her favourite. Only six months ago, before he'd left for Isfahan, she used to give him a goodnight kiss every evening before he went to bed. Now he had a black moustache and long hair.

Fakhri Sadat had raised Jawad herself. She hadn't wanted him to get too involved in the mosque, the bazaar or politics. She had raised him to think for himself, so he could choose his own path. Now she could reap the rewards. Her son didn't look like a religious fanatic, and she was pleased that he'd let his hair grow a bit longer. He seemed to take after his uncle Nosrat more than his father.

In all the years that he'd lived at home, he'd never shown the slightest interest in the affairs of the mosque. Fakhri Sadat was glad that Aqa Jaan considered Shahbal, and not Jawad, his successor. What she didn't know, because Aqa Jaan hadn't told her yet, was that he was disappointed in Shahbal and was now pinning his hopes on his son.

It had been several months since Shahbal had phoned Aqa Jaan. He'd called him at the bazaar, but had dialled the number of the warehouse rather than that of his office. Someone from the warehouse had come running in to tell Aqa Jaan that he was wanted on the phone.

'Who's calling?'

'A businessman from Tehran.'

'Why did he call the warehouse?'

'He says he tried your number several times, but there was no answer.'

Aqa Jaan went to the warehouse and picked up the phone.

'I apologise for the inconvenience, Aqa Jaan, but I was afraid your phone might be tapped. I called to tell you not to worry if I don't come home for a while. I've got a couple of things going at the moment. I just wanted to hear your voice. Will you give my love to everyone?'

'I will. And may God watch over you!'

There was no need for Shahbal to elaborate. Aqa Jaan understood why the call had to be kept short.

Still, the last thing he wanted to do was to talk to Fakhri about it now. This was her evening, and he didn't want to spoil it.

It was a pleasant evening. They lingered at the table and everyone was in a good mood. Normally Zinat would have told them a story, but she wasn't home tonight. What Aqa Jaan didn't know was that she had secretly been in contact with the fundamentalists in Qom. Her instructions were to form the women's devotional groups into a tight unit, under the guise of teaching them about the Koran.

To keep the tradition going, Muezzin took over Zinat's role and told them a story about the prophet Yunus:

One day a disillusioned Yunus left his house for good. His followers were both saddened and surprised. Yunus reached the sea, saw a few travellers boarding a ship and decided to go with them.

The ship sailed for three days and three nights. On the fourth day the sky suddenly turned dark and a huge fish rose up out of the water, blocking the ship's way. The passengers didn't know what to do: the fish wouldn't move. Then an older traveller, a veteran of many sea voyages, spoke up. 'One of us has sinned. The fish will not let us pass until we offer up the sinner.'

'The fish has come for me,' Yunus said. 'Throw me into the sea and the rest of you can sail on.'

'We know you,' a few of the passengers said. 'You're a righteous man. You could never have blasphemed. We knew your father, too. He was also a God-fearing man. No, you are not the one the fish is seeking.'

But Yunus knew that he was. 'This is between me and my God,' he said. 'That is why the fish has come.'

He climbed up on the railing and leapt into the water. The fish swallowed him whole and disappeared beneath the waves.

They were still mulling over the story when they heard a strange sound coming from the courtyard. Aqa Jaan cupped his hand behind his ear.

'What's that I hear?' Muezzin asked. 'What's that sound?'

Aqa Jaan went outside and saw that the sky had become strangely dark.

'I hear a horde of insects,' said Muezzin.

'Locusts!' Aqa Jaan shouted. 'Close all the doors and windows!'

But it was too late. Thousands of locusts flew into the house, and the air turned brown, as if the house had been hit by a desert storm.

The women flung on their chadors and raced from room to room, closing doors and windows.

Ahmad hurried into the library, while Aqa Jaan raced down to the cellar to close the shutters.

The locusts landed on the roofs, the trees, the plants in the garden, even in the *hauz*, and began to devour everything in sight.

Every once in a while locusts descended on Senejan from such faraway places as Mecca. Only after they'd stripped the city bare did they move on to the grapevines by the river and finally disappear behind the mountains. No one had ever seen such an enormous swarm of locusts as they did that day. Only the old people could recall hearing their parents talk about such devastation.

One of the books in the library described a plague of locusts that had taken place fifty years ago:

The locusts came in droves, millions of them, and the world went dark. Even though they were as big as your finger, you couldn't see them when they were on the ground, because they were the same colour as the soil, but when they moved, it looked as though the ground itself was moving.

People went up to their roofs and banged on pots

and pans in hopes of scaring them off, but the locusts didn't seem to hear them. So they lit fires and hoped the smoke would drive them away, but that didn't work either. So then they took out their Korans and read the surah about the Valley of the Ants.

Solomon, it was said, once came upon such a mass of ants that the valley floor looked as if it were covered with a black carpet. Solomon's messenger, the hoopoe bird, flew over the valley and cried, 'Ants! Didn't you hear? The man who just spoke to you is Solomon. He speaks the language of animals. He is on his way to the queen of Sheba. Haven't you heard of this beautiful queen? Step aside! Clear the road so the troops can pass! Step aside for Solomon and the beautiful queen of Sheba! You are about to witness a great event. Step aside!'

At first nothing happened, but then the mass of ants began to move. They crept back into the earth and were never seen again.

Only when daylight came did the locusts fly off towards the mountains. Every plant and tree in the garden had been stripped bare, and there were fish bones floating in the *hauz*. Even the grandmothers had been spirited away by the locusts.

It's a sign that something terrible is about to happen, thought Aqa Jaan as he viewed the damage from his window. Locusts come for a reason.

He slipped his hand into his pocket and wrapped his fingers firmly round his Koran.

Zaman

A s Muezzin lay in bed, he chanted a surah to himself:

> By the sun and its morning glow!
> By the moon that follows in its wake!
> By the day when it shows its glory!
> By the night when it conceals the light!
> By the sky and He who made it!

Seven days had gone by since the locusts had descended on the city. But Muezzin was still in bed.

'Why have you shut yourself up in your room, Muezzin?' Aqa Jaan enquired from behind the closed door. 'Why won't you come out?'

'I don't dare.'

'Why not? What are you afraid of? What's happened?' Aqa Jaan asked, and he entered the room warily.

'The clock in my head has stopped ticking. I've lost my sense of time, of *zaman*.'

'You're just tired, Muezzin,' Aqa Jaan said. 'It's your work. You're upset because your pottery isn't selling well.'

'No, it's not the pottery; it's the locusts. My clock stopped ticking when the swarm arrived. I don't dare go out any more. I panic whenever anyone asks me what time it is.'

*   *   *

The shopkeeper who used to sell Muezzin's pottery on consignment had cancelled his contract. The market had been flooded with so many cheap plastic goods that there was no longer any demand for his ceramics. And yet Muezzin couldn't stop making things. He kept churning out plates, bowls, water jugs and vases, and stacking them in the cellar. When the cellar was full, he started piling them between the plants in the garden. And when the garden was full, Lizard helped him to stack them on the roof of the mosque.

Muezzin stayed in bed for three more days. On the tenth night, his clock suddenly started ticking again.

'Three minutes past twelve,' he muttered. He was so relieved that he immediately sat up in bed.

He heard a noise: the clang of the front gate. Then footsteps crossing the courtyard to Aqa Jaan's study.

'Shahbal,' he realised instantly.

He stood up and was about to shout a greeting, but then thought better of it. Shahbal must have his reasons for going to see Aqa Jaan so late at night. He would have to be patient. Shahbal would come and see him soon enough.

Aqa Jaan's first thought when he saw Shahbal in the doorway was: he's changed. All traces of the boy who had once lived in the house were gone. There was now a man standing before him.

Aqa Jaan stood up, embraced Shahbal and offered him a chair. 'How are you, my son? You've forgotten us. I haven't heard from you in months.'

'It's a long story, Aqa Jaan, but I'll make it short. I'm happy and everything's all right.'

Aqa Jaan knew that he mustn't insist, so he kept his

reply simple. 'Good, that's all I need to know,' he said, and he paused, to allow Shahbal to continue if he wanted to.

'The university is currently in an uproar,' Shahbal began. 'The American vice-president was in Tehran today for a visit. Students blocked the road from the airport to the palace, but the riot police broke up the demonstration. Then the students regrouped and tried to storm the American Embassy, but they were stopped by a special task force. There were a few scuffles, and a couple of Molotov cocktails were thrown through the windows. The embassy burst into flames. Then a helicopter came down and started to fire randomly into the crowd. Two students were killed and dozens more were wounded. The police are now looking for the students who led the demonstration. They've all fled. So have I. I'd like to hide in the mosque for a few days until things have calmed down, unless you object.'

'Why would I object?' said Aqa Jaan. 'You were right to come home. You're safer here than anywhere else. I can help you better here than in Tehran.'

'Thank you.'

'For what?'

'I don't live here any more, but whenever I feel unsafe or insecure, you're the first person I think of. This house has always been my haven. Thank you for giving me a sense of security. And for raising me. When I was living here, I didn't really know who I was. Now I do. You've made me into the strong person I am today.'

Aqa Jaan was touched by Shahbal's remarks. 'Not only do you have a good head on your shoulders,' he replied, 'but you can also express your feelings.'

'There's something else I'd like to tell you,' Shahbal said. 'This afternoon, when the train pulled into Qom,

I saw an incredible scene. Hundreds of young imams were holding a demonstration in the train station. They were standing on the tracks, blocking the trains, and shouting, "*La ilaha illa Allah!* There is no God but Allah!"

'I've never seen such a demonstration! Their voices were so strong and powerful! What I saw in Qom today was a totally new kind of resistance. The ayatollahs have changed their tactics. Imams who used to turn their backs on modern inventions like trains were now standing on the railway tracks. One young imam scaled the wall in the waiting room and pasted a picture of Khomeini over the shah's portrait. Someday the great event we've all been waiting for is bound to happen . . . Have you been in touch with anyone in Qom?'

It was an unexpected question. No, he was no longer in touch with anyone in Qom, and no ayatollah had phoned him during the past year. Now that Shahbal had told him about the demonstration, he felt as if a train full of ayatollahs had left the station, and he had missed the train.

It was thirteen minutes to one when Muezzin heard footsteps in the alley. The footsteps sounded familiar, but he couldn't quite place them. Then he heard someone fumbling at the lock on the front gate. He got out of bed, padded barefoot into Aqa Jaan's study and whispered, 'I heard a noise in the alley. Someone's at the gate!'

Aqa Jaan immediately turned to Shahbal. 'Go and hide in one of the minarets!'

Shahbal gave his father a quick kiss, went up to the roof, took a blanket out of the shed, opened the trapdoor in the left minaret, crawled inside and closed the door behind him.

Aqa Jaan saw a bewildered-looking Lizard standing in the middle of the courtyard. His clothes were soaking wet. 'You can't stay here!' he whispered to him. 'Go upstairs!'

Outwardly calm, Aqa Jaan strode to the gate and opened it. A man wearing a hat and a pair of dark glasses was standing on the pavement with a key in his hand. He seemed vaguely familiar, but Aqa Jaan couldn't remember where he might have seen him.

'I think we've met before,' Aqa Jaan said, 'but I don't see very well in the dark. Can I help you?'

The man took off his hat. Only then did Aqa Jaan recognise him, though it took a moment for it to sink in. It was Khalkhal! He had aged.

'*Salaam aleikum*,' Khalkhal said.

For a moment Aqa Jaan wasn't sure how to react. After all, Khalkhal had destroyed Sadiq's life. He had abandoned her when she was pregnant with Lizard and had gone to Iraq to be with Khomeini. Now, after all these years, suddenly here he was again.

'What can I do for you?' Aqa Jaan said coolly, stepping outside and shutting the gate behind him.

'I've been travelling round the country, spreading Khomeini's message. This afternoon, I met with a group of merchants here in Senejan. I thought I'd see you there, and was surprised when you didn't turn up. I'm leaving later tonight for Iraq, but I have one request: may I speak to my wife?'

'She's not your wife, not legally. When a man abandons his wife and has no contact with her for several years, the marriage is officially dissolved. You're an imam; you ought to know that. You have no right to see her.'

'I know, but I thought she might be willing to see me anyway.'

'I'll decide that! And I'm telling you, she won't see you!' Aqa Jaan heatedly exclaimed.

'But I have a son, and I do have a right to see him.'

'That's true. But it would be better for us all if you turned and left and we could forget you ever came here,' Aqa Jaan said in a slightly calmer tone of voice.

'To be honest, I wasn't planning to come. I was already in my car, ready to drive off, when I realised I couldn't go without seeing them. I understand your anger, but you know that I was forced to leave my family because of the intolerable political situation in this country. The Americans are running the show. We must be prepared to sacrifice ourselves, our wives and our children in order to overthrow the regime, or else we'll never achieve our goal. I had no choice, but I can live with the consequences.'

'I don't have to stand here in the middle of the night and listen to your drivel!' Aqa Jaan snapped, and he pointed to the street.

Khalkhal glared at Aqa Jaan from behind his dark glasses. 'If you want me to go, I will,' he said. 'But we'll meet again some day!'

And he turned on his heel and left.

Aqa Jaan went to bed and told Fakhri about his unexpected meeting with Khalkhal. They discussed it briefly, but were both too tired to go into it further.

The next evening Fakhri knocked on the door of Aqa Jaan's study. 'I need to talk to you.'

'Come in,' said Aqa Jaan, a little taken aback.

Fakhri came in and stood in the middle of the room to deliver her bombshell: 'I think that Zinat has been in touch with Khalkhal, and that Khalkhal has been meeting Sadiq, with Zinat's knowledge and consent.'

'What? I can't believe it!' Aqa Jaan said, stunned. 'Are you sure?'

'I suspect that Khalkhal and Zinat are in cahoots. I think that he's even put her in contact with Qom. Zinat has had a taste of power. I can tell from the way she's been acting. Have you noticed that she's stopped going to our mosque? Beware of Zinat; I don't trust her. She's been doing some strange things lately.'

It might very well be true, thought Aqa Jaan, but how could I not have noticed?

'I shouldn't be telling you this,' Fakhri continued, 'but now that this has come out, I think there's something else you ought to know. Khalkhal and Sadiq met quite recently, and, if you ask me, they did more than just talk. Sadiq has a bounce in her step again.'

'What? That's impossible! It's just silly women's gossip.'

'No, it's not. You notice every little change in the bazaar, so why can't you see the changes in your own household? Every time I hear Zinat's footstep on the stairs, I automatically reach for my chador. I don't dare wear any make-up when she's around. It's like having a strange man look at me. I don't know what she's up to or who she's in touch with, but she looks at people in a different way. I have the same feeling when our devotional group gets together. Nobody dares to speak up when Zinat's there. I used to enjoy our meetings, but now they're dominated by a bunch of rude women who talk about nothing but the sharia. And Zinat is the ringleader.'

Aqa Jaan sank deeper into his chair.

There was a knock at the door.

'Who's there?'

'The cinema is smoking.' Qodsi's voice could be heard from the other side of the door.

'What are you doing out so late at night?' Aqa Jaan asked.

He jumped up and opened the door.

A thick layer of smoke was hanging over the centre of town, and fire engines were racing noisily towards the fire.

Aqa Jaan's first thought was: Khalkhal! He didn't mention his suspicions to Fakhri, but quickly changed into his street clothes, hurried outside and headed into town.

There were police cars everywhere, and ambulances were taking the wounded to the hospital. A bomb had exploded in the cinema. Three people had been killed and more than a hundred had been wounded.

A week later another bomb exploded, this time in a cinema in Isfahan. There were even more dead and wounded. The regime didn't issue an official statement, nor was the incident mentioned in any of the newspapers.

Forty days after the attack in Isfahan, a huge bomb went off during the premiere of an American film in the country's largest cinema, in the southern city of Abadan. Four hundred and seventy-six people died, and many more were injured.

The news made the headlines of newspapers throughout the world.

The shah could hear Khomeini's footsteps coming closer and closer, and yet it never occurred to him that the mosques and bazaars could have rallied round Khomeini in such a short time. Although he was kept informed of developments, his underlings always scrupulously avoided mentioning the possibility of a popular uprising. The shah was told only that his people were contented and grateful. His Western allies were confident of his ability to govern. He saw no reason to worry about the bombings.

The eyes of the world were focused on Iraq, where Khomeini was living in exile. During the Friday prayer, the Persian service of the BBC broadcast the following message from Khomeini: 'We are not responsible for the bombings. We don't commit such atrocities! The secret police are behind the attacks.'

The broadcast was of historical significance, for it was the first time an imam – an ayatollah – had ever delivered his message over the radio. Khomeini might be old, but his voice sounded as militant as ever. Not once did he say the word 'shah'. Instead, he referred to the shah disparagingly by his middle name, Reza: 'Reza uses harsh words. Let him. He's a nobody, an errand boy! I'm going to come and fling him out on his ear. I'm not defying him; he isn't worth it. I'm defying America!'

The BBC announced that a demonstration would be held in Tehran on the following Friday. The news came like a bolt from the blue. The shah couldn't understand why contented people would want to demonstrate – or how an uprising could take place in a country so tightly controlled by the police and the security forces.

On that famous Friday thousands of shopkeepers from Tehran's bazaar made their way towards Majlis Square, where the Parliament was located. They were joined by thousands of others, who spilled out of the mosques at the end of the Friday prayer and poured into the side streets.

When the square was full, the crowd began to move in the direction of Shah Square. The first row of demonstrators was made up of young imams. A few feet ahead of them, walking all by himself, was a newcomer: a relatively young ayatollah in a noticeably stylish imam robe.

The more traditional imams usually paid little attention to their appearance, but this ayatollah was obviously different. He walked with his head held high, his beard neatly clipped and his white shirt carefully ironed. But the most eye-catching feature of all were his yellow imam slippers.

Nobody knew who he was. This was the first time he'd been seen in public. He'd arrived in Iran only last week, having travelled from Iraq via Dubai, disguised as a businessman in an English suit and hat.

This first trial demonstration had been an instant success. According to the BBC, one hundred thousand people had demonstrated against the shah in the streets of Tehran. A younger generation of imams had clearly been in charge.

A picture of the remarkable imam was splashed across the front pages of all the morning papers. 'Who is this man?' read the headline in *Keyhan*, the country's leading daily.

His name was Ayatollah Beheshti. He had been born in Isfahan and was – at the age of fifty-five – one of the youngest ayatollahs in the Shiite hierarchy. A highly motivated man, he was head of the Iranian mosque in Hamburg, the most important Shiite mosque in Europe.

He had also been the first imam to hear the footsteps of the approaching revolution, and had immediately left his mosque and gone to Iraq to assist Khomeini.

Having lived in Germany for years, Beheshti had an insider's view of the Western world. This is exactly what the ageing Khomeini needed to help him realise his dream of an Islamic state.

Beheshti understood the value of folk tales and the power of photographic images. His plan was to focus the attention of Western television on Khomeini and then to weave his magic web: 'An elderly imam sits on a simple Persian rug. He lives in exile, dines on bread and milk, and defies America!'

Unlike Beheshti, Khomeini was so ignorant of the modern world that he still had trouble saying the word 'radio'.

It was nearly nightfall when Beheshti knocked on the door of Khomeini's house in Najaf. Khalkhal opened the door.

'I am Beheshti, the imam of the mosque in Hamburg,' he said, introducing himself. 'I have come here to talk to the ayatollah.'

In those days nothing happened in the Khomeini household without Khalkhal's consent. Pilgrims were always coming to the door, hoping to meet the ayatollah. Khalkhal had never met or heard of Beheshti, but he was immediately struck by his air of confidence and his stylish attire. 'What do you wish to speak to the ayatollah about?' he enquired.

'I understand your curiosity, but I have no intention of discussing this matter with anyone but the ayatollah.'

Khalkhal ushered Beheshti into the guest room and ordered the servant to bring him some tea. 'I hope you don't mind waiting,' he said.

Khomeini had never met Beheshti either, but he had known his father. The old man was dead, but he had once been the head of the influential Friday Mosque in Isfahan.

'The ayatollah was a friend of your father's,' Khalkhal

reported back to him. 'He's looking forward to meeting you.' And he escorted Beheshti into the simply furnished library, where the ageing ayatollah was seated on his rug.

Beheshti came into the library, bowed to the ayatollah and shut the door behind him.

Paris

Alef Lam Ra.
We shall never know in advance
What Your plans are.
I shall follow You.
I shall follow You with my head bowed.

No one had seen it coming, no one had been expecting it and no one knew exactly what was going on, but one day the ageing Ayatollah Khomeini suddenly appeared out of nowhere at Charles de Gaulle Airport in Paris.

There were four of them: Khomeini, Beheshti, Khalkhal and Khomeini's wife, Batul.

During the fourteen years of his exile in Iraq, Khomeini had never once left the city of Najaf. He woke up every day at five-thirty, said his morning prayer and read the Koran. At seven-thirty his faithful wife brought him his breakfast, after which he worked in his modest library until twelve-thirty. Then it was time for the noon prayer. After lunch he took a short nap, then went back to work until four.

Late in the afternoon he received visitors, mostly Iranian carpet merchants who had travelled to Iraq on business, though some were Islamic dissidents disguised as merchants. They carried messages back and forth, so that Khomeini could maintain his secret contacts with the ayatollahs in Qom.

During the winter, he spent the day in his library, but during the spring and summer he went out at six o'clock, after it had cooled down a bit, to work in his garden.

Later in the evening, he washed his hands and face, put on his robe and went to the Imam Ali Mosque, with his wife walking several feet behind him.

And now here he was in Charles de Gaulle Airport, leaning on a trolley by a baggage carousel.

After they had all collected their bags, the owner of the largest Persian carpet emporium in Paris drove them to a house in Neauphle-le-Château, where he had arranged for them to stay.

Approximately sixty years ago, Khomeini had left his native village and gone to Qom to become an imam.

In those days there were no cars in his village, much less roads for them to drive on. He walked through the mountains to the city of Arak, where he was planning to take a stagecoach to Qom, for it was not until decades later that Reza Khan, the father of the present shah, modernised the country and, with the help of the British, built a railway system.

When Khomeini reached Arak, he was surprised to see a lorry filled with pilgrims on their way to the holy city of Qom. The Armenian driver offered him a lift. It turned out to be an unforgettable trip, but when Khomeini finally reached Qom after the bumpy ride through the hills, he felt sick from the diesel fumes.

Later, after becoming an ayatollah, he had himself driven around in an elegant Mercedes, but every time he stepped into the car and caught a whiff of diesel fuel, his nausea returned.

And now, as he was being driven to the quiet suburb through the streets of Paris, he smelled it again.

Beheshti, who had organised everything in advance, pulled out his appointment book and picked up the phone.

He dialled the number of a young Iranian journalist who worked for the American television network ABC and informed her that Khomeini had moved from Najaf to Paris. He explained that from now on the ayatollah would be leading the revolution from Paris and offered her a scoop: ABC could be the first network to interview Khomeini in Paris, but she had to decide quickly, or else he would call the BBC.

The next day an ABC van pulled up in front of Khomeini's house in Paris.

It was late afternoon in the city, but early evening in Iran.

Am Ramazan rode excitedly into the alley, hopped down from his donkey and hurried into Aqa Jaan's study. 'Khomeini is in Paris!' he exclaimed. 'He's going to be on television any moment now!'

'He's where?'

'We can watch it in the Hajji Taghi Khan Mosque. Are you coming?'

Aqa Jaan didn't want to go to the Hajji Taghi Khan. It was the mosque everyone was going to these days. It had become the centre of political upheaval in Senejan.

Only the elderly still attended Aqa Jaan's mosque. But the Hajji Taghi Khan Mosque was so full that people had to stand outside. Young imams from Qom held fiery speeches there every night, whipping the masses into such frenzy that they poured out into the streets to demonstrate.

'I'm sorry,' Aqa Jaan said to Am Ramazan, 'I'm busy right now. I'll come later.'

And yet he was curious. He felt obliged to be a witness. To see everything, record it in his journal and save it for posterity. He *had* to be there. So he put on his coat and hat and set off for the Hajji Taghi Khan.

The mosque was packed and hundreds of people were milling around outside the gate. He sought a dark corner where he wouldn't be noticed, then reproached himself: 'You're not a thief, so why are you hiding in the dark? Go in and see what's happening.'

He pushed his way through the crowd. The men were in the courtyard, the women in the prayer room.

At a certain point he realised he wasn't making any headway, so he turned round and went up to the roof. There he found a spot with a good view of the mosque. Three large television sets had been mounted high up on the wall so everyone could watch the unprecedented event.

Aqa Jaan was reminded of the portable television that Shahbal had brought home years ago so that he and Alsaberi could watch the moon landing. The conversation he'd had with Shahbal was still fixed firmly in his mind.

'May I have a word with you, Aqa Jaan?' Shahbal had asked him.

'Of course, my boy. What's on your mind?'

'The moon.'

'The moon?'

'No, I mean, television.'

'Television?' Aqa Jaan had said in surprise.

'An imam needs to know what's going on. He has to keep up with current events,' Shahbal had replied.

Alsaberi had died and Khalkhal had taken his place. Then Ahmad had come, and now there was this.

*   *   *

There was a flurry of movement by the gate.

'*Salla ala Mohammad wa ale Mohammad!*' shouted the men standing in the street.

Aqa Jaan looked down at the gate. A group of bearded men in stylish suits came into the courtyard and ushered a young imam over to the television screens, where Khomeini's interview would soon be shown. Aqa Jaan recognised the men: they were the merchants who had taken control of the bazaar.

A woman came up to the men in the suits, exchanged a few words with them and went back into the prayer room. It was Zinat, but because she was so far away and wearing a black chador like the other women, Aqa Jaan hadn't recognised her.

A young bearded man switched on the television sets. The crowd held its breath, and people craned their necks to get a better view.

At first the camera showed the quiet streets of Neauphle-le-Château. Then you saw a couple of French women go into a supermarket. Next a school bus drew up to a bus shelter, where you could see a brightly coloured ad of a sleek young French woman. Two girls with rucksacks got out of the bus and stared straight into the lens. The camera then panned to a house and showed the trees, the pergola, the garden.

At last Khomeini appeared on the screen. He was sitting on a Persian rug.

The crowd in the mosque went wild and shouted in one voice, '*Salaam bar Khomeini! Salaam bar Khomeini!*'

Back in those days you couldn't watch a live foreign broadcast on Iran's state-controlled television network, but the organisers had put a satellite dish on the roof of the mosque. The images were being beamed in from neighbouring Iraq.

The camera zoomed in on Khomeini's face. It was the first time people had actually seen the ageing ayatollah who wanted to oust the Americans.

Few people knew Khomeini personally, and no recent pictures of him had ever been published. Since no one knew exactly what he looked like, the camera stayed on his face for a long time. He had a long grey beard, and his face glowed in the light of the cameras, which made him look like a saint.

He started to stand up. Someone – probably one of the camera crew – offered him a helping hand, but he waved it away and got to his feet unaided.

He went out into the garden, where two rugs – a large one and a small one – had already been spread on the ground. He took off his shoes and stepped onto the small rug. Then he reached into his pocket, took out a compass and tried to find the east, but couldn't see the needle. So he patiently put on his glasses, consulted the compass, and turned to face Mecca.

Beheshti was standing behind him, on the large rug. Khalkhal had deliberately kept out of sight. He knew that, as Khomeini's most loyal adviser, it would be better to remain anonymous.

Khomeini's wife, Batul, shrouded from head to foot in a black chador, came out for the prayer and took her place behind Beheshti. The camera focused on her for a moment, and she stood as still as a statue. Then the scene shifted to a green hedge, where a few French women and their children were watching in amazement.

Within days a horde of journalists from all over the globe descended on Neauphle-le-Château, thereby focusing the attention of the world on the approaching revolution.

Until then Beheshti and Khalkhal had been the only

men at Khomeini's side, but within twenty-four hours of the interview seven more arrived from America, Germany, England and Paris. For a while they formed the new Revolutionary Council.

Later, after the shah had been toppled and the revolution had been won, they were appointed to top government posts. It was these men who became president, prime minister, minister of finance, minister of foreign affairs, minister of industrial affairs, chairman of the Parliament and chief of the newly formed secret police.

What became of these seven men? Within a few short years, one was executed as an American spy, another was imprisoned for corruption, three of them were assassinated by the Resistance, the man who'd served as president fled to Paris, where he requested political asylum, and shortly thereafter the prime minister was dismissed from his post.

In Tehran millions of people took part in demonstrations being held almost daily. It seemed that no earthly power could prevent Khomeini's return.

The face of the country changed almost overnight. Men grew beards and women enveloped themselves in chadors.

Massive strikes in the oil sector brought the country to an economic standstill. Workers abandoned their machines, students stopped attending classes, schoolchildren left their schools and everyone took to the streets.

The revolution also left its mark on the house of the mosque.

Zinat openly distanced herself from the family, and Sadiq went out more often. Both she and Zinat often attended mass gatherings of Islamic women.

Sadiq, who had never worn a headscarf inside the house,

now swathed herself in a chador when she was at home. She used to spend all of her time indoors, cooking and taking care of Lizard. Now she dropped everything in order to go out. She came home late, grabbed a bite to eat and went to bed.

Aqa Jaan went to the bazaar every day, but the carpet business was the last thing on people's minds. He felt himself to be more and more of a stranger in his own shop.

The storerooms were stacked with rugs that should have been posted to other countries weeks ago. The corridors and workrooms were filled with yarns and other materials that should have been sent to the workshops in the outlying villages.

His trusty office boy, whose job it was to usher customers into his office and bring them tea, had grown a beard. He no longer came to work on time, and left the building at odd moments, saying only that he had to go to the mosque.

The employees had cleared out one of the offices and turned it into a prayer room. They had removed the desks and chairs, put down a few rugs and hung a large portrait of Khomeini on the wall. They had even brought in a mosque samovar and set it on a table.

No one did any work. His employees hung around the shop all day, discussing the latest events. They drank tea in the prayer room and listened to the BBC's Persian broadcasts so they could follow the developments in Paris.

Aqa Jaan could see that his business was on the brink of collapse, but he was powerless to do anything about it.

At home he saw that Fakhri Sadat no longer sparkled. She had lost her customary cheerfulness. She used to go into town periodically to buy new clothes, especially nightwear, but her shopping sprees were now a thing of the past.

Aqa Jaan always enjoyed watching Fakhri standing in front of the mirror, feeling her breasts to see if they were still firm. But she didn't do that any more, and she also stopped wearing her jewellery. One day she tidied up her jewellery box, which had always lain on her dressing table, and put it away for good.

Nasrin and Ensi were also victims of the change. No one seemed to notice that Aqa Jaan's daughters had reached a marriageable age and were still not spoken for.

Aqa Jaan missed Shahbal. He wanted to talk to him, to pour his heart out to him, but he didn't get the chance. Shahbal came home for a quick visit every once in a while, then left again. Aqa Jaan knew that he was no longer attending classes. He tried to approach him a few times, but he got the feeling that Shahbal didn't want to talk to him.

And yet he trusted him. He knew that Shahbal would eventually come back to him.

Aqa Jaan had taken to going down to the river and strolling along its banks in the dark. He remembered his father's advice: 'When you're feeling sad, go down to the river. Talk to the river, and your sorrows will be borne away on its swift current.'

'I don't want to complain,' Aqa Jaan said to the river, 'but there's a lump in my throat the size of a rock.'

His eyes were stinging. A tear rolled down his cheek and fell to the ground. The river caught it and bore it away in the darkness, without telling a soul.

Tehran

Aqa Jaan was in his office at the bazaar. The office boy had just brought him a glass of tea when he heard a sudden commotion downstairs in the workroom. The employees had left their posts and were watching the two o'clock news.

'What's going on?' Aqa Jaan called.

'The shah has fled!' the boy yelled up the stairs.

'*Allahu akbar!*' someone exclaimed.

There was no mention on the news of the shah fleeing, so apparently it had been a rumour, yet it was such a persistent rumour that the regime had been compelled to put the shah on television. He was shown receiving some of his generals, which only aggravated the situation. The shah, who used to appear on television every night, had been absent a great deal in recent months. Now people couldn't believe their eyes: he had grown thin and looked like a man who was terrified of losing all he had.

The rumour had contained only a small grain of truth.

The next day a new rumour was making the rounds: 'Farah Diba is fleeing to America with the children!'

This wasn't entirely true. Farah Diba wasn't fleeing with the children; her mother was.

A street war was about to break out in Tehran. The protestors were getting close to the palace. According to army intelligence, the mullahs were planning to attack the palace, so the shah had asked Farah Diba to leave the country and to take the children with her.

She refused. 'I'm not going to abandon you at a time like this.'

'I'm thinking about the children's safety, not my own,' the shah replied.

'Then we need to come up with a different plan. I'll ask my mother to go with them,' was her answer.

While a helicopter was conveying the shah's children from the palace to a nearby military base, where they would be flown out of the country in an air-force jet, Nosrat was taking the night train to Senejan.

The train drew into the station at four o'clock in the morning. Nosrat took a taxi to the house, then tiptoed into the guest room and fell asleep.

In the morning Lizard came to his room and woke him up.

'I've got something for you,' Nosrat said, and he took a pair of leather gloves out of his bag. 'Here, put them on, then we'll go to the bazaar and get something to eat. I'm starving.'

Lizard put on the gloves and crawled into town on his hands and feet alongside Nosrat. When they reached the giant statue of the shah on horseback, Lizard looked at Nosrat to see if it would be all right for him to climb onto it. Nosrat winked, and a few seconds later Lizard was seated in the saddle behind the shah.

Lizard was the only person who'd ever had the nerve to do such a thing.

At first no one noticed, but soon people stopped to stare. When he realised that he had a crowd of enthusiastic onlookers, Lizard got bolder. He leaned forward, threw his arms round the horse's neck and pretended to gallop. Then he leapt from the horse's neck to the shah's head, slid down the horse's long tail and hopped back into the saddle – all with such extraordinary agility that he looked more like a monkey than a lizard.

More and more people gathered round, and they were all clapping.

Two policemen came striding up, but didn't dare to intervene. One of them reported the incident on his walkie-talkie. A while later a van pulled up with a squad of riot police, but since they hadn't been ordered to disperse the crowd either, they merely kept an eye on things. The situation in the country was so tense that anything they did could trigger a riot.

On the one hand, it could be viewed as a minor incident in which a crippled child had climbed onto the statue of the shah. On the other hand, his innocent antics were not without political overtones.

The weakness of the regime was obvious to everyone who saw Lizard cavorting on the horse. Yet no one could have suspected that the shah's statue would soon be toppled by a hysterical mob.

The next day the front page of the local newspaper featured a picture of Lizard, dangling from the neck of the royal horse. Within an hour the paper had been sold out – for the first time in its history.

Everyone who read the article hurried over to the mosque to see Lizard with their very own eyes. They usually found him sitting on the roof.

It was a turning point in Lizard's life. He had always been in the habit of climbing to the top of one of the minarets – where the storks used to have their nests – to read his books. Now he had an audience.

*   *   *

No one had ever come to the mosque to demonstrate, but nowadays hundreds of young people came every day to see Lizard.

'You're a bad influence on him,' Aqa Jaan grumbled to Nosrat on the phone.

'What do you mean? I don't see the problem.'

'He climbs into the minaret like a monkey. He's turning into a major attraction here in Senejan.'

'Let him do something he enjoys. Besides, it might help to improve the mosque's image.'

'We're talking about a mosque, not a circus. We shouldn't make ourselves more ridiculous than we are already. First that business with Ahmad, and now Lizard.'

'I'll talk to him,' Nosrat said.

Two nights later Nosrat once again took the night train to Senejan.

He had no way of knowing that this was the last trip he would ever make to his home town with a head full of black hair. The next time he came, his hair had turned grey and his face had changed so much that no one recognised him.

Nosrat asked Lizard to come to his room. He had a handful of flyers with a black-and-white photograph of Khomeini on the front, which he stuffed into the boy's pockets. 'The next time a lot of people are gathered outside the mosque,' he instructed him, 'climb into your minaret and toss these flyers down to them. You got that? See, like this,' he said, flicking his wrist. 'All of them in one throw.'

At eleven-thirty Lizard climbed into the minaret. After a few wild leaps to attract everyone's attention, he tossed the flyers to the crowd. Nosrat, positioned on the roof, began snapping pictures of the swirling flyers and the people trying to catch them.

The images appeared in every major newspaper in Iran.

It was the first time a photograph of Khomeini had ever been published in a newspaper. The regime was caught off-guard, but was unable to take any action since the newspapers were united in their support of the publication. Aqa Jaan bought the papers and tucked them into the chest in which he kept his journals.

Nosrat and his camera were on hand for every major event. The photographs he took of these landmark moments were printed daily in the newspapers.

He also had a cine camera, which he'd used to film the first big demonstration in Tehran, the one that had been led by Beheshti, who had crossed the border illegally to lead it. Nosrat had done a good job of documenting the presence of the ayatollahs and conveying the strength of their leadership.

When you watched his film reports, you could see what was in store for the nation.

Nosrat regularly sent his extraordinary footage to the Revolutionary Council in Paris. As a result, he and Beheshti developed a close working relationship. Beheshti began phoning him at home to tell him when a demonstration was going to be held so Nosrat would be sure to film it.

The Council then arranged for a man who worked at the airport in Tehran to function as a secret go-between. Nosrat was instructed to hand him the pictures and film rolls, which were then put on the next flight to Paris.

Nosrat was supposedly neutral, but sometimes he wondered which side derived the most benefit from his work. Was he making propaganda for Khomeini? No, he wasn't committed to any person or any cause. Religion meant nothing to him. Nor did politics. He thought only of his camera. Other people's wishes or his own personal viewpoint didn't matter. He simply recorded what he saw.

Nosrat was also secretly in touch with Shahbal. He often gave him photographs, which Shahbal then published in his underground newspaper. One time they ran into each other at a demonstration and had a long talk. Nosrat had read Shahbal's newspaper, so he knew that his party was sharply divided on the issue of the Islamic state that Khomeini was hoping to establish.

As Khomeini's displays of power escalated, the leftist underground factions were confronted with the question of how to deal with him. Should they support Khomeini, or should they align themselves against him? Heated debates resulted in a painful break-up: a tiny minority refused to support Khomeini, choosing instead to continue their work underground, while the majority opted to lay down their weapons and support Khomeini's anti-American crusade.

Shahbal, who had left the university long ago, sided with the majority.

The turning point came on the seventeenth day of the month of Shahrivar. The ayatollahs in Tehran had joined forces in an effort to get as many people as possible into the mosques. At eight o'clock that Friday evening the worshippers left their mosques and marched to Parliament Square, shouting slogans all the way. Both Khomeini supporters and the regime were determined to show their strength.

As thousands of demonstrators headed towards Parliament Square from every corner of Tehran, soldiers left their barracks, determined to teach the protestors a lesson.

The man in charge, General Rahimi, was sitting in an

army jeep parked in a corner of the square, keeping an eye on things from behind his dark glasses. When every inch of the square was packed with protestors, he ordered his tanks to block off the side streets so the crowd wouldn't be able to escape.

Meanwhile, the unsuspecting demonstrators were passing out flowers to the soldiers, which the soldiers gladly accepted. 'Peace! Peace!' the crowd roared. 'Peace, soldiers!' And the officers in the square waved peacefully back.

What the crowd didn't know was that the goal of the demonstration was actually to seize and occupy the Parliament. Nosrat had been informed ahead of time and already had his camera in position.

As soon as the first row of demonstrators reached the Parliament, a handful of young men started to climb the fence. Sharpshooters on the nearby roofs opened fire, and the young men fell to the ground, dead.

People fled every which way, screaming, 'La ilaha illa Allah!'

Despite the mad scramble, dozens of other young men ran towards the gate and tried to scale the fence, but the sharpshooters shot them down as well.

'La ilaha illa Allah!' the protestors cried, pushing and pulling the fence, trying to tear it down so they could get inside the building. But before they got the chance, the army opened fire on the crowd from all four corners of the square.

Within minutes, there were hundreds of dead and wounded.

Nosrat, safely ensconced on a nearby balcony, recorded the incident on film.

The soldiers chased after the demonstrators, shooting everyone in sight. Women pounded on the doors of houses, begging to be let in, while men climbed onto roofs and into trees, and children crawled under cars. The streets were strewn with shoes, jackets, caps, cameras, head-scarves and hundreds of black chadors.

Nosrat captured it all: the general in sunglasses giving the order to shoot, the young men falling off the fence, people crawling through drainage ditches, people trying to flee over the blockades, the tanks rolling into the square from the side streets, the scattered bodies.

Seven minutes later a hush fell over the square. All those who could flee had fled, and hundreds had sought refuge in nearby houses. Only the dead and the wounded remained.

The general removed his dark glasses, cast his eye over the scene of the battle and ordered the square to be cleared. Then he got back in his jeep and drove to the palace to deliver his report to the shah.

His orders to his men were clear: no reporters were to be allowed in the square and any cameras that were found were to be destroyed on the spot.

As soon as the general left, Nosrat escaped via the rooftops.

Three days later ABC broadcast Nosrat's film clip. More than seven hundred people had died.

Aqa Jaan followed the events on Lizard's television.

The shah, shocked by the incident, addressed the nation: 'I have heard the voice of the revolution! I have heard the voice of my people. Some mistakes have been made. To restore order I shall appoint a new prime minister. I ask my people to be patient a while longer.'

His voice trembled. His speech was rambling, and he stuttered.

A few days later he did appoint a new prime minister. Khomeini rejected the man, however, so the new cabinet lasted only a few weeks. The shah cast around for another candidate, but no one dared to side openly with him.

Bowing to the inevitable, the shah handed power over to the military. General Azhari, the most pro-American general in the army, put together a military cabinet and declared a curfew in Tehran.

To flaunt the order, Khomeini called on everyone to go up to their roofs at night. Millions of Iranians obeyed his call, climbing onto their roofs and shouting, 'Death to America! *Allahu akbar!*'

Why wasn't Aqa Jaan up on his roof? Wasn't he opposed to the regime? Wasn't he pleased that the shah was on his way out and Khomeini on his way in?

What would the neighbours think if no one in his family went up to the roof?

'Fakhri!' Aqa Jaan called.

But people were making so much noise that she didn't hear him.

'Girls!'

Nasrin, his elder daughter, came out to see why they'd been called.

'Everybody's up on the roof. I'm going up to ours. Where's your mother? Don't you want to come too?'

On the stairs he bumped into Lizard. 'Would you go down and get Muezzin for me?' Aqa Jaan asked him.

Lizard scurried down to the cellar to fetch Muezzin.

A little while later Aqa Jaan, Muezzin, Fakhri Sadat and her two daughters – encased in black chadors – stood on the roof and shouted along with everyone else, '*Allahu akbar! Allahu akbar!*'

Lizard sat at the edge of the dome and stared in astonishment at the hysterical masses.

* * *

The shah did his best to find a reputable politician who would be able to reconcile the cabinet. No one seemed willing to undertake such a difficult and hopeless task.

At last he managed to persuade Bakhtiar, the second most important man in the National Front, to serve as prime minister. But Bakhtiar had one condition: he would accept the offer only if the shah agreed to leave the country immediately for an indefinite period of time.

The shah agreed. From that moment on things happened swiftly, as if an avalanche were sweeping down a mountain and dragging everyone and everything along with it.

The next morning when Aqa Jaan arrived at the bazaar, the shop was buzzing with excitement. The shah was leaving!

Aqa Jaan joined his employees, who were clustered round a television. The shah and Farah Diba were at Tehran Airport, surrounded by a group of officials.

Bakhtiar shook his hand and wished him a pleasant journey.

A military officer suddenly threw himself at the shah's feet, kissed his shoes and begged him not to leave. The shah was so moved that tears rolled down his cheeks.

Another man took out a Koran and held it over the shah's head for him to walk under – the traditional Iranian way of wishing your loved ones a safe journey.

The shah kissed the Koran and walked beneath it on his way to the plane. Farah Diba kissed the Koran and followed her husband. They boarded the plane, and it flew off towards the border, escorted by two fighter jets.

Thirteen days later Aqa Jaan, Fakhri Sadat, Nasrin, Ensi and Lizard sat glued to the television, watching mechanics at a French airport prepare a Concorde for Khomeini's history-making return.

Bakhtiar had warned the ayatollah that his plane wouldn't be given permission to land, but Khomeini had cast his warning to the winds. 'Bakhtiar is a nobody. I will decide what happens! I'm going to appoint a revolutionary cabinet. I'm coming home!'

Early in the morning millions of people streamed to the airport in Tehran, where the Concorde was scheduled to land. One of them was Shahbal. He wanted to see this momentous event for himself and write an article about it.

Nosrat, standing in an open jeep with a film camera on his shoulder, was being driven to and fro by a man with a beard. He was the only cameraman allowed to film the arrival at such close quarters.

The Concorde came into view above the airport.

'*Salla ala Mohammad! Khomeini gosh amad!* Welcome, Khomeini!'

The plane landed, the door opened and Khomeini appeared at the top of the stairs. He waved modestly.

'*Salaam bar Khomeini!*' the crowd roared.

Aqa Jaan left the house. In the alley he ran into Ahmad. Without knowing why, he took him into his arms and gave him a brief hug. Neither of them could have guessed what the future held in store for them.

Qadi

'*A staghfirullah, astaghfirullah, astaghfirullah, astagh-firullah, astaghfirullah, astaghfirullah, astaghfirullah, astaghfirullah, astaghfirullah, astaghfirullah, astaghfirullah, astaghfirullah, astaghfirullah,*' Khalkhal chanted to himself as he headed towards Khomeini's room.

People chant '*astaghfirullah*' when they've committed a sin or are afraid they're going to, or if they want to avoid a confrontation but know they'll have to face it anyway. Sometimes it's simply an expression of astonishment at an unexpected turn of events or a request for God's forgiveness.

Or you chant it, as Khalkhal was doing now, when you're sure you're about to make an irrevocable mistake.

Khomeini had no desire to live in the shah's palace. Instead he chose to occupy a room in a seminary in one of Tehran's poorer neighbourhoods.

It was dark when he came in and sat down on his rug. Someone brought him a glass of tea and some dates. After his first sip of tea, he asked for a pen and piece of paper.

He spent half an hour in his room by himself, then sent for Khalkhal. Khalkhal sensed that it was urgent. He shut the door behind him, knelt before the ayatollah and kissed his hand.

Khalkhal was the first person to perform this act of

obeisance since Khomeini had been welcomed back to the country as its leader. It was his way of saying that he would carry out whatever mission Khomeini chose to send him on.

Khomeini whispered to him to come closer. Realising that the ayatollah wished to impart secret information, Khalkhal leaned forward until their heads were almost touching.

'I appoint you to be a *qadi*, a judge. You are now Allah's judicial envoy,' Khomeini said, and he gave him a document.

Khalkhal's hands began to shake.

'America will do everything in its power to destroy us. The vestiges of the old regime must be wiped out. Eliminate all those who oppose the revolution! If your father rises up, eliminate him! If your brother rises up, eliminate him! Destroy all that gets in the way of Islam! I have appointed you as my representative, but you are responsible only to God. Show the world that the revolution cannot be undone. Begin at once. There is no time to waste!'

Khalkhal kissed Khomeini's hand again, then stood up and hurriedly left the room to begin his mission.

Even though it was night, Khalkhal put on the dark glasses he had bought in Paris.

This Khalkhal bore little resemblance to the Khalkhal who had set off a riot in Senejan to prevent Farah Diba from opening a cinema. With his black turban and long black beard, which had recently begun to go grey, he now had an aura of power. As Allah's judge, he would inspire fear.

An hour later, with some files tucked under his arm, he stepped into a waiting jeep, which drove him to the city's largest slaughterhouse, where thousands of cows and sheep were slaughtered daily to feed Tehran's burgeoning population.

The top officials of the old regime had been arrested and brought to the slaughterhouse in the greatest of secrecy. The regime was so terrified that the Americans would try to liberate the prisoners that they had brought them to this stinking hellhole and thrown them in the stalls beside the cows.

Khalkhal entered a dark, bare room. In the middle were a table and two chairs – one for Allah's judge and another, much lower, for the accused – and a ceiling lamp, placed in such a way that its yellow glow would light only the face of the accused.

There was little time. By dawn it had to be clear to the world that the old regime was gone for good and that the Americans would have no opportunity to restore the shah to power.

Khalkhal laid a file on the table. 'Bring in the accused!' he said to the guard.

The first to be brought in was Hoveyda, the shah's former prime minister. He was led into the room in handcuffs. Hoveyda had served as prime minister for fourteen years. He had rarely been seen without an orchid in the lapel of his elegant suit, or without his walking stick and pipe. Now he was dressed in a filthy pair of pyjamas.

There was a third person in the room: a masked photographer, who kept circling round Hoveyda, taking pictures of him from every angle.

'The accused may be seated,' Khalkhal said curtly, and he lowered himself into his chair.

Hoveyda sat down.

'You now find yourself before Allah's judge,' Khalkhal said, his voice as hard as steel. 'Your case has been reviewed. You have been sentenced to death. Do you have anything to say to that?'

Hoveyda, who had been received as a guest of honour by the American president; Hoveyda, who had been given three standing ovations by the American Senate; Hoveyda, who had studied law at an American university, couldn't believe that this stinking stall was a courtroom. And so he made no reply, though his lips moved involuntarily, as if he were smoking an invisible pipe.

'Did you say something?' Khalkhal asked.

'No,' Hoveyda replied numbly.

'The accused is hereby sentenced to death!' Khalkhal said. 'The execution is to be carried out immediately!'

Hoveyda, still not quite realising that he was about to be executed, was led away by two guards.

They took him to the warehouse behind the main slaughter room, which was stacked with thousands of hides from freshly slaughtered cows. The stench was so bad that you had to hold your nose. The guards propped Hoveyda up against the wall between the stacks of hides and tied a blindfold over his eyes. According to Islamic custom, he was offered a glass of water, but he waved it away.

Hoveyda trembled in his pyjamas, still unable to believe he was going to be executed. He thought they were simply trying to frighten him. He heard Khalkhal's footsteps in the corridor, and a moment later Khalkhal came in and signalled to the guards to kneel and aim their rifles.

'Ready, aim—' Khalkhal began.

'I'm innocent!' Hoveyda cried in a broken voice. 'I demand to see a lawyer!'

'Fire!' Khalkhal ordered.

Seven shots rang out. Hoveyda slumped to the ground. His head struck the damp stone floor of the warehouse, and the photographer rushed up to take pictures of his bullet-ridden body.

Khalkhal returned to the interrogation room and called for the next prisoner.

The former chief of the secret police was led in. He had heard the shots and was so frightened that he could barely walk.

'Sit down!'

The guards lowered him into the chair.

'Are you Nassiri?'

There was a long pause. 'Yes,' he said at last.

'Were you the chief of the secret police who ordered the arrest, torture and death of hundreds of resistance fighters?'

Nassiri made no reply.

'Were you chief of the secret police?' Khalkhal repeated.

'Yes,' he said softly.

'Allah's judge hereby sentences you to death!' Khalkhal exclaimed. 'The execution is to be carried out immediately. Is there anything you wish to add?'

The dreaded Nassiri, whose very name had made people quake, began to cry and beg for mercy, but Khalkhal motioned to the guards to take him away.

Nassiri was led to the warehouse where Hoveyda had just been executed. The guards blindfolded him, offered him a glass of water and stood him against the wall.

'Take your positions!' Khalkhal commanded.

The guards knelt and aimed their rifles at Nassiri.

'Fire until you have no more bullets left!' Khalkhal thundered.

Shots rang out, and the guards fired until they had no more bullets left, thus ensuring that the body stayed upright until the firing stopped. Only when the last bullet had been pumped into Nassiri's body did he fall into a stack of fresh cowhides, where he sprawled, face down, with his arms outstretched.

Khalkhal kept going until dawn, until all of the ministers and high-level officials who had been arrested and imprisoned in the slaughterhouse had been executed.

When he was through, he washed his hands and ordered breakfast. Boiled eggs, milk, honey and freshly baked bread were brought in on a silver tray and placed in front of him, along with the morning edition of the paper.

The front page had a picture of the blindfolded Hoveyda, his arms held wide as the first bullet slammed into his chest.

In one week Khalkhal met with fifteen young imams from Qom. They were all students at a seminary, where they were studying Islamic law.

He appointed them as Islamic judges and sent them out to the larger cities to try those officials of the former regime who had been directly involved in crimes against the people. All fifteen judges had his permission to show no mercy.

There was a knock on Aqa Jaan's door. He hadn't come home yet from the bazaar, so Lizard opened the gate. Three armed men wearing green headbands came charging into the courtyard. They were soldiers in the Army of Allah – a militant faction formed during the revolution to carry out Khomeini's orders.

'Where's Ahmad?' one of the men snapped at Lizard.

Fakhri Sadat, who was in the kitchen, could see the men through the window, but couldn't go out and talk to them because she wasn't wearing a chador. She opened the window and shouted to Lizard, 'Would you please bring me my chador?'

He scuttled off and came back with it. She put on her chador and went into the courtyard. 'Gentlemen,' she said, 'how can I help you?'

'Where's Ahmad?' one of them repeated in an insolent tone of voice. 'We've been ordered to bring him in.'

'Bring him where?'

'To the Islamic Court.'

Just then Ahmad emerged from the library. Dressed casually in his long cotton shirt rather than his imam turban and robe, he headed towards the *hauz*. The men raced over to him.

Startled, Ahmad asked them what they were doing in his house.

'We've been sent to pick you up. You're going to be tried before an Islamic court.'

'Why? What for?'

'We don't know.'

'I'm not going anywhere,' Ahmad said, and he knelt by the *hauz* to wash his hands.

The men seized him from behind and started dragging him towards the gate.

Ahmad struggled to free himself. 'What's the meaning of this?' he cried. 'Let me go!'

But the men ignored him.

Ahmad squirmed around until he was facing Mecca. 'Help me, Allah!'

Fakhri Sadat quickly ordered Lizard to shut the gate. As he was closing it, Jawad, who had arrived home last night, came careering down the stairs.

'Phone Aqa Jaan!' Fakhri Sadat said to him. 'Hurry!'

Then she went over to the men and planted herself in front of them. 'What do you think you're doing?' she said. 'This is the imam of the mosque! You should be ashamed of yourselves!'

At the sound of Aqa Jaan's footsteps in the alley, Lizard re-opened the gate. He was trying to tell him something in his usual gibberish when Aqa Jaan suddenly saw two men trying to overpower the struggling Ahmad. 'Stop it!' he yelled. 'Stop it! What do you think you're doing? Let go of him!'

Muezzin also came hurrying into the courtyard, while Nasrin and Ensi watched from upstairs. Aqa Jaan pulled one of the men off Ahmad, but Ahmad lost his balance and fell over. He scrambled to his feet and was about to make a dash for the roof when one of the men kicked him so hard that he fell down again. This time the man grabbed him, shoved his knee in his back and handcuffed him.

Lizard cowered, bewildered, next to Muezzin.

Aqa Jaan tried to reason with the men. 'I'll bring him to the court myself. I don't want him to be dragged off in handcuffs. I'm Aqa Jaan, you can trust me, I'll go with you. This isn't the proper way to do things.'

One of the men shoved him aside. Jawad quickly inter-vened and tried to keep his father from shoving him back. 'Leave it,' he said. 'You've done all you can.'

'Allah! Allah! Allah! Allah!' Aqa Jaan exclaimed as the three men pushed Ahmad roughly into a jeep.

'Which court are you taking him to?' Aqa Jaan called out helplessly.

But the jeep roared off, leaving his question unanswered.

Fakhri Sadat, weeping, was led upstairs by her daughters.

Jawad tried to get Aqa Jaan to come into the house, but he refused.

'This is a disaster,' Aqa Jaan said. 'I have to find out where they're taking him.' And he rushed off through the gate.

*　　*　　*

The men blindfolded Ahmad and drove him to a secret location, which had been turned into an Islamic court only the day before.

When they removed the blindfold, Ahmad saw that he was standing in a dimly lit room. He had no idea where he was, though he knew he had to be in a cellar, because he'd counted thirteen steps on the way down.

There were no windows. The walls were covered with large strips of black cloth on which sacred texts had been scrawled in white paint.

The only furniture consisted of a table and two chairs. A green flag – the symbol of Islam – had been nailed crookedly to the wall behind the taller of the two chairs.

Ahmad was ordered to sit on the low chair. The men left him alone in the airless room, with a yellow lamp shining down ominously on his face.

For one long hour he sat there, waiting for something to happen.

The silence and the uncertainty were terrifying.

He heard a door open somewhere, and there were hurried footsteps on the stairs.

A guard came in. 'Stand up for the Islamic judge!' he bellowed.

Ahmad stood up. He could just make out the figure of a young imam, who promptly sat down across from him.

'The accused may be seated!' he snapped.

Ahmad sat down and tried to see if he knew the imam. But he was so blinded by the lamplight that he couldn't get a clear look at his face.

'I'm going to read out your name,' the judge began. 'If it is correct, you may say yes. Then I'm going to ask you a few questions to which you must reply.'

'I am the imam of the Friday Mosque,' Ahmad said.

'Before you start, I would like to have my robe and turban brought to me. If not, I refuse to answer your questions.'

'You are Ahmad Alsaberi, the son of Mohammad Alsaberi.'

Ahmad maintained a stubborn silence.

'As an active member of the secret police,' the judge continued, 'the suspect has committed the worst crime an imam can commit.'

'That's not true!' Ahmad burst out. 'I haven't done anything!'

'We're got the evidence in here,' the judge said, holding up a file.

'Then it's been falsified. I should know whether or not I've done anything wrong, and I don't have any crimes on my conscience.'

'We have proof that you were working hand in glove with the shah's secret police,' the judge said.

'You can't have proof, because I wasn't working with them. As an imam I have contacts with all kinds of people – everyone from beggars to the chief of the secret police. You have no doubt received reports of those contacts, but they could hardly be considered evidence in a court of law! I was the imam of the mosque during turbulent times. Whenever I gave an inflammatory speech, the secret police showed up on my doorstep and read me the riot act. A judge wouldn't consider that to be evidence either. I've done nothing wrong.'

'You're an opium addict,' the judge replied.

'That's not a sin,' Ahmad retorted. 'Most of the ayatollahs in this country are opium addicts.'

'We have proof that you smoked opium with top men in the secret police.'

'True, but that's all I did.'

'They gave you money. That's been documented.'

'Only in my official capacity as an imam. People confide in me and give me money for a variety of reasons. The secret police also gave me money, but I turned every last cent of it over to the mosque.'

'You've had improper relations with women on numerous occasions.'

'I've had relations with women, but always according to sharia law.'

'I have in my possession photographs which clearly show you smoking opium and cavorting with prostitutes.'

'The secret police set me up in order to discredit me, but I . . .'

Up to this point he'd tried to give convincing answers to the judge's questions, but in the harsh light of the lamp it was obvious that his hands were shaking, and that tears were oozing out of his eyes and rolling down his cheeks.

Soon he began to stutter and leave his sentences unfinished. It was the opium. He'd never kicked the habit. Instead, he'd bought a modern electrical pipe in Tehran so that he could smoke opium in secret wherever he wanted to. Aqa Jaan knew, but had decided to turn a blind eye.

If he'd had his usual fix, he would have been able to defend himself more eloquently. But they'd arrested him at the wrong moment, just when he'd been about to smoke his pipe before going to the mosque to lead the prayer.

Now that he was under so much pressure, every nerve in his body was crying out for opium. It felt like an elephant was standing on his chest.

Usually he kept a little chunk of opium in his robe for emergencies. If he'd had it with him now, he could have swallowed it and felt halfway normal, but when they hauled him off to the Islamic Court, he'd been wearing only a long cotton shirt.

In desperation, he patted the pockets of his shirt, but they were as empty as a desert.

He tried to loosen his collar so he could breathe more easily, but his fingers refused to cooperate. His forehead was beaded with sweat. His ears began to pound, the sound faded away and he no longer heard the judge's voice. Everything went black before his eyes, and he slid from his chair.

The next morning his wife took their child and went home to her parents.

The Donkey

No indeed, they shall soon know!
And again no, they shall soon know!
We made the night as a covering.
And we made a glowing lantern.
We sent down torrents of water from rain-soaked
  clouds.
And we warned you of imminent torment,
A day when man shall see what his hands have
  wrought.

For the next month Aqa Jaan searched the city and talked to everyone he knew, but he found no trace of Ahmad. Everyone had heard about Ahmad's arrest, and rumours were spreading through the city like wildfire.

'What are you going to do next?' Fakhri Sadat asked Aqa Jaan.

'Maybe we should wait for it to blow over,' he said. 'Especially in these uncertain times. You ought to come down to the bazaar one of these days and see how the merchants all avoid me. My reputation is at stake.'

Aqa Jaan jumped when the doorbell rang.

There was something different about the ring, as though the messenger of fate were at the door.

'Who's there?' Aqa Jaan asked, his voice trembling.

'Open up!' demanded a male voice.

'Who's there?' Aqa Jaan asked again.

'We have a message for Aqa Jaan.'

He opened the gate. Outside stood a bearded man, toting a gun.

'What can I do for you?' Aqa Jaan enquired.

'The imam would like to speak to you,' the man replied.

'Which imam?'

'The one in the jeep.'

Aqa Jaan walked over to the jeep. 'Welcome to my home,' he said through the window to the young imam in the back. 'Come in if you like. We can talk in my study.'

The imam got out. Aqa Jaan ushered him into his study and offered him a chair.

'Normally you would have been invited to come down to the Islamic Court,' the imam stated calmly, 'but we don't have much time. I'm here to deliver a message and to make a request that must be complied with at once.'

'What do you mean? What kind of request?'

'The court has reached a decision, and I've come to inform you of its ruling. I'll read the document aloud.'

Aqa Jaan, assuming that it was about Ahmad, suddenly felt relieved at the thought that there might be room for negotiation after all.

The imam reached into his pocket, took out an unsealed envelope, removed the sheet of paper inside, carefully unfolded it and began to read:

In the name of Allah, who shows no mercy to sinners who refuse to heed his word, and in the name of our leader Ayatollah Khomeini.

The Islamic Court has ruled that, effective immediately and for an indefinite period of time, the Qa'im

Maqam Farahani family is to be relieved of all further responsibility for the Friday Mosque in the city of Senejan.

Aqa Jaan was so shocked he leapt to his feet. 'That's impossible! The mosque belongs to us!'

'The mosque belongs to God,' the imam stated serenely. 'A mosque is never anyone's personal property. You should know that!'

'But we have documents showing that the land and the mosque belong to this house. It says so in our family deeds. We inherited the mosque. I have proof!'

'Calm down. Those documents have no legal validity, because the mosque belongs to us all. Your family has merely been its custodian. It hasn't been bestowed on you as a divine right. Now that we have an Islamic government, the judge can rescind earlier rulings. Your supervision of the mosque is no longer required. Further discussion is out of the question. The Islamic Court has revoked your family's right to the mosque. The house and the mosque are to be separated. You and your family may continue to live in the house, but I have come to collect the keys to the mosque. Are you prepared to hand them over?'

'No!' Aqa Jaan said. 'I can't hand them over and I won't. What's the meaning of this? You're destroying us all! Do you have to insult us too?'

'If you don't hand over the keys right now, I'll order the men I have posted outside to come in and get them.'

'You're not getting them from me!' Aqa Jaan said firmly.

The imam left and went back to his jeep, where he ordered his men to go in and get the keys.

Three men came into Aqa Jaan's study. They started

towards his desk, but Aqa Jaan, who was standing in the middle of the room, blocked their way. 'Get out!' he screamed. 'Get out of my house!'

The men pushed him aside and began to search the room.

'This is pure theft!' Aqa Jaan shouted at the man who was dumping the contents of his drawers on his desk, and he shoved him away.

Jawad, having heard the noise, rushed in and dragged his father away, then stood between the two men to prevent them from coming to blows.

The men took every key they could find and then left. But they didn't get their hands on the key to the treasure room, because Aqa Jaan always kept it in his pocket, next to his Koran.

Three days later, as evening was drawing to a close, a helicopter flew over the mosque. Inside it was Ayatollah Araki – one of the dozens of ayatollahs sent to the major cities by Khomeini to oversee the implementation of the sharia. Each of the ayatollahs had been granted unlimited powers. Answerable only to Khomeini, they were referred to as *Jomas*, or Friday, imams, since they operated from the *Jomah*, or Friday, Mosques.

In the streets below, hundreds of believers raised their arms towards the helicopter and shouted '*Jare imam gosh amad!* Welcome, friend of the imam!'

The helicopter landed on the roof, and a group of men from the bazaar trooped up to greet the ageing ayatollah, while the hundreds of Islamic fundamentalists in the mosque's courtyard beat their chests and shouted, '*Janam beh fadayet Khomeini!* We will sacrifice our souls for you, Khomeini!'

Two armed young men rushed over to help the ayatollah

down the stairs, and he was carried into the mosque on the shoulders of the faithful.

Aqa Jaan, not wanting to miss the ayatollah's arrival, had stealthily opened the trapdoor to one of the minarets, crawled inside and climbed up to the spot where Nosrat had once made love to a woman. From his lofty position he stared down at the scene, taking in every detail, while the green light of the minaret shone on his face.

The mosque had again become the centre of activity in Senejan. Every Friday evening people came to the mosque from miles around to hear the ayatollah speak.

Ayatollah Araki was the most powerful man in the city. His appointment book was always full, and no decision was ever taken without his approval. His autocratic rule extended to everything but the Islamic Court.

The Islamic judge operated independently, though he did consult with Khalkhal in special cases. In fact, he had phoned him to discuss Ahmad's case. Khalkhal's advice had been clear: 'You're the judge. Close your eyes and give your verdict!'

Nevertheless the judge had gone to the mosque, handed Ahmad's file to the ayatollah and asked his opinion. The ayatollah had studied the file in between two prayer services and agreed with the judge's proposed ruling. 'He is an imam, so he has to be punished more severely than ordinary citizens. *Wa-assalaam!*'

The following day a jeep drove around the city from dawn until early afternoon, blaring an announcement from the loudspeaker: 'Attention all believers in Senejan! Come to the main square at two o'clock. The judge will announce his verdict in the case of Ahmad Alsaberi, a former accomplice of the secret police. This will be the first public sentencing under sharia law. God is merciful, but also cruel when He has to be.'

Aqa Jaan was standing in the courtyard by the *hauz* when he heard the announcement. He froze. All at once his legs went numb, and he had to clutch the lamp post for support.

Fakhri Sadat had also heard the announcement. 'What should we do?' she asked, appalled.

'Nothing,' Aqa Jaan said. 'Only God can help us now. For the last month I've gone round knocking on doors and kissing everyone's hand, but it didn't help. Nobody knows what goes on in the Islamic Court. The cases are always tried behind closed doors.'

'Why hasn't Zinat done anything? She has friends in high places.'

'I don't think there's much she *can* do. Even she doesn't know who the judge is and who's behind the trials. Besides, she's on their side. She can't make an exception for her own son.'

'Why not? You've told me often enough that he's innocent.'

'I don't know, Fakhri. I just don't know any more!'

'But Ahmad is her son. Why should you have to call on people and kiss their hands, while she's hidden somewhere? For that matter, where is she? And why is she hiding, even from you?'

'Fakhri, there's been a revolution, not just an ordinary transfer of power. And because of that, there's been a radical change in the way people think. We're going to see things we never would have thought possible in ordinary times. Human beings are capable of the most inhuman behaviour. Look around you; everyone's changed. You can hardly recognise them any more. I can't tell if they've suddenly dropped their masks or put on new ones. God only knows what happened to Zinat. Who would have thought she'd ever achieve any kind of prominence?'

'Prominence? What do you mean by "prominence"?' Fakhri snapped.

'She has power, she makes decisions, she organises things. God knows what else she's doing.'

'She's no one special. She's ugly. All the women she works with are horrible, the kind of women that no one looks at twice. They're all ugly!'

'Fakhri!'

'Zinat is ugly on the inside,' she said, ignoring Aqa Jaan's rebuke.

'This isn't the time to discuss it. I'm going to the square to see what's happening. Maybe I can still do something to help Ahmad.'

'Don't go. He's going to be humiliated in public. Stay home until the storm has died down.'

'I have to go. It's my *life*. Humiliation is the least of my worries.'

Before he left, Aqa Jaan said his prayers. Then he put on his hat and, with his chin held high, went out to meet his fate.

It was crowded in the square. He found a spot beneath a tree, where he had a good view of the platform on which the sentencing would take place. People were talking to each other, curious as to how the sharia would be implemented.

Three army jeeps drove up and disgorged their load of Revolutionary Guards, then a black Mercedes rolled into the square. One of the guards opened the door and a young imam stepped out. The guards escorted him to the platform, where he seated himself on a tall chair. 'Bring in the prisoner!' he ordered.

Ahmad was led out from behind an improvised green curtain. He looked frail and unkempt. It had been weeks since he'd had any opium, and it showed in his lined face and stooped shoulders. He looked like an unwashed tramp. If the judge hadn't announced his name, nobody would have recognised him.

The crowd stared in disbelief at Ahmad Alsaberi, once their beloved imam, the man who used to receive hundreds of love letters.

First the judge called for silence, then he began to read his verdict: 'Ahmad Alsaberi has been found guilty of collaborating with the secret police of the former regime. Of collaborating with Satan! This is an act of treason against Islam and against the mosque that he was appointed to serve. However, because he doesn't have any blood on his hands, he has been sentenced to only ten years in prison!'

There were gasps and cries from the crowd. Again the judge called for silence, then resumed his reading: 'The offender is hereby relieved of his duties. Since he will no longer be allowed to work as an imam, his robe and turban have been taken from him.'

Ahmad trembled in his filthy shirt.

'Because he was the imam of the Friday Mosque, and was therefore expected to set an example to others, he will be given an extra punishment,' the judge said. He paused, then suddenly exclaimed, 'Bring in the donkey!'

The guards led a white donkey out from behind the stands.

There were mutterings from the crowd: 'What are they up to now? What are they going to do to him?'

The donkey took one look at the mass of people and refused to take another step. The guards had to push it onto the platform.

Aqa Jaan recognised the animal. It was Am Ramazan's donkey!

Just then a group of militants wearing green headbands bearing the words 'Soldier of Khomeini' came bursting into the square, shouting, 'God is great! Death to the henchman of the shah!'

Above the tumult, the judge cried: 'The offender is to be seated backwards on the donkey and taken to the Friday Mosque. This is a merciful punishment for a man who has defiled his imam robe!'

There was a shocked silence. Everyone stared in horror at Ahmad, who kept his eyes glued to the ground.

Aqa Jaan took out his handkerchief and wiped the sweat from his brow. He couldn't believe they were actually going to make Ahmad ride backwards on a donkey through Senejan!

Ahmad had admittedly done some foolish things, but Aqa Jaan didn't believe he'd ever been a henchman of the shah. It would be totally out of character. But why didn't Ahmad speak up? Why didn't he object? Why didn't he defend himself?

Aqa Jaan pushed his way towards the platform. 'Ahmad!' he cried loudly. 'You're not a traitor! Defend yourself!'

Everyone stared at Aqa Jaan.

'Say something!' he cried, louder this time.

At the sound of Aqa Jaan's voice, Ahmad seemed to snap out of his trance.

'Quiet!' the judge ordered.

'Speak up, Ahmad!' Aqa Jaan said.

'Quiet!' the judge ordered again.

Two guards came over and seized Aqa Jaan.

'Wake up, Ahmad! Say something! Do it for me! Do it for us! For the mosque!' Aqa Jaan shouted as he tried to shake off the guards.

'You're the imam of our mosque, defend your—' he cried. But before he could finish his sentence, one of the guards twisted his arm behind his back and pushed him to the ground, face down.

'Ahmad! Do something for us!' he called, as the guards held him down.

Two of the merchants from the bazaar ran up and dragged Aqa Jaan out from under the hands and feet of the guards, then led him back to where they'd been standing.

Ahmad, summoning all his strength, raised his arms in the air and addressed the crowd. 'I swear by the Holy Koran that I am innocent!' he cried.

'Be quiet!' the judge ordered.

'I swear by the mosque that I've never been a henchman of the shah!'

'Shut up!' the judge roared, truly angry now.

'I have never—' Ahmad began. Just then two guards grabbed hold of him and started to lift him onto the donkey, but the animal shied away. One of the guards jabbed it so hard with his rifle that the donkey stumbled and fell, then scrambled to its feet again.

An old man wearing a green headband and holding a weapon stepped forward. He stroked the donkey's head, then held the animal still while the guards hoisted Ahmad into the saddle.

Aqa Jaan couldn't believe his eyes. The old man in the uniform was Am Ramazan! Their former gardener had become a soldier in the Army of Allah! It was inconceivable. Am Ramazan had not only let them use his donkey to humiliate Ahmad and break his will, but he had even volunteered to hold the animal still.

He ought to be ashamed of himself. Why, he still had the key to their house! How could people change so quickly?

Aqa Jaan was so upset that he began to chant the Al-Mursalat surah like a madman:

Woe, that day, deniers of truth!
By the tempests tempestuous!
By the dispersers dispersing!
By the sunderers sundering!
What you are promised shall come to pass.
When the stars become dim.
When the heavens are torn asunder.
When the mountains are scattered to the winds.
Woe, that day, deniers of truth.

The donkey moved off. Ahmad was weeping soundlessly. Someone threw a stone that hit him in the head.

Aqa Jaan could bear it no longer. He ran after the donkey and hurled himself in front of it. 'Stop!' he said to the crowd. 'You can't throw stones! He hasn't been sentenced to a stoning! Where's that accursed judge?'

One of the guards gave Aqa Jaan a shove, which sent him sprawling to the ground. But he got back up again, with surprising agility for a man of his age, and ran towards the donkey.

The guard stuck out the lower end of his rifle and blocked the way.

Another stone was thrown. This one struck Ahmad's right ear. Aqa Jaan took out his Koran, thrust aside the guard and ran over to Ahmad. Positioning himself in front of his nephew, he held up his Koran and shouted, 'In the name of this book, do not stone him!'

The guard snatched the Koran out of his hand and hit him across the face with it. The blow sent Aqa Jaan reeling, but he quickly regained his balance. He grabbed Ahmad round the waist and tried to drag him off the donkey, pulling so hard that they both fell to the ground.

While two of the guards were lifting Ahmad back onto the donkey, the other guards were kicking Aqa Jaan. Their heavy boots thudded into his stomach, back and legs.

The donkey trotted off towards the mosque, and the crowd followed along behind.

Aqa Jaan lay curled up in agony, chanting:

> *Oh, you cloaked in your mantle!*
> *Oh, you muffled in your garment!*
> *You may lie*
> *On the ground no longer.*
> *Stand up!*
> *By the moon,*
> *And by the morning when it dawns!*

He placed his palms on the ground and rose painfully to his feet.

The Cow

In the beginning was the Cow. The rest was silence. At least that's what the ancient Persians believed, which is why the columns in the old Persian palaces in the province of Fars are crowned with the heads of cows.

When the Cow died, the rest of creation emerged from her body. Plants and animals sprang up out of her flesh.

After a while this belief disappeared and was replaced by others. Fire became sacred and the Cow faded into the background.

Fires were still burning brightly in the fire temples in the mountains when Zoroaster, the first Persian prophet, was born in Yazd. Zoroaster announced that neither the Cow nor Fire was to be worshipped. There was one supreme deity, he said, and he gave him a name: Ahura Mazda. Fire became the symbol of Ahura Mazda on earth. The prophet also presented his people with the holy book of Zoroaster, the Avesta.

Centuries later, Muhammad proclaimed Islam. The ancient Persian beliefs were suppressed and the Fire was extinguished.

The Cow and the Fire have not been worshipped for fourteen hundred years, but they still live on in the Persian spirit.

Islam had created a rift in Aqa Jaan's family. For the past eight centuries the house had been united in its struggle against the enemies of Islam, fighting the battle from the pulpit of the mosque. Now, for the first time, the family's foe was Islam itself.

The revolution had more or less ended, but Shahbal still hadn't come home.

Nosrat was doing well, working day and night to carve out a position for himself as an Iranian filmmaker in the new Islamic Republic. He didn't have time to come home. He didn't phone any more either.

Zinat had thrown herself so zealously into Khomeini's brand of Islam that she was rarely at home. She broke off all contact with the family. They had no idea what she was doing.

Muezzin, who didn't feel well, went on trips more and more often.

Jawad was often away from home. Though he didn't tell his family, he was spending much of his time in Tehran, where he was in touch with Shahbal. He'd always secretly sympathised with the leftist movement and with the struggle that Shahbal was now actively engaged in.

'Why don't you come home?' Jawad asked Shahbal.

'When Khomeini was living in Paris, he promised to tolerate others. Now that he's in power, he's forgotten his promise. To him, leftists are blasphemers. There's no room for dissent in his regime, so we've toned down our rhetoric and gone underground. Khomeini can't be trusted.'

Nasrin and Ensi, the daughters of Aqa Jaan, also decided to leave. They were hoping to find a place in Tehran. No woman in the family had ever lived on her own before, but Nasrin and Ensi were no longer content to sit at home and wait for a husband.

Fakhri Sadat had always been protective of her daughters. She hadn't insisted that they attend mosque regularly, and she had sent them to the best schools in

Senejan. After secondary school, both girls had gone on to teacher's training college. In the normal course of things, they would have graduated by now and be working as teachers. But schools and universities had shut down when the revolution began. When they re-opened, Nasrin and Ensi weren't allowed back in.

The new regime had unleashed a cultural revolution in factories, offices, schools and universities. Anyone not considered Islamic enough was sent home. Nasrin and Ensi were the first students in their class to be dismissed, mostly because of Ahmad's disgrace and Aqa Jaan's spirited defence of him.

For a while the girls went on living at home, but there was no future for them in Senejan.

'Nasrin and Ensi want to move to Tehran,' Fakhri Sadat announced to her husband one night as they were getting ready for bed. 'They've come to me to ask me what I think.'

'We can't send two young girls to Tehran by themselves!' Aqa Jaan said.

'What are you planning to do? Keep them here for ever?'

Aqa Jaan didn't reply.

'They have no future here. You've got to let them go.'

A few days later Nasrin and Ensi went to see Aqa Jaan in his study and told him that they wanted to find jobs in Tehran and that he shouldn't try to stop them.

'All right,' said Aqa Jaan, 'I won't stand in your way.'

So they moved to Tehran, where they found rooms with a former classmate.

Aqa Jaan continued to go to the bazaar every day, but things had changed. The men, who had all grown beards, spent most of their time competing for the mullahs' favours. Insolence had become the norm; no one showed Aqa Jaan the slightest bit of respect. Ever since his office boy had started coming to work in a militia uniform, Aqa Jaan didn't dare phone anyone when he was in the room.

In the past, when he had gone to the villages to check up on his workshops, he had always been given a royal welcome. Now the villagers didn't even come out to say hello.

One day an old friend of his from Isfahan stopped by and found him bent over the papers on his desk. Aqa Jaan had aged so much he was unrecognisable. He had turned into a broken, grey-haired old man.

He tried to keep working as usual, but his heart wasn't in it. He didn't have the energy he once had either, so he started going home earlier and pottering about the garden. Sometimes he went down to the cellar and spent hours poking around. One day Fakhri Sadat went looking for him. 'What have you been doing down here all this time?' she asked.

'I've never had the time to look through these trunks.'

'That's enough for today. Go and wash your hands. I've just made tea.'

He washed his hands and face in the *hauz* and went into the kitchen to drink tea with Fakhri.

'Be patient,' Aqa Jaan advised her, when she began to moan about her children's future.

'How can I be patient when all three of my children have left home with no future prospects and we don't even know where they are half the time?'

'Our children are not the only ones. Thousands of others are suffering the same fate. That's how life has always been and always will be. The only remedy for that is patience.'

'Your faith gives you the strength to be patient, but it

doesn't help me. I'm weak and filled with doubts. I hardly dare to say it, but I doubt if God sees our struggles.'

'Be strong, Fakhri. Don't stray into the darkness. You need to hold on to your serenity.'

'Everyone acts out of self-interest, everyone tries to protect his own territory. You're the only person who's always been honest, and where has it got you? The cellar! You used to be the most important man in the bazaar, your word was gold, and how do you spend your time now? Rummaging through the junk in the cellar!'

'I wish you wouldn't put it like that,' Aqa Jaan said, stung.

'I'm sorry, but you know what I mean. My point is, where are your friends, the powerful men of the bazaar? Why aren't they doing anything to help you?'

'I don't need their help,' Aqa Jaan retorted.

'Everyone has abandoned you. Where's Zinat? Where's Muezzin? And, most of all, where's your brother Nosrat? Have you heard from him lately?'

At that very moment, Nosrat was standing in the shower, thinking about the contribution he could make to Persian cinema. He knew he'd never achieve anything without Khomeini's approval.

Then, while the water was pounding on his head, he had a brilliant idea. 'A cow!' he shouted out loud. 'That's it!' He turned off the water, grabbed a towel, dried himself, got dressed and hurried outside, where he hailed a taxi and had himself driven to the former palace that now served as Beheshti's headquarters.

Nine months had gone by since the beginning of the revolution and Khomeini still hadn't decided what he was going to do about the cinemas. They had been boarded shut and, like the brothels, declared unclean.

Nosrat and Beheshti had worked so closely together that they were on familiar terms. Beheshti had nothing against cinemas. When he lived in Germany, he used to sneak off occasionally to see a film. Still, he didn't think this was the right time to broach the subject with Khomeini.

'But I've got the perfect solution,' Nosrat said to Beheshti. 'All we have to do is take the imam to see a film. That way he can see for himself that a cinema and a brothel are two very different things.'

'Be realistic,' Beheshti said. 'What film could we show him that would make him approve of the cinema?'

'*The Cow*!' Nosrat said.

'The cow?'

'The very first honest-to-goodness Persian film. I'd even go so far as to say that it's an Islamic film.'

'And it's called *The Cow*?'

'Yes, *The Cow*! It's a Persian classic. It's not a master-piece, mind you, but it's the best film to show the imam. After all, the archetype of the Cow is familiar to every Persian, even to Imam Khomeini. I'll line up a cinema, and you can make sure the imam gets there. Islam could have a great influence on the film industry. I have big plans. If Khomeini approves of the film, an independent film industry will spring up from the heart of our culture. The Shiites have a unique way of looking at things. With our ancient Persian culture as our guide, we'll soon conquer cinemas all over the world!'

'We can talk about the rest of the world another time. First we have to convince the imam to see the film.'

'We'd better hurry. There's not much time. Now that the cinemas have been boarded up, the carpet merchants have launched a nationwide campaign to buy up the build-ings and convert them into mosques.'

'We'll never get the imam to set foot in a cinema.'

'Then we'll do it the other way round. We'll bring the cinema to the imam.'

Beheshti smiled. 'That's a good idea,' he said.

'This is history in the making. Khomeini will like the film. It takes place in the countryside. It'll remind him of his youth.'

The next evening Nosrat showed up at Khomeini's residence in the northern hills of Tehran, carrying a projector and balancing a screen on his shoulder.

Beheshti ushered him into the imam's study. Khomeini was sitting on a rug, leaning against the wall with a cushion at his back.

Since the revolution, Nosrat had grown a beard and his hair had turned grey. He'd also started wearing an artsy kind of hat. People usually knelt before Khomeini and kissed his hand, but Nosrat was an exception. He took off his hat and gave the ayatollah a brief nod.

Beheshti introduced him. 'This is the cameraman whose coverage of the revolution was broadcast all over the globe. He's very reliable. He comes from a good, pious family and has interesting ideas about the cinema. I'll leave you two alone.'

When Beheshti had gone, there was a silence.

Nosrat put down his things and looked for a place to hang up the screen. He took a hammer out of his pocket and, without asking permission, nailed the white screen to one of the walls with two small nails.

He moved a table away from the wall and set his projector on it. Then he placed a chair in the middle of the room and turned to Khomeini. 'Would you please sit in this chair?'

'I'm fine where I am,' Khomeini said, somewhat irritated.

'I know, but the chair is part of the experience.'

Khomeini stared at him in astonishment. No one had ever spoken to him like that before. But he knew that Nosrat was a photographer, and he also knew that there were two people you should always listen to: your doctor and the photographer. So he got up and seated himself in the chair.

Nosrat closed the curtains and turned off the light, plunging the room into darkness.

Then he switched on the projector.

The reel began to turn. It was an old black-and-white film. The first image to appear on the screen was that of a cow. It mooed – something Khomeini hadn't been expecting. Then a farmer came into view. He kissed the cow on the head, stroked its neck and said, 'You're my cow. My very own sweet cow. Come, let's go for a walk.'

The farmer set off, and the cow followed him to the pasture. There the farmer took out an old-fashioned pipe, sat down beneath a shady tree and began to smoke. He gazed contentedly at his grazing cow. Then a woman in a headscarf appeared.

'*Salaam aleikum*, Mashadi!'

'*Salaam aleikum*, Baji. Come and sit in the shade, it's hot today. I was just about to take my cow to the river. It was too hot for the poor thing in the cowshed. How are you doing, Baji?'

The woman sat down beside him in the shade of the tree, and they stared at the cow in companionable silence.

There was nothing fanciful in the film, and yet there were several magical scenes, in which you could see ordinary village life. The story itself was simple, but what made it so moving were the villagers' primitive living conditions.

It was a fitting film for Khomeini's new Islamic Republic,

because there wasn't a single sign of modern life in the village. The women all wore chadors and the Koran reigned supreme. There was no running water or electricity. No music could be heard and no one owned a radio. It was the perfect film for Khomeini to begin with. He could recognise himself, his parents and his former fellow villagers in the film.

The story is about a childless farmer who adores his cow. One day the cow falls ill. The wise men of the village advise him to have the cow slaughtered before it gets worse, but he refuses to listen.

One day, when the farmer is away, the cow drops dead. The villagers decide to bury the animal at once, before the farmer returns.

When he comes home and asks about his cow, everyone tells him that it wandered off. The farmer panics. He spends days looking for the cow. When he doesn't find it, he decides his life is no longer worth living, and he stops eating.

The wise men of the village go to his house to comfort him and explain that it's not right for a human being to mourn the loss of a cow. But the farmer is so upset that he thinks he's turned into a cow. As the wise men enter his house, he begins to moo with grief. The wise men take out their handkerchiefs and wipe away their tears.

When the film was over, Nosrat turned on the light, just in time to see Khomeini reach for his handkerchief.

On the following Friday every ayatollah in the country made an unusual announcement at the end of his sermon: 'Tonight a film is going to be shown on television. The film is called *The Cow*, and it's been approved by Imam Khomeini. Islamic believers are allowed to watch it!'

327

People who didn't have televisions flocked to the teahouses that evening to watch the film. It was a red-letter day in the history of Iranian cinema.

Aqa Jaan watched the film along with Lizard in the shed on the roof. It was his first film too. After he saw the cow and the farmer and the poverty-stricken houses, he had a hard time believing that this was the highly acclaimed cinema he'd heard so much about.

Shahbal and Jawad saw it together.

Nasrin and Ensi watched the film along with their former classmate.

Sadiq saw it in the company of a handful of Islamic women in Tehran, where she'd gone for a visit. With his sister's help, Khalkhal had arranged for Sadiq to spend some time in the capital.

Zinat Khanom was staying at the house of Azam Azam, who had hired her to work as her assistant in the women's prison. She had recently denounced Ahmad, declaring publicly in the mosque that she was ashamed of her son.

Zinat wasn't alone in her denouncement. The television was full of devout parents who turned their backs on any child of theirs who dared to oppose the ayatollahs. Everyone was talking about it; no one understood it. Were the parents motivated by religious conviction? Or had they been brainwashed by the mullahs?

The day after Zinat denounced Ahmad, Ayatollah Araki called her into his office for a private talk. 'Zinat Khanom,' he said, 'you are an example of the kind of Islamic woman this city needs. You are a real *mahajjabeh*. Holy Fatima is pleased with you. Now listen carefully. I order you to turn the women of Senejan into model Islamic women. I want all of them to look and act like Zinat Khanom. Is that clear?'

'Yes, Ayatollah!' Zinat said, and she sprang to her feet.

Zinat and six other fanatical women set up a morals committee and began to Islamise the behaviour of women in public places.

Most of the women in Senejan put on a black chador when they went out, but many young women had no desire to obey the Islamic regime and refused to wear a chador. The city was patrolled by the newly formed morals police, who cruised around in jeeps and checked to see whether the women in the streets were dressed according to the *hijab*.

In each jeep were two veiled women and one armed man. The moment they spotted a woman who was wearing make-up or whose clothing didn't meet Islamic standards, they leapt out of the jeep, raced over to her and stopped her for questioning. If she listened to their advice and adjusted her chador or headscarf, they let her go, but if she protested, they arrested her, threw her in a waiting van and drove her to an undisclosed location to teach her a lesson.

All of the women who were arrested were brought to Zinat. She and Azam Azam had devised various ways to terrorise the women. For example, Azam Azam would smear syrup on their legs and Zinat would lock them in a dark, cockroach-filled room. Girls who talked back would be put in another dark room, where squeaking mice would scurry over their bare feet.

Recently Zinat had taken a rough towel and scrubbed the lipstick off a woman's mouth with such force that her lips had bled.

On the night that everyone was glued to the television, watching *The Cow*, a group of Islamic students, acting with Khomeini's approval, climbed over the wall of the

American Embassy compound and burst into the building. In a lightning raid, they arrested the ambassador and sixty-five employees, who had been staying in the embassy as a security measure. To make sure that the Americans couldn't try to free them in a large-scale military operation, the hostages were later transported to a number of secret locations.

As an added precaution, the most important hostages were driven to Qom, Isfahan and Senejan.

In the middle of the night Ayatollah Araki of Senejan was awakened in his bed by his assistant.

'Get dressed,' the assistant whispered. 'You have a visitor.'

'Who?' the ayatollah asked.

'A very young imam who says he's been instructed to tell you a state secret.'

The ayatollah flung on his clothes. The young man was standing in the living room, waiting for him.

The ayatollah held out his hand and the young man kissed it. 'I'm a student at the University of Tehran,' he said. 'I have a secret message for you from Ayatollah Khomeini.'

The ayatollah brought his head close to the student's.

'There are three cars parked out front,' the student whispered in his ear, 'with seven blindfolded Americans inside.'

Ayatollah Araki put on his turban and grabbed his walking stick. 'I'm ready,' he said.

He got into one of the vehicles, and they drove off into the desert.

Representatives of the Iranian and American governments met, with the Swiss as mediators, to discuss the release of the hostages, but the negotiations dragged on for months with no result. Khomeini had two non-negotiable demands: the extradition of the shah, so he could be tried in an Islamic court, and the release of billions of dollars in Iranian oil revenues that had been deposited in American banks.

The Americans were unwilling to extradite the shah, since they knew he would be executed by the ayatollahs. Nor did they wish to release the Iranian assets, which had been frozen in America and elsewhere. Negotiations were broken off. After that there was a long silence.

One hundred and seventy-two days later, six American transport planes flew through the night sky above Senejan. No one saw them; no one heard them. Half an hour earlier they had taken off from the deck of an American aircraft carrier in the Persian Gulf and, with Saddam Hussein's permission, flown to Iran through Iraqi airspace. They were headed for a secret air-force base in the desert.

The Americans had been informed of the hostages' hiding places by a spy in Khomeini's inner circle. The plan was for the shah's former commando units to free the hostages, after which they would be brought to the base by helicopter and then flown out of the country in transport planes.

But the rescue attempt was a disaster. Khomeini was the only one with a ready explanation: divine intervention. 'Allah stopped them!' he cried the next morning when it was announced that America's top-secret military operation had failed. 'Our country is under the protection of Allah,' he continued calmly. 'Why can't the Americans understand that? It's very simple: God struck down the enemy!'

It seems that several helicopters, damaged by a dust

storm, had landed on the runway. As one of them tried to lift off, it skidded into a transport plane, and the two aircraft had burst into flames. The desert had been the scene of a raging inferno, though no one had witnessed it.

Eight US servicemen died and four others were wounded. After the crash the remaining transport planes had flown directly back to the carrier.

A shepherd, curled up beneath a tree by an old water well at the edge of the desert, was jerked out of his sleep by an unfamiliar sound. He sat up and peered into the inky darkness. A column of smoke was rising into the starry sky.

He climbed into the tree and saw a distant fire. Realising that there must have been some kind of catastrophe, he left his flock and ran to the nearest village. Half an hour later the villagers were all standing on their roofs, staring at the blazing fire.

The village imam hurried over to the mosque, opened the door, picked up the phone – the only one in the village – and dialled Ayatollah Araki's number. 'Flames are shooting up out of the desert! Our village elders have never seen anything like it. Something terrible must have happened!'

The ayatollah immediately ordered the commander of the Islamic Army to drive into the desert and check out the fire. Forty-five minutes later the ayatollah picked up his red phone and called the Khomeini residence in Tehran. 'Flames are shooting up into the sky! It looks like a couple of planes have crashed, but the heat is so intense we can't get any closer!'

Before Tehran could put together a reconnaissance team and dispatch it to Senejan, the villagers had ridden out to the scene on their donkeys and tried to rescue the wounded.

The authorities still didn't know exactly what had happened when Radio Moscow made an announcement on its six a.m. news: 'Two US aircraft crashed in the desert of Iran near the city of Senejan.'

Muezzin, who always tuned in to the morning news, heard the announcement, but failed to grasp its significance. Only when he heard the word 'Senejan' in the repeat broadcast did he go to Aqa Jaan and say, 'Two US aircraft crashed in the desert!'

Iran's state-controlled television opened its two p.m. news with a live report from the crash site. First the camera zoomed in on the bodies of the Americans, then Ayatollah Araki appeared on the screen. Clutching a Kalashnikov in his right hand, he gave an impassioned speech. 'Islam is a miracle,' he began. 'Even after fourteen hundred years, Islam is still a miracle!

'Last night American planes entered our country from Iraq. They turned off their lights and flew in the dark, using the latest electronic equipment to avoid our radar. They planned everything down to the last detail and calculated everything on their super-intelligent computers, but they forgot to include one thing in their calculations: the Koran! We don't need ultra-modern computers to make such calculations. We don't need electronic eyes to monitor everything. There is One who watches over our country, there is One who protects us, there is One who takes care of things while we sleep, and that is Allah.

'America has computers, we have Allah.

'America has reconnaissance planes, we have Allah.

'America! If you want to know who crashed your planes, read the Al-Fil surah:

A-lam tara kayfa fa‘ala rabboka be’as-habi alfeel.

Did you not see what your Lord did
To those who rode the elephants?
Did He not confound their treacherous plan?
He sent against them flocks of birds,
Which pelted them with clay pellets,
And left them like a field of half-eaten stalks.'

Al-harb

Five months later, at around noon, three Iraqi warplanes flew over Tehran, flying so low that you could see the pilots in the cockpit. Everyone fled in panic at the deafening and altogether terrifying sound.

The planes bombed the airport. And with this surprise attack Iraq declared *al-harb*, war, on Iran.

The Iraqi army had crossed into Iranian territory the night before and occupied strategic targets in the southern oil-rich province of Khuzestan. Iran's most important gas and oil refineries were now in the hands of Saddam Hussein.

The regime was shocked. People couldn't believe it. Only after the first televised images had been broadcast, showing Iraqi tanks in front of Iranian oil refineries, did it begin to dawn on everyone that it wasn't just a threat, but an actual war.

Khomeini appeared on television and urged all those who owned a rifle to report immediately to the nearest mosque. 'It is jihad!' Thanks to his call to arms, a large army of believers was mobilised within twenty-four hours. Thousands of men – both young and old, but none with any military training whatsoever – were crammed into buses and driven to the front.

Meanwhile, American spy planes, flying high above the war zone, had started photographing the movements of the Islamic Army and passing the information on to Saddam Hussein. As a result, Iranian troops were repeatedly bombed by Iraqi planes.

Khomeini, unbowed by defeat, inspired his people with courage. 'Only death can save us now. America is monitoring our every move from above. We have no choice but to lay down a bridge of corpses that will eventually lead us to Iraq.'

An army of believers, clothed in burial sheets, took up their weapons and paved the way to the Iraqi army. The Iranians finally reached the Iraqi troops and began a war that would last for eight long years and result in the deaths of millions of soldiers on both sides.

The ayatollahs feared that the opposition would make use of the war to topple the regime. Khomeini had always been wary of the leftist movement. He thought of their supporters as enemies of Allah and the Koran, so was waiting patiently for the right moment to crush them once and for all. In turn, the leftist opposition was secretly plotting to weaken the Islamic Republic and remove the fanatical ayatollahs from power.

To safeguard the home front, the regime decided to destroy the leftist movement there and then. Khalkhal was the first to be informed. 'Tear it out by the roots!' Khomeini ordered. 'Show no mercy! Stamp out all those who oppose Islam!'

In less than an hour the leaders of the Communist Tudeh Party – all of whom had supported Khomeini – had been arrested. Yet the regime didn't manage to get its hands on the leaders of the various underground groups. After the revolution, they had been radicalised and had debated whether or not to rise up in arms against the regime.

The Tudeh Party, which had opted not to fight, had walked into the trap Khomeini had set for them.

Three nights later, the party's elderly leader – thin, grey and unshaven – was paraded on the Islamic-controlled television as on object lesson. His spirit had been broken. It was evident that he'd been taken directly from the torture chamber and placed in front of the camera. He begged to be left in peace.

It was a grisly scene, a cleverly edited videotape intended to frighten people. And it worked, for on that same night the remaining members of the Tudeh Party fled to the borders and escaped.

In Senejan, Ayatollah Araki had been ordered to clear out the Red Village.

The Red Village was in its heyday. It had declared itself an autonomous zone with its own rules and regulations – an enclave in which young men and women had set up an idealistic Communist state of their own. After the harvest, they divided the crops equally among the villagers. In the evening people gathered in the village square and read aloud the poems of the Russian poet Vladimir Mayakovsky.

On the night of the attack, the villagers were sitting in the square, watching a Russian film, when all of a sudden someone shouted: 'Tanks! They're coming to get us! Block the road!'

But it was too late for barricades. Within seconds the square emptied. Some of the villagers fled to the mountains, others went inside and locked their doors, and the few who had rifles hidden somewhere got them out and climbed up to their roofs.

A helicopter appeared above the village. Shots rang out

from the roofs, causing the helicopter to veer off sharply and fly away.

Tanks rumbled into the village. Hundreds of armed Revolutionary Guards appeared out of nowhere and stole through the darkness, taking up strategic positions. Meanwhile, two helicopters circled overhead, shining their searchlights on the roofs and firing at everything that moved.

The villagers hadn't been expecting such a large-scale attack. The Revolutionary Guards kept watch on the doors and windows, and fired at anyone who tried to escape. The people on the roofs fired back with fanatical zeal, but their shots were answered with grenades, which blew the roofs sky high.

There was no point in prolonging the struggle. One by one the doors of the houses opened, and the villagers came out with their hands up.

Those who had fled to the mountains were hunted down with jeeps. Anyone who refused to surrender was shot.

That night, dozens of men and women were arrested and hauled off to jail. One of them was Aqa Jaan's son, Jawad.

Khalkhal was flown to Senejan by helicopter to try the prisoners. As Allah's dreaded judge, he sowed death and destruction wherever he went.

The sun had not yet risen and the citizens of Senejan were still in their beds when nine young men from the Red Village were executed.

The city awoke in a state of a shock. Parents whose sons or daughters had been arrested hurried off to the prison to find out if their children had been executed.

The bodies were released to the families. But according

to the sharia, the corpses were unclean and could not be buried in official cemeteries. So fathers drove into the mountains, where they hoped to give their sons a decent burial.

Aqa Jaan didn't realise that Jawad had been arrested. He thought his son was in Tehran. It never occurred to him that Jawad might be among the prisoners.

He did know one of the boys who'd been executed – the son of the vaccination specialist whose office was opposite the mosque. Aqa Jaan was thinking of the stricken family and reading the Koran when the phone rang. He lifted the receiver.

'I'll keep it short,' a man said without introducing himself. 'I'm a friend of Jawad's. He was arrested in the Red Village. He's probably going to be executed. If there's anything you can do to prevent it, you need to do it fast. Once he comes before Allah's judge, it will be too late,' and he hung up.

Aqa Jaan's hand shook as he replaced the receiver. Hundreds of thoughts were racing through his head. He wanted to shout for Fakhri, but he couldn't speak. His son had been arrested! Why hadn't he been informed? Who was the man who phoned him? Where had he been phoning from?

As far as he knew, Jawad had gone to Tehran. What on earth had he been doing in the Red Village?

And how could he keep his son from being executed?

He didn't know where to start. He picked up the phone to make a call, then put it down again.

He grabbed his coat, jammed his hat on his head and started to leave, but just as he was going out the door the phone rang again.

'Excuse me,' the same voice said. 'He's in the city jail.

The judge will come back in a few days to try the rest of the prisoners. You need to hurry.'

'But what was he doing in the Red Village? And who are you?'

'We were there together. I managed to escape in time; he was arrested. You've got to act quickly. Sorry, I can't talk any longer, I've got to go,' the man said, and he hung up.

Aqa Jaan hurried towards the gate, but halfway there he turned around and came back. 'Fakhri Sadat!' he called.

There was no answer.

'Fakhri Sadat!' he called louder.

Fakhri, who could tell from his voice that something was wrong, hurried downstairs.

'Brace yourself for some bad news,' Aqa Jaan warned her. 'Jawad has been arrested!'

Fakhri nearly fainted. 'Arrested? Why?' she gasped.

'A friend of his just called. Jawad was arrested in the Red Village.'

'What was he doing there?'

'I don't know.'

'Maybe he went there with Shahbal. Where's Shahbal?'

'I don't know that either,' he said. 'But we have to do something before it's too late!' He started towards the door, then stopped. 'I don't know what to do or where to go.'

'Go to the mosque!' said Fakhri Sadat, her face as white as a sheet. 'Talk to the ayatollah!'

Aqa Jaan opened his mouth to say something, then shut it again. He hadn't been inside the mosque, not even to pray, since it had been taken away from him.

Swallowing his pride, he went over to the mosque, but the ayatollah wasn't in his office. 'Where's the ayatollah?' he asked the new caretaker.

'He cancelled his appointments and won't be coming in for a while. He doesn't want people pestering him with questions about the executions.'

'How can I get in touch with him?'

'I don't know. Nobody knows. He has more than one address.'

Aqa Jaan went into the grocery shop opposite the mosque.

'Aqa Jaan! What can I do for you?'

'Do you know where the ayatollah lives? I need to get hold of him right away!'

The grocer took pity on him. '*La ilaha illa Allah*,' he said. 'I'm not supposed to tell anyone, but why don't you try the mansion that used to belong to the former chief of the secret police?'

Aqa Jaan took a taxi to the house.

Armed guards were posted outside. He went up to the gate, but the guards told him they couldn't let him through and advised him to use the intercom that was connected to the house. He pressed the button. It took a while before someone answered.

'What do you want?' snapped a gruff voice.

'I'd like to speak to the ayatollah.'

'Write him a note and stick it in the letterbox on the right-hand side of the gate.'

'I'd like to talk to him personally.'

'Everyone wants to talk to him personally, but that doesn't mean they're allowed to.'

'But this is an emergency. I'm Aqa Jaan, the former custodian of the Friday Mosque. Tell him that, and I'm sure he'll agree to see me.'

'I don't care who you are. The ayatollah doesn't have time to see anyone. Besides, he's out, and I don't know when he'll be back.'

Stumped, Aqa Jaan stood helplessly by the intercom.

'Don't just stand there! Move!'

He walked back to the city. For the first time in his life, he was completely at a loss.

He stepped off the kerb, and a car slammed on its brakes. The driver rolled down his window. 'Are you trying to kill yourself, or what?' the man yelled.

'I'm sorry,' Aqa Jaan said. 'I wasn't paying attention.'

The driver recognised him and saw his look of despair. 'Where are you going? Maybe I can give you a lift,' he offered.

'Me? I'm on my way to the jail, if it's not too much trouble.'

'Which jail? The old one or the new one?'

'I don't know. The one where the executions were held.'

'The old one, then. Get in!'

The old jail, on the outskirts of the city, was surrounded by a massive stone wall. The car stopped in the square in front of the jail and Aqa Jaan got out. The tall iron gate was shut, and aside from three guards who were posted on the wall, there wasn't a soul in sight.

It wasn't dark yet, but the floodlights suddenly came on.

'No one's here,' the driver said. 'Let me take you home.'

Aqa Jaan didn't seem to hear him. He went up to the gate and hunted for the bell. There wasn't one. So he pounded on the gate with his fist. There was no answer. 'Is anyone there?' he shouted.

'I'll be glad to drive you home!' the driver repeated his offer.

'Sir!' Aqa Jaan called up to one of the guards on the wall. The man pretended he hadn't heard him.

'Sir!' he called again, louder.

The driver got out, walked over to Aqa Jaan and took him by the arm. 'I think you'd better go home now,' he said. 'You can come back tomorrow.'

He helped him into the car, drove him into town and dropped him outside the mosque.

Back home, Aqa Jaan had another idea. 'Fakhri!' he called, with a note of urgency in his voice, 'put on your chador!'

'Why?'

'We're going to see Am Ramazan!'

They hadn't seen him for a long time. They didn't know exactly what he was doing these days, only that he wore a uniform and that he had let the ayatollah use his donkey. Aqa Jaan rang the doorbell, but there were no lights on and it didn't look like anyone was at home.

He rang again. This time he heard footsteps in the hallway. The door opened and there stood Am Ramazam, who now had a long beard. He was carrying a gun. In the darkness of the hallway, he seemed bigger than he really was.

Aqa Jaan and Fakhri Sadat were the last people he'd been expecting to see.

'Could we come in for a moment?' Fakhri Sadat asked.

'Be my guest,' Am Ramazan said.

On the wall was a large picture of Khomeini, and the room was filled with framed portraits of other ayatollahs.

'We need your help, Am Ramazam,' Aqa Jaan said. 'Jawad has been arrested. Would you be willing to do us a favour?'

Am Ramazan looked surprised. He had been their gardener, and they had always been good to him. Now they were standing before him, humbled, asking for his help. 'What can I do? I'm not sure I can be of any use.'

'I need to talk to Ayatollah Araki. Can you arrange an appointment for me? It can't wait. I have to see him now, tonight, before it's too late.'

'Tonight? That's impossible,' he said. 'I mean, I don't

know, wait a minute. Please sit down. Fakhri Sadat, would you like some tea?'

He went over to the telephone, which had only recently been installed, and dialled a number. 'It's me,' he said. 'I'd like to make an appointment with the ayatollah. Can you set it up for me? No, not for myself, but for an acquaintance . . . Yes, I know him well, I've known him for years. It's important . . . Tonight, if possible . . . I understand. And tomorrow? Okay, in the mosque, after the sermon? No, before the sermon is better.'

Tears sprang to Aqa Jaan's eyes.

It was Friday, so hundreds of people were heading for the mosque. Aqa Jaan stood by the door and waited, but Ayatollah Araki had been delayed. Just as the ayatollah was about to leave, his red phone had rung.

'Iraq used chemical weapons against our troops this week,' the ayatollah heard the Friday Prayer Leader say. 'Thousands of soldiers have died, including three hundred men from Senejan and nearby villages. The bodies will be arriving in Senejan tomorrow.'

Ayatollah Araki's black Mercedes drew up in front of the mosque, and two Revolutionary Guards got out. Aqa Jaan moved towards the car, but one of the guards stopped him.

'I have an appointment with the ayatollah,' Aqa Jaan said.

'Get out of the way!' the guard barked.

The ayatollah looked at Aqa Jaan, but had no idea who he was.

Aqa Jaan removed his hat and bowed. The ayatollah swept right past him.

'I have an appointment with you,' Aqa Jaan explained.

The ayatollah paused, glanced back at him and walked on again.

Aqa Jaan started to run after him, but was seized by one of the guards. 'I'm the former custodian of the mosque!' he cried.

The ayatollah signalled for the guard to release him.

Aqa Jaan hurried to catch up with him. As they neared the mosque, the ayatollah held out his hand. At the entrance to the prayer room, Aqa Jaan took his hand and kissed it.

The worshippers, who had stood up to greet the ayatollah, saw Aqa Jaan kiss the ayatollah's hand. They also saw the ayatollah stop for a moment to listen to him. Everyone in the room noticed that Aqa Jaan was still talking when the ayatollah stalked off in annoyance. They all watched as Aqa Jaan clutched the ayatollah's robe and was roughly shoved out of the way by the guards.

The ayatollah strode directly to the pulpit and stood on the first step. A guard handed him a rifle, which he held throughout his speech, to symbolise the fact that the country was at war.

'Saddam, who is not the true son of his father, has bombed our pearl in Isfahan!' he began. 'Saddam is a nobody, a bastard who dances to the tune of the Americans. America is taking revenge! America is using Saddam as a war machine! Saddam is not bombing our mosques, America is!

'Bomb us, America! We are not afraid of you. Destroy our historic places of worship, America! We are not afraid of you!

'Saddam is a mere hireling. He is afraid of us, afraid of our army, afraid of your sons.

'Prepare yourselves, believers of Senejan, for I have painful news. Saddam has used chemical weapons against our sons! Prepare yourselves, mothers, prepare yourselves, fathers, for we shall soon bury your sons! Your sons who are now being welcomed by angels in Paradise!'

'*Allahu akbar! Allahu akbar!*' the worshippers cried.

'God is great! Victory will be ours! We will conquer Baghdad, but we will not stop in Baghdad. We will strike at America in the heart of Zionism and liberate the Al-Aqsa Mosque in Jerusalem!'

'*Allahu akbar! Allahu akbar!*' the crowd roared.

'We are living in difficult times, but your sons are making history. I congratulate you on the death of your sons!

'Watch out, mothers, stay alert, fathers, for we are fighting on two fronts. Our sons are fighting Saddam on one front, while here at home we are fighting the Communists – a small but no less dangerous enemy in our midst. We will weed them out and destroy them as well!'

Pointing his rifle at Aqa Jaan, he thundered, 'Punish them! And show them no mercy!'

'*Allahu akbar!*'

Aqa Jaan, who was kneeling on the ground, felt the weight of the mosque on his shoulders. With his back bent, he mumbled:

We worship You and ask You for help.
Guide us to the straight path,
The path of those upon whom You have bestowed
  Your grace,
Those whose portion is not wrath and who do not
  go astray.

Afterwards, when Aqa Jaan told Fakhri Sadat how he'd been treated by the ayatollah, she flung on her chador.

'Where are you going?'

'To see Zinat. She *has* to help us!'

'She won't. She didn't lift a finger to help Ahmad and she won't lift a finger to help Jawad. The world has been turned upside down. Khomeini has called for a jihad. Anyone who says a word against the regime is supposed to be reported to the authorities. Mothers have even turned in their own children.'

'But Jawad hasn't done anything!'

'Don't be so naïve, Fakhri, that's what every mother says. He hasn't lived at home for a long time. We don't know what he's been up to or why he was in that village.'

'I'm going to see Zinat anyway.'

'Zinat has publicly denounced Ahmad in the mosque. If she talks about her own son that way, she's not going to help yours.'

'We have to go; we have no choice. We'll go together.'

Zinat was still working in the women's section of the prison. She put the prisoners under such pressure that they finally snapped and were prepared to pray seven times a day. They also shamelessly betrayed their friends, one after another.

One night, when Zinat had unexpectedly stopped by the house to pick up the last of her belongings, Aqa Jaan's voice came to her out of the darkness. 'Why are you creeping around, Zinat? Why don't you talk to us? Why won't you say hello to us any more?'

Zinat didn't answer, but kept walking towards the gate.

Aqa Jaan stopped her.

'You can't just walk away. I demand an answer. People are saying bad things about you behind your back. They say that you've become a torturer. Is that true?'

At last Zinat broke her silence. 'People are free to say whatever they like. I'm simply doing my duty, and obeying the wishes of Allah!'

'Which Allah do you mean? Why don't I know that Allah?'

'Times have changed!' Zinat hissed, and she yanked open the gate and left.

Zinat felt good. In fact, she had never felt so good. She didn't care what people were saying about her. After all, she wasn't doing anything wrong! After Ahmad's arrest, Zinat had secretly met with Khalkhal in Qom. It had been a crucial meeting, a turning point in her life. Sometimes she'd wondered if she were on the right track, but Khalkhal had swept away her doubts.

'A great revolution has taken place,' Khalkhal had said. 'After 2,500 years the Persian empire has finally been torn up by the roots and replaced by Islam. We're working hard to set up the first Shiite republic. If we let this opportunity slip by, Allah will punish us unmercifully. Allah has two faces: a merciful one and a cruel one. Now is the time for the cruel, terrifying face. It's the only way to keep Islam alive. We're plagued by enemies, so we have no choice. You have to opt for Islam and forget everything else. Your son, your father, your mother – none of them matters any more. You will be rewarded by Allah in Paradise.'

The women of the morals police, who were under Zinat's command, were housed in the former mayor's residence.

When Aqa Jaan and Fakhri arrived there, they found a group of parents huddled in the courtyard, come to plead on behalf of their arrested daughters. Fakhri Sadat adjusted her chador to make sure that not a single strand of hair was showing, then walked towards the steps. She was stopped by two women in black chadors.

'What do you want?' one of them asked.

'I'd like to speak to Zinat Khanom.'

'*Sister* Zinat!' the other woman corrected her.

'I beg your pardon,' Fakhri Sadat said. 'Of course, I meant Sister Zinat!'

'Sister Zinat is busy. She isn't seeing anyone just now.'

'I'm here on family business. I need to speak to her.'

'She doesn't have time. Not for families, not for anyone.'

'I'm her sister-in-law. And that's Aqa Jaan, her eldest brother-in-law. I need to speak to her right away. If you'd let her know we're waiting, I'm sure she'll talk to us.'

'I'll see what I can do. But go back and wait with the others.'

'Of course,' Fakhri agreed.

Zinat, looking down from her office through a gap in the curtains, had already spotted Aqa Jaan and Fakhri. She knew that Jawad had been arrested. She also knew she wouldn't be able to help him.

Although Khalkhal phoned her from time to time, she wasn't able to phone him. She didn't know exactly what he did, nor did she realise that he was Allah's dreaded judge.

Would she help Jawad if he were really in danger? She trembled at the thought of her own impotence. No, she couldn't help him. She was in no position to put a stop to such things. She could only carry out orders. And Khomeini had made his orders clear in his speech to the morals police: 'Today Islam is resting on your shoulders. If necessary, you must sacrifice your own children!'

Zinat looked down at the courtyard again. 'I don't want to see them,' she told the guard. 'Tell them I'm not here.'

The guard went downstairs. 'Sister Zinat isn't here,' she told Fakhri Sadat. 'She's gone out.'

Fakhri was frantically looking around, not knowing what to do next, when her eye fell on one of the windows.

A woman was peeking through the curtains. Zinat! The curtains jerked shut.

'She *is* here,' Fakhri said. 'I just saw her at that window.'

'No, she's not,' the guard said firmly. 'I just told you she wasn't. Now go home!'

Aqa Jaan tugged at Fakhri Sadat's arm. 'Come, let's go!'

'No! I'm not leaving, I'm staying here! I have to speak to Zinat,' she said.

'Leave this instant, or I'll call the guards!' the woman said.

'Zinat!' Fakhri called.

A bearded guard came out and pushed Fakhri towards the gate with his rifle butt. 'Get out! Now!'

'Zi-n-a-a-a-a-a-a-t!' Fakhri wailed at the top of her lungs.

The guard hit her with his rifle. Fakhri stumbled and fell against the gate, which caused her chador to slip to the ground. Aqa Jaan grabbed the man by his collar and shoved him against the wall. The female guard screamed for backup, and two armed men came running towards Aqa Jaan. Zinat leaned out the window. 'Don't hit him!' she cried. 'Let him go!'

Aqa Jaan scooped up Fakhri's chador and wrapped it around her. 'We're going!' he said.

Khalkhal arrived in the city late that afternoon.

Now that so many soldiers from Senejan had been killed by chemical warfare, this was a good moment to try the opponents of the regime.

He interrogated the prisoners in the former stable of the old jail, which still reeked of horse manure. The walls were lined with horseshoes, saddles and bridles. Khalkhal always picked the most macabre locations.

Three young men were led inside. Within fifteen minutes, Khalkhal had delivered all three verdicts: the first was sentenced to death, the second was given ten years in prison and the third fifteen years.

A young woman was next.

'Name?'

'Mahbub.'

'You were arrested while trying to escape. Why were you running away?'

'I was running away because I was afraid I was going to be arrested.'

'What had you done that made you think you were going to be arrested?'

'I hadn't done anything.'

'We found flyers in your handbag!'

'That's not true. I didn't have any flyers in my handbag.'

'You were arrested in the Red Village. Do you live there?'

'No.'

'So what were you doing there?'

'Visiting friends.'

'What are their names?'

'I can't tell you that.'

'You mean you *won't* tell me. Fine. Are you sorry for what you did?'

'I didn't do anything wrong, so I have nothing to be sorry for!'

'If you sign here and say you repent, I'll reduce your sentence.'

'If I didn't do anything wrong, why should I have to sign anything?'

'Six years!' said Khalkhal. 'Next!'

She was taken out and Jawad was led in by an armed guard.

'Name!' Khalkhal said, without looking at the accused.

'Jawad!'

'Your father's name?'

'Aqa Jaan!'

Khalkhal's head jerked up, as if he'd been stung by a bee. He stared at Jawad through his dark glasses.

Jawad was unable to see him, because of the bright light shining in his eyes. Khalkhal's pen rolled off the table and onto the ground. He leaned over to pick it up, and in that brief moment Jawad caught a glimpse of the judge's face.

There was something familiar about it, Jawad thought.

Khalkhal leafed through his papers, clearly stalling for time. 'Water!' he shouted to the guards who were posted outside.

The two men, assuming they'd been ordered to remove the prisoner, came in, grabbed hold of Jawad and were about to drag him out of the room.

'Leave him here and bring me a glass of water!' Khalkhal snarled.

I know him from somewhere, thought Jawad. His voice sounds familiar.

One of the guards placed a glass of water in front of Khalkhal and left. Khalkhal took a sip. 'You have a file as thick as my arm,' he said. 'You're an active member of the Communist Party. You're the mastermind who works behind the scenes. At the time of your arrest, you were carrying a gun that had fired three bullets. You were seen shooting at a helicopter. These are serious offences for which you can receive the death penalty. Do you have anything to say to that?'

'It's a pack of lies. Furthermore, I don't recognise the authority of this court. What you're doing is illegal. I have the right to a lawyer! The right to defend myself!'

'Shut up and listen!' Khalkhal snapped. 'I've already spent more time on you than on the others. Your file contains a long list of serious offences.'

'They're obviously trumped-up charges, because I didn't have a gun on me, and I certainly wasn't shooting at a helicopter.'

'I don't have time to discuss this with you. I advise you to listen carefully to what I'm about to say. Is that clear? I know your father, and I'm willing to help you if you agree to cooperate.'

It's Khalkhal! Jawad suddenly realised. Khalkhal is Allah's judge!

He was aghast. His mouth went dry and his hands began to shake.

Khalkhal knew that Jawad had recognised him. 'Listen to me, young man. The bodies of more than three hundred soldiers are being brought here tomorrow from the front. All young men of your age. While they were out fighting the enemy, you were shooting at our helicopters. I don't care who you are. I'd sentence my own brother to death if I had to. But I'm making an exception in your case because I know your father. Now I'm going to ask you three questions. Think carefully before you answer. If you're smart, you'll give the right answer. This is the first – and it will be the last – time I've ever given anyone this chance.

'The first question is: Are you a Communist, or do you believe in Islam?'

The gravity of Khalkhal's words hadn't sunk in, and Jawad was still seething: 'I'm not going to answer that question! Judges aren't allowed to ask such questions. Besides, this isn't a courtroom; it's a stable!'

'Think before you talk,' Khalkhal said, clearly disappointed. 'The second question is: If I reduce your sentence, will you pray seven times a day along with the other prisoners?'

'Prayer is a personal matter, so I won't answer that question either,' Jawad retorted.

'Question three: Will you sign this form, stating that you're sorry for what you've done?'

'Why should I repent when I haven't done anything wrong? No, I won't sign it.'

Khalkhal was in doubt. He wanted to save Jawad, but only if he agreed to cooperate, at least to some extent. 'I'm going to give you one more chance,' Khalkhal said. 'I advise you to make use of it.'

He took a Koran out of his pocket and handed it to Jawad. 'If you swear on the Koran that you weren't carrying a weapon and didn't fire any shots, I'll reduce your sentence. If you refuse, I'll have you executed at once!'

'You've had hundreds of innocent people executed! And that's a crime. A crime in the eyes of the Koran. I refuse to cooperate. The fact that you know my father is all the more reason to say no. I'm ashamed of your deeds. I refuse to accept any favours from you. You feel guilty about the way you've treated my family, but I'm ashamed of you. You're the monster who abandoned his wife and disabled child, the bully who beat and tormented his own wife. I will never kneel before the man who had hundreds of Kurds executed in one day. I wouldn't be my father's son if I did. Put away your Koran, I don't need it!'

'Death!' Khalkhal bellowed.

The guards rushed in and led Jawad to the room where the executions were carried out.

One of the guards put a blindfold over his eyes and stood him up against the wall. Jawad didn't think for a moment that he was going to be shot. He thought that

Khalkhal was just trying to frighten him into signing a confession.

The guards left him standing there for a while with his blindfold on, which made him even more sure that they were just trying to frighten him. Besides, he hadn't been carrying a weapon and hadn't fired at a helicopter, so they had no right to execute him. He heard footsteps, which he suspected were Khalkhal's. He was no doubt coming to interrogate him some more. Jawad was convinced that Khalkhal would spare him, that he would call off the execution.

But Khalkhal didn't come over to him. Jawad expected him to say, 'That's enough. Take off his blindfold and throw him in prison.'

Instead, Khalkhal barked out an order: 'Take up your positions!'

Two guards knelt and aimed their rifles at Jawad.

Jawad stood up straight and squared his shoulders so Khalkhal could see that he wasn't afraid. He knew Khalkhal wouldn't go through with it.

'Ready . . . aim . . . *fire*!' Khalkhal commanded.

Shots rang out. At first Jawad didn't feel the bullets slamming into his body. I was right, he thought, they were just trying to frighten me.

Then he slumped forward and fell to the ground.

And then he laid down his head and closed his eyes.

The Mountains

Aqa Jaan had gone to collect Jawad's body, which was now lying in a delivery van parked in front of the house.

Fakhri Sadat stood by the window and looked down at Muezzin, who was anxiously pacing the courtyard. In the frame of the window, she looked like a black-and-white photograph of a grieving mother.

Persian custom demanded that she weep and wail, beat her head and tear out her hair. Then the other women would rush over and take her hand, and they would cry and comfort one another. But that was forbidden. The regime did not allow executed prisoners to be mourned openly.

Aqa Jaan had no idea where he was going to bury Jawad. He had spent all afternoon on the phone, trying to get permission to bury him in the city, but no one had dared to go out on a limb to help him.

There was the sound of feet in the alley. Although Muezzin listened carefully, he didn't recognise the footsteps.

A key turned in the lock, the gate creaked open and in came Shahbal. Lizard hurried over to him.

Muezzin also went over to his son, embraced him and wept silently on his shoulder.

Shahbal had heard the news. It was dangerous for him to come home, but he'd set off for Senejan the moment the message had reached him.

Aqa Jaan came out of his study and greeted Shahbal as he always did. He didn't show the slightest flicker of emotion, making Shahbal wonder if he'd driven three hundred miles for nothing.

'Thank God you're here,' Aqa Jaan said. 'You're just in time. Who gave you the message?' He went on without waiting for an answer. 'We have to hurry! I've got him in the van by the gate.'

In the lamplight Shahbal saw his fears confirmed by the haunted look in Aqa Jaan's eyes. It was a familiar story: a corpse, a father and no grave.

He took him by the arm and embraced him. 'You have my condolences, Aqa Jaan,' he said as he wept. 'My poor Aqa Jaan . . .'

Shahbal, feeling guilty for having encouraged Jawad, had been afraid that Aqa Jaan would shun him.

'It was God's will, my boy,' Aqa Jaan said. 'Come, let's go. It will be dark soon. We don't have much time.'

Shahbal was holding the key to the van, a sobering enough fact, but until he'd seen Jawad for himself, he couldn't believe that he was really dead.

Shahbal opened the rear doors. There he lay, wrapped in a white shroud. He was curled up on his right side, with his hands between his thighs. He looked cold. Shahbal undid the shroud so he could see his face. It was definitely Jawad, with a bullet hole in his left temple.

'We have to hurry,' Aqa Jaan said.

Shahbal slid in behind the wheel.

'Where are we going?' he asked as they drove out of the alley.

'That way!' Aqa Jaan said, pointing to the mountains in the north.

Shahbal didn't know what his uncle's plans were, but

he was sure of one thing: Aqa Jaan wasn't the kind of man who would let his son be buried in a deserted spot in the mountains.

He would have liked to share his grief with his uncle, but Aqa Jaan looked so preoccupied he didn't dare disturb him. Instead, he kept driving silently towards the mountains.

'Do you have a plan?' he asked after a while.

'We're taking him to Marzjaran,' Aqa Jaan said.

'Marzjaran?' Shahbal was surprised. 'Whatever for? The villagers are all Khomeini supporters. We can't ask them for a grave!'

Aqa Jaan made no reply, and Shahbal knew from his uncle's silence that he must have consulted the Koran before leaving, opening it to a random page and letting his finger fall on a random verse. Since his decision was based on faith and superstition, rather than on reality, further discussion was pointless.

The track wasn't really meant for cars. Actually, it wasn't a track at all, but a couple of ruts left by the local bus.

Marzjaran, the village closest to the city, lay at the foot of the mountains, behind the first foothill. Shahbal drove up the hill and cautiously wound his way down the other side. He could already see a few scattered houses.

It was cold. The tall mountain peaks were covered in snow. Darkness hadn't fallen yet, but the mountains cast a dark shadow over the village. The houses were made of stone: if you didn't know there was a village there, it would be indistinguishable from the rocks. When they got nearer, they saw smoke coming out of the chimney of the bathhouse – the only sign of life.

In a place like this, people were always waiting: for

someone to come or for someone to leave, for a birth or for death.

Sleepy Marzjaran was forever waiting for an event of some kind. Only then did it wake up and stir itself.

Shahbal drove into the village. There was no need to announce their arrival. An unfamiliar vehicle driving down the hill was sure to be noticed. After all, who would come here in the dead of winter? It had to be an enemy, a fugitive or a man in search of a grave.

Suddenly they heard barking. A pack of dogs bounded furiously off a boulder and came charging towards them, followed by three warmly dressed men with rifles.

'Allah!' Aqa Jaan exclaimed.

The dogs barked and blocked the road, while the men approached the van.

'Stay here,' Aqa Jaan said to Shahbal as he got out.

He went up to the men, intending to talk to them, to tell them that he knew the imam of their village. He put out his hand, but they ignored him, choosing instead to march over to the driver's side and glare at Shahbal. Then they moved to the back, obviously intending to open the rear doors.

Aqa Jaan hurried round to the back, the frantically barking dogs at his heels. Shahbal leapt out of the van, but Aqa Jaan swiftly pushed the men aside and stood with his back to the doors. One of the men grabbed him by the sleeve and pulled him away, while the other two swung open the doors. One of the dogs jumped inside and sank its teeth into the shroud. Shahbal grabbed the jack, which had been lying next to the body, and hit the dog so hard that it sprang out of the van, whimpering.

Shahbal was livid. He shoved the men away from the door and positioned himself in front of it, guarding the body, his hand wrapped tightly round the jack.

359

Outraged at his bold behaviour in *their* village, all three men attacked him. Aqa Jaan tried to stop them, but they were too strong. Shahbal did his best to ward off the blows until a group of villagers, awakened by the noise, finally separated them.

Aqa Jaan raised his hands in supplication. 'I'm begging you for a grave,' he said. 'I have the body of my son with me.'

No one made a move or said a word. It was as if they were made of stone. Three statues stared at him in disbelief.

'There are no graves for sinners here!' one of them exclaimed. 'Go away!'

'I'm begging you for—'

'Go away, I said!' the man roared, and he strode angrily towards Aqa Jaan. Shahbal snatched up the jack, but Aqa Jaan took it from him. 'Let's go,' he said.

They got in the van, and Shahbal turned it around.

When they had put enough distance between themselves and the village, Shahbal glanced over at his uncle. He was huddled in his seat – a broken man. He could tell by the way he was huddled in his seat. Aqa Jaan had turned to his Koran for advice, and it had let him down. He looked like an old bird that no longer dared to fly.

Darkness had fallen. Shahbal drove aimlessly through the mountains, not knowing where to go until Aqa Jaan suddenly sat upright and took the Holy Book out of his pocket. He had obviously found his strength again. He opened his Koran and slid his fingers down the page like a blind man. After a few minutes, he said calmly, 'We'll go to Saruq.' Then he slipped the book back into his pocket.

Shahbal disagreed. There was no difference between

Saruq and the village they had just been to. They could go to a hundred different villages, and the result would always be the same.

Aqa Jaan didn't want to bury his son without honour. He was hoping to find an official grave for him, but it was asking the impossible.

After a while Shahbal broke the silence. 'They won't help you there either,' he said. 'We need to accept it.'

Aqa Jaan remained silent, pretending he hadn't heard him.

Saruq's cemetery lay outside the village, in a remote and bleak spot.

'Wait here,' Aqa Jaan said. 'I'd better go into the village by myself.'

Shahbal got out, stood next to the van and watched his uncle walk towards the houses. He's right, he thought to himself, I'm ashamed I didn't think of it sooner. We haven't done anything wrong! Jawad mustn't be buried in secret!

He picked up the jack and waited. Then he heard voices and saw five men carrying lanterns. They were old men, walking side by side with Aqa Jaan. There were no dogs.

He could tell by the set of Aqa Jaan's shoulders that he hadn't been able to convince them either. They were friends, escorting him out of the village as an expression of sympathy. But they knew that there were informers and spies everywhere and that there would be hell to pay if they allowed the body to be buried in their village.

They came up to Shahbal to say hello and offer their condolences, but Shahbal was in no mood for sympathy. He was furious, and filled with a sense of helplessness. He opened the van door and sat behind the wheel. Aqa Jaan said goodbye to the men and climbed in beside Shahbal.

They had just driven off when they heard a shout.

'Stop!' said Aqa Jaan.

Shahbal stopped. Aqa Jaan rolled down the window. One of the men came running up, panting. 'You should go and see Rahmanali,' he said. 'He's the only one who can help you.'

Aqa Jaan nodded a few times to show his agreement.

'Drive to Jirya,' Aqa Jaan said to Shahbal. 'We're going to see Rahmanali.'

Jirya was indeed the most likely place for them to find a grave, because the village lay within the family's domain. Many of Aqa Jaan and Fakhri Sadat's relatives still lived there, and it was also where Kazem Khan was buried.

They should probably have driven straight to Jirya to begin with, but the Koran had not pointed them in that direction. Now that Rahmanali's name had come up, Aqa Jaan was sure it was the right place.

Rahmanali was a wizened old man with a long grey beard. He was one hundred and four years old and reputed to be a holy man. It was said that he performed miracles and brought dying children back to life. His word was law in Jirya, and everyone knew it. Anybody who asked him for refuge was sure of safety. His house had been declared holy by the villagers, and they were proud of him. When no one else could be counted on, Aqa Jaan could always go to Rahmanali. They knew each other well. Aqa Jaan often stopped by to see him when he was in Jirya and gave him money whenever he needed it.

* * *

They bumped and bounced along a narrow dirt track, afraid that the van would slide into a ravine or get stuck in a rut. Jirya was high up in the mountains, near the snow, and the cold was unbearable. The heater did nothing to dispel the chill. Aqa Jaan kept casting worried glances at the body in the back.

Just before they reached Jirya, Aqa Jaan turned to Shahbal. 'Switch off your lights and pull in behind this rock. We're not going to drive into the village. I'll go and look for Rahmanali, while you stay here.'

'Let *me* do it,' Shahbal said.

'It will be better if *I* talk to him.'

'I don't want you going there alone.'

'What else can we do? We can't leave the body here by itself.'

'I don't trust anyone, not even in this village. Times have changed. If someone sees you, they'll know what you've come for.'

Aqa Jaan's hand slid into his pocket, making sure he still had his Koran.

'We don't have a choice. I'll manage,' he said, and he left.

He trudged through the snow and across the wooden bridge that spanned the river. By coming in on foot, he wouldn't alert the dogs. The icy wind blowing across the snow lashed his hands and face.

One thought was uppermost in his mind: let me reach Rahmanali before the fundamentalists see me. If they try to stop me, I'll yell his name so loudly that Rahmanali will be sure to hear it, even if he's sleeping more soundly than he ever has in his life.

He entered the village as quietly as he could. There

were four blocks to go before he reached the square where Rahmanali lived.

The dogs had picked up his scent. An unfamiliar smell in the middle of a cold winter night spelled trouble. A dog behind him suddenly began to bark. It was bound to wake up the entire village. What should he do: run or keep walking? At the second block a huge black dog jumped over a wooden fence. 'Allah!' He burst into a run.

Every dog in the village was now barking like mad. The black dog was chasing after him, so Aqa Jaan speeded up. Ahead of him he saw a group of surprised villagers. Two men tried to bar his way, but he pushed them aside. 'Rahmanali!' he shouted. He was running as hard as he could. His heart was pounding in his throat, and his eyes were so filled with tears he couldn't see a thing. Blindly, he headed towards the square. Everyone knew where he was going.

'Al-l-a-a-a-a-a-h! Rahmanali! Refuge! I'm seeking refuge for my son!'

Three armed men suddenly came out of an alley. One of them hit Aqa Jaan on the back of his leg, so that he tripped and fell in the snow. 'Who are you?' the man demanded, and he shone a torch in Aqa Jaan's face.

They recognised him immediately, helped him to his feet and walked him back to the van, where a few villagers were gathered on top of the rocks.

This was preposterous. Aqa Jaan couldn't believe it was really happening. This was his village. His family was buried here. Why were they treating him like this? The revolution had brought out the worst in people. You couldn't trust anyone any more, not even your own brother or sister. He'd read a lot of books about the lives of kings, so he knew that such people had always existed. Treachery and wickedness were part of human nature.

Aqa Jaan climbed back in and Shahbal turned the van around.

'Let's go home,' Aqa Jaan said.

'Home?'

'I'll bury him in the courtyard, under the cedar tree.'

Shahbal wanted to say something, but he couldn't find the words.

He carefully wound his way down the mountain. Eagles were soaring overhead – their first flight of the day. They had been awakened by the sun, which was slowly beginning to rise over the mountain peaks. The light wouldn't reach the city for at least another hour.

They needed to hurry, but Shahbal didn't dare drive faster. Every time he braked, the van skidded and Jawad's body bumped against the front seat.

Suddenly, a mile or so behind him, he saw a car. The driver was flashing his lights. Aqa Jaan had noticed it too. 'Pull over. Something must be wrong.'

Shahbal stopped and they got out. He grabbed the torch and signalled to let the driver know he'd seen him.

The car vanished behind a few rocks, then came back into view.

'It's a jeep!' Shahbal exclaimed.

The jeep stopped. The driver turned off the lights and got out. It was a man, wearing ordinary clothes, except for a French beret and knee-high boots. He rushed over to Aqa Jaan, uttered a gentle '*Salaam*', embraced him and kissed him on the forehead. 'Give me the body,' he said. 'I'll bury Jawad on my estate. But we've got to hurry. It'll soon be light.'

Shahbal was puzzled. The man was obviously an old friend of Aqa Jaan's, but Shahbal didn't know him.

'Help me get him into the jeep,' the man said to Shahbal.

Working together, the three of them loaded the body into the jeep.

The man embraced Aqa Jaan again, patted Shahbal on the back, hopped into his jeep, skilfully turned the vehicle around and drove off into the mountains.

Aqa Jaan and Shahbal stood by the empty van and watched until the jeep had melted into the darkness. The eagles circled the van one last time, then flew up high into the sky.

All-Wise

The house was shrouded in grief, as though a black chador had been drawn over it. No one talked, no one cried, no one broke the silence. Except for one person who chanted the All-Wise, All-Knowing surah over and over again:

> Oh, you, you are possessed!
> There is nothing, but we have its treasures with Us,
> And We send it down only in fixed measures.
> We send forth the pollinating winds,
> While they are heavy laden.
> All-Wise! All-Knowing!
> It is We who give life and death.
> It is We who know those who came before
> And those who shall come after.

Sorrow wilted the plants, a few of the fish floated belly-up in the *hauz*, and the old cat died on the roof of the mosque.

Meanwhile, there had been a wave of executions. The opponents of the regime were buried outside the cities, at the foot of the mountains. No one was allowed to visit their graves. The eyes of the nation were focused on the martyrs at the front. Week after week, hundreds of bodies were transported to the cities during the Friday prayer.

The crow was the first to break the silence in the house.

It flew up into the air and cawed loudly, signalling the arrival of a visitor.

Fakhri Sadat was in the kitchen, cooking dinner. Lizard opened the front gate.

An unknown man in a worn suit and hat came in and walked towards the *hauz*.

Fakhri Sadat stared in surprise at the stranger walking so calmly past her window.

The man stopped by the *hauz* and stared at the fish. Then he strolled around the courtyard with his hands behind his back, pausing first by the stairs, then peering through the window of the guest room, and at last continuing on to the Opium Room, where he tried the door to see if it was unlocked.

Fakhri Sadat opened the kitchen window. 'Are you looking for someone, sir?'

He didn't answer, but moved in the direction of the library.

Fakhri wanted to run after him and find out what he was up to, but she was frightened.

'Muezzin!' she called. 'A stranger is wandering around the courtyard! Will you come up here and find out what he wants?'

Lizard, who had been lying under the tree and keeping an eye on the visitor, scuttled down to the cellar to fetch Muezzin.

The man disappeared behind the tree, where Fakhri couldn't see him.

Suddenly she heard a loud banging noise.

Muezzin came up from the cellar, holding his walking stick, with Lizard at his side.

'A man in a suit and a hat just went towards the library. I think he's trying to break down the door,' Fakhri Sadat said. 'Can you hear him?'

Muezzin hurried over to the library. 'What do you think you're doing?' he demanded. 'Who are you? You can't just come barging in here!'

Fakhri Sadat put on her chador and went outside. The man was pounding a rock against the door, trying to smash it in.

'What does he look like?' Muezzin asked Fakhri Sadat.

'I can't see his face. He's standing in the shadow.'

'Does he have a beard?'

'I don't think so. All I can see is his hat.'

Muezzin started to go over to him, but Fakhri stopped him. 'I think he's mad! He might be a tramp!'

'Go and get Aqa Jaan!' Fakhri said to Lizard, who had clambered up the tree, where he was monitoring the man's every move.

He leapt from the tree to the roof and disappeared.

Muezzin brandished his walking stick. 'Who are you?' he repeated. 'What are you doing here?'

There was no answer.

'Stop that, you idiot!' Muezzin said. He waved his walking stick again. 'Stop banging on the door, you bastard, or I'll beat the shit out of you!'

But the man didn't stop. Muezzin was about to hit him when Fakhri Sadat cried, 'No, don't! He's mentally ill!' And she dragged Muezzin away by his coat.

Only when Aqa Jaan arrived on the scene did the man stop pounding. 'What's going on here?' he asked. Since the man was standing in the shadow of the library wall, Aqa Jaan couldn't see him very well. 'What's your name, sir?'

There was no response.

'Step away from the shadow so I can see you,' Aqa Jaan said. 'Give me your hand, I won't hurt you, I'm just going to lead you out of the shadow.' Aqa Jaan calmly took the man by the arm and led him into the sunlight.

'Would you like something to drink? Are you hungry?'
The man's eyes filled with tears.

Those eyes were familiar . . .

'Allah, Allah!' exclaimed Aqa Jaan. 'Fakhri, it's our Ahmad!'

Muezzin reached out to touch him. He ran his fingers over Ahmad's hat and down his face, then pulled him close and wrapped him in his arms.

Fakhri Sadat laid her head on his shoulder and wept. 'Oh, Ahmad!' she said. 'Our Ahmad! Let's go inside. What have they done to you? How dare they! Come, everything will be all right.'

Aqa Jaan unlocked the library door for him, but Ahmad didn't go in. Instead, he shuffled over to the guest room, opened the door, went inside, took off his shoes and sank down on the bed.

'Let him sleep,' Fakhri said to Aqa Jaan and Muezzin.

Khalkhal had arranged for Ahmad's early release from prison, but the life had been drained out of Ahmad. After his arrest, his wife and child had gone back to live with her parents, and her influential father – a staunch supporter of the regime – had arranged a divorce and seen to it that his daughter had been awarded custody of the child. Ahmad had been robbed of his fatherhood.

The next morning Fakhri Sadat called him for breakfast, but Ahmad was still unresponsive. So she went to his room, helped him out of bed and brought him outside, where she lovingly washed his hands and face in the *hauz* and led him to the library, so he could see that the door was now open.

He went in and shuffled past the bookcases, running his finger over the spines of the books. He switched on the antique reading lamp on his desk and touched his chair, but didn't sit down. Then he went out again and shuffled over to his old room, where he looked at his bed, his chair and his notebook – the one in which he used to jot down his ideas for the Friday prayers – and then sat down on the bed.

He sat there all day, staring vacantly into space. Aqa Jaan brought him some food and tried to talk to him, but he could see that Ahmad wasn't ready to talk, that he needed to be left alone for a while.

That night Ahmad packed his suitcase and left.

Lizard saw him leave and hurried over to alert Aqa Jaan. But it was too late. He had gone.

The Mujahideen

There was fierce fighting at the front. Iranian troops had recaptured a number of strategic areas and opened a new front in Iraqi territory, but it looked as though they'd never be able to oust the Iraqis from the vital oil cities of Khorramshahr and Abadan. Saddam used bombs and chemical weapons to keep the Iranians away from those cities.

The leftist opposition had been almost completely wiped out, but there was one organised group that the regime had so far left untouched: the Mujahideen. The members of the Mujahideen were devout Muslims, though their interpretation of the Koran differed from Khomeini's. In public they pretended to support the regime, but in secret they were amassing weapons, so that they could strike when the time was right.

Khomeini declared them to be public enemy number one and warned that they were out to destroy the government from within. Now that Iran was fighting an endless war and growing weaker by the day, he wanted this internal foe to be eliminated once and for all. Because the Mujahideen were Muslims, however, Khomeini couldn't simply make them disappear.

An emergency meeting of the Executive Committee of the Islamic Republic was called to discuss the matter. They reached a unanimous decision: the Mujahideen, like the leftist opposition before them, were to be wiped out at once.

Jeeps were driven in the middle of the night to the

homes of the Mujahideen leaders. Armed agents burst into their homes from the rooftops, but not a single leader was found. They had all fled.

Clearly, they'd had advance warning. It seemed that the Executive Committee had a spy in its midst.

The chairman, Ayatollah Beheshti, called another committee meeting. He assumed that the spy wouldn't show up, thereby giving himself away, but all of the members were present and accounted for. They spent a long time discussing the possible source of the leak.

'I think I know how the information was leaked and who leaked it,' said one of the members, a man known for his keen mind and decisiveness. The other men looked at him in surprise and waited breathlessly for him to reveal the name.

He surreptitiously slid his black briefcase, which was under the table, closer to Beheshti's feet, then stood up. 'I have proof,' he said. 'It's in my office. I'll go and get it. I won't be long.'

As soon as he left the conference room, he tore down the stairs, raced to his car, jumped in and roared off.

Before he even turned the corner, there was an explosion. The building behind him collapsed, sending up a huge cloud of fire and smoke, and killing every one of the committee members.

The news was announced on the radio. Crowds gathered round Khomeini's residence to express their sympathy. He came out on the balcony and calmly delivered a speech. '*Enna lellah wa enna elayhi raje'un*,' he began. 'This time the Americans worked their evil through the Mujahideen. But it doesn't matter, because Allah is on our side! I have appointed a new committee. We will not let anyone or anything stand in our way!'

The hunt for the Mujahideen supporters began at once. There was a spate of random shootings. Mujahideen sympathisers blocked off a few streets in the centre of Tehran and reached for their weapons. Street fighting broke out between the Mujahideen and the security troops.

Everyone who was arrested that day was summarily executed the very same night.

The next week, the chief of the secret police met with Khomeini to inform him of an urgent security issue. He knelt before Khomeini and kissed his hand. 'The Mujahideen have managed to infiltrate the government at the highest levels,' he whispered. 'While our attention was focused on the front, they took over the most strategic posts. They've even penetrated your inner circle. I've put together a list of suspects in high ministerial positions. With your permission, I'll notify the prime minister and have the suspects arrested at once.'

Khomeini put on his glasses, examined the list and gave his permission for everyone on it to be arrested.

The chief of the secret police went directly from Khomeini's house to an undisclosed location, where a cabinet meeting was being held. First he spoke with the prime minister, relaying the gist of his conversation with Khomeini, then the two of them went to the cabinet meeting to inform the ministers.

The chief of the secret police came right to the point. 'I've just come from the house of Imam Khomeini,' he said. 'I spoke to him in private, and he knows I'm here. I'm expecting a phone call from him at any moment. I've also spoken with the prime minister. The Mujahideen have infiltrated our—'

Just then the phone rang. The chief set his black brief-case on the table, excused himself and went into the adjoining office to take the call. He picked up the phone. 'Yes, it's me,' he said, speaking loud enough for everyone in the next room to hear. 'I've just spoken to the prime minister. Yes, I have it with me. No, wait, I may have left it in the car. Would you hold on for a moment? I'll go and get it.' He raised his voice at the end to make sure everyone heard him. Then he put down the phone, left the room, went down the stairs, got into his car and drove off at great speed. Nobody suspected a thing, since they had no way of knowing that history was repeating itself. The explosion shook the ground for miles around.

The Mujahideen's fight against the regime continued. Week after week, bombs went off at random places throughout the city. But the regime was still going strong, despite the fact that Khomeini's hand-picked cabinet had fallen for the same trick. When the Mujahideen realised that, they deliberately set out to create chaos in the city, setting fire to buses, banks and government buildings, and shooting as many functionaries as they could.

After a while their strategy began to look more like political suicide, for the Revolutionary Guard retaliated by arresting scores of sympathisers and ruthlessly shooting anyone who tried to escape. Within days, hundreds of members of the Mujahideen had been summarily executed.

The Mujahideen then abandoned the streets and switched to another tactic. This time they concentrated on acts of revenge. Focusing their wrath on the ayatollahs in the major cities, they set out to liquidate them one by one.

After the ayatollahs of Isfahan and Yazd had been assassinated, the Mujahideen stunned everyone by killing Ayatollah Mortazavi. An Islamic philosopher and one of the regime's most important theorists, he held no political office of any kind. Instead, he taught young imams.

One day, when he was walking to his seminary, he was greeted by a young man: '*Salaam aleikum*, Ayatollah.'

'*Salaam aleikum*, young man,' the ayatollah replied.

'I have a message for you.'

'Oh? What is it?'

'Your interpretation of the Koran is about to end!'

'What do you mean it's about to—'

'I mean *now*!' the young man said, and he fired three shots.

The chain of assassinations sowed fear and confusion in the regime. No one knew who the next target would be or where the next assassination would take place.

The ayatollah of Ghazvin was likewise singled out. His own cousin pulled the trigger. Only a few days before it happened, the ayatollah, worried about his security, had asked his cousin to be his chauffeur.

The ayatollah had spoken out against the attacks. 'America is killing us, Saddam is killing us, the Mujahideen are killing us. But they haven't killed our spirit! We taught America a lesson once before, and now it's time to teach Saddam and the Mujahideen that same lesson!'

That night, after his impassioned speech, his cousin drove him home. 'We're going through such terrifying days,' the ayatollah sighed.

'And such terrifying nights,' the cousin said as he drove into a side street.

'Where are you taking me?' the ayatollah asked.

'To hell!' the cousin said. And he pumped him full of bullets.

Nobody was safe any more. All it took was a whisper of suspicion against your neighbour, and he or she was immediately carted off to jail. The opposition went underground. Everyone who could possibly escape tried to flee the country.

The Mujahideen weren't the only ones behind the assassinations. The armed factions of the leftist opposition carried out their own acts of revenge.

Despite the widespread fear, the ayatollahs refused to give in to the terror. They went about their business as usual. This was also true of Ayatollah Araki of Senejan. Everyone knew that he was a potential target, so he was surrounded by bodyguards.

Araki was a fanatic who wanted to turn Senejan into a model Islamic city. He spoke with loathing of the families of the men and women who had been executed, and he had given Zinat carte blanche in the women's prison. She tortured the women until, at a sign from her, they lined up like robots and turned to face Mecca.

The residents of Senejan held their breath and waited for this hated ayatollah to be assassinated.

They didn't have to wait long.

The sun had just set, and the heat in the courtyard was making way for the cool evening air when the door to Aqa Jaan's study opened softly and someone came inside. Aqa Jaan, sitting in his chair and reading a book, thought it was Lizard.

He looked up. The last time he'd seen Shahbal had been the night they'd taken Jawad's body to the mountains for burial. Shahbal had left immediately afterwards. Now, here he was, standing in the study.

Aqa Jaan took off his glasses. 'I wasn't expecting you. When did you get home?'

'Just now.'

'Have you seen your father?'

'Not yet. I happened to be in Senejan and thought I'd drop by.'

There was a tremor in his voice.

Fate, Aqa Jaan thought, was about to strike again.

The door opened softly a second time and Lizard crept in. He could see by the look on Aqa Jaan's face that he wasn't welcome, so he quietly shut the door behind him and sat down outside.

'What do you mean you happened to be in Senejan?' Aqa Jaan said.

'I had a couple of things I needed to do here, so I thought I'd take advantage of the opportunity to come by and say hello.'

'Why don't you sit down? Here, have a chair.'

'I can't stay long. I have to leave soon. Actually, I came to say goodbye.'

'Goodbye? Why? Where are you going?'

'I'm not sure. I have to wrap up some unfinished business, then I'll probably be leaving the country for a while. I wanted to see you before I left. I'm sorry, but I . . .' He looked at his watch. 'I've got to go.'

'What are you trying to tell me, my boy?'

Through the window Aqa Jaan saw the silhouette of Muezzin, though he made no move to come in.

'Shall I ask your father to join us?'

'No, there's not enough time. I'll phone him later. You're the one I came to see. I'm worried about you. But I've got to go now. Someone's waiting for me,' he said.

Aqa Jaan sensed that something was wrong. It was still early in the evening. Why didn't Shahbal have time to say goodbye to his own father? Why did he keep glancing at his watch? There was something odd about his solemn goodbye.

Then suddenly it dawned on him. He knew what was going to happen. Ten minutes from now the prayer would

378

begin in the mosque. Ayatollah Araki's Mercedes would be arriving shortly.

'It's time to go,' Shahbal said, and he gave him a hug.

Aqa Jaan hugged him back, and as he did so, he felt the hard outline of a gun. With unexpected swiftness, he pushed Shahbal against the wall and yanked the gun from his waistband.

'What's got into you, Shahbal?' Aqa Jaan enquired fiercely.

Lizard rose to his hands and feet.

'I don't need to spell it out for you, Aqa Jaan,' Shahbal said, his face as hard as steel. 'There's no time. Give me back the gun, please, before it's too late!'

Aqa Jaan felt powerless to resist. He wanted to shout, 'You can't do this! Get out of my study!' But he couldn't. He realised to his horror that he didn't want to stop Shahbal, that a part of him actually approved.

Shahbal wrenched the gun from Aqa Jaan's hand.

Aqa Jaan wanted to snatch it back, but Shahbal held him at arm's length with his free hand. 'Don't say anything! Don't do anything!' Shahbal said. 'Save your words for later. Wish me luck!'

Dazed, Aqa Jaan suddenly found himself alone in his study. He felt as if he'd momentarily stepped out of his life. For one long minute he'd been unable to move or to say a word.

Shahbal squatted next to Lizard, kissed him and hurried outside, where he bumped into his father and accidentally knocked him down.

Shahbal knelt, took his father's head between his hands and planted a kiss on top of it. 'I'm in a hurry, Father. I'll call you later!'

Lizard scuttled off behind Shahbal.

* * *

The ayatollah's Mercedes pulled up a few feet away from the mosque.

Shahbal was standing in the darkness of the alley, waiting.

Three bodyguards got out and took a quick look around. They didn't see anything suspicious, so one of them opened the door, while the other two started walking towards the mosque.

Shahbal slipped the gun out from under his waistband. Lizard, who had been crouching silently behind him, began to crawl towards the Mercedes. Shahbal wanted to stop him, but it was already too late. Lizard, scrabbling along on his hands and feet, was heading straight for the ayatollah. The bodyguard, who had just helped the ayatollah out of the car, recoiled at the sight. The ayatollah took a step backwards and shouted, 'Scram!' as if Lizard were a stray dog.

But Lizard crawled up to him anyway and stuck his head under his robe, which completely unnerved the man.

'Ayatollah!' Shahbal yelled.

The ayatollah looked up in surprise, not sure where the voice was coming from.

Three shots rang out. The ayatollah raised his hands, took two steps backwards and fell to the ground.

The bodyguards pulled out their guns and started shooting wildly at anything that moved.

'Al-l-a-a-a-a-a-a-a-a-a-a-a-a-a-a-a-ah!' It was the voice of Aqa Jaan on the roof.

A motorcycle came roaring round the corner. Shahbal hopped on and it sped off.

The ayatollah's body lay in front of the mosque. His turban had fallen a few feet away, near the spot where Lizard now lay stretched out on the pavement. He no longer looked like a lizard, but like a little boy asleep in the dark, amid the pool of blood that was seeping out of his body.

Aqa Jaan knelt beside him, kissed his cold cheek, lifted him up and cradled him in his arms.

Tayareh

Whenever you were in the courtyard, you heard aeroplanes flying overhead. They took off in Tehran, crossed the desert and flew down to the Persian Gulf, where they continued on to Europe or America. On the return trip they usually took another route, crossing the Gulf of Oman and entering Iran at Bandar Abbas.

When the children were small, they used to sing a song whenever they heard a plane, looking up at the tiny, mysterious bird in the sky and singing:

> *Tayareh, tayareh,*
> Where are you going, *tayareh?*
> Who is on board, *tayareh?*
> When will it be my turn, *tayareh?*

Fakhri Sadat was sitting on the bench by the *hauz*, knitting. Since Lizard's death, the jumper she'd been making for him had been left unfinished.

Aqa Jaan was working in the garden, burying his sorrow in a pit along with the dead leaves.

Suddenly a passenger plane flew over the house, so low the noise was deafening. The sun glinted off its broad wings and lit up Fakhri's face, the trees, the *hauz* and the windowpanes.

Aqa Jaan, fearing that it was a bomber, grabbed his wife's arm and dragged her down to the cellar. They peered up at the sky through the trapdoor, but the plane had already disappeared.

When they got over their fright, they saw Muezzin standing by his workbench. For once his hands weren't covered in clay. Instead, he was dressed in a navy-blue suit and hat, and had already donned his usual travelling glasses. There was a suitcase at his feet.

'Are you leaving on another one of your trips, Muezzin?' Fakhri asked, saddened.

'I can see that you're all packed,' Aqa Jaan said. 'Where are you going this time?'

'You're the man who records everything,' Muezzin said. 'Make a note of this: I'm moving out.'

'You're moving out?' Fakhri echoed in surprise. 'Why?'

'I hear the boy crying, all night long. He's dead, but he still comes down to the cellar and plays around my feet when I'm working. He's buried in the garden, but I see him sitting in the cedar tree. At night he weeps outside my door and crawls through my sleep.'

Fakhri Sadat began to sob quietly. 'It's the same for us. We hear him in the garden too, but that doesn't mean you have to move out.'

'I don't want to, but the house is telling me to go. It's turning me out. Look at my hands – I can't make a thing any more. The cellar is piled high with my work, the garden is full of my vases, my plates are stacked up on the roof. Nobody buys my pottery. I'm being chased out. Let me go, brother, and wish me luck.'

Muezzin embraced Aqa Jaan, kissed Fakhri, picked up his suitcase and went up the cellar stairs. He paused for a moment in the courtyard and listened to the familiar sounds. 'Old crow!' he yelled. 'Take good care of the house. I'm moving out!'

*   *   *

After Muezzin had shut the gate behind him, three warplanes flew over the house with a thunderous roar and were swallowed up in the clouds.

'Iraqis!' said Aqa Jaan.

But they weren't Iraqi warplanes. They were Iranian air-force jets in hot pursuit of the passenger plane.

The president of Iran, Bani-Sadr, was inside the plane. He was trying to flee the country, and the jets were hurtling through the sky at top speed in an attempt to stop him. A week ago, Khomeini had accused him of working for the Mujahideen and dismissed him from office.

Bani-Sadr had gone into hiding, and the Mujahideen had devised a master plan for smuggling him out of the country. They had planned the escape down to the last detail and even informed Saddam Hussein of the flight, so that Iraqi aircraft would be standing by to escort the ex-president's plane through Iraqi airspace.

The three Iranian jets didn't catch him. Bani-Sadr's plane reached Iraq in the nick of time and flew on towards Europe.

Four and a half hours later, when the plane was approaching Paris, the pilot radioed the control tower: 'This is an emergency. I have the president of Iran on board, and he's requesting political asylum.'

The control tower passed the message on to the airport manager, who immediately contacted the French president, then asked Bani-Sadr a few questions, which he answered in flawless French. 'I am the elected president of the Islamic Republic of Iran,' he announced. 'I have on board with me the leader of the Mujahideen. I am requesting political asylum for myself, the leader of the Mujahideen and the pilot.'

The plane circled above Paris while the airport manager and the French president discussed the matter.

Bani-Sadr, who had a PhD in economics from the Sorbonne, had lived in Paris for years. In fact, he still had the key to his Paris apartment. He had been doing some postgraduate work when Khomeini had left Iraq and moved to Paris.

During his studies, Bani-Sadr had come up with an economic model that combined capitalism and Islam. His plans were ideal for Khomeini, who knew absolutely nothing about economics.

When Khomeini flew from Paris to Tehran, Bani-Sadr was one of the seven men educated in the West who went with him. Later he was elected the first president of Iran.

The plane was circling Paris for the fourth time when the airport manager informed Bani-Sadr of the decision: 'The French government has agreed to offer asylum to you and your fellow passengers. Your plane may land. Welcome to France.'

Bani-Sadr's escape was the lead story on French television that night.

Khomeini had just come to the end of his evening prayer when Rafsanjani, then commander-in-chief of the armed forces, knelt by his side and broke the news to him.

Khomeini stood up and immediately launched into another prayer. Now that he had been informed of this unfortunate news, he hoped that an extra prayer would bring him closer to God. He needed Allah's advice. After he'd uttered the last *rakat*, his eyes gleamed. He turned to Rafsanjani. 'Our moment of glory has come!'

*   *   *

Ever since the war began, the Iranian army had been waiting for the right moment to liberate the occupied city of Khorramshahr. The largest oil refinery in the Middle East was located in its strategic harbour. Up to now the operation had been impossible, because American satellites relayed every movement in and around Khorramshahr to the Iraqis.

'Allah is on our side,' Khomeini said to Rafsanjani. 'We will liberate Khorramshahr. The moment has come. Call a meeting of all your generals!'

Saddam had toasted his good fortune and was on his way to a cabinet meeting to break the news of Bani-Sadr's escape to his ministers when the Iranian army attacked Khorramshahr simultaneously from six sides.

Thousands of Iraqi and Iranian soldiers were killed. The streets were lined with corpses. After half a day of heavy fighting, two Iranian soldiers managed to tear down the Iraqi flag on top of the refinery and replace it with the green flag of Islam.

The Iraqis regrouped, but the ayatollahs unexpectedly opened a new front: the Iranians attacked the Iraqi harbour of Basra. The Iraqi soldiers were so shaken by the news of the invasion that they went on the rampage, destroying every house in Khorramshahr and torching the trees before retreating in a vain attempt to save Basra.

After this historic victory, Khomeini appeared on television and was seen to be smiling for the first time. He gave thanks to Allah and congratulated the parents of the fallen soldiers on their sons' bravery.

Millions of people took to the streets to celebrate the liberation of Khorramshahr. They set off fireworks, drove around in cars, honking and flashing their lights, danced on top of buses and treated each other to biscuits, sweets and fruit.

The rejoicing went on until deep in the night. It was the first nationwide celebration since the ayatollahs had come to power.

A full moon shone that night, comforting those who had suffered the pains and sorrows of war. Not everyone was rejoicing, however. Some people took advantage of that joyful night to exact revenge.

The light of that same moon shone down on a salt-water lake near Senejan, where the half-submerged body of Zinat Khanom lay. There was a note in a plastic holder round her neck: 'She forced young unmarried women who had been sentenced to death to sleep with an Islamic fundamentalist before being executed. She has been tried and punished here at this salt lake, at the express wish of the mothers whose daughters were unwillingly made brides on the last night of their lives.'

Soon the moon would fade, and the sun would take its place. A flock of desert birds would spot Zinat's body by the lake and circle noisily above it.

A traveller riding by on a camel would stop at the lake to see what had attracted the birds' attention. And he would get down from the camel, kneel by the corpse and read the note.

Akkas

Aqa Jaan strolled along the banks of the river. Instead of going back to bed after the morning prayer, he had come here for a walk. He sat down on a mound of sand to rest. Despite the cold, a woman was washing her feet in the river.

She dried her feet on the hem of her chador, put on her shoes and approached Aqa Jaan. 'Do you have any change?' she said. 'I don't have any coins to put in my mouth.'

'Qodsi, is that you?'

The once so young and lively Qodsi now looked old. Her hair was grey, her face wrinkled.

'I haven't seen you for a long time, Qodsi. Where have you been? How's your mother?'

'She's dead,' Qodsi said sombrely.

'When did that happen? Why wasn't I told?'

'She just up and died one day,' was all Qodsi said.

'How's your sister?'

'She's dead too.'

'Your sister too? When? What did she die of?'

There was no reply.

'Where's your brother?'

'He's dead too.'

'What's all this you're telling me?'

'But you won't die,' Qodsi prophesied. 'You will stay until they've all gone and come back again.'

She turned and walked away.

'Where are you going, Qodsi? You haven't told me the latest news.'

'Seven men are left. Three of them will come, one will go, one will lie where he is, one will die and one will sow. But you will stay until they've all come and gone,' she replied, without turning round to look at him.

Aqa Jaan stood up and continued his walk.

Who was going to come and who was going to go? he wondered.

Suddenly he thought of Nosrat.

During the turbulent nights of the terror, only one man had had access to Khomeini's nights: Nosrat.

Khomeini and Nosrat would shut themselves off from the harsh reality of daily life, and Nosrat would transport him to another world, in which there were no Iraqi jets, no bombs and no executions.

Nosrat beguiled him with his cinema. He showed him documentaries and nature films about birds, bees, snakes and the river of stars. It was their secret. No one else knew what went on behind Khomeini's closed door.

Khomeini was the leader of the Shiite world, a man who could move millions of people with a single speech, but he was lonely. He spent all day, sometimes all week, by himself in his study.

He was a charismatic leader, and in turn everyone was always doing their best to impress him. Everyone except Nosrat, that is. Nosrat tried to be himself, in the hope that it would bring him closer to Khomeini.

Khomeini knew nothing of maths and lacked even the most rudimentary knowledge of physics, but he was curious about such things as light, the moon, the sun and space exploration. He was particularly interested in meteorites.

Nosrat, the *akkas* – the photographer – brought Khomeini into contact with a wondrous world he had never known before. He transformed Khomeini's lonely nights into colourful and captivating nights in which he could forget his troubles.

The first thing Nosrat did when he came into Khomeini's room was to take off his jacket, hang it on the coat-rack and start talking about whatever films he'd brought along. 'I have a couple of short films for you tonight,' he began one evening. 'Unique documentaries about the life of two animal species. One is about the social hierarchy of ants, and the other is about apes. I'm sure you're going to enjoy them. You'll be amazed at how much their behaviour resembles ours! After that, I have a fascinating film about the rocks floating around in space. There are billions of them, and every once in a while one of them crashes into the earth. It's brilliant!'

Khomeini looked at him in surprise. Even his own son didn't feel this much at ease in his presence. He had heard that artists were a different breed, but Nosrat was the first artist he'd ever met.

Nosrat's function could be compared to that of a *malijak*, a fool, in the court of the ancient Persian kings. The fool was the only one who had access to the king's private chambers and was free to say and do whatever he pleased, as long as he kept the king amused.

'What's the name of that television network?' Khomeini had asked him once.

'Which one?'

'That American network. The one that interviewed me a couple of times.'

'You mean CNN?'

'Yes, that's the one,' he said.

'What about it?'

'Oh, nothing. I've been told that the presidents of major countries have televisions in their offices and that they're always tuned to CNN.'

'That's true. I'm surprised you don't have a television.'

Khomeini had neither a radio nor a television in his study. The news was always brought to him in written form.

'I assume they speak only English on CNN?'

'There's also an Arabic channel. It's like CNN, except that it broadcasts the news in Arabic,' Nosrat told him. 'I'll bring you a television set, and you can watch it in your room.'

The next day Nosrat brought in a portable television and set it up in Khomeini's clothes cupboard, where no one would be able to see it. He showed Khomeini how to turn it on and off, and how to change the channel.

'As long as it's tuned to the Arabic channel, it will be fine,' Khomeini said in a furtive whisper, as if this were some kind of covert operation.

Several weeks later Nosrat received an unexpected call from a CNN reporter who knew about Nosrat's close ties to Khomeini. They agreed to meet in a teahouse by the station. Nosrat told him about his work, and at the end of the conversation the reporter asked him cautiously if he might be interested in making a documentary about Khomeini.

'What did you have in mind?' Nosrat enquired, surprised.

'A human-interest story.'

Nosrat's jaw dropped. For a long time he'd been thinking of doing something along those lines, but had decided it couldn't be done.

'CNN wants a thirty-minute special devoted to Khomeini's private life,' the reporter said. 'Of course we'd pay you a fat fee in American dollars.'

Nosrat wasn't interested in the fee, what appealed to him was the human-interest angle. This was probably the opportunity of a lifetime, but he'd never be able to pull it off.

'Forget it,' he said. 'He'd never give me permission to film him.'

'You can always try,' the reporter replied. 'Think about it, and let me know if there's anything I can do.'

'Okay,' Nosrat agreed.

The scenes he wanted to film were already running through his head. He was so excited that night he couldn't sleep. He would have liked to talk it over with someone, but didn't dare, for fear that he'd jinx the project.

One night, while Nosrat and Khomeini were strolling along the lake behind Khomeini's house, Nosrat regaled him with information about satellites. He explained what they were and how they worked, and told him that, thanks to such technological advances, people could now see the president of the United States live on television, sitting in the Oval Office and drinking a cup of coffee.

'Human beings are curious,' he went on. 'And to satisfy their curiosity, they invent things like satellites and launch them into space. They want to know everything about everyone, including you. For example, where you live, how you live and what you eat. There's nothing wrong with curiosity.'

Nosrat tried to lay the groundwork for his request, but he knew that the moment he said 'CNN', the word 'America' was sure to follow. He was afraid that if he broached the subject, he'd no longer be welcome, that

Khomeini would order him to pack up his equipment and go.

But he was too obsessed by the idea to stop. He always had his camera with him, so that night, after he'd come into Khomeini's room and switched on the TV for him, he surreptitiously pressed the red button on his camera and filmed Khomeini, sitting barefoot on the floor behind the door of his wardrobe, secretly watching television.

Over the next few months, Nosrat filmed dozens of short fragments: Khomeini walking along the lake and looking at the ducks, sparrows chirruping as they flew past his head, Khomeini stumbling over a log and his turban falling off and rolling into the lake, the ducks paddling over to the turban and plucking at it.

In one of the scenes Khomeini is lying ill in bed. He's sleeping on his side, with his face turned towards Mecca, exactly as the dead are laid to rest in Islamic graves. His wife comes into the room. She gently feels his forehead, then leaves without saying a word.

In another shot you see him pacing up and down in his living room. He goes over to the sink, washes his hands, takes out his Koran and intently studies one of the pages. When he's through, he picks up his pen, writes a few lines, puts the note in an envelope, seals it and calls his wife. 'Batul!'

She comes in. 'Make sure the general gets this,' he says, and he hands her the envelope.

She takes it, tucks it beneath her chador, and hurries out.

It didn't take long for Khomeini to realise that Nosrat was surreptitiously filming him. And Nosrat, for his part, was sure that Khomeini had tacitly given his consent.

* * *

One day the CNN reporter phoned Nosrat. 'I haven't heard from you, so I guess you decided not to accept our offer.'

'I've got some great footage,' Nosrat blurted out.

Fifteen minutes later the reporter was at his door.

Nosrat was so enthusiastic he didn't realise he was being monitored by the new secret police. It never occurred to him that they might know about his contacts with CNN.

The reporter came in. Nosrat made some tea, slid one of the tapes into the video recorder and sat down.

The reporter couldn't believe his eyes. 'Fantastic!' he said.

Before they'd viewed even half the tape, five armed men lowered themselves onto the balcony from the roof, kicked in the door, stormed inside and arrested Nosrat and the reporter. Two of the men were ordered to search the house. Anything remotely suspicious was packed into boxes and carted off.

The CNN reporter was deported the next day. Nosrat was put in a cell to await further questioning. Only then did he discover that the secret police were taking the matter much more seriously than he'd thought. He knew that he'd taken huge risks and that the charges were serious, but he was counting on Khomeini to bail him out.

Nosrat did his best to convince the interrogator that he had a great deal of respect for Khomeini and had been motivated by genuine regard.

He explained that the footage was of historical value and therefore an important part of the country's cultural heritage.

He stressed that it had never been his intention to sell the material to the Americans, but that he had acted solely out of his love of cinematography.

He swore that he had remained faithful to both Khomeini and his camera.

And he hinted that Khomeini was aware of the fact that he was being filmed and that he could prove it if necessary.

Nosrat's defence seemed plausible. And they would have believed him if they hadn't discovered another tape in his house – a tape so shocking and beautiful that Nosrat hadn't known what to do with it. He'd hidden it behind the beams in his studio in the hope that no one would ever find it, and had promptly erased it from his mind because the thought of discovery was too awful to contemplate. Now the secret police had found it.

'Be careful, Nosrat,' Aqa Jaan had frequently warned him. 'Women are bound to be your downfall.'

Nosrat was always on the lookout for a special woman, whose beauty he could capture on film. It had never occurred to him, however, that that woman would turn out to be Khomeini's wife.

The interrogator laid the tape down on the table in front of him. Nosrat paled when he saw it. He knew that the game was up and was gripped with fear.

What had he seen in the old woman that had made him suddenly, reluctantly, let his camera roll?

Batul was the wife of the most powerful man in the Shiite world, but she herself was utterly powerless.

Nosrat couldn't explain how it had happened, but that powerless woman had silently forced him to film her, to record her movements, to preserve her image so that one day she might be shown to the world.

All her life Batul had worn a veil. No stranger had ever seen her hair, her hands or her feet. And that is why she sometimes felt the need to show herself.

At first Nosrat hadn't realised what was going on. When he knocked on the door of their living room, Batul always opened the door and welcomed him with a smile. She was about twenty years younger than Khomeini, which you could clearly see in her face. She assumed the role of a gracious hostess – something devout wives didn't ordinarily do – and yet Nosrat knew she wasn't doing it because of him, but because of his camera.

Batul was beautiful, and she wanted her beauty to be noticed. She yearned to be seen through the lens of a camera.

Her wish was the same as that of every other Iranian woman who had suffered centuries of male oppression and had never been given the chance to display their beauty.

She and Nosrat had reached a tacit agreement. He filmed her in silence.

Thousands of pictures of Khomeini had been printed in the newspapers, but not even one small photograph of Batul had ever been published. It was as if she didn't exist.

One scene on the videotape showed Batul standing by the window and looking out at the lake. She had exchanged her black chador for a milky white one with blue flowers. Nosrat zoomed in on her face, on the silvery hair that could just be seen. Then she slowly let her chador slip down to her shoulders. It was a revelation.

But it was another scene that sealed Nosrat's fate. The door to Batul's room had been standing ajar. He had filmed the room, showing in the corner a single bed and a nightstand, on top of which lay a small hand mirror and a blue tin of Nivea.

The interrogator picked up the video recorder and slammed it down so hard on Nosrat's head that Nosrat crumpled, unconscious, to the floor.

*　　*　　*

After that it was silent.

Silence spread across the land.

Saddam Hussein stopped bombing the cities, and Khomeini no longer consulted the Koran to decide whether or not to advance further into Iraqi territory.

Silence reigned supreme. There were no more executions, and no more assassinations. Everyone was tired. Everyone needed a rest.

The First to Come

By the mountain!
Is this sorcery?
Is this sorcery
Or are you blind?
By a book inscribed
On an unrolled scroll.
By the much-visited house.
By the canopy raised high.
By the swirling sea of fire.
Woe, that day, deniers of truth!
The mountain, the mountain!

How many years had passed by? How many months had elapsed?

Who had come? Who had gone?

No one kept track of the years any more, and there was no point in counting the months. Time stood still for the grief-stricken, for the dead and for those who mourned them.

It also stood still for those who gardened to forget their grief and those who prepared hallowed dishes so their sorrow could be divided into more manageable portions.

The country seemed to be at rest. And yet one person,

a man with a loaded gun tucked into his belt, was now riding through the desert on a camel so that he could mete out justice to the judge.

Once that had been done, the sorrow might truly come to an end. Only then would time again be set in motion and would we see how many years had passed since some had come and some had gone.

During the long period of silence, Khomeini gradually lost his memory. One day he no longer recognised even those closest to him.

Rafsanjani and Khamenei, the key men in his government, seized power and gradually forced Khomeini into the background.

Khalkhal had been the first to realise that Khomeini was becoming senile. One day he had knelt beside him and noticed with a shock that Khomeini no longer knew who he was.

Khalkhal was the only person at the top who operated independently. He was seen as an extension of Khomeini. As long as he was under Khomeini's protection, he was powerful, but without it, he was nothing. It was time for him to step down.

Besides, the wave of executions had served its purpose. The regime had flexed its muscles sufficiently. It had driven the Iraqi occupier out of the country and eliminated the opposition. Now stability was called for. There was no more need for a judge as hated as Khalkhal.

The regime would have to find him another position, though that would be far from easy. Many people in the Mujahideen and the leftist movement knew about his role and about the heinous crimes committed on his orders. They were lying in wait, hoping to assassinate him.

If he'd been able to choose, he would have gone back to Qom to teach Islamic law at a seminary, but that was out of the question now. He knew that his mission was coming to an end, just as it had for Khomeini.

Khomeini wasn't dead yet, but he belonged to the past. Khalkhal had no future, and the present had no need of him. He would have to go back to the past. The only question was how.

Fortunately, Khomeini's successors did find a way to send Khalkhal back to the past. The Taliban were busy setting up an Islamic regime in neighbouring Afghanistan, using force to impose an antiquated sharia on the country.

In those days there were close ties between the Taliban and the ayatollahs in Iran. They met from time to time to discuss how to go about strengthening their position against their common enemy: the West.

The regime came up with the idea of offering Khalkhal's services to the Taliban. After all, the fanatical Taliban would consider him an asset.

It was a perfect solution, and Khalkhal eagerly accepted it. The Taliban's extremism appealed to him, so he packed his bags and, disguised as a merchant with a hat and a beard, took the train to the border city of Mashhad, where he spent the night at an inn. The next evening a Taliban fighter picked him up and drove him – now clad in traditional Afghan garb – across the border and on to Kabul, where the leader of the Taliban gave him a warm welcome and offered him a house.

Khalkhal's life changed completely. He was now able to breathe more freely. Officially he worked for the Municipal Archives. In secret, however, he was an important figure in the Taliban hierarchy.

He enjoyed the anonymity of Kabul. At last things were quiet enough for him to devote more time to Islamic law. He spent his days in the ancient library of the Municipal

Archives, studying the Islamic documents that had been sent to him specially from the royal libraries of Saudi Arabia. After a few months he married an Afghan woman and began to adjust to married life.

He was happy. His new life suited him. He walked freely through Kabul and went into the shops, something he'd never done before. He also spent a lot of time visiting his in-laws. No one knew about his past. To the outside world, he was an Islamic researcher writing a book on the history of Islam.

He didn't realise that people were still looking for him and that his crimes had not been forgotten.

Shahbal was one of the people searching for Khalkhal. Unfortunately, the trail had gone cold.

Only three members of the steering committee of Shahbal's party were left. The others had all been arrested or executed or forced to flee. During the last hurried meeting of the remaining members, Shahbal had been ordered to liquidate Khalkhal. Later it appeared that this was the last decision ever taken by his party.

Shahbal was anxious to avenge Jawad's death. He couldn't forget the long cold night in the mountains when he and Aqa Jaan had gone in search of a grave. The humiliation was unbearable. He had to do something, or he'd never have another peaceful night. Only after this deed had been done would he be able to pick up the thread of his life again.

Since the shooting of Ayatollah Araki, no one in the family knew where Shahbal was. Aqa Jaan thought he'd fled the country and was living in Europe or America.

But Shahbal hadn't fled. He was still in Tehran. He'd grown a beard and was driving one of the city's many orange taxis. It was too risky for the members of the underground movement to drive their own cars, so they generally relied on taxis to get them where they wanted to go.

Shahbal had been driving the taxi ever since he joined the editorial board of the party's newspaper. He used it not only to get around the city, but also to earn a living.

So as not to jeopardise its security, the steering committee no longer held any meetings. Instead, the handful of members who were left occasionally exchanged information at a teahouse in Tehran's bazaar. During one of these brief encounters, Shahbal was told that Khalkhal was living in Kabul.

'I should have guessed!' he said. 'Who gave you this information?'

'The Tudeh Party,' answered one of the men, and he handed him a piece of paper with Khalkhal's address on it.

The Tudeh Party had also been disbanded, after having been all but decimated by the regime. However, former members of this Russian-oriented party still had contacts with Iran's Communist neighbour to the north, the Soviet Union.

Shahbal knew what he had to do.

During the years of the Communist regime in Afghanistan, the leftist underground groups in Iran had developed strong ties with Afghan sympathisers. After the takeover by the Taliban, most – but not all – of the Communists had fled to the Soviet Union. It took Shahbal several months to arrange to be smuggled into the country by a group of Afghan rebels.

One night he rode through the desert on a camel until he reached the Afghan border. He left the camel in the stable of an inn, then walked to a rendezvous point, where an Afghan was waiting for him on the other side of a barbed-wire fence. After they had exchanged passwords, the man showed him where to crawl under the wire and into Afghanistan.

He hopped onto the back of the man's motorcycle and they drove for half an hour until they reached a shepherd's hut. The Afghan went in and came back out with a set of clothes. After Shahbal had changed into the traditional Afghan garb, they drove to the nearest town, so he could catch a bus to Kabul in the morning.

Even though it was autumn, it was snowing high up in the mountains. An icy wind lashed Shahbal's face. The man bought him some fresh bread and dates and made sure he boarded the bus.

After many gruelling hours of winding mountain roads and endless stops, the bus finally reached the centre of Kabul. Shahbal got out and went to a café to get something to eat. He ordered a bowl of thick soup and gulped down several glasses of freshly brewed tea.

He'd hardly slept for the last three nights, so he went to a small hotel near the café and crawled into bed, only waking when the desk clerk knocked on the door the next morning to make sure he was all right. Because the hotel didn't have a bath or shower, he wandered around looking for a bathhouse. Before he'd gone far, he came across a mosque, where he managed to scrub off most of the dirt and grime. After that he had lunch in a nearby teahouse.

The Municipal Archives were only a few blocks away. The building was closed to the public, but Shahbal could see lights on inside.

Khalkhal's office was on the top floor. He was the only person there. His desk was by the window, so every time he looked up from his work he could see people walking in the street. He went to work early in the morning like the other employees, but when the building closed at four, he worked on for another hour. He was always the last to leave.

Shahbal recognised him the moment he came out, despite his Afghan clothes. He had gained a lot of weight, but Shahbal knew it was Khalkhal from the way he walked.

Night had just fallen. Shahbal followed him, keeping safely out of sight. Khalkhal went into a bakery and came out with a fresh loaf of bread under his arm. Then he strolled over to a street vendor and bought a bunch of grapes – the last of the season. Shahbal followed him all the way home, then checked the surroundings and returned to his hotel.

The next evening, Shahbal went back to the house. He was hoping Khalkhal would be alone, but when he looked through the window, he saw him sitting on the floor with his Afghan wife, eating dinner.

Shahbal couldn't wait. He had to act quickly, before the Afghan secret police found out he was here. He walked around for a while, to allow Khalkhal time to finish his meal.

The next time he looked through the window, he saw the woman in the kitchen. There was a light on upstairs. It was now or never, so he crawled through the window and tiptoed towards the kitchen, but the woman, who was doing the washing-up, must have heard him, because she turned. Her eyes widened in fright when she saw a man with a gun standing in the doorway. Before she could scream, however, Shahbal grabbed her and clamped his hand over her mouth. 'Don't scream!' he whispered. 'I'm not going to hurt you. Listen to me. Your husband is an Iranian criminal, who ordered the execution of hundreds of innocent people. Don't make a sound, and you won't get hurt. Do you understand my Persian?'

The terrified woman nodded.

'I don't have much time. I'm going to tie you up and put some tape over your mouth. If you move, I will shoot you. Do you understand what I'm saying?'

Again, the woman nodded.

'Good,' he said, and he tied her up and left her sitting on the kitchen floor. Then he tiptoed up the stairs to the room where he'd seen the light.

At the top of the stairs he peered through the crack in the door, holding his gun firmly in his hand. Khalkhal, wearing his reading glasses, was sitting at a desk, reading a book and taking notes.

Shahbal opened the door softly and went in. Khalkhal, thinking it was his wife with the tea, didn't look up. But when he didn't hear her voice, he took off his glasses, turned around and saw an Afghan pointing a gun at him.

'Don't move!' Shahbal ordered.

The moment he heard the Persian words, Khalkhal knew that his attacker wasn't an Afghan. Dumbstruck, he stared at Shahbal.

Shahbal took off his Afghan cap. 'Mohammad Al Khalkhal! Allah's so-called judge!' he said, his voice as cold as ice. 'I have been ordered by the Underground Court to execute you!'

Khalkhal recognised Shahbal and tried to speak, but his mouth had gone dry. He knew that the end had come. No one could help him now. He mumbled a few words.

'What did you say?' Shahbal asked.

Khalkhal pointed to the glass of water on the table.

'Go ahead,' Shahbal said.

His hand trembling, Khalkhal took a sip of water.

'May I stand and face Mecca?' he asked, in a flat voice.

'Yes, you may.'

Khalkhal stood up. He took one step in the direction

of the window and, turning towards Mecca in the waning light, began to chant:

> *The companions of the right,*
> *And the companions of the left.*

Shahbal fired. The bullet struck Khalkhal in the chest and sent him reeling. He clutched the windowsill for support and went on chanting:

> *Oh, he who strives for Him shall meet Him.*
> *When the heavens are rent asunder*
> *And the stars are scattered—*

Shahbal fired two more shots. Khalkhal's hand jerked up and he let go of the sill, then keeled over. As he lay writhing on the floor, he chanted almost unintelligibly:

> *The first to come will be the first to arrive,*
> *And they shall be nearest to Him*
> *In the Gardens of Bliss.*

Shahbal raced down the stairs and quickly untied the woman. 'Go!' he said. 'Run to your family!'

The woman fled the house.

Shahbal let himself out, hurried down to the corner and turned left. Then he slowed his steps and walked calmly through the dark alleys to the centre of Kabul. There he bought a loaf of freshly baked bread and a bunch of grapes, then boarded the late-night bus to Pakistan.

The bus drove through the dimly lit streets. Kabul was beautiful. One day he would come back to this mysterious city.

The Gardens of Bliss

A *lef Lam Mim Ra*. Years went by, and the house's sorrow grew like the trees in the garden.

The American hostages had long ago returned to their own homes and their own beds. Khomeini had died.

The war had ended, and America – having failed to achieve its objective through Saddam – had grounded its spy planes.

The migratory birds still flocked to the city and flew over the house of the mosque, but since no grain had been put out for them, they continued on their way.

Aqa Jaan's daughters were living in Tehran. They had been quietly married during the frantic years of the war and the executions. Ensi had given birth to a son, whom she named Jawad in honour of her brother. She came home from time to time with her husband and laid the baby in her mother's arms.

Fakhri Sadat, who had once thought she would never get over her grief, kissed her grandson. 'Aqa Jaan!' she called excitedly one day. 'Come and look! He's the spitting image of Jawad!'

The old crow heard her and circled above the house. The fish in the *hauz* leapt out of the water for joy, the cedar tree smiled and stood a bit straighter, the birds flew down and perched on its branches, and the wind blew the fresh smell of spring wildflowers down from the mountains. Aqa Jaan put on his hat and coat, picked up his walking stick and went off to the bazaar to buy a box of biscuits.

When was the last time he'd blithely bought a box of biscuits?

It had been the day the grandmothers left for Mecca.

On one of those lovely spring days, Aqa Jaan drove his old Ford out of the garage and, for the first time in his life, washed it himself. He put Fakhri Sadat's suitcase in the boot and helped her into the front seat, then slid behind the wheel and drove to Jirya.

At one time almost all the women in Jirya, young and old alike, had woven carpets for Aqa Jaan and given him a royal welcome whenever he visited the village. There had also been a time, however, when they refused to give him a grave for his son.

Fortunately, those days were now over, for when he parked his car and he and Fakhri Sadat crossed the village square, the villagers made way for them and bowed respectfully.

Now that the wave of violence had stopped, the war had ended and the dust of the revolution had settled, people were able to take stock. They could see what the years of strife had cost them. Families had been destroyed by political division and death. Prisons were crammed with opponents of the regime. Unemployment had soared and food was scarce.

Aqa Jaan had never told Fakhri what had happened that night in the village, but she had heard the story from her relatives.

'I still don't understand how people can change from one day to the next,' she said, as they walked towards the house that used to belong to her father.

'They're simple people. Most of them are illiterate.

The shah did nothing to help them, and neither will the ayatollahs. I don't blame them. Besides, this is where we have our roots. Our dead are buried here. When things go well, we get the credit; when things go badly, we get the blame.'

The Islamic Army had commandeered their ancestral home, so they spent their first night at the house in which Fakhri had grown up. It now belonged to her sister.

The next day they set out for Kazem Khan's house, strolling side by side through the almond groves. The trees were covered with pale pink blossoms, and the birds twittered merrily, as if they were celebrating the end of the sorrowful era. The old part of the village was the same as ever, but young couples had started building houses on the hills.

Jirya was known for two things: carpets and saffron. Sweet-smelling saffron flourished on these hills. In the old days, when the only way to get to Kazem Khan's house was by horseback, the hillsides had been covered with yellow saffron plants. Now the lower slopes were dotted with hundreds of simple stone cottages. During the shah's reign, people had started to build a water reservoir on the highest hill, but the project had long since been abandoned.

'The almond trees have become old and gnarled,' Fakhri remarked.

'So have I,' Aqa Jaan replied.

Before the onset of winter, the village girls used to go out to the hills and pick the saffron threads, which were as valuable as gold. They sang happily as they worked, and at the end of the day their hands were stained a brownish yellow and their bodies smelled of saffron.

The girls from Jirya were popular with the boys from other villages. Their suitors soon discovered, however, that Jirya girls were reluctant to leave the village.

During the long cold winters, the girls stayed inside and wove carpets. When spring came, they flung open the windows, and then you could hear them giggling and singing.

The windows were open now, but there wasn't a sound. Singing was no longer allowed.

Aqa Jaan and Fakhri Sadat passed an old walnut tree, a sign that they weren't far from Kazem Khan's house, which had been built on an elevation overlooking the saffron hills.

In the distance they saw two men on horseback galloping towards them. When the men were nearly upon them, they reined in the horses, dismounted and led the horses over to Aqa Jaan. There was a strong family resemblance between the two men. They bowed and said *salaam* to Aqa Jaan, then fell silent.

Aqa Jaan didn't recognise them. He shot a quizzical glance at Fakhri.

'It's the two deaf sons of the couple who used to work for Kazem Khan,' she said, and she smiled.

Aqa Jaan returned their greeting and, gesturing, asked after their wives and children.

The men signed back that their wives were doing well and that the children had grown. 'The horses are for you,' one of the men gestured. 'To use while you're staying here.'

Aqa Jaan smiled at Fakhri. 'They're offering you a horse,' he said. 'Do you think you're up to it?'

'Absolutely not!' Fakhri said, and she laughed. 'You might still be able to ride, but I can't. I'm not as young as I used to be. I wouldn't dare get on a horse these days!'

'Their wives have invited you for a visit,' Aqa Jaan said.

'Good, I accept with pleasure,' Fakhri signed. 'Tell them I'll come.'

The men handed over the reins and started back home on foot.

Kazem Khan's house glittered like a jewel among the gnarled trees, as was only proper for the house of the village poet. Kazem Khan had been buried at the bottom of the garden, beneath the almond trees. His grave was now blanketed with blossoms.

When Kazem Khan was still alive, the birds used to sit outside the window of his opium room and sing until he opened the window and let out the smoke. After he'd finished his pipe, he'd say, 'Go home now, birds, and sleep well!' And off they'd fly.

Kazem Kahn's former servants had readied the house for Aqa Jaan and Fakhri. They ate outside, talking about Kazem Khan and laughing at how he used to win the hearts of the mountain women by writing them poems.

That evening the former servant delivered a message to Fakhri Sadat. 'Some of the women would like to come by and say hello,' she said. 'If you don't mind, that is.'

'Which women?' Fakhri asked, surprised.

'The ones who used to weave carpets for you.'

The women of the village had always looked up to Fakhri, admiring her beauty and pleasing manners. She was still well liked.

'What time would they like to come?'

'Now, if it's convenient.'

Aqa Jaan retreated to Kazem Khan's library.

The old women were the first to enter the house. They kissed Fakhri Sadat and seated themselves on the floor. Then more women came in, this time in groups. They too kissed Fakhri and sat down. Fakhri was astonished. She knew most of the women by sight, since they had all worked for them at one time or another, but then a group of seven women came in and embraced her. These were the girls who had once woven sample carpets for her.

'What a lovely surprise!' Fakhri exclaimed. 'Your visit brings the light back into my heart. I wasn't expecting this. I thought you'd all forgotten me.'

One of the old women stood up to speak. 'Fakhri,' she began, 'you've suffered a lot of pain. We know that. You lost your son, and we denied him a burial place. We'll have to live with that for the rest of our lives. Tonight we've come to ask you to stop mourning. We've brought you a dress. We beg you to put away your mourning clothes and wear this dress instead. We should have done this a long time ago.'

The woman handed her a brightly coloured floral-print dress. Fakhri looked down at her black mourning clothes with tears in her eyes. She was speechless. She wept silently, her hand covering her mouth.

Just as she was about to go upstairs and show her new dress to Aqa Jaan, she saw a group of men coming up the steps. They were the village elders, all of whom had at one time worked for Aqa Jaan.

One of them knocked on the library door and asked if they could come in.

'Please do,' said Aqa Jaan. 'You're more than welcome!'

They trooped into the library and sat down on the creaking chairs by the window. After a long pause, one of the men spoke up: 'Aqa Jaan, almost every family in the village lost a son during the war. Our children are all buried in the cemetery. We refused your son a grave, and that troubles us greatly. Please forgive us!'

'God is all-knowing and all-forgiving,' Aqa Jaan said soothingly. 'I've never blamed you. Your visit has eased my pain. I've always believed in human goodness. Thank you all for coming here today.'

The old man took out a white shirt. 'The time for mourning has come to an end,' he said. 'Please accept this gift and put your black shirt away.'

That night in bed, Fakhri lay her head on Aqa Jaan's chest. 'What a lovely evening,' she said. 'I'm so happy! Now I can come and visit our village again!'

They looked out of the window at the star-filled sky.

'The villagers have made amends. The older ones have learned from their experiences, and it's made them wise. The rich traditions of this place have served as the basis of their wisdom. They know how to heal old wounds.'

'Some of the women are coming over tomorrow to put a henna rinse in my hair,' Fakhri said excitedly. 'It's supposed to bring good luck.'

'I'm glad,' Aqa Jaan said. 'You deserve to be happy.'

And they fell asleep in each other's arms.

Aqa Jaan was awakened the next morning by the chirping of the birds. After his prayer, he put on the white shirt the villagers had given him and strolled around the garden. He felt good. He looked at the blossom-laden trees and felt the strength flowing back to his legs. He stopped by Kazem Khan's grave, knelt down, picked up a pebble, tapped it against the tombstone and recited one of his uncle's poems:

Ruzgaar ast keh gah 'ezzat dehad
Gah khaar daarad
Charkhi baazigar az-in baazichehaa besyaar daarad.

And so life toys with you,
Sometimes loving you,
Sometimes humiliating you.

A delightful breeze was blowing from the mountains. Suddenly Aqa Jaan remembered last night's dream. He'd dreamed of Hushang Khan.

Hushang Khan was an old friend of his, a nobleman who lived high up in the mountains. Khan was the man who had come to their rescue that night, the man who had driven up in his jeep and taken Jawad's body away for burial.

He lived in an old fortress in a village that belonged to him, a village far away from all the other villages in the mountains.

Aqa Jaan had not been back to the mountains since the night that Hushang Khan had driven off with Jawad's body. He knew that patience was called for, that one day the time would come.

Now, as he knelt by his uncle's grave, he remembered his dream. The strong scent of the blossoms sent memories of Jawad, of his sweet smell, wafting through Aqa Jaan's soul.

He led one of the horses out of the stable, heaved himself into the saddle and galloped off towards Sawoj-Bolagh.

Hushang Khan was about sixty years old. The son of a powerful nobleman, he was a remarkable individual who had turned his back on his father and refused to have anything to do with the regime of the shah.

Hushang had four wives, each of whom had borne him five children. He had turned his domain into a kind of closed colony, which was almost entirely self-sufficient.

He owned a jeep and a few tractors, and raised cows, horses and sheep. There was a small winery in the cellar of his house, where he produced wine for his own consumption.

He had no contact with the outside world, except for friends who came to see him from time to time. His circle of friends included writers, poets and musicians from such places as Isfahan, Yazd, Shiraz and Kashan. To them his door was always open. They hiked through the mountains with him, smoked his opium, drank his home-made wine and enjoyed the fruit from his garden.

There was no road to his village. Somehow he managed to get his battered jeep over the rocks and up the steep inclines, but no one else even tried. His guests usually took a bus to Jirya and hired mules to take them the rest of the way.

Hushang Khan had once been a student in Paris and had lived there for a long time. One day, however, he'd simply packed his bags and returned to the mountains.

He always wore knee-high boots, a French beret and cologne from Paris. Every morning he climbed to the top of the mountain to see the sunrise. He kept his radio tuned to a French station, so he could listen to the news and the music.

Even though he had four wives, he lived in the fortress by himself, surrounded by his belongings.

The mountains around Sawoj-Bolagh were enveloped in mystery. There was a crater in the highest mountain, and an ancient volcano still belched out smoke. The fortress, which had been built on the slope of one of the mountains, overlooked an arid valley.

On the way to the fortress there were three mysterious

caves, each of which housed a remnant of Persian history. In the deepest recesses of the first cave was a simple stone statue of King Shapur, an early Sassanid king. Carved in the wall of the second was a lion battling the king of the Achaemenids, who was seated on a bull. The third cave contained a chiselled relief depicting King Darius – the greatest king of all.

Green flags emblazoned with Koran verses fluttered outside the entrance to the caves, to welcome the pilgrims who made their way up the mountainside on mules to see the carvings.

Eagles soared high above the caves, keeping an eye on all that went on. The pilgrims liked to think of them as the guardians of the caves.

At the top of the mountain was a huge bell that Hushang Khan's visitors could ring to let him know they were coming. Aqa Jaan rang the bell and waved his hat in the direction of the village. 'Kha-a-a-a-a-a-a-a-a-n!' he called, and his voice echoed through the valley beneath the fortress.

The children playing outside the fortress heard his cry. 'What's your na-a-a-a-a-a-a-a-a-me?' they called back.

'Aq-a-a-a-a-a-a-a-a-a J-a-a-a-a-a-a-a-a-a-n!'

They raced inside to tell Hushang Khan that a guest was about to arrive.

Meanwhile, Aqa Jaan, leading his horse by the reins, climbed a bit higher.

Before long Hushang came galloping towards him, waving his beret. When he got closer, he leapt out of the saddle and embraced Aqa Jaan.

'Welcome, my friend! What a pleasant surprise! My house is yours!'

They started off towards the fortress on foot.

'Tell me, friend, what brings you here?'

'Believe it or not – a dream,' Aqa Jaan told him.

'What kind of dream?'

'Just a dream I had last night. Fakhri and I have been staying in Jirya.'

'Why didn't you bring her along?'

'Because I wasn't planning to visit you. I only decided to ride up here this morning, when I remembered my dream.'

'What was it about?'

'I've forgotten, except for one part: I was standing by the bell and watching you ride down into the valley. I rang the bell, but you didn't hear it, so I rang it again, even louder. You still didn't look up. Then, with a lump in my throat, I kept ringing that bell until everyone in the mountains could hear it, except you. I don't remember what happened next.'

'I know what happened next. Follow me and I'll show you,' Khan said, and he sprang onto his horse and rode off towards the valley.

The valley was as dry as a bone. As far as the eye could see, there was nothing but dirt and dark-brown rocks, without a single sign of life. Khan deftly made his way down the hillside. When they reached the bottom, they dismounted and Khan strode off towards the valley floor.

'The soil in this valley is so parched that even if you got the Persian Gulf to flow through it, you wouldn't quench its thirst,' Khan said. 'Still, the soil is incredibly fertile. I have a dream: one day I'm going to transform this valley into the Garden of Eden. I'd like to show you something. Do you think you're ready to see it?'

'To see what?'

'Something that's bound to be painful, but also wonderful!' He clambered over a few boulders, and Aqa Jaan followed along behind him.

'Nature has performed a miracle,' he continued. 'Here the soil is arid, but behind the fortress, it's soft and moist. Shall I tell you a secret? As strange as it may seem, there's a huge water reservoir beneath the fortress.'

'A water reservoir?'

'Yes, a water reservoir! I don't know how it was created or where the water comes from. Maybe from the snow-capped mountains to the north. It's the secret of my domain. No one knows about it. I only discovered it myself about three years ago, when a French friend of mine came for a visit. He's a geologist. He was curious to see where the water in the well came from, so he lowered himself into it on a rope. When he came back up, he said, "There's gold beneath your fortress." "Gold?" I said. "Water!" he explained. "There's an aquifer running beneath this soil, and that's as good as gold."'

'I haven't told anyone,' Khan said. 'I'm afraid that if the ayatollahs get wind of it, they'll confiscate my fortress and throw me out. I plan on keeping it a secret for as long as I live. Still, I've been conducting a little experi-ment, with the help of one of your relatives.'

'Oh, who?'

'I'll tell you later. Anyway, I went out and bought a powerful water pump and a long hose. You can judge the results for yourself. Close your eyes, and I'll take you there. Brace yourself, and follow me!'

Aqa Jaan closed his eyes, hesitantly took hold of Khan's arm and allowed himself to be led behind a cliff.

'You can open them now,' Khan said.

Aqa Jaan opened his eyes, and was stunned by what he saw. Stretched out before him was a vast garden. It was filled with fragrant flowers in every colour of the rainbow, dotted here and there with blossoming trees.

'I don't believe it!' Aqa Jaan said.

'The volcano warms the soil, and it's rich in minerals. The cliff shelters the garden from the wind and the cold. This is just the beginning of my dream for this valley. You had a dream last night, but you can't remember exactly what it was about. Well, I'll tell you what it was about. Look over there. Beneath that tree, up by those rocks, is your son's grave. It doesn't have a tombstone yet, but it's covered with flowers and fallen petals.'

Aqa Jaan clutched Khan's arm to steady himself.

'Ordinary birds don't dare to come in here,' Khan went on. 'This is the domain of the eagles. They fly above the valley and keep watch over it.'

Aqa Jaan's eyes were swimming with tears. He stared at the apricot-coloured flowers growing on top of the grave, in such thick clusters that they seemed determined to conceal it. Tears rolled down Aqa Jaan's cheeks. He knelt by the grave and kissed the ground:

Alef Lam Mim Ra.
He governs the world.
He is the one who spread the soil
And lifted up the mountains
And made the rivers flow.
He raised up the heavens
Without any pillars that you can see.
He made the sun and moon do his bidding,
Each one moving in its course
For an appointed time.
He governs the world.
He causes the night to envelop the day
And the day to envelop the night.

He made fruit of every kind in pairs,
Two and two.
And on the earth are plots of land,
Adjoining one another, and gardens of vines,
And fields sown with corn, and palm trees,
Growing out of a single root or a cluster,
All watered by one stream.
He governs the world.
Such things are signs for those who understand.
Alef Lam Mim Ra.

'Thank you, Khan,' Aqa Jaan said. 'Thank you, my friend. My heart is filled with happiness.'

'I know something else that will make you happy,' Hushang Khan replied.

'Nothing can make me happier than this.'

'Don't be too sure. As I told you a few minutes ago, I had help. Help from a man with the strength of an elephant. Without his tireless efforts, this garden would not exist. Would you like to see him? Come with me. He's driving a tractor on the other side of the fortress. We're ploughing a new field, sowing it with sunflowers. That French friend of mine brought me some seeds from France. Our native sunflowers don't grow very tall here in the mountains, but these French ones shoot up into the sky. Soon this field will be covered with thousands of suns, and every one of them will produce fat, juicy seeds. Last year we had a test plot, so this year we expect to press our own sunflower oil from those seeds.

'The man you're about to see is a genius! He works day and night, ploughing, sowing, repairing equipment, giving me advice. He's the best worker I've ever had!'

Leading the horses by the reins, the two men walked slowly to the other side of the hill. When they reached a clump of trees, Khan tied the reins to a branch. 'Let's surprise him,' he said. 'Walk softly.'

They crept through the trees to where the man was working.

'Don't move,' Khan whispered.

Aqa Jaan looked at the man on the tractor. His face was hidden by a hat. When the tractor came to a tree, the man stopped, got out and strode over to the tree, where he'd left his lunch. There was something familiar about the way he carried himself, the way he walked.

Khan smiled.

The man grabbed a loaf of bread, sat down on the ground, leaned back against the tree and looked up at the sky, his face bathed in sunlight.

'Ahmad!' Aqa Jaan exclaimed. 'It's Ahmad!' He took a few steps forward and studied the man more closely. No, he wasn't mistaken. It was Ahmad: the son of the house, the imam of their mosque!

'Go to him! Embrace him!' Khan urged him.

Two eagles glided overhead and started circling above the field.

Aqa Jaan stepped into the open. Suddenly Ahmad saw Aqa Jaan walking towards him. He leapt to his feet and stared at him, speechless.

Aqa Jaan reached out and folded Ahmad into his arms. 'You've become a farmer! And a modern one at that! You drive a tractor, you smell of diesel oil and you have the hands of a mechanic.' Aqa Jaan beamed with joy. 'You've gained experience and can now see life from a different perspective. Thank you, Allah, for this blessed moment!'

Ahmad was still too stunned by Aqa Jaan's sudden appearance to speak. His hands trembled as he wiped the tears from his eyes.

'Everything will be all right, my son,' Aqa Jaan said.

'This will all end one day, I swear. Then the mosque will be restored to us and you will go back to your library.'

'He doesn't want to be an imam any more,' Khan said, smiling. 'Let the ayatollahs have his turban and his robe! Come, he has work to do. You and I are going to have lunch. You both need to recover from the shock.'

Aqa Jaan, flabbergasted but overjoyed, walked back to the fortress with Khan. 'You're a true friend, Khan. You've done so much for me that I hardly know how to thank you.'

'You don't have to thank me, though there *is* one small thing you can do.'

'I'll be glad to. Just say the word.'

'We'll talk about it later. We have plenty of time.'

They reached the fortress, and the children greeted Aqa Jaan with whoops and cries. 'I swear you've had a dozen more children since the last time I saw you,' Aqa Jaan said.

'I don't know about that,' Khan laughed. 'You'd have to ask their mothers.'

Khan led Aqa Jaan into an elegant sitting room, where the candles in the tulip-shaped sockets of a crystal chandelier were burning brightly and the light was bouncing off an antique mirror. The room was pleasantly warm, and the antique Persian carpets on the floor added even more comfort and colour. The furniture dated back to the Renaissance, and had lost none of its splendour. A massive bookcase was lined with French and Persian books.

'I hope you're planning to stay for at least a week,' Khan said.

'I wish I could, but I can't. I've left Fakhri all by herself in Jirya. She's arranged to meet a couple of women today, and she doesn't know I'm here. I just told the servant that I'd be back late.'

'I understand, but you can't leave now. I'll send someone to fetch her.'

'I don't think she's ready to deal with this yet. She's only just starting to feel better. I never told her that you took Jawad's body that night. She still finds it hard to talk about his death.'

'That's perfectly all right,' Khan said. 'I'll send someone to tell her that you're going to spend the night here. She can sleep at her sister's, can't she? You shouldn't let women get used to sleeping in your arms! Let her sleep by herself for one night; it will do her good.'

Just then two servants came in with lunch on a round silver tray.

Later that afternoon, Aqa Jaan went back to the field. He and Ahmad walked through the mountains, talking about everything that had happened in the intervening years.

Afterwards, Khan took Aqa Jaan to see his wives, who welcomed them with tea and home-made biscuits. They stayed to eat dinner with the oldest wife.

When they'd finished eating, they went back to the fortress, where Khan showed him into the drawing room. The candles had already been lit.

'You're my guest of honour,' Khan said. 'Sit down, I'll be back in a moment.'

Aqa Jaan suddenly felt a wave of melancholy wash over him. The stressful day had taken its toll. He stared blankly at the floor and waited for the return of his host, who came back a few minutes later carrying a bottle coated with a fine layer of dust. He set the bottle on the table, reached into the cupboard and took out two gold-rimmed goblets.

'You and I have several reasons to celebrate tonight. I can see from your face that it's been a sad, but wonderful, day.'

Aqa Jaan, who had never drunk a drop of alcohol in his life, shook his head. 'I don't drink,' he said.

'You're making a mistake. A few hours ago you wanted to thank me, but you didn't know how. It's very simple: join me in a drink. Let that be your expression of gratitude. Listen, my friend, this is the oldest bottle of wine in my cellar. I've brought it up to share with you. My father laid it in the cellar thirty years ago. I've been waiting all these years for an evening that I knew would come, for just the right person, for a friend. No, don't interrupt me. I know it's against your principles, but I'd like the two of us to drink a toast to your son, who is buried here, and to Ahmad, who is happy and healthy and driving a tractor. Tonight is a special night. I won't let you ruin it with religion. I'm going to pour you a glass of wine. Don't say a word. I'll raise my glass, you'll raise yours, and then we'll drink.'

He uncorked the bottle and sniffed the wine. 'Allah, Allah, of course you shouldn't be forced to drink something you don't want to, but I'd be delighted if you would drink this wine with me.'

Aqa Jaan was silent. First Khan poured a small amount in his own glass. He picked it up and swirled it around. 'This wine smells as sweet as the paradisiacal rivers of wine mentioned in the Koran.'

Aqa Jaan stared at him in silence.

'Don't look at me like that!' Khan said. 'There's nothing wrong with what I just said. You're not the only one who's read the Koran. I've read it too – in my own way. The Koran says a lot of things about Paradise. It promises us handmaidens – beautiful women with lips tasting of milk and honey who will pour out divine libations. Here, raise your glass in a toast. One day this wine will be offered to you in Paradise!'

Aqa Jaan didn't reach for his glass.

'I'm a sinner from way back, but you aren't,' Khan said. 'I wouldn't ask you to do anything sinful. This wine was made out of grapes from my own vineyard. At harvest time the most beautiful girls in the mountains come here to pick the grapes and pour the wine into the old clay jars in the cellar.'

Khan took a sip and savoured it. 'It's unbelievable,' he said. 'In this wine you can taste the particles that make up the volcano, the particles that make up the universe. You can even smell the hands of the girls who picked the grapes. Take a sip, Aqa Jaan!'

When Aqa Jaan didn't lift his glass, Khan decided not to press him any further. He went outside.

Bats were swooping across his property, wheeling above the tractor parked on the hillside. He saw Ahmad walking towards the stable, with something slung over his shoulder. He sipped his wine and listened to the sounds of the night. His children were still playing outside. He heard his daughters chasing each other through the darkness. Years ago he had lived in Paris. It had been a time of great upheaval, with demonstrators marching through the streets, existentialism in its heyday and Simone de Beauvoir captivating *tout le Paris* with her books. He'd been happy, he'd fallen in and out of love a dozen times and his French friends had welcomed him as if he were a Persian prince. He could have lived in Paris for ever. But after a while the tide turned. He wasn't happy any more: he longed for home, for the hills of his youth and the women of the mountains. Paris was beautiful, but its beauty was not for him. He stored up his memories of Paris and went back to his fortress, this time for ever.

Carrying his wine goblet, Khan walked down his village's only street. After a moment he turned and saw

Aqa Jaan standing by the window. Was he sipping the wine? Khan wanted to go in and find out, but something held him back.

The poignancy of his last years in Paris unexpectedly stole over him. He didn't want to be alone with his sorrow, so he went to the house of his youngest wife, in whose arms he always found peace. He knocked, and she opened the door. 'Why do you look so sad?'

'My friend's sorrow has rubbed off on me,' he said.

She asked no more, but took him into her bed and let him lay his head in her lap.

The next morning the aged servant led Aqa Jaan to the royal bath chamber. He stepped into the bath and felt the hot tiles beneath his feet – a moment of joy after an unusually long night. The water came up to his chin. He slid down beneath the surface for a moment, then came back up and chanted:

> *The first to come will be the first to arrive*
> *In the Gardens of Bliss.*
> *They shall recline on sofas studded with jewels.*
> *Passing among them will be maidens*
> *With big expressive eyes,*
> *Like pearls in their shells,*
> *Who will go from one to another*
> *With chalices and goblets of wine,*
> *Which cause neither headache nor intoxication.*
> *They shall have whatever fruits they desire,*
> *And the flesh of fowls.*

He plunged back under the water, so that it gushed over the sides of the bath. He opened his mouth wide and stayed underwater for a long time, as if to cleanse himself of sin. This time when he came up, he was gasping for air. He shouted, as hard as he could, 'In the gardens of bliss!'

He got dressed, put on his hat and motioned for the servant to bring him his horse. Then he sprang into the saddle and galloped off.

He Is Light.
Light Upon Light

The story of the house of the mosque is far from over, and yet it resembles real life in one respect: we must all bid it farewell.

There's a phrase that often crops up at the end of Persian tales: 'Our story is over, but the crow still hasn't reached its nest.'

One day, when Aqa Jaan was at his office in the bazaar, he received an unusual letter. It had a foreign postmark. He was surprised. It had been a while since he'd received business letters from abroad. But this letter was different: he didn't recognise the stamp. German stamps were always very grand, with portraits of musicians or philosophers or drawings of historical monuments, but this stamp featured a bouquet of bright red tulips.

Aqa Jaan took a magnifying glass out of his drawer and examined the stamp. Maybe it was from Switzerland. He recalled sending a consignment of carpets there years ago.

The envelope filled him with hope. Still, you could never be sure, for bad news was always lying in wait, ready to pounce at any moment. He put the letter aside and asked the office boy to bring him some tea.

* * *

When he had finished his tea, he took out his letter-opener and carefully slit open the envelope. Inside was a letter written in Persian with a fountain pen:

Dear Aqa Jaan,

Salaam! Salaam *from the bottom of my heart.* Salaam *with a hint of longing for home.*

My dear Aqa Jaan, I'm writing to you from a country I never expected to live in. If I were you, I'd say that it was God's will that led me here. But I'm not you, so I chalk it up to a series of coincidences. Anyway, what's done is done, and you taught me to accept things as they are.

I must confess that I carry your words of wisdom around with me always, like a beloved set of beads.

Your words have given me hope and helped me to survive so that I could build a new life, make something of myself and be a true son of the house of the mosque.

My dearest Aqa Jaan, I long for the day when I can open the door to our house and walk inside. I still have the key, which I carry with me always.

You taught me to face up to my problems, and to work hard and be patient. I have followed your advice.

I left our house, but I haven't turned my back on it. I live in Holland now, and I dream of the day when you and I can walk along the canal in front of my apartment. That day is bound to come. It must!

You always told me to dream and to make my dreams come true. I intend to do just that. There are secrets I can share with you only in the freedom of this city.

One night you will be here, and I will invite my friends over to meet you. I've talked about you so much they feel they know you already.

My dear uncle, I'm still writing. For the last few years, I've spent all of my time committing my stories to paper. I have done this for you and for our country.

I write in another language now, and I don't know whether I should apologise or jump for joy. It just happened, it wasn't in my power to do otherwise. Actually, writing has been my salvation. It was the only way I could express the suffering and pain that you and our country have undergone. Even though I write in a new language, I still try to imbue my stories with the poetic spirit of our ancient and beautiful language.

Forgive me.

My dearest uncle, I dream so often of the house and of all of you that I seem to be living there more than here.

You won't die. You will stay until they've all gone and come back again.

Shahbal

That night Aqa Jaan put on his coat and hat, picked up his walking stick, left his study and went out into the courtyard.

It was cold. The *hauz* was frozen and the tree branches were encased in a thin layer of ice.

The dark-blue sky was studded with stars stretching all the way to Mecca. Aqa Jaan walked across the courtyard and gingerly mounted the stairs to the roof.

The old crow recognised his footsteps and cawed, but stayed in its nest, watching his every move.

'Thank you, crow! I'll be careful,' Aqa Jaan said as he passed the dome on his way to the mosque.

The crow cawed again.

'Thank you, crow. It's good of you to remind me. No, I won't switch on the light. The treasure room is our secret.'

Clutching the wooden rail, he went down the steps and into the mosque. Then he tiptoed through the darkness until he came to the vault and cautiously opened the door. He couldn't see a thing. For a moment he wondered whether to turn on the light, but decided against it. He crept down the stairs and groped his way to the door of the treasure room.

It was eerily silent. The only sound was that of his footsteps and the tapping of his stick.

Finally, he stopped walking. He fumbled with the lock, and a moment later the hinges creaked and the heavy, ancient door opened.

His silhouette was dimly visible in the inky blackness. Then he stepped into the treasure room and was swallowed up in the darkness.

He walked across the red carpet and stopped beside the last coat-hook in the long row. Taking Shahbal's letter out of his pocket, he knelt down and slipped it into the chest. Then, breaking the silence, he chanted:

> *He is light.*
> *His light is like a niche with a lantern.*
> *The glass is like a shining star,*
> *Lit by the oil of a blessed olive tree.*
> *Its oil is almost aglow.*
> *Light upon light!*

Acknowledgements

A few chapters in *The House of the Mosque* begin, just as some of the surahs in the Koran do, with the names of letters from the Arabic alphabet, such as *alef*, *lam* and *mim*. At first glance, they seem to be meaningless, but Islamic scholars have written countless volumes about them. They are thought to be secret numbers, a kind of code to the universe that will unlock the secret of creation.

The story quoted at the end of the *Mahiha* chapter is based on a paragraph in a short story by the Iranian writer Jalal Al-e Ahmad.

The poems in the *Family* chapter are taken from *Een karavaan uit Perzië* (A Caravan from Persia), edited and translated by J.T.P. de Bruijn, Amsterdam: Bulaaq, 2002.

All the passages from the Koran have been reworked. I've taken them out of context, mixed the lines of one surah with lines from another and translated them freely, using a number of different source texts and consulting various interpretations.

Although *The House of the Mosque* is based on historical fact, all the references to real people and actual events should be read according to the conventions of fiction.

Translator's note: The passages from the Koran are a composite of several different English translations, including an online version translated by Yusef Ali. I am particularly indebted to Tarif Khalidi, *The Qur'an*, London: Penguin,

2008. Its poetic elegance makes it a pleasure to read.

I wish to thank Diane Webb for her editorial advice and R.M. McGlinn for his assistance with the transliteration and translation of Farsi into English.

Glossary

aba Iranian-style robe

akkas photographer

Allahu akbar God is great

Ankahtu wa zawagto I ask you to be my wife. (The traditional words recited by the groom during a wedding ceremony.)

astaghfirullah God forgive me

azan the call to prayer

Enna lellah An expression you say when someone has died. It's short for '*Enna lellah wa enna elayhi raje'un*', which means 'To God we belong and to Him we return.'

Eqra Read. (The first surah revealed to Muhammad begins with this word.)

esfandi fragrant seeds of wild rue that are burned to chase away evil spirits

hauz hexagonal pool or basin of water used for ablutions

Hayye ale as-salat Hasten to the prayer

hijab an Islamic dress code for women

Inshallah God willing

La ilaha illa Allah There is no God but Allah.

Mobarak inshallah Blessings, congratulations

mahajjabeh a veiled woman, and by extension a model Islamic woman

mahiha fish

Qabilto I consent. (The traditional words recited by the bride during a wedding ceremony.)

qadi judge

rakat one unit of prayer

Salla ala Mohammad wa ale Mohammad Blessed be Muhammad and the House of Muhammad.

Salaam aleikum Peace be upon you. (A traditional greeting.)

Salaam bar Khomeini Greetings to Khomeini.

siegeh Under Shiite law a man may have a maximum of four wives. In addition he's allowed an unlimited number of temporary wives, who make a marriage contract for a period ranging anywhere from one hour to ninety-nine years. These *sigeh* wives have no inheritance rights and are not officially registered with the city or the mosque.

tayareh a swiftly moving object, such as a bird, boat or plane

toman Iranian unit of currency

Wa-assalaam That is all.

zaman time